LAST
Stand
FOR GENEVIEVE

LAST
Stand
FOR GENEVIEVE

THE LAST SERIES
KAYMIE WUERFEL

Copyright © 2024 by Kaymie Wuerfel

The moral right of the author has been asserted.

All rights reserved. No part of this book may be reproduced or used in any manner without written permission of the copyright owner except for the use of quotations in a book review.

This is a work of fiction. Names, characters, places, and incidents either are the product of the author's imagination or are used fictitiously. Any resemblance to actual persons, living or dead, events, or locales is entirely coincidental.

First published in March 2024 by Kaymie Wuerfel

Cover design by coversbyjules.crd.co
Editing and formatting by Allusion Publishing (http://www.allusionpublishing.com)

Paperback ISBN 978-0-6457951-2-7
E-Book ISBN 978-0-6457951-3-4

www.kaymiewuerfel.com
Instagram: @kaymiewuerfelwrites
TikTok: @kayywuerf

PLAYLIST

Brooke

Wait - M83

Evermore (feat. Bon Iver)– Taylor Swift

Innocent (Taylor's Version) - Taylor Swift

What Was I Made For? - Billie Eilish

Daylight – David Kushner

Gilded Lily - Cults

idontwannabeyouanymore - Billie Eilish

Lust for Life (ft. The Weeknd) - Lana Del Ray

Radio - Lana Del Ray

Clean - Taylor Swift

Connor

ocean eyes – Billie Eilish

Always In My Head - Coldplay

how u make me feel - Montell Fish

Use Somebody - Kings of Leon

Sex On Fire – Kings of Leon

Time After Time – Cyndi Lauper

Falling in Love (ft. Andrew Langston) - Dennis Kruissen

Free Fallin' – Tom Petty

AUTHOR'S NOTE
(& Content Warnings)

Before embarking on this journey with these characters, you should know that it touches heavily upon struggles with addiction, violence, threats of SA and the power that grief and survivor's guilt can have over one's mind.

I promise that you will laugh just as much (or more) than you want to cry. However, if these topics are highly triggering for you, I recommend reading one of my others.

This story was inspired by someone I knew, who if not for their willpower of iron, could have so easily become just like Brooke, and fallen prey to the medications they were given while they healed.

Life can be a slippery slope, and even the best of us can lose our footing. My hope is that Brooke's story will make you, my reader, feel seen and maybe just a little less alone.

To the souls who feel lost.

I believe that you will find your way again.

CHAPTER ONE

Now - Brooke

"Please state your full name for the record."

"Brooke Anderson."

"Would you raise your right hand?"

I raise it.

"Do you swear to tell the truth, the whole truth, and nothing but the truth, so help you God?"

"I swear." There's no going back now.

The judge nods, accepting my oath and motions for the attorney to begin. "Please proceed."

I'm relieved to see that today, it's not the prosecuting attorney I'd had the displeasure of encountering that...*other* time. A small mercy.

"Well, Ms. Anderson, we are here today because of you. I think you can begin by explaining why that is." The prosecutor's voice isn't cruel, but it's not gentle.

I take a moment to gather myself.

Today, I took care to put my best foot forward. My blonde hair is gelled into a sleek, low bun. I went shopping for makeup for the first time in years, hoping my skills from plastering on a full face of it every day in high school remained. I wasn't disappointed, but I wasn't impressed either. Anyone else could say I did a fantastic job of it, but they don't know how well I used to transform my face. Now, it feels like nothing but a mask, concealing the rot underneath.

My outfit was chosen with just as much attention, I had to shop for that too. Simple. Straightforward. Sleek. I've got a black turtleneck on, a black blazer, and trousers. Although this outfit should be illegal to wear in Florida, I look sharp. I can't have a hair or *word* out of place today. Everything needs to be seamless.

The attorney is standing in front of me now, looking at me expectantly.

I know what he wants me to explain. It's something I've locked down and buried as deep as anyone can bury anything. This story was never supposed to go anywhere besides my grave, with me. I had never planned to bring this to light, because that would require having to relive every single moment which led up to me being here, in a courtroom again.

How much pain can a person take?

These days it seems like I'm on a treadmill, running as fast as I can, but never getting anywhere. My past is still *right* behind me, ready to drag me under at every turn. Coming here today is my *last* effort to escape it, my *last* stand.

So, I clear my throat, making my voice strong, no matter how much I'm quivering on the inside. "In high school I had a 4.0 GPA, full-ride scholarship offers to not one, but *three* Ivy League universities. Not a bad mark on my record or report card. I'd never even been tardy." I think back to the days where I was the golden child, the golden student, the golden girlfriend. Before.... *everything*. None of it means a goddamn thing anymore.

"I'd never touched drugs. Not even alcohol or cigarettes." I think of my father, the reason I never came within an inch of substances.

"Toward the end of senior year, when I was eighteen, there was an... accident." I know I'm incapable of saying her name aloud, even after five years, so I don't even try. "I lost my little sister."

"How is this relevant?" The prosecutor questions.

I do my best not to flinch at the ability of the justice system to disregard lives so easily, as if the story of a teenage girl losing her life too early is only important if it directly pertains to what *they* want to know. "If you let me continue, you'll see the relevance for yourself. Please."

He glances at the judge and then nods at me to continue.

"I broke thirteen bones. They put me into an induced coma for a week after the accident, giving me the only chance at survival." I try not to scoff under my breath, remembering how people would glance at me with such awe, telling me how lucky I was to be alive. "As you can imagine, there was a certain level of physical pain when I woke up. The morphine helped, as long as they kept pumping it into my system. In the end, it wasn't the physical pain that broke me."

I solidify my face into the frozen setting I've been practicing in the mirror for weeks...for years. "When I found out that my sister didn't make it, for a while I didn't feel anything. I don't think anyone is mentally equipped to process that level of loss." I push the emotion down, pausing until I feel disconnected from the brimming emotions, and I can pretend I'm not discussing my own life. Just like I've practiced.

"I'm still waiting to see the relevance, Ms. Anderson." The prosecutor reminds me why I'm here.

I hate that I'm sharing this with *these* people. The people who throw away lives like it's just another day in the office. I want to get up from this stand and get as far away as I can from this courtroom, so I can restitch the emotional sutures I've brutally torn open by coming here today.

"After spending a few weeks in the hospital, I was sent home. I had enough morphine in my system that I don't remember getting home. I just woke up one day, back in my room, in my bed, where I remained for several more weeks."

"Get to the point or we will be done here." He is losing his patience.

I close my eyes, returning to that day.

That day I took the tiny step which set me on this trajectory.

CHAPTER TWO

Now – Connor

'll have to find one hell of a lay to put this trainwreck of a night behind me. There's nothing a good root can't fix. I'll find a nice-looking girl and get that shitty performance out of my head for good.

We thought playing at this music festival was going to be the big break that we needed, but of course, Jayden messed it up for all of us. I'll lose my shit if he keeps going on like this, raving all night before gigs, destroying his vocal cords. I've about had enough. The whole band has.

I shake my head and light another ciggy. We're supposed to have a sound between *Mumford & Sons* and *Kings of Leon,* where the raspy whining is meant to be appealing, *not* like he's going through puberty. My mate Ryder, who only listens to screaming stuff, did a better job of it the last time Jayden screwed us, and he stepped in.

If we were really in a tight spot, I could step in. My voice isn't bad, but singing on stage while playing guitar is different from a little acoustic bit for a girl I'm about to toss into the sheets. My mates back home in Sydney would be floored, seeing how easy it is to get with girls here.

That's one of my favorite things about America. All I have to do is say a few sentences, thicken up my accent a bit, and use too much slang. They're pretty much ready to go right then. Occasionally, I get one who's a bit tougher, but it's nothing my guitar and go-to song for hookups can't fix. I'm not a good guy, but at least I'm an honest one.

And the last thing I need tonight is to take a chance with someone new and wind up with a mediocre lay. It needs to be nothing short of mindblowing to fix this shit in my head. Performances like this always bring back my father's words from the last time I saw him, the night I chose living on the street over living in his home.

See you when you fail, Son.

Yeah. I need a *really* good lay.

I open up my contacts, scrolling through the numbers that were worth saving, but not because I might want to take them on a date. They're not alphabetized by their names, which are only tacked on at the end so I'm not a total cunt. They're alphabetized by, shall I say, *specialties.*

Anal Annie

Yeah, not tonight.

Blowy Becca

Ha. I've always liked that one.

Connor: U up?

I keep scrolling, needing a backup.

Better Blowy Bianca

Even better. I send off the message.

Connor: U up?

What's the harm in getting a backup for my backup? Who else have we got?

Flexible Felicity

Yeah, okay.

Connor: U up?

"Connor, tell me you're not doing what I think you're doing," Theo says as he approaches.

I quickly close my phone, slipping it into my back pocket and smiling up at him, even though I know there's no fooling my best friend. My chosen brother. "Oi, don't come over here just to bust my balls."

Theo rolls his eyes. "Tonight wasn't bad, man. Ara and I really enjoyed it. She's learned most of the lyrics to your songs."

Theo knows what this kind of night does to me, and he's trying to make me feel better, but we both know that it never helps. There are only two things that usually do: writing new music, or previously discussed activities, which I'm hoping text me back soon.

"Where is Ara anyway? Assaulting a food truck somewhere?" I say lightheartedly. I've never seen my brother happier, and the girl deserves the world for that, as far as I'm concerned. Even though it took them so long to get together, it started giving *me* blue balls.

Theo laughs. "I think she saw a sign about a fried Oreo somewhere."

We both cringe.

"Well, thanks for checking on me, but I'm good. Really." Even my bullshit alarm is going off.

Theo nods, putting his hand on my shoulder, not convinced. "Well, let me know if none of the girls work out. We can get wasted and play Mario Kart."

"They always work out," I say with a wink.

It may be disgusting, but it's true.

"I'm gonna go find my girl," Theo says as he starts to walk away. "Call me though, if you need me."

"I'll be too busy!" I call after him.

Theo has always thought that I was the one to save him, but he's never realized that it was the other way around. He gave me a home and a family, just when I believed I'd have neither.

I feel my phone vibrate several times, and my usual smirk takes its rightful place. Pulling it out of my pocket, I find that all three girls have already answered, all game. As usual. My confidence might be excruciating to those around me, but it's justified. I just never let myself wonder what Lara would think of me now.

Blowy Becca is out, since Better Blowy Bianca is in.

I shoot her a message, not the type to ghost anybody.

Connor: Sorry, think I just got food poisoning.

Down to two, now.

Better Blowy Biana or Flexible Felicity?

I grab another ciggy from the pack, placing it between my lips as I search for my lighter. Fuck, where did it go? I swear, I always lose these things as fast as I replace them. I'm so busy looking for the little fucker that I don't see the figure approach, until they've literally grabbed the cigarette from my mouth and thrown it in the dirt.

"Oi, what the fuck!?" I'm about ready to fight whatever nut who's just wasted a perfectly good smoke, but come to a quick halt when I find one *hell of a* woman standing in front of me.

The first thing that stops me dead is how different she looks than the rest of the ladies at this festival. She doesn't have an ounce of makeup on, and not a *sliver* of skin on display, aside from her face. This girl is wearing a fucking *turtleneck*, a far cry from my yellow t-shirt and ripped jeans, yet every cell in my body just stood up to attention.

She's got this rare kind of beauty about her, prominent features that are still pleasant. Her hair is pulled into a tight, slicked-back bun, giving me an uninterrupted view of her face; eyes are the kind of blue you see at the bottom of an iceberg, with lips slightly too big for her delicate chin, with a pert little nose that gives you the urge to boop it, after it scrunches up all cute and shit.

Boop it? The fuck?

This chick is bad news. I need to walk away. Shrugging away from the giant speaker I'm leaning against, I move to do just that.

"You're welcome." She says all proud, like she did me a grand favor. "The moment you turn to an addiction, you've lost yourself."

"What are you going on about?"

She rolls her eyes. "If you can get addicted to something, chances are it's not good for you."

"And where did you get the idea that what I do, or don't do, is any of your business?"

"I'll never not step in, if I feel I should."

"No need to step in here. I'm doing just fine."

"Is that why you've been standing here, chain smoking for an hour?"

"You've been watching me, aye?" The thought of her hanging back in the shadows, watching me, sends a shiver down my spine.

"More like suffering from secondhand smoke."

I grin. This one has fight in her, and I'm starting to think she might be worth the trouble. "Want to get out of here?"

There is a slight crack in her icy façade, but I can't get a read on her. "You don't even know my name."

"Connor West." I introduce myself, turning up my accent and putting on my best smirk. "What should I call you, *Sheila?*"

If another Aussie heard me now, they'd probably want to puke and revoke my citizenship, up until the point where they see how well this works. She looks at me for a second and I wait for her to smile, get that flirty look in her eyes, or check me out. Instead, she makes a gagging noise and walks away, giving me pause.

This routine *always* works.

I speed up and walk after her. "Already have plans tonight?"

"No, but that pick-up line gave me secondhand embarrassment, and the fact that it probably works makes me lose hope in my own gender."

"Well, you're right about one thing, it does work." I keep my smirk on, my accent thick. She's putting up a bigger fight than I'm used to, but I can't lose faith in the routine.

"Then I guess tonight will be a lesson on how to take a loss."

She's walking so fast that I haven't managed to fully catch up to her yet. I do a little jog, finally getting in front of her. *You don't chase girls. They chase you.* My phone is incessantly buzzing from the evidence, as we speak.

I let my accent go back to its new normal, slightly less strong after living here for so many years. She's a toughie, this one. The routine will still work, I just need to customize it for her. Let her think she was too smart to fall for a pick-up line, make it her idea.

Yeah, I know I'm a toxic piece of shit.

"Look, I'm not asking you to leave a toothbrush at my place, I just want to show you a good time."

"Listen...Connor, was it?" My name on her tongue does something to me. "I'm not interested in whatever you think you have to offer. Maybe try one of your groupies. I'm sure they'd enjoy a good ride."

Her tone is cold, serious. Her blue eyes have turned into daggers of the sharpest kind, made from ice and shooting straight for me. She's not *playing* hard to get, she *is* hard to get. No way am I taking this girl to bed tonight.

"You're right, okay? I'm a total dick, I won't try to deny it. But yeah, this usually works for me." I let out a breath, rubbing my hand through my sandy brown hair, which has gotten too long. "Tonight, it was...it was a bad night for me."

She snorts. "Yeah, what was with your singer?"

I groan. "I knew it was bad."

LAST Stand FOR GENEVIEVE

"Yeah, that guy was lying to you. Your set was shit."

"Fuck me dead. I know it was." I can't hide how much it guts me.

Her eyes soften, only slightly. "*You* weren't bad, it was just obvious that you were the one carrying the vocals, and your drummer was too pissed with the lead to keep his shit straight."

The assessment is spot on. "Are you in the music business?"

She looks at me like I'm an idiot. "No, I just know how to use my eyes, ears, and my brain, unlike the people you're probably used to."

I smirk. "They've got other talents though."

She gags again. "You're disgusting."

"I'm honest, though."

"No point in being honest if you're still spewing bullshit."

Is it her mission to repeatedly hand me my ass? And why do I like it? "Want to get some hot chocolate? No expectations, just a chat."

"It's like ninety degrees and two-hundred-percent humidity. I don't want to torture myself."

"Says the girl in a turtleneck," I say with a smirk.

Her façade cracks, the tiniest bit, almost as if that's as close as she gets to smiling these days. Why do I want to know why? You have rules for a *reason*, Connor. Walk. Away.

Except I don't have to because she beats me to it.

"Where are you running off to?" I keep my feet planted, refusing to chase her again. I have at least that much dignity.

"Somewhere with better company."

AKA away from me. This night is right and truly fucked. I pull my phone out of my pocket and chuck it into the nearest bin, not bothering to see who texted me back, just because I'm feeling dramatic.

Her words haunt me all the way home.

Somewhere with better company.

Fuck me.

CHAPTER THREE

Then - Brooke

Mom finally went back to work today. I don't think she was ready, but we were struggling financially before the accident, and now with the medical bills? I don't know how we'll ever recover.

As a single mom for the past four years, and the only parent worth a damn long before that, she has almost always had double the pressure to provide for me and....her. Though it's just the two of us now, I think the medical bills racked up to be more than our house and everything in it. No matter how many extra shifts she takes, there's no way out of that hole.

I was planning to become a doctor, to help people and maybe make enough to take some stress off Mom, too. I'd planned to work hard and get into a position where I could help not just Mom but also... her. But what good are the hundreds of thousands in education costs, years of study and training, to end up in a medical field that can't save the ones it should?

I glance at the clock.

5:25 pm

Mom will be home soon, and she threatened to cut my TV cables if I hadn't eaten the food in the fridge by the time she got home. I don't eat these days unless she is there to physically force me. Today she managed to find the one thing that still matters enough to threaten me into doing so.

I spend most days completely passed out, thanks to the blissed unconsciousness that comes with pain medication. When it comes to those few hours between doses, I rely on *The Golden Girls* playing on loop. My TV is probably the one thing which I'd prefer didn't go away.

LAST *Stand* FOR GENEVIEVE

Maybe I don't have to actually eat the food, I can just make it look like I did. I've seen *Law & Order*, I can fabricate some simple evidence. I could wrap it in a paper towel and dump it in the trash. It's not that I'm intentionally starving myself, I'm just never hungry.

How long I've been home, I couldn't tell you. Everything has been a blur of pain and blackouts these days. The only thing I'm sure of is that this is the first time I've tried to leave my corner of the top floor.

When *she* was a baby, Mom wanted to be close to her nursery, giving me the master bedroom. Even though we grew up, we loved our rooms and never switched back. I'll have to make it down the hall and past their room —I mean *Mom's room*—to get to the stairs. Half of my body is still plastered in casts, so it'll be slow going at best.

Mom's room. That will never not be weird. Fate is fucked up. I was the one who didn't have my seatbelt on, got thrown through a windshield, and rather than finishing the job like it should have, left me here to waste. But the precious cargo in the other part of the car?

The one who was supposed to make it out?

She gets ripped away.

I close my eyes, not letting myself think about that night any further. If I can make it down to the kitchen in time, at least I'll have Dorothy, Sophia, Rose, and Blanche to keep me company until I can pass out again. This is what I've been reduced to.

Rolling onto my least broken side that has just one arm plastered, I move my good leg toward the edge of the bed and gently move it over the side. Using the weight of it as leverage, I lift my torso diagonally into a sitting position.

I'm supposed to use crutches still, but the plaster seems sturdy enough. I can barely manage the crutches on flat ground with my bad arm, I won't attempt using them on the stairs. I'll just scoot down on my ass. Finally managing to get into a standing position, I put most of my weight on my right leg, using the walls to balance with my good arm.

One. Painful. Wobbling. Step. At. A. Time.

Though it takes me a while, I finally pass Mom's room on my left. I close my eyes, making sure I don't get a peek of the empty room coming up on my right from my peripherals. I realize too late that I should have held my breath, too.

Her delicate, floral scent comes all the way out to the hallway to greet me. I'd recognize it anywhere.

Tulips. Pastels. Books. Spring. Life.

I freeze, keeping my eyes squeezed shut.

It's not real.

It's not real.

It's not real.

It's just another hallucination.

For days after the accident, I thought it was one big cruel joke. I didn't believe that she was gone, no matter how much Mom cried. The doctors worried about my stability when I started seeing her in the hallways or walking past my hospital room, smiling at me from the chair in the corner as I healed. She would bring her favorite book to read aloud when we got bored, whispering and turning a bit too pink when it got to certain scenes.

I made the mistake of telling someone. They told Mom I needed medication, threatened her with child neglect if she didn't oblige. Mom remained strong, telling them that drugs of any kind were never the answer. She insisted on giving me time to heal on my own, naturally.

Except I'm with the doctors on this one. I am crazy.

Unless... she really is here. Maybe she's standing right in front of me, all I have to do is open my eyes. Is this when I finally wake up from this never-ending nightmare?

I open my eyes, a sob racking through my body at what I find.

Her door is open.

Her room is perfectly intact.

Her bed is still made, besides the wrinkled spot from where she was laying, studying for her history exam. Her history book, neatly closed a few inches away, notes still inside.

Everything is exactly as she left it.

Before I....before I convinced her to go on a drive with me anyway. Saturdays aren't for studying, I told her.

My back hits the wall behind me. I don't even register the pain as I slide down to the ground. For the first time, I believe it. The nightmare isn't a nightmare. I'm not waking up from this reality. She really is gone.

And I'm the one who put her in that car.

I can't take this. I can't feel this. I'd rather break every fucking bone in this body than endure another moment of this pain. Before I know what I'm doing, I'm crawling toward Mom's room, pain shooting through every nerve ending as I drag my crippled leg behind me.

I don't know where she's hidden the painkillers, but I know her well enough to figure it out. We can't afford one of those fancy safes, so I know I'll be able to get to it.

Managing to use the bedpost to pull myself up again, I take in the room around me, as the sobs continue their agonizing racks upon my body. Mom would put it somewhere that would be extremely difficult to get to in my current state. I wipe my face, trying to clear my vision.

Mom will be home soon, meaning I don't have much time. If she finds me in here like this, she'll never give me another pill for the rest of my life.

Think, Brooke.

The tallest shelf will be in her closet, requiring something to stand on, which will be next to impossible for me and thus, likely her first choice in hiding spots. I look around, realizing the only thing to stand on is a swivel chair at her desk. This is a disaster waiting to happen, but if I succeed, I won't have to feel if I break anything else in the process.

I limp over, rolling it into her closet.

Once inside, I find an old shoe box with the word "photos" scrawled above the barcode. I put my good knee on the chair first, grabbing the back with my good arm. The chair moves around uncontrollably. Another sob racks through me, strong enough to hurt my still-healing spine, but nothing close to the unbearable suffering caused by my emotions. Getting these pills is the only way I can keep doing this, the only way I can stay here for Mom.

I realize soon enough that I won't be able to get up without putting actual weight on my broken leg. Clenching my teeth, I prepare for the pain and put all my weight on it as I lift my good leg to the seat of the chair, trying to straighten as steadily as I can...

The chair twists suddenly, sending me to the ground, head cracking against the shoe rack. My broken bones scream, the sound and feel of it echoing throughout my entire body, probably adding weeks to my recovery.

Rather than resist it, I endure it. In fact, I welcome it as it gives me a different pain to focus on, a pain that will pass if I can grit my teeth and breathe through it. Nothing like the memories which are capable of endless torture.

After a minute, I lift myself up again to try one more time. My body cries out in response, but I manage to stand, placing my foot on the chair and haul myself up once again. My broken arm is placed against the nearest wall, steadying myself and the chair, which is begging to swing me off of it, as I reach for my reward.

Opening the box, I find the pill bottle resting atop the last picture I have with my father, just the two of us, before the addiction ruined him and drove him away from us. I know why she put this here. If I ever reached the point where I was trying to sneak pills behind her back, she wanted to remind me what it would do to me.

I pause.

This is everything I swore I would never be. It's why I turned down every drink in high school. Every hit. Every pill. Every smoke. Nothing would own me. I pick up the picture of my dad and me, thinking that maybe she was right in putting this here.

Then I see the one below it.

It was supposed to be the second fail safe, reminding me who I wouldn't want to disappoint. Something cracks inside my chest. I slam the picture back into the box.

She isn't here to be disappointed.

She won't feel anything ever again.

And just like that, Mom's fail safe becomes the thing that pushes me over the edge. It's only an hour before my next dose anyway. I just need to sleep. I need to be numb for a while. It doesn't mean that I'm addicted.

Fumbling with the bottle, I finally get it open.

For a minute, I do nothing but stare at the pill in my hand. The garage door will be opening any moment, it's now or never. I close my eyes, swearing to myself that this will be the only time. Never again. Only this one time.

I swallow the pill.

CHAPTER FOUR

Now – Connor

"Come on, Ms. G. Haven't I always been good to you?" I flash my best smile, the one that never lets me down, with just the right amount of cheekiness.

Ms. G arches her brow. "I've seen you, you know? With all those girls."

My smile widens. "None of them ever complain."

She rolls her eyes. "God help us all."

I've almost got her.

"Please, Ms. G, you should have *seen* this girl." Unfortunately, my desperate pleading isn't fabricated, it's not just a show because I *am* desperate to find her.

She shakes her head, but it's less emphatic.

One more round of begging and I'll have her. I just need to make her think I'm not only looking for a hookup, even though that's all I'm capable of. "I haven't been able to stop thinking about her."

This girl—whom I will lose my mind over if I have to keep referring to her like that—has been haunting me. She's invaded all my thoughts, all my actions. I haven't been able to focus on writing new music for the band, and we need it badly. We need something new, something different. Except my head is stuck on an icy, uptight blonde.

I haven't even been able to enjoy a ciggy, which up until this point has basically been written into my DNA. Somehow, every time I pick one up, her words run through my head, and for some reason it *gets* me. This is so *fucked.*

Ms. G sighs, saving me from the bloody fuck job which is my head. "If you are anything short of a gentleman to this poor young lady whom I'm about to sic you on, I will have something to say about it."

I can't withhold my victorious grin as she clicks print.

Ms. G works for the main office of Vortex, the company which is almost wholly responsible for putting on the bigger shows we get invited to open for. Since we haven't gone big yet, the shows are still considered fairly small, meaning the event organizing, ticketing, set lists, and getting sponsors are all managed in-house by Vortex.

For the first time, I feel grateful for it.

It's the only way I would have the balls to come in here and ask Ms. G to print the list of ticket holders from last week. It's the only way I wasn't told to fuck off and get reported to the police for being a creep. Anyone else would have. Not Ms. G.

She gives me one more disapproving look before she hands me the list. "This goes nowhere else, right?"

"What goes nowhere else?" I say with a smug grin.

"Exactly. Now get that accent and smile out of this office, it's too warm." Ms. G starts fanning herself with her mousepad.

I can't help but chuckle. She's adorable. "Thanks heaps, Ms. G."

She just rolls her eyes and keeps fanning as I make my way out of the office.

Okay, *Ice Queen*.

If you thought you had the last word, you've got another thing coming.

● ● ●

"Uhh. You good, bro?" That's concern laced into Theo's voice, and I get why.

I don't know what time it is, I don't even know what *day* it is. I've destroyed our living room. There are papers scattered everywhere, covered in colorful highlights, having gone through about three highlighters. Ran them fucking dead, marking off each name as they got eliminated.

First, I crossed out all the strictly male names. The gender-neutral ones were a bit harder, but I still managed. She didn't seem like a Taylor or Alex, anyway. The only issue is after going through the gender-neutral ones and the strictly female, I've now crossed off *every* name on the list.

Every. Single. One.

Usually, when I get in my head like this, I can just go outside and chain smoke, but Ice Queen stole that, too, along with the rest of my sanity. That last bit is what explains the twenty unsmoked cigarettes scattered about among the mess.

Theo must take my silence as confirmation that I've deep dived into a real nutter. He approaches slowly, dropping onto the floor next to me. "Walk me through it. Sometimes it helps to have an exterior perspective."

"This is a list of everyone with tickets to our last show. I went through every name and every social media account under each one. I checked Facebook. Instagram. TikTok. Twitter. Even fucking *LinkedIn*. Mate, do you know how *painful* it was to go through LinkedIn?"

Theo smirks. "I can only imagine. Did you check the gender-neutral names?"

I groan. "Been there, done that."

He lets out a low breath. "How long have you been here?"

"I couldn't answer that, even if I wanted to."

"She got under your skin pretty good," he says, somewhat awed. Theo knows my style, and this is not it. I've lost my goddamn mind.

We're quiet for a few minutes. Maybe it's hours.

"What if she's not on this list because she didn't have a ticket?"

I shake my head. "Yeah, nah. Ice Queen isn't the type of girl to jump a fence, trust me. She was wearing a *turtleneck*."

Theo chuckles, but thankfully doesn't ask about the nickname. "You're going after a girl who wears turtlenecks?"

I put my head in my hands.

"That's not what I meant anyway," Theo continues. "I meant, what if she wasn't *attending*. What if she was *working*?"

My head shoots up.

It would explain why she isn't on this list, why she was wearing a turtleneck to a show, and it may even be why she turned me down. She was *working*. She must be an executive at Vortex. There's a chance that my routine isn't broken after all, because if she really was working, she could've never accepted.

"You're a bloody genius." I grab Theo by the neck. "What time is it? What day is it?"

Mercifully, Theo doesn't comment on my lack of basic orientation. "Tuesday. Four o'clock. PM."

That means I haven't slept since Sunday night.

Vortex doesn't close for another hour. I can make it.

I jump up from the floor and jog to the door. "I'll be back!!"

• • •

"Nope. Nope. NOPE. Absolutely NOT." Ms. G is playing hard to get today. "I can't give you access to a list of Vortex employees."

"Ms. G, you have to give me *something*. I'm a man who's lost his marbles."

"I could lose my job for that. I won't be risking that so you can get some tail."

I love when Ms. G uses words like tail.

"If I lose my mind, I can't perform. Surely Vortex doesn't want to lose their talent. If you think about it, you're just doing what's best for Vortex."

She shakes her head. "The court of law and basic privacy wouldn't agree."

"*Please*, Ms. G, I'm *begging* you." It might be the nicotine withdrawals driving me to such lengths, but I am not above getting on my hands and knees for this woman.

She sighs. "Describe her to me."

I don't let myself dwell on the fact that her face is permanently etched into my mind.

"She has the most clear, striking blue eyes I have ever seen. Almost like the water in the Maldives, but if it was frozen into an iceberg." I'm lost in the description immediately. "She doesn't wear makeup. Not even a *drop*. She has blonde hair, the natural kind, but I can't tell you the length because it was so tightly wound up in a little bun. Her nose is...well, perfect. Her lips are the only *unproportionate* part of her and a bit pouty. She's got this amazing bone structure...and she smells like lavender."

Ms. G has a big, horrible grin on her face. "Mr. Connor. I believe you're about to find yourself in trouble with this one."

Even Ms. G knows I'm fucked.

"Unfortunately, there is no one who works here that *remotely* matches that description." She looks disappointed for me, like she really does want to help me find her.

LAST *Stand* FOR GENEVIEVE

I reach up and pull my hair in frustration. "Surely, there is some executive here who closely matches it, or maybe she works in publicity?" Though, I've never met anyone in that industry who doesn't build a new face with makeup.

Ms. G shakes her head. "Not from Vortex."

I walk a little circle, the jitters really getting to my head. The fact that I haven't eaten, slept, or taken a piss in over twenty-four hours doesn't help.

Ms. G groans. "I'm definitely going to lose my job for this."

I turn to her, putting my hands together, uttering a prayer to the God of one-night stands. "Ms. G. Thank you. Thank you. Thank you."

"You better invite me to the wedding," she says, printing some papers.

"Er, sure. No worries." Ms. G doesn't need to know marriage will never be in the cards for me. I already had my chance at that and lost it.

She pulls back, just as I reach for the papers. "Not a word. To *anyone. Ever.*"

I mime sealing my lips with a zipper and bow to her, my savior.

She hands them over. "No more little visits, Mr. Connor."

I give her my smile, which I know is her favorite, as I back away. "Maybe you can come over for a shrimp on the barbie sometime."

My Aussie ancestors just turned over in their grave, hearing me say that fucking blasphemy, which was invented by Americans *for* Americans. If they'd really done their research, they'd know we don't even say "shrimp" down under, but my words hit their mark, Ms. G beginning to fan herself with her mousepad, just as I intended. She loves my harmless flirting and I owe her at least that.

Exiting the building, I feel more jittery than before, needing to eat something and find a urinal before I dive down this hopefully more fruitful hole.

I don't even bother with attempting a smoke.

• • •

"This doesn't make sense," Theo says, absolutely stumped.

"Mate, I'm gonna lose it in a minute."

Theo decided to go through the next list with me. He's been typing the names and flashing me the photos for hours. This list is much smaller than the ticket holders, but it's still not a small job.

19

"That was the last name on the list you gave me." He looks thoughtful. "You're sure this is all the names of the people working the show?"

"Yeah. Those were the only people listed under the representatives of sponsors, vendors, and publicity attendance."

"What about the actual staff?"

"What do you mean?"

"You know, the people *working* the festival. Security, ticketing booth, trash duty, toilets...."

I shake my head. "I've *worked* both the trash duty and toilet duty on festivals, she doesn't strike me as the type who would sign up for that."

Though she didn't strike me as a trust fund brat with a closet full of Prada, like the kind who frequent Ryder's bar, I would be more likely to believe *that* over trash duty.

"Well, maybe you were wrong," Theo says simply.

I decide to entertain him, though I'm positive it will lead to more disappointment. Going through the ticketing staff first, I cross off every single one because I know them all. I cross off the guys on security next, I know them too. Toilet duty is next, but they're the same dudes I roughed it with when it was the only work I could get.

I start on trash duty, one name that I don't recognize clanging through me.

Brooke Anderson.

I rip Theo's laptop from his grip, making him chuckle, typing in *Brooke Anderson* into the Facebook search. There are hundreds, just in Tampa Bay, but none of them are her.

I check Instagram.

Nothing.

TikTok.

Nothing.

Twitter.

Nothing.

LinkedIn.

Nothing.

"Shit! She's not here," I say, angry now. "I guess I'll try Google next, but it's usually only famous people or criminals on there."

"Did you check Pinterest? Every girl has a Pinterest."

I open Pinterest and type in *Brooke Anderson*, scrolling through a few until I find a private profile, every pin hidden. All I can see is a tiny photo icon.

Her face is turned to the side, hair covering most of her face, but that's her.

Every cell in my body wakes up, comes back to life.

I found her.

Brooke Anderson.

CHAPTER FIVE

Then - Brooke

Something cold and wet presses against my forehead, attempting to pull me out of my deep unconsciousness. My welcomed oblivion. The place I wish I could stay forever.

I start to stir. Everything hurts and it hurts *bad*. I must be having another nightmare.

"How are you feeling, sweetie?" My mom's gentle voice leads me back. I finally open my eyes, finding that we're in my room. Mom is pressing a damp rag to my forehead, eyes full of concern.

Right. My life *is* the nightmare.

I close my eyes again, wishing I could disappear. The events from yesterday—or whatever day that was—roll through my mind. Pain and soreness have become as typical as breathing for me, but the fall is to blame for making things even worse. The fall I took when I was... when I was sneaking an extra pill.

My mom brings her hand to my cheek with a loving stroke, having no idea what I did. Adrenaline floods in, caused by the fear that she already knows, followed closely by guilt.

So much guilt.

I try not to think about it, but it presses in harder, sending a wave of severe nausea straight to my gut. My palms are sweaty. My body temperature is rising. My heart is beating too fast. The thought of my violation is making me physically ill.

Mom must think I'm unwell, which is why she's in here with a damp rag, cooling me down. She doesn't realize that it's *my* fault. There's no bacteria or virus, just me, violating her trust in me and my trust in *myself*, because I'm not strong enough to face reality.

I slowly open my eyes, trying to get a read on her expression. There's no trace of anger or betrayal, but maybe she's just going easy on me since she thinks I'm ill.

No, she wouldn't sugarcoat this kind of thing no matter how sick I was.

She must not know. Yet.

What if I didn't put everything back exactly how I found it? If the chair was crooked at her desk, would she have guessed what I'd used it for? Would she count the number of pills in the bottle just to be sure?

My heart is pounding so hard, every other sound becomes canceled out. The room starts to spin, my chest feels too heavy. I feel the sweat trickle down the back of my neck, as I lock down my emotions, trying to stop the panic.

"Sweetie, are you sick?" Her sweet voice somehow finds a way to reach me. My sweet, sweet mom. My *strong* mom.

We have lost the same people.

She lost the love of her life to drug addiction, forced to watch him change into a completely different person than the one she fell in love with. She lost him little by little, every single day and still found the strength to shield us from it.

Then she lost... *her.*

Yet here she is, putting one foot in front of another, finding it in herself to keep going. Neither of us admit that we lost *me*, too. My body is still here, but I'm not. I think it may be permanent, but Mom must still have hope.

"Sweetie, can you hear me?" Her voice has taken on a panicked tone, urgency.

I nod my head. "Yeah."

The bed shifts as she lets out a breath and relaxes. "I was worried there for a second."

I crack open my eyes just in time to see her glance at the clock, full of worry. She has to go to work now. She doesn't want to leave me, but she has no choice. The bills won't pay themselves. Death would have been much cheaper.

"Mom, I'll be fine."

She looks at me apologetically. "I wish I could stay, sweetie."

I don't. "It's okay, Mom. Go to work."

"I have to." She squeezes my hand. "I'll get you some things before I go. I'll be right back."

She walks out of my bedroom and I try to sit up, hating what I've become in her presence. Well, really anybody's presence.

When you're the one who lives, people look at you like you're a miracle destined for greatness, since you were the one who was chosen to survive. They look at you, expecting an amazing person who deserves it, who feels *lucky*.

But I'm not destined for anything great. I'm not part of anything bigger. I'm not going to change the world. I don't feel *lucky*. Instead, I get to endure excruciating pain, a few months of burdening the only person I have left, following it up with a lifetime of unending pressure.

My mom's entire life revolves around taking care of me now. Making sure I eat. Making sure I breathe. It's a fast track to no dignity or self-respect, especially when you can't get up easily to go to the bathroom.

I have become *everything* she focuses on. The thought that if something happens to me, she will be utterly alone, haunts my every move. She tries not to, but I know she watches everything I do with the fear that it could be the thing that takes me away.

Getting sick is no longer just getting sick.

Crossing the street is no longer just crossing the street.

Getting into a car is no longer just getting into a car.

All survival *is*, is becoming the source of another person's anxiety and the constant feeling that you're responsible for what was lost. Your life is no longer for yourself. It's for them. It doesn't matter whether you want to be there or not, because you're all they have left.

I've managed to reach a sitting position on the side of the bed by the time my mom walks back in, hands full of vitamins, cold medicines, and a tall glass of water. "Sweetie, I know it isn't fun, but I need you to take all of this today. We need to beat this sickness head on."

She never says the words, but what she is really saying is that she needs me to stay alive.

"Okay." I put slight pressure on what's supposed to be my good leg and wince. My ankle must have been injured during the fall. Stretching my back sends my spine screaming all the way down to my hips.

The fog from unconsciousness has started to clear, and I'm terrified of what it's left in its wake. Everything hurts so much more than I've ever remembered it hurting. Is it from the fall or has it somehow been intensified in my mind?

My emotions are...all over the place. It's different from how I've been feeling; the hopelessness, the depression. No, it's not that. I feel...on edge. I have this weird impatience flowing through my entire body, as if I'm just waiting for something to set me off.

I feel...*all wrong.*

The thought of experiencing this for an entire day… I know in my bones that I can't. Looking at the clock gives me instant relief. I only have to make it through an hour before my next dose of oblivion. I'm so relieved that I forget to be sickened by it.

"I brought something else that I thought you might like." My mom's voice is hesitant, but genuine. She thinks that whatever she has behind her back may bring me happiness.

I do my best to sound like I care. "What is it?"

Mom slowly reveals what she's carrying and places it on my lap.

The silence is deafening.

Tulips. Pastels. Books. Spring. Life.

Her favorite book, the one she read to me in my hospital room in the alternate reality where I'd let her stay home to study.

My mom shifts on her feet in front of me, clearly starting to worry that maybe I'm not ready for this. She's right. I'm not ready. I will never be ready.

"It's been almost a month, Brooke. I'm worried that you're not processing this in a healthy way."

"Healthy?" My whisper is raspy, one of death.

"Brooke. I love you so much." There's a but coming. "I've given you time, but continuing to bottle up this grief will only make things worse. You have to walk into the grief and let yourself feel the pain, to-"

"It's not the pain, Mom." My voice scares me, I don't recognize it. A weird feeling courses through me, like I've dropped off that ledge where I've been standing in my mind since I woke up. "I wish it was just the pain."

"Then what *is* it, sweetie? *Talk* to me."

I remain silent, not trusting what I will say and not wanting to hurt my mom, as something builds beneath my skin.

"Brooke…she wouldn't want this for you."

The feeling erupts, pulsating throughout my entire body and mind. The rage. The anger. The urge to ruin everything the way *she* was ruined. It pushes against my skin, pushes against my mind.

I do my best not to scream. "She can't *want* anything! She's *dead.*"

My mom's face contorts into sheer agony, the echo of my words making me sick. The look on my mom's face makes me sick. *I* did that to her. But I don't know how to stop. She needs to leave before I can hurt her even more.

"Please leave." I want to get on my knees and beg for her to leave.

I won't be able to live with what I do if she stays any longer, needing to be alone until I can figure out what the hell is happening to me.

"Brooke. We have to remain strong. We are all we have left," Mom says the last part with a soft sob. I want to hug her, comfort her, promise her that she still has me, that she always will.

Instead, I do the worst thing possible. "It's easy to be strong when all you have to live with is *grief.* You have *no idea* why I feel the way I do." My voice is getting too loud. "NO IDEA!"

Mom's crying now. "Then tell me. *Please.* Just tell me everything."

She will hate me if she finds out that it was my fault. My mom takes my silence as something that it most definitely isn't: consideration.

"Everything happens for a reason, and some things are out of our control."

Her words are like acid, coating my skin, setting me on fire. Everything goes quiet besides the sound of the pin falling to the floor. I release the grenade and destroy what I have left.

"There is NO reason! No reason will EVER be good enough! How can you even SAY that!? You think ANYTHING would be more important than her life!?"

I know that's not what she meant, but I say it anyway.

"No. I-" My mom is shaking her head. The tears cascading down her face. "No, that's not-"

"It's never been the PAIN, Mom." I'm still screaming. "It should have been ME. I shouldn't even be here right now. I don't WANT to be here, but now I'M FORCED TO because of YOU."

My mom is silent. Broken.

I did that. I'm the one who broke her.

She needs to leave before I hurt her even more. If that's even possible.

I launch the book into the wall.

Mom flinches, not at the crash, but at the fact that her only daughter has just become something she can no longer look at. She drops her head and leaves my room. Soon, I hear the front door close behind her.

The guilt pours back in, sending me to the toilet faster than the pain can even stop me from moving. I hurl nothing and everything into the toilet bowl as the thoughts barrel into me.

The sound of squealing brakes and crunching metal.

Hurl.

She's gone.

Hurl.

It should have been me.

Hurl.

Becoming my father.

Hurl.

Destroying all my mom has left.

Hurl.

In this moment, I know that I'm losing myself.

There is only one way to make this stop.

I crawl away from the toilet to steal another pill.

I crawl away to lose myself for good.

CHAPTER SIX

Now - Connor

I was so focused on finding Brooke's name that I didn't think about how I would actually find her, once I had it, in the physical sense. Guess I assumed I'd see her Instagram posts about where she brunches or goes out and stage a run in. A meet cute.

Except the only thing I've got is a private Pinterest account.

I don't know what to make of her. *Brooke Anderson.*

I've never bothered with a hookup that requires so much work. See, I'm not one of those guys who works to break through someone's walls and then ghosts them. Nah, that's fucked up. The girls I hookup with are DTF. They know where it begins and ends with me: sex.

Just sex. End of story.

As long as I'm honest about my intentions, none of them ever have a reason to complain. Playing guitar...it makes you *good* with your fingers and thankfully, my skills make up for my complete lack of ability to develop feelings. The girls who are looking for feelings, I give 'em a righteo and wish them luck finding Prince Charming. It'll just never be me.

Most assume that my aversion stems from a bad breakup or toxic relationship experience. Nah, never had to go through any of that crap, thankfully. Theo has his own theory, but I banned him from spouting philosophical shit in my direction. I don't know why people have the urge to try and figure out the "why," as if that can change the "it."

The bottom line is that things are much simpler when you leave feelings out of the equation. It's really that easy. I don't need a Freudian analysis to explain it to me.

My rules have never failed me.

No feelings. No relationships.

That's why it's been... a while since I've put in this kind of leg work. I'm not sure if it's a good idea. Part of me knows it's one of my worst to date, but sometimes the bad ideas turn out to be the most fun.

I haven't even thought through what I'm going to do or say when I find her.

Brooke doesn't strike me as my usual DTF type. She doesn't strike me as the relationship type either. Is that why I'm acting fucking wacko? Because she's the first girl I've never been able to figure out at a glance?

Mix that with nicotine withdrawals, and it explains why I've gone fully mad.

I just need to get her *out* of my head, starting with figuring out what's going on in *her* head and why someone who looks like they could have it all is working trash duty at a festival. No judgment from my end, I worked that gig for ages before meeting Theo and getting this life handed to me so that I could pursue my dreams.

Brooke could be doing the same, pursuing a dream.

Maybe she has a prick of a father like I do, who wants her to be a doctor, regardless of what she wants, so she's going it on her own. Or maybe she is a trust fund baby, but wants a taste of the real world, while proving she can make it without anyone's help. Maybe she's a criminal on the run, that could be hot.

All I know is that I need to find her. Figure her out. Get a good bang in, if I'm lucky. Then, I can smoke a pack of ciggies, make up for lost time, and move the fuck on.

What I *can* get a read on, though, is that Brooke is wound up tight. *So* fucking tight. I'd guess it's been... years. And bloody hell, would I like to be the one to...

"Oh, *God*, the look on your face makes me want to hurl." Ara's dry tone pulls me out of my Ice Queen fantasy. I'd like to travel back in time to thank myself for dressing in my thick jeans today, or she really would be hurling right now.

I grin. "There's only one reason why girls gag around me."

"Oh my fucking hell. I have to bleach my brain now," she says as she plops down on the other couch across from me, crossing her legs and putting a pillow in her lap, which means she plans to stay for a while.

I chuckle. Ara's become like a sister to me over the past year. I've never seen my brother so...*fulfilled*. A distant, far away part of me used to wish for what he has. Almost had it once.

"Theo with his agent?" I ask.

My boy has skyrocketed in every way, not just finding his soul mate. His book was an instant bestseller, currently under negotiations for film adaptations with several heavy hitters in the film industry. When he's not helping me stalk Brooke, which is a field he has *considerable* experience in according to Ara, he's in back-to-back meetings.

Ara nods with a proud smile. "This is going to be huge for him. I can't *wait* to see what he does with it."

"I couldn't be happier for him."

Her expression softens. "I know."

Ara knows our past. Knows how deep our bond goes.

A while after she and Theo got together, she moved in. It was one of the first times we'd ever hung out just the two of us, Theo went out to get popcorn for their date night. I about fell over when she suddenly embraced me, thanking me for saving the life of her soul mate, for keeping her happiness safe until she found it. Then pulled away awkwardly, apologizing for being a hug slut, said it was something new for her.

I decided to tell her the story from *my* perspective. How Theo had looked when I found him on what was supposed to be his last night on this earth. Somehow, I'd known just by looking at him why he was sitting there in the middle of the night, looking out at the water.

I'd been put there to stop it by whatever fates may be. Then I told her what Theo had saved *me* from that night, which ended up in both of us crying. I may be a man, but I've still got fucking tear ducts.

The look on Theo's face when he walked in that night, finding the two of us sitting on the couch, hugging respective tissue boxes as snot ran down our faces is something I'll never forget. Ara jumped him right there.

LAST *Stand* FOR GENEVIEVE

Once I realized they weren't coming back for the popcorn or the movie they'd rented, I ate it all in a sad attempt to drown out my feelings while I watched the worst chick flick of all time, by myself.

"What about you?" Ara asks, bringing me back to the here and now.

"What about me?"

"You look like you got kicked in the dick recently. Tinder date gone wrong?"

I snort. Theo sure knows how to pick them. "Tinder is treating me just fine, thank you."

Ara sends me a pointed look. "What's got you looking like you're tied in knots, then?"

I groan, not wanting to get into this with her. She's going to bust my balls, but I don't think I have a choice. And, she's probably the only person who has a shot at giving me helpful insight into Brooke's female brain.

An evil grin spreads across Ara's face. "It's about a *girl*, isn't it?"

I chuck a pillow at her, but she catches it and throws it back faster than I can block, hitting me straight in the face. Here it comes.

"So? Big Booby Britta not cutting it anymore?"

I roll my eyes, knowing she's only just begun. If I could travel back in time, there's only two things I would change. One of them being the ONLY time I've ever left my phone on the counter, screen unlocked. Ara went straight to my contacts and has never let me live it down.

"What about Tatted Titties Tara?" She cackles.

I get comfortable, not sure how long this is going to take.

"Did you tire of Strap-On Sadie??" She's howling now, making these up as she goes. Even I find it hard not to join in when she gets like this, her laugh is contagious. I've never been able to believe that there was a time she rarely did it.

"What about-" Ara can't breathe enough to get the words out, and I'm barely holding in my grin now. She finally screams, "What about CLITTY CLARA!?"

I lose my shit and finally join in. "Not even Dildo Diana can fix this mess in my head." Ara's laughing so hard I can't tell whether she's sobbing or still laughing. Even *my* stomach aches from it.

"Whew," she says, trying to get oxygen down while wiping her eyes. "I'm sorry. I couldn't help myself."

I give her a minute to steady herself and then successfully chuck the pillow this time, hitting her square in the shoulder. "Hey!!!"

I laugh again. "This is serious."

This sobers her. "Shit. It's about a girl and it's serious?" She's quiet for a moment, contemplative. "Oh fuck, you finally got an STD, didn't you?"

I groan, pulling my hair in frustration. "Let me know when you're done being mean."

"Okay, done. Tell me."

I take a deep breath. "I met a girl-"

"HOLY SHIT! Sorry. Shutting up. Continue, please."

I shoot her a look. "I met a girl, and I can't figure her out. Which is... unusual for me."

She smirks. "The routine didn't work, did it?"

"There is nothing wrong with my routine, something is up with this one, and I don't know what it is."

"Right, of course. *Definitely* not the routine," she says dryly.

"I need to figure out what it is, though, or I'm going to lose my literal fucking mind."

"Sounds like she got under your skin instead of your sheets," Ara says, a bit less sarcastic now, knowing this is unprecedented. "Tell me what happened."

I launch into the story of how I met Brooke, the lengths I've gone to thus far just to find out what her name is. Ara has this shit-eating grin plastered on her face, throughout the entire retelling, making me nauseous, *obviously*.

"This doesn't mean what you think it does," I tell her. "I'm still looking for the same thing. Just sex. I just have to... work a bit harder this time."

She nods, like I just spouted a crock of emu shit.

"I'm serious, Ara. My rules haven't changed. They never will."

"I wouldn't dream of it," she says with a wink. "So how do you plan on finding her?"

"I was hoping you could help with that. Maybe talk to her over Pinterest for me."

She snorts. "Oh, wait, you're for real?"

"Yes, I'm for real," I say in a mock American accent.

She cackles. "No way in hell, dude. Make your own Pinterest account."

"Please."

"Well, since you said please... still no. I want to see Bewitching Brooke torture you some more. It's only healthy."

"Ughhhhhh. You were supposed to *help* me, not make it worse."

She shrugs. "Connor, until you realize that this could be different, that there might be another reason than your dick that's inspiring you to put in this much effort, I'll be remaining on the sidelines."

"You're right, there is another reason," I hedge, throwing her off. "I want a *fucking* cigarette!"

Ara lets out a low whistle and stands, not even questioning my outburst. "Good luck with that Pinterest account. Word of advice, don't make your username something cringy like *ConnorLovesBoobs69*. Probably won't help your case."

"I hate you." She knows I don't mean it.

"See ya, Cunt." Ara tosses over her shoulder, leaving me to my misery.

She's right. I don't see another way around it. So, I figuratively cut off my balls and shelve them, download the Pinterest app, and create an account. I consider my username for a moment. It *has* to be perfect. It'll be the only chance to get my foot in the door.

I could be straightforward.

AussieConnorLovesCigarettes

She would know who I was that way, but not sure it's the best approach.

I could take the comical route. Girls use this app for house crap, right?

ConnorLovesThePropertyBrothers

The fact that I know who they are takes me down a notch on my own peg.

Scratch that.

Think.

Think.

Think.

I've got it.

ConnorLovesTurtlenecks

It's funny, sends a message, and she'll know exactly who I am.

I create my account and start their profiling survey so they can hack my brain in that creepy way social media platforms do. Maybe I'll save some stuff so she can get to know me a little, hopefully smooth over the stalker bit. Bloody hell, there's some cool stuff on here.

I make a board for musician aesthetic inspo. I don't know what that means, but it sounds like something chicks would dig. Now that I look at it, I could probably do one of these outfits for my next gig.

Save.

Wow, I would *kill* for one of these custom guitar designs. I'll save it, so I can find it later and reward myself when we land our first record deal.

Save.

I keep scrolling. This amp skin is sick.

Save.

I'm about fifty pins in, when I remember why I got onto his app from hell. Brooke wants to talk about addiction? This qualifies because I'm not going to be able to put it down. Balls permanently shelved.

Clearing my head, I go to the search bar and type in Brooke Anderson.

Scrolling all the way to the bottom, I find that tiny icon, where I can barely make out that nose of hers. The outer edges of her lips. Lips my body is screaming to feel anywhere. *Everywhere.*

I click "request" and wait.

CHAPTER SEVEN

Then - Brooke

I realized that I'm going to have to get smarter about this.

After my outburst this morning, my mom may become suspicious. I'm hoping that she chalks it up to the "new me." Maybe she will blame it on the fact that I wasn't feeling well. She might even think that this morning was a sign of progress, of "opening up."

If I'm honest with myself, I have no idea where all of that came from, but I know for sure it wasn't progress. It wasn't "opening up". I'm not usually the person to lash out and say things that harm the people I care about. That *was* new for me.

Thankfully, once I'd taken another pill, that edginess and the jitters seemed to ease. I didn't feel so guilty anymore. I didn't feel like I just destroyed the last thing which mattered to me. I felt...*better*.

I *swear* that I'm not going to keep this up for long, only long enough until I can function on my own. When I take a pill, I believe that things will get easier. It gives me room to breathe. Things aren't pressing on me so much. I even felt like listening to music today as it carried me into unconsciousness.

My mom would be somewhere between devastated and furious if she knew how I was coping. She would drag me to the hospital and chain me up until it was all out of my system. That's only because she wouldn't understand that I'm doing it *for* her.

She wants me to feel better. I feel better when I take the pills.

So, I will let her think that I've made progress. I will cover my tracks in case she gets suspicious, using the pills as my crutch for *just* a little while longer. What happened this morning can never happen again, and the only way I can ensure that it doesn't is by taking them.

I won't get addicted because I'm not that kind of person.

I'm not a criminal or a deadbeat. And I'm not my father.

I just need to feel better.

And I need to manage it without getting caught.

Mom would notice the bottle slowly emptying out, and climbing onto a chair to reach the pills each time is too much of a risk. Not only could I take another bad fall, but it increases the odds of leaving a trail of evidence. Thankfully, I have a plan.

Slowly and painfully, I make my way to the medicine cabinet at the end of the hallway, just outside of my room. Opening the child-safe bottles is not the easiest when you've still got one arm in a cast, but I'll make it work. I've got all day.

After opening every single bottle, I realize that not one leftover prescription looks enough like *my* pills to replace what's in the bottle. None are quite the right size or shape. They're either capsules, too oval shaped or too chunky. My mom isn't an idiot.

I limp back to my room to strategize, having no idea how to cover this up in a way where she won't figure it out. Finally, I reach my bed, taking care not to sit too fast. The physical pain is starting to come back, which is never a good sign because it means the other pain isn't far behind.

Looking at the clock, I realize that today's dose didn't last as long as yesterday's did. Surely, it's a coincidence. I couldn't develop a tolerance that quickly, could I?

The book I threw at the wall this morning is still on the floor, where it will stay until my mom decides to put it back where it belongs. Thoughts, the kind I don't want, start to stir, and I need to look anywhere but at that damn book.

I glance at the clock on my bedside table, making sure I counted the hours correctly. Maybe I read it wrong since it's practically covered by all the vitamin bottles my mom dumped on it—wait. *The vitamin bottles.*

Unscrewing the first bottle, it's not even close. I reach for the second bottle, having barely had time to put the other one down without dumping it all over the floor. Once again, not even close. I do this with all five bottles and come up empty each time. Nothing looks remotely similar to my pills.

Until it hits me.

When I first got my period, I used to get lightheaded all the time. My mom would say it was because I was lacking iron, and she would make me swallow iron tablets.

Iron tablets.

They were red. Not too thin. Not too thick. You wouldn't be able to tell the difference in color unless you held them right next to each other.

Fucking iron tablets.

• • •

The iron tablets were as good as it's going to get. At a glance, nobody would know the difference. I just need to make sure I don't do anything to make my mom suspicious enough that she takes a closer look.

I've just finished counting and sorting the pills I need to replace when I hear the garage door open, sending my stomach straight into my feet. Mom isn't supposed to be home yet. It's only been a few hours since she left. I should still have the majority of the day to finish cleaning up my mess. Now, I have about ninety seconds.

If my mom is home early, it means she was worried enough to check on me, likely before she does anything else. I need to move *now,* otherwise this is going to be over before it starts.

Standing as fast as I can from the swivel chair I've pushed into Mom's closet, I put the iron tablets into my prescription bottle, praying that she never decides to take a better look. My heart pounds as the sound of the car engine echoes in the garage.

My remaining pills go into the now-empty iron bottle, leaving me with a handful of leftover iron tablets. I don't have time to decide what to do with them, so I put them into the pocket of my sweats followed by the iron bottle, that way I can make better use of my hand.

I glance at the swivel chair and the shelf where this box needs to be returned to, instantly feeling sick. If I fall, my entire plan is ruined. I won't be able to finish putting things away or get back to my room in time.

Mom will not only find me here, obviously having taken a dose without her permission, but she will see the lengths I was going to in order to cover my tracks. She will know this isn't the first time and take me to the hospital, where they'll stop me from feeling better.

The engine cuts off. I don't have long.

Taking one last look at the swivel chair, I clench my teeth and put all of my weight on my still-healing leg. I manage to pull myself up in one fluid motion, causing the chair to move only slightly, before I can grab a rack for balance. The garage door begins to close as I place the box back where it belongs. I can't afford to make sure it's in the perfect spot or facing the right direction.

Rolling the chair back to Mom's desk on the other side of her room, I move as fast as my injured body and the carpet allow. The door from our garage opens with a jingle of keys, leaving me less than thirty seconds to get back to my room before she finds me in the hallway, or worse, in here.

I grit my teeth, reaching into my pocket to steady the bottle so it doesn't make a sound as I run. It's bulky and slow, with pain lashing through my legs and spine, but I make it back to my room before her footsteps reach the midway point of the stairs, allowing her a direct view of the hallway.

"Brooke?" My mom calls out, only a few steps left to go.

I lower myself into my bed, trying to make everything look dull and hopeless as it has for weeks. It's a task and a half, trying to calm my breathing and eyes, which are too wild. At the last minute, I realize the iron bottle, now full of pills, will make a sound from where it remains in my pocket if I move the slightest bit. Just as I go to place it on the side table, my mom walks in, eyes zeroing in on the bottle of secrets.

She caught me. She caught me. She caught me.

I've never lied to my mom. I don't even know what I could say to explain this situation. There's nothing I *could* say, actually. I'm busted. Instinctively, I snatch the bottle back into my grasp as if she's going to try and take it away.

"I'm glad to see you're taking the vitamins, even if you waited until I came back through the door." She gives me a disapproving look.

Vitamins?

Oh.

"Let me help you." Mom moves to sit next to me on the bed and I'm frozen. She reaches for the iron bottle, having to pry it from my hand. "Come on, don't be stubborn. Let me help you."

I couldn't stop her if my life depended on it, and in a way, it does. She is holding my pills. One good look and everything is over. I will have to endure what I've been enduring for weeks now, and there will be no more coming up for breath.

Going under is probably a better way to put it.

My mom is saying things to me as she unscrews the lid, but I can't hear anything over the pounding in my ears, the screaming silence in my mind as I wait for her to discover what I've done.

She dumps out one tablet.

Then two.

My heart stops.

Mom doesn't spare it a second glance as she screws the lid back on and reaches for the next bottle. One by one, she dumps more tablets and capsules into her hand until she's got an entire balanced diet in her palm. Plus, my pills.

"Brooke, give me your hand."

I don't know how long I've been frozen, but I finally find my muscles and reach out my hand. She dumps everything into it, passing me a glass of water immediately after.

"I'm not leaving until you've swallowed every single one of those." She crosses her arms to show that she means business.

Glancing down at my palm, there are two pills mixed in with the vitamins. I've never taken more than one at a time, not to mention what I already took earlier. I don't know enough about drugs to know whether this endangers my life or not. So, I stall.

Swallowing every other pill in my hand, I pretend to choke on the last, shaking my head. "I'll have to take these later, I'm afraid I'll choke."

My mom shakes her head. "Your body needs it now." She reaches into her pocket, pulling out a strawberry Go-Gurt. My favorite. "This was supposed to be my peace offering, but it'll help them go down if you chew them a bit first."

My mom feels that *she* is the one who has to apologize, that *she* is the one who has done something wrong. I take it from her and try to manage a smile, but don't even get close. "Thanks, Mom."

Fate is fucked up. This is the one thing my mom would *never* want for me, and the universe is twisted enough to make her the one pushing it down my throat. My mom smiles. She thinks she's helped me, done something good here. The Go-Gurt does nothing to conceal the awful, bitter taste taking over my mouth, but I manage to hold back my grimace.

"I love you, honey," Mom says as she brushes my cheek. "We'll talk more when you feel better."

While I should be feeling gratitude for her unconditional love and comforting touch, all I can think about is whether the box of pictures, containing the pill bottle, is facing the right direction. It's all I can think about until the high comes and carries me away to places greater than I've ever known.

CHAPTER EIGHT

Now – Connor

It's been twenty-four hours.

Brooke hasn't accepted my Pinterest request yet.

She's probably just making me sweat.

I'm fine. I like a challenge.

• • •

It's been forty-eight hours.

She'll accept it today.

• • •

Seventy-two. Fucking. Hours.

Why am I counting?

• • •

Ninety-six hours.

Must be an old account.

If she doesn't accept today, I'll let it go.

One-hundred-and-twenty hours.

Weird. I can no longer find her account.

Me: I think she deleted her account.

Ara: Nope. It still comes up for me.

Me: My app must be glitching then.

Ara: It's not glitching. You've been blocked.

Blocked!?

I need a fucking cigarette.

CHAPTER NINE

Then - Brooke

I came down for breakfast today.

Mom almost fell out of her chair when she saw me hobbling toward the table. Her face and body were frozen in shock for all of five seconds before she launched into motion, pouring me a bowl of my favorite cereal.

She's attempting to play it off, trying to act like this isn't a big deal, me getting out of bed. Mom is quiet, probably afraid of saying something to jinx it and lose the progress she believes I'm making.

Don't worry, Mom, as long as I keep taking the pills, I'll keep coming for breakfast.

I'll be able to pretend I'm still the daughter you've always had.

I'll keep making you happy.

She places the bowl in front of me and quietly takes a seat in her usual chair. I avoid looking at the empty chair to my right, the reason I haven't been able to stomach making it down here.

Chewing those pills that first time, well, I thought it was going to be the death of me. Luckily or unluckily, I'm still here. I'd thought taking more than one might give me an overdose, but it didn't.

I never would have guessed what chewing them was going to do. When I usually take them, there's a coating that prevents it from going into your system all at once. It lessens the high and prevents the pain over a number of hours. So instead of dying, I discovered that it enhances the high.

I felt even better. The highs became higher, but the lows have become so much lower. There's nothing worse than the feeling of that happiness dissipating and returning to the nightmare. It's taken all my strength not to take everything in one go, to wait before my next dose, but the knowledge that it would make me run out sooner keeps my discipline intact.

So I just have to be careful to keep my regimen, so that the lows don't happen when my mom is home. She can never be the collateral damage that comes with coming off a high.

The downside is that since I'm chewing more pills, there are less remaining each and every single day. Running out is something I can't afford. I need a plan.

With my spotless track record, I wouldn't know the first thing about how or where to get more. Getting another prescription is not an option. Mom would never allow it, and my plan only works if she doesn't know *why* I'm feeling better.

Meaning, I'll need to figure it out on my own, likely forcing my hand into doing something illegal, getting involved with *actual* addicts. It'll be a tough pill for me to swallow, pun not intended.

Crossing that line is something I may not be capable of. There would be no coming back from it. I'd be just like my father, and the thought of that makes me sick after spending so many years hating him for what he became. Maybe not all of me has been broken if I can still find it in myself to care about that.

Looking up from my cereal bowl, I find my mom looking at me with tears in her eyes. She quickly looks down, no doubt trying to conceal it from me. The pills are working their magic, allowing a spurt of happiness to hit my heart, seeing her blossoming hope. They don't let me focus on what kind of state I've had to be in for coming down here to create such a response in her.

The pills shield me from it, let me have this high for a while longer.

My mom clears her throat. "How is your cereal?"

She's walking on eggshells. I hope I can make her feel like she doesn't have to do that anymore.

"It's yummy." It feels weird to speak, like I'm out of practice. After the never-ending screaming for those first few days after the accident, my voice stopped working entirely.

Mom smiles and goes back to her own breakfast. She is so beautiful. I don't think she realizes it anymore, but she is. People always say I look just like her, but I've always thought of myself as a bad knock-off of the original.

LAST Stand FOR GENEVIEVE

She has the kind of beautiful blonde hair that women pay thousands for, a golden mix of near whites, honey, and maple syrup. The crystal blue of her eyes are a stark contrast against her naturally glowy, golden skin.

Growing up, moms used to ask her what hairdresser she went to, what her secret to perfect skin was, who her dermatologist was, where she got her Botox and lifting injections. She would always laugh and say the beauty must come from the love shining out of her.

My dad was her soulmate. They met as kids, were friends all the way into middle school, until one summer they were forced to spend it apart, before the days of FaceTime and texting. She told me the story so many times, of how they were reunited on the first day of freshman year.

Time froze as they ran to each other, straight into an embrace and shared their first kiss, just like it happens in the movies. Over those three months apart, they realized what they had was something more than friendship. They couldn't spend another summer, or minute, apart.

They got married on my mom's eighteenth birthday and had me shortly after. She said they never worried about the future or money because as long as they had love, they had everything. Love made them strong enough to overcome anything life threw at them.

We were the culmination of that love. Mom used to say that every love we had in our lives, and every love our children would have, would be an extension of theirs, and because of that, their love would last forever.

I've never understood how my dad could throw away something as powerful and beautiful as what they had. Mom said it wasn't because he was a bad person, but he suffered from something in his mind, an illness which he didn't think had a cure. He tried finding ways to cope, but before he knew it, the thing which he had turned to is what destroyed him.

When he left, my mom had no doubt he only wanted what was best for us and left for no other reason than that. It wasn't because he didn't love us. She believed he only wanted to do right by us, and he wasn't what we needed at that time.

I hated him anyway.

After he left, I asked why she didn't date. My mom said that he would find his way back to us when he was ready, and she would be waiting when he did.

I thought she was insane and never understood how she didn't hate him the way I did. But maybe she was right, maybe he wasn't a bad guy. Maybe he was trying to be better in the only way he knew how.

Even though I understand him a little more now, I will never be as weak as him. I'm doing this *for* my mom. I would never let it become the thing to take me away from her. I'm stronger than that, stronger than he was.

Mom is looking at me again, eyes shining. "I love you so much, Brooke."

She wouldn't if she knew. "I love you, too, Mom."

"Any plans for today?" she asks like there may finally be an answer.

I shrug. "Maybe watch some more *Golden Girls*."

"That sounds good." She's quiet for a moment, which means she's deliberating whether or not to say something more. "How's your leg?"

My heart turns thunderous. Does she know I fell? Did she figure it out somehow?

"Still healing, but fine." Do I dare ask? "Why?"

"I thought if it's getting easier to walk, maybe you could go outside a bit, get some fresh air."

I let out a breath. "Yeah, I could maybe do that." Actually, it's a good idea, a great idea even. I need to start finding options on where to find more pills. "I'll go for a walk later today."

My mom smiles again and nods. Crossing that line may be worth it.

If something makes someone happy, a good person like my mom, is it still bad? Where is the line drawn between good and bad? Right and wrong? Does someone's situation and reason behind their actions make something any less evil?

My mom smiles again, almost as if it's a sign.

I will cross any line I've previously drawn for myself, as long as it keeps her smiling.

One of us deserves to be happy.

CHAPTER TEN

Now – Connor

This is a new low. Even for me.

Not the job, of course. I don't consider myself to be above any sort of work. If it makes money and serves a purpose, then it's worthy of my time. So no, it's not the job.

It's *why* I'm here, doing it.

As I sit here scraping scum from the bottom of a garbage bin, all I can think of is the *audacity* someone has to have to walk up to a stranger and take a cigarette straight out of their damn mouth.

Shaking my head, I try and fail to get her out of my head. My neck is going to need an adjustment after how many times I've tried to shake loose of her. I'm starting to think she took my balls along with the cigarette that night.

Fucking Ice Queen.

A chunk of muck sloshes out, hitting the ground with a slop, sending rubbish water flying onto my face. "Fuck!" I chuck the bin, not caring about the noise while I slew every curse I can muster. For an Aussie, that's a lot of fucking cursing.

Wiping my face with the sleeve of my tee, I make my way to the outdoor sink to wash my hands. Wherever she is, I hope Ice Queen is suffering as much as I am right now. She blocked me because I got under her skin, too. There's no other explanation.

She knows she won't have the strength to resist me, and accepting my follow request would have been cracking open the door. I hope she's being accosted by thoughts of my lips, my hands, my fingers, the way that I am by thoughts of hers. The confidence that she is just as affected by me is the only thing keeping me going right now.

Then, the moment I get my hands on her, I'll make one hundred percent sure she is as *affected* as I have been since that night. I'll lead her through a master class of tantalizing torture until she is nothing more than sensations, begging me for release and screaming my-

"Connor, wipe whatever the hell that is off your face before you need to go change your pants." Joe's stern, no bullshit tone rips me back to where I'm standing, next to an entire line of rubbish bins waiting for scraping.

Joe has the gruffest exterior of anyone I've ever met, never got him to crack a smile once, despite my best attempts over the years. Most people think he's an asshole, but I'll never forget when he let me stay on his couch indefinitely, until his wife made him choose between her or me. I never let him decide, grabbed my shit then and there, not wanting his kindness to cause him any more trouble.

Joe always gets the phone numbers of people who work trash duty. He claims that it's so he can reach you if you don't turn up when you're supposed to, but I think it's because the people who work for him usually aren't in the best situations, and he wants to be able to reach them if he's worried.

All in all, it means that he's got a phone number that I appear to need more than oxygen. Or sanity. Or dignity. He knew it, too, that he had a bargaining chip I'd do almost anything for.

The cunt used it.

One-hundred-and-five bins to scrape.

This is usually reserved for someone on trash duty after they've messed up big or the fate of whatever sad soul drew the short straw. Today it's my fate, thanks to Ice Queen. After days of little sleep, no cigarettes and no coffee, the layer of muck is the cherry on top. I must look terrible.

"You look terrible," says Joe.

"I haven't had a cigarette since my last show."

He lets out a low whistle. "This Brooke girl must have really put you through the ringer."

I give him a pointed look and reach for the next bin, ignoring the shock waves that just went through my chest at the mention of her name.

"Hopefully I took her number down correctly. Imagine you did all this for a wrong number."

I glare at him. His mouth twitches in response, as close to a smile as he'll get.

"Let me know once you've finished."

I pick up the next bin and start scraping.

• • •

How does one come across not-stalkery when they clearly had to be a bit stalkery to get the phone number? I decide to go with what's on my mind, and pray it's enough to crack open that door she keeps frozen shut.

Connor: I haven't had a cigarette in way too fucking long.

I toss my phone on the couch, preparing for another torturous three-day battle of wills. Except, my phone dings not even forty seconds later.

Ice Kween: You quit?

Holy shit. She answered. Consider the door bloody cracked.

The fact that she didn't have to ask who this was shows me that I have been on her mind, too. She may have even expected this. I pump one arm into the air in celebration, and then take a deep breath. I have one shot and I'm walking on thin ice. Pun not intended.

Connor: Not intentionally.

Ice Kween: You should be thanking me.

Connor: And why is that?

Ice Kween: I was the catalyst.

Connor: That's a tad presumptuous.

Ice Kween: Is it? When did you smoke your last cigarette?

I groan. Admitting this gives her the advantage, but *not* admitting it would be insecure. I hate that she's right. Ice Queen was undoubtedly the catalyst, and I've been so focused on finding her, in the hopes of getting her out of my system, that I haven't unpacked what it all means.

Connor: The festival.

Ice Kween: Interesting. Something get under your skin?

That was almost flirty.

Play it cool, Connor. You're in the goddamn door. Don't ruin it because you're thinking with your dick instead of your brain.

Connor: No hard feelings, by the way.

Ice Kween: For what?

Connor: For blocking me on Pinterest. I was looking for some kitchen inspo.

Ice Kween: Glad I didn't hurt your feelings.

Ice Kween: And sure you were.

Ice Kween: How did you get my number?

Connor: As if I'd tell you.

Ice Kween: Joe, then?

Shit.

Okay, I know this is about to sound misogynistic, but I swear it isn't. Women always crack the shits over it before I finish explaining, even though they end up agreeing with me.

Chick flicks provide great research into the female brain. They've ingrained into their mind that it makes sense to fall in love (or in my case, hook up) with the geek after he gets a makeover, or the jock after they've helped him with his homework. That's because women, at the end of the day, are admittedly much better than men at basically everything, but *especially* projects.

People assume that I use this information for manipulative purposes to play with feelings. Actually, it's the opposite. I'm always upfront with women, and it's up to them to take it or leave it. I've never shared my insight with ghosting douche bags who'd use it to break the hearts of women, either.

If anything, it helps me *avoid* breaking hearts. I can spot exactly when someone wants to turn me into their long-term project, hoping to be the one to cure me of my aversion of feelings. I'm incurable and I don't need to add to whatever they're already talking about in their therapy sessions, so I steer clear.

Instead, I situate myself as a side quest on their project for *themselves*. Most women want to explore themselves sexually, experiment a little, before settling down. As long as they're okay with it ending there, I happily oblige.

With Ice Queen, though...it feels *different* somehow. She seems incapable of feelings, let alone warmth of any kind. So, I have no qualms over using what I know to get my foot in the door, since neither of us are at risk of catching feelings.

Speaking of feelings. I have a text to answer.

Connor: Okay, maybe my feelings are a little hurt. But I know how you can make it up to me.

Ice Kween: Not a chance in hell.

Connor: I'm not asking you on a date.

Ice Kween: Then what do you want?

Connor: I'm still having all the cravings of nicotine, I'm just not having the nicotine.

Ice Kween: See what I meant about addictions?

Connor: Yeah. I do.

Ice Kween: I know I'm going to regret this.

Adrenaline courses through my veins in anticipation. My heart starts pounding.

Ice Kween: Meet me tomorrow morning. 10AM. Target on Dale Mabry. It's NOT a date.

My foot is in the fucking door.

Connor: Wouldn't dream of it, mate.

Ice Kween: Please refrain from using your deranged language while you're at it.

I smirk.

CHAPTER ELEVEN

Then - Brooke

It's been a while since I last looked in the mirror. A big change from staring into it for at least two hours before school every morning. Making sure that every eyelash and brow hair was in the perfect place was something that used to consume me. I'd spend hours getting the flawless shadow of contour and precision-winged eyeliner. Every. Single. Day.

That's what mattered to me then: perfection. I wouldn't stop until I achieved it. The perfect makeup. The perfect outfit. The perfect grid on my Instagram with the perfect filter for the perfect mood. The perfect straight-A student. The perfect cheerleading captain. The perfect quarterback boyfriend, making us the perfect high school couple. The perfect friends. The perfect life.

In all honesty, the makeup was nothing but a mask, along with everything else. It was all a futile effort to convince myself that I had things to live for, while I wasted the precious time I could have spent with *her*.

When I returned home, I found myself surrounded by everything that reminded me of how much time I'd wasted. Trophies, medals, and pictures documenting how I'd spent that time with meaningless people, who never even bothered to visit me in the hospital.

I'd be lying if I said I'm not a little scared at what I'm going to find in my reflection now. The traces of that life, those masks, being long gone.

I reach for the mirror, grabbing it from where it's been stored, tucked between the basin and the wall, where my mom put it before I could bash it in. Casting my eyes down, I manage to avoid looking as I hang it back on the wall.

LAST *Stand* FOR GENEVIEVE

Deep breath. I look.

I'm barely recognizable. No wonder my mom was resorting to threats to get me to eat again. My love for pasta used to leave my body pretty full, but my activities kept me toned and shaped. Now, my cheeks are shallow. My lips have thinned. My skin has taken on a lifeless pallor. My hair is dead and stringy. Even my eyes, which used to be crystal blue like my mom's, have lost their light. I close them, as the haunted image of what I've become follows me into the shower, the rustling of grocery bags that I have taped around my casts my soundtrack.

Mom won't be happy if I keep looking like a corpse. I need to start eating again, put some weight back on. It'll require some level of care going back into myself. For Mom, I can do it. Slowly, I wash my hair and my face one-handed, letting my mind wander the way it does in the shower. Shaving just isn't going to happen while I'm still plastered up. Just another reminder of what I've lost.

There's not even peace in a hot shower.

The water cuts off as I twist the faucet and towel off, careful not to slip. I'm not supposed to take another pill now, but I need it. Mom is still downstairs, and I can't have her seeing the effects that looking in the mirror has had on me.

I pull my flare yoga pants over the bulky cast and a large t-shirt over my head, not bothering with a bra since my boobs are too small these days to worry about anyone seeing them through a shirt this big. A baseball cap and backpack finish off the look.

Coming face to face with my biggest foe, the hallway, I close my eyes and hold my breath, using the wall to my left as my only guide. I need to get past *her* room in order to get to the stairs. The next high is on the horizon, it's in my system already, only a little longer until it kicks in. One step at a time, I make it through the hallway and down the stairs.

Mom is grabbing her keys as I make it to the bottom. Her keys clatter back to the counter as she leans against it for support, almost as if she is witnessing a miracle. Then, she smiles.

My efforts were worth it.

"Can you drop me off downtown on your way to work?"

Mom is shocked into silence for a second, either at my request or the sheer volume of words in that sentence. She shakes it off, clearing her throat. "Of course, sweetie. Do you need some money?"

Money. I hadn't even thought of that. Better to accept her offer at a time where it won't cause suspicion, especially when I'll likely have to use my own reserves soon. "Maybe just a little."

Mom digs into her bag before handing me a ten-dollar bill. "Don't spend it all in one place," she says with a wink.

I try to muster a smile, but fail. Mom smiles back, so she must know I tried.

• • •

Downtown looks the same. Mom dropped me on the same corner she'd always drop me on, when I used to go out with friends. It's weird to remember that not *that* much time has passed. It feels like years, but it's only been a matter of weeks.

The pill is working its magic, making me feel better again. I won't waste it trying to process my feelings from this morning. I need to direct it toward finding *more*. I look around, not knowing where to begin. It's not like I can go on Yelp and look for dealers with five stars.

Mark has the best crack and flawless customer service.

If I was a person trying to acquire illegal substances, which I realize that's exactly what I am, where would I go? Taking in my current surroundings, I keep that question front and center in mind.

I probably *wouldn't* go to the children's clothing store, although that would be one hell of a front. So would Starbucks. Even the restaurant across the street. They're just not...*realistic*. I can't just walk into one of these places and go "Hey, anyone got some spare pills?"

Sigh. This is going to be a waste of time.

There's a bench a little farther down the block, so I start my hobble over, not wanting to aggravate my leg more than I need to while I'm figuring out what to do. Just as I'm about to take a seat, I spot a somewhat familiar figure on the other side of the street.

I'm not sure I believe in fate, but this is one hell of a coincidence, finding Lloyd Perkins, known druggy at my high school. I could recognize that hunch anywhere, almost like his body is permanently trying to hide what he's doing from watching eyes. If anyone would know where to find pills, it would be Lloyd.

He's too far for me to catch up to him with my leg in its current state, nor do I think I should walk up and ask for it. Obviously, I don't know what the protocol is, but approaching someone in the middle of the street, asking for drugs in the light of day, doesn't scream good move.

Plus, I doubt Lloyd would help me anyway. We weren't friends. I treated him little better than trash. He would probably laugh in my face, seeing how far I've fallen, and take pride in refusing to help me. I would deserve it.

Following him seems like a better plan. See where he goes. That would at least point me in the right direction without asking for his help.

I stand up, hobbling after him as quickly as I can. If I remain on this side of the street, I risk losing him, but if I cross now, there's a higher risk of him spotting me. Ugh. What I can't risk is going home exactly how I started: almost no supply left and no other way to keep making my mom happy.

Fuck it. I cross the street.

My adrenaline is pumping with the knowledge that it could all be over if he turns around. I'd never be able to keep up if he decided to run, and I don't think another opportunity like this will present itself. I'm extra careful, making sure I don't follow too close.

Every now and then I stop to "window shop" in hopes of appearing less suspicious, while I keep my peripherals on him. He's made several turns already, so I'm happy that I crossed when I did, having never been able to keep up if I hadn't.

Lloyd abruptly turns a corner again. I wobble a little faster, hoping that he doesn't take another turn before I can glance around the corner and see where he goes. Except as I peek around, Lloyd is nowhere in sight. I take a step around the corner, walking a few steps into the alley which leads to a dead end.

My heart is pounding as I turn in circles, looking for any clue as to where he went. Did I turn too early? As I turn to head back to the main road, someone covers my mouth from behind and drags me farther into the alley, away from help.

I'm only dragged a few feet before being released, landing in a puddle which smells worse than sewer. I stagger back as pain lashes through my injured leg, catching myself on the aged brick walls, covered in graffiti. From where I'm standing, all I see are overflowing, unattended dumpsters spilling their contents onto the asphalt, and a dead end.

The only way in or out is on the other side of whoever dragged me down this alley.

The adrenaline coursing through me says I should scream, use whatever strength my broken body can muster to get away. But as I turn, my mind slows, confusion muddling my fear when it's Lloyd standing there.

He looks different than the last time I saw him. My eyes subtly drift as I try to pinpoint what's changed. Lloyd's sunken eyes, still set too far apart, framed by dark circles and bony features are exactly how I remember them. His nose is still bent to the right, lips thin and pressed together. His skin is still too pale, but it's missing that clammy shine which I once considered so revolting. Nearly everything about him appears the same.

Unease settles in my stomach with the realization that maybe he hasn't changed much after all, just the lens I look at life through has. The lens which portrayed him as trash, up to who-knows-what with who-knows-whom, nothing but a disease infecting society.

Something dark begins to stare me in the face: I'm no better.

Trash? Not quite.

Diseased? Maybe.

Repulsive? Only to myself.

There is a truth here, which I can no longer ignore. Something happened to Lloyd. He may have been hurt or even worse, someone he cared about was hurt. The pain was too excruciating and he needed to disappear. How could I have judged him so harshly before?

Thankfully he speaks, not allowing my thoughts to descend further.

"Why is Brooke Anderson, Captain-Goody-Two-Shoes, following me into an alley in a bad part of town?" Lloyd's eyes catch on my good hand, as it jitters before I tuck it behind my back. His eyes reach mine again and I find understanding, coated in disappointment.

Though I didn't expect pleasantries and a warm embrace, being met with disapproval, especially from Lloyd, has taken me off guard. Regardless of our history, I thought he'd jump at the possibility of a new regular, or at least be happy at the prospect of being able to make a quick buck.

"I think you know why." My words are barbed wire, not appreciating how the roles have reversed as I stand on the other end of his judgment, learning how it feels. "And you, of all people, have no right to look at me that way."

LAST *Stand* FOR GENEVIEVE

"I heard about Genevieve." Lloyd swallows. "I'm sorry."

My ears begin to ring, my chin trembling. "I'm here for one thing, Lloyd, not a reunion."

He shakes his head, somber. "I can't help you with that."

Unsure where his bleak outlook is coming from, I try again. "I need you to."

"You're a good person going through a hard time, it's not worth throwing your life away."

"If you don't sell them to me, then I'll just find someone who will." I can't believe I'm having to convince him. "It might as well be *you* who benefits from my…situation."

"Brooke, you can still turn around." Lloyd runs his scrawny hand through his limp hair. "Go back home to your mom and get help. You don't have to see this through."

"Fuck you, Lloyd. I'm not here for philosophical bullshit." Anger surges up, readying to explode out of me. I wipe a bead of sweat from my brow, becoming more agitated by the second. "I came here for pills. I intend to leave with them."

It's pity which enters his eyes then. "The more steps you take off the trail, the harder it'll be to find your way again."

"Did you get that off a self-help pamphlet?" All I see is red. "Just give them to me, Lloyd."

"I got clean, Brooke." He sighs, defeated. "I don't have anything to give you, even if I wanted to."

I slap the brick wall, the pain centering me. "Why didn't you start with that?"

"Believe it or not, I was hoping to talk some sense into you, maybe even prevent you from falling into the same trap I did." Lloyd looks at the ground, running his worn boot through a puddle of muck. He laughs humorlessly. "I figured the only reason you'd be following me, of all people, was because you needed something. At least I was right about that."

Part of me stings at his words, at how terrible I've been. Never once did I stop him in the hallway with a hand to his shoulder and ask him if he was okay. Day after day he walked by me between classes, buried in troubles, and the only thing on my mind was making sure I didn't get too close to him. And now here I am, berating him for treating me with the kind of decency I never showed him.

"Well, now that you see that talking me out of it is impossible, can you at least point me in the right direction?"

He shakes his head. "I won't be the one to doom you."

"Enough with the dramatics. I'm going to find someone who will help me." I don't make it five steps before I'm slammed into the wall, rough bricks cracking against my skull.

Lloyd's eyes are pleading, imploring. "You have *no idea* the life you're trying to jump head-first into. The Brooke I knew wouldn't have come within a *mile* of this, and Genevieve would have never let her."

"Get off of me!" I struggle to get free, but he slams my shoulders back.

"You've seen what pills do to someone, what it does to their families when they inevitably leave. I know what happened with your father."

"Fuck you." I need to get out of here.

"How low are you willing to go, Brooke? When you get so desperate you'd rather have pills than oxygen? What are you willing to do?"

"Let me go!!"

"Will you hurt people? Because I did."

"That's because you're a psycho!!"

"And soon you will be too." Lloyd grabs my chin, forcing me to look him in the eye. "Or you can turn around and go back home. You can HEAL."

I whimper, shaking my head. "I can't. I can't."

"Then are you prepared to debase yourself? To lose every last shred of self-respect you hold?"

"Screw you!"

"Are you prepared to spread your legs, open your mouth, and let someone take what they want, just for a high?"

"You're sick!"

"I'm not anymore, but I was." Lloyd pulls back roughly, dropping my chin and letting me fall to the ground. "This life, the pills and what you become desperate enough to do, they will ruin everything good. They leave nothing in their wake."

"I have nothing left anyway!!" I scream from where I've landed on the ground.

"What if it were Genevieve?" Lloyd's voice softens with his question. "What if it were Genevieve in this alley, what would you want me to do? Would you have me help her get what you're asking for?"

Squealing breaks.

I begin to crawl.

Crunching metal.

I don't stop. I *can't* stop.

Lloyd doesn't say anything more, but his words blare through my head, over and over, until I can barely see through the throbbing. Using only my good arm, I continue to pull myself toward the main road, finding a rusted pipe screwed into the bricks to pull myself up with on the way.

What if it were Genevieve?

Pain becomes a welcome escape as I hobble back out into the clueless world, tears streaming down my face, throat raw with screams I couldn't contain.

What if it were Genevieve?

It doesn't matter, because now I only have one purpose. My mom needs me. The pills are the only way. I leave Lloyd behind in the alley, but his words follow me, haunt me, stalk me, all the way home, until oblivion makes it all disappear.

CHAPTER TWELVE

Now - Connor

As I stand here, feeling like I'm waiting for a cold front, I can't help but wonder if I went with the right coffee for Ice Queen. *I'm* even stomaching a Starbucks, just to have the chance to show her I'm not a total twat. It'll be a wasted effort if I guessed wrong.

My gut tells me that she is straightforward, not the picky-eater type. It's almost like she has this air of survival, of doing what needs to be done. That kind of person wouldn't muck around with oat-milk-soy-rainbow-puke-frap-puccinos.

She would go basic. Simple. Mostly black coffee, maybe a dash of cream. No sugar.

Aaaaaand I've officially lost my mind. This is just going to give her more ammo to annihilate me with. Just as I'm about to chuck her coffee into the nearest bin, I feel her. It's as if the entire atmosphere just shifted when she walked through that door.

Her icy, blue eyes instantly find mine, sending electricity throughout my entire body. Her gait is frustratingly steady, unrushed, as she makes her way toward me. Her eyes remain on my face, almost intently, as if she isn't allowing herself to look anywhere else.

Interesting.

"I got you something," I say, holding out her coffee. Her eyes flatten, taking on the dull cold which I've decided is my least favorite. She's obviously assumed that I haven't paid any attention at all. "It's decaf."

LAST *Stand* FOR GENEVIEVE

Her brows lift in surprise, which is the most expressive motion I've seen from her thus far. I'm not sure whether I should be celebrating, or punching myself in the dick, for being so awful, that doing something thoughtful causes such astonishment.

"Thanks," she says simply, taking the cup from my hand, cautious to avoid even the smallest physical contact. She takes a hesitant sip, and her brows lift again, higher this time. "Decaf coffee with a splash of cream and no sugar?"

I nod.

She seems momentarily off put, but not necessarily in a bad way. "How'd you know?"

I think about my serial killer evaluation and shrug. "A wild guess."

"Well, thanks." She takes another sip and glances at my cup. I don't know how, but I already know what she's thinking.

"Mine is also decaf." This time her eyes meet mine, and below the ice, I see it, a smidge of curiosity.

She takes another sip and walks off.

Uh, okay. I grab a trolley and by the time I've wrangled the thing to face the right direction, I have to jog to catch up with her. "So, what's new?"

Eye roll. "You mean aside from some creep starting to use his addiction as a cheap excuse to try to get me into bed?"

Ice Queen's overly direct, cold words go straight to my dick, which is just fucking weird. I've never been into the chase, nor had to resort to it. Instead, I chalk it up as an oddball symptom of nicotine withdrawals, when paired with caffeine withdrawals. Yeah, that's it.

"I'm starting to think *you're* the one who spends all their time thinking about me getting you into bed," I shoot back.

"You wish." She stops, pinning me with a glare. "Unfortunately for me, I can't walk away from anyone who needs help, regardless of whether I *want* to or not."

I want to know why. I want to ask her what happened. But I'm smarter than that. "So how *do* we fix me?"

Ice Queen must have one hell of a bullshit meter, because I hear the sliver of vulnerability which creeps into my voice and she sighs in defeat, hearing it too. "Are you *actually* trying to quit?"

"Erm." Maybe this isn't the time to tell her about my obsession. "I'm not particularly quitting because I don't want to smoke anymore, but yeah. I guess I'm quitting." For now.

"Why do you smoke?" She starts walking again. I follow.

"What do you mean, why do I smoke?"

"What does smoking solve for you?"

I shrug. "Helps my struggling musician look? Gets the girls? I don't know."

Eye roll. "I mean, what happens emotionally that gets you reaching for the next one?"

"Is this you auditioning to become my therapist?" A wicked smile spreads across my face. "I wouldn't mind getting onto a couch behind a locked door for you."

Snort. "Do you ever answer anything seriously?"

I can barely process her question following the snort. I'm too tied up on the little fissure to come up with something clever, so I offer her something of mine in return. "I reach for a cigarette when something becomes… a lot."

She nods. "We can help your body to slowly learn to live without the highs."

I clap my hands together and rub them, like we're cooking something good here. "That's the best thing you've said all day."

She stops again, turning to face me. "But *you* will have to learn how to carry *yourself*, without the crutch."

I don't do deep. Yet something in her crystal blue eyes has me in a choke-hold. It's not pity or disdain or even pleading. It's just plain understanding. My hands develop a mind of their own and I have to aggressively shove them into my pockets to avoid doing something catastrophic, like touching her face.

There's not a blonde hair out of place from her slicked-back bun to blame it on. My hands would serve no purpose other than to run across her smooth, unblemished skin and trace her lips that are too full for her face.

Her eyes move from mine and travel to my hair, which has always been too wild and curly for me to gel or style. I can't help but wonder what it would feel like for her fingers to slide into the strands, pulling…

The sound of a text coming through rips us from our, uh, whatever the fuck you'd call that. I clear my throat and Brooke takes a jerked step back as if she's just accidentally touched a hot stove.

LAST Stand FOR GENEVIEVE

I pull out my phone, seeing the text which came in from *Fantasy Faith* and crack a grin before putting it back in my pocket.

Good. This is familiar. This is what I need. Not whatever was happening a second ago.

"Who is Fantasy Faith?"

Someone is nosy. "Ah, she likes to reenact scenes from a particular type of book where-"

"Never mind. I don't want to hear any more."

I laugh.

A pause. Then curiosity wins out. "But you named her that *in your phone?*"

"What's the harm in a little organization?"

She shakes her head. "I don't know how you manage to convince anyone to sleep with you."

"Easy. I stick to my niche."

"Your *niche?*" She says it like it's a disease she can catch just from saying the word.

"Yeah. My niche." I shrug. "I don't fuck around with feelings. The women know what they're getting themselves into. And trust me...." I drag the words out just a little, looking her up and down while I do. "I take pride in there being no complaints when I'm done."

Gulp. *Round one for Connor.*

Ice Queen grabs a few little boxes from where they hang on the shelves and shoves them to my chest. "This is what you need to get your body through the withdrawal. Your mind, though? I don't think there's any fixing what's up there."

I'm starting to get the hang of this. I can count on Ice Queen to be extra icy after any sort of headway. A snort, a twitch of the lips, maybe a gulp here and there, and within seconds she's more venomous than ever.

"You love me that much already?" I say with a little smirk.

Deadpan. Blink. "Okay. We're done here."

I step in front of her. "Going so soon?"

"I came here to help you with one very specific thing, not to hang out."

She tries to side-step me, and I step in tandem, predicting her move. "You're not enjoying yourself even a little?"

Ice Queen shoots me another glare and tries to fake me out, but I predict that, too, remaining directly in front of her. "Come on, I paid seven dollars, *plus* tax, for the world's worst cup of decaf coffee. The least you can do is help steer the trolley."

There. *Indecision.* It didn't take as much convincing as I'd expected. I was ready to get down on one knee in the classic proposal pose until I garnered enough attention that she would have to say yes just to avoid embarrassment.

"I mean, if you don't walk around Target buying things you definitely don't need, have you really even *gone* to Target?" The side of her mouth twitches, and everything disappears as I zero in on it as it slowly pulls a tiny bit more to the right.

"Fine. Whatever."

I realize then that I won't be leaving this store until there is a smile so warm, not even her glacial walls can chill it.

• • •

"Please tell me we aren't headed to the toy section."

I chuckle. "Not sure Target sells the kind of toys I'd be interested in."

That generates a slap. It's not affectionate. It doesn't linger. Yet it sends shockwaves over my body, generating over and over from the point of contact, leaving me in a daze that lasts for several aisles.

We pass by some kitchen utensils, and she reaches for an ice tray. I can't resist. "You're telling me the icy cold that follows you around isn't enough to freeze some cubes?"

"Har. Har." She drops it into the cart, bored.

And that's how, with only one little sentence, I create a monster.

Brooke throws a baby bottle into the cart next. "For your next tantrum."

I snort, intending to let her have the last word, but the universe intervenes, putting something in my path that I'm just not a strong enough man to pass by.

Walking over to the rack, I pick up a little girl's shirt plastered with a big picture of Elsa shooting ice from her fingers. I mock shock, walking it over to Ice Queen, where I look back and forth between the shirt and her, just long enough to where she gets a little irritated. Then I point to her and the shirt, "I mean, the resemblance is uncanny."

And I throw it into the cart.

LAST *Stand* FOR GENEVIEVE

Her face doesn't move an inch, but humor gleams in her eyes.

As we walk by a utility cart piled with items to put back, she grabs a box of Band-Aids and chucks them into the trolley. "For your ego, when I block your number next."

I move over to the same pile of junk, grabbing a globe and giving it a little twirl, stopping it with my finger pointing to Antarctica and an obnoxious gasp. "Look! Your homeland!"

She acts exasperated, but I know she isn't. Somehow, I can already tell the difference.

Brooke disappears down the aisle for pets and comes back, holding a black studded collar, chucking it into the trolley. "Surely you have a Colleen or Cleo in your contacts who's into collars?"

A stupid, stupid grin takes over my face at her sheer brilliance and ability to slap a pile of my own shit into my face. The knowledge that I could spend an entire day with Ice Queen, fully clothed, and have this much fun sends warning bells off in the back of my mind. But I can't curb my eagerness to continue, just to see what she comes up with next.

The men's section comes up on my left and I grab the thickest, heaviest jacket Florida has to offer. I toss the hanger into the trolley and don the jacket. "Just preparing for your next mood swing."

Snort. That little sound has no right to affect me the way it does.

Ice Queen disappears down one of the many home goods aisles and comes back with a little rug so plush I want to take off my shoes and give it a go. She chucks it into the cart, deadpan. "To soften your next walk of shame."

Another stupid, stupid smile. I grab the next thing closest to me, which happens to be a heated blanket, throwing it into the trolley. "I don't even have to explain this one."

Eye roll. Brooke walks ahead to the beginning of the outdoor section, tons of camping gear, survival kits, and bug spray on display. She grabs some anti-itch lotion and chucks it into the trolley. "Surely you've got sores and rashes of all kinds, this should help."

It's not lost on me that she is absolutely smashing me in this little battle of wit. It's her humor and dry delivery that is sending me. I shake my head a little, wondering what the fuck has gotten into me. Maybe I'm coming down with something, or maybe I just have to do whatever it takes to get this demoness expunged from my mind.

I stop, pointing to the display of a model showing us how exhilarating it is to stand next to a tent. "This is called a smile. I'd buy you one, but sadly they're not for sale."

Ice Queen turns before I can see the proof, but I know that almost cracked her, sort of in the way it happens when you tell a child not to smile. She disappears down the next aisle and comes back with some sort of heavy-duty fishing pole. "Just in case Tinder isn't pulling enough catfish."

At first, I'm frozen. The wit. The execution. Then, the sound of the pole crashing into the trolley, unleashes my howl. I clutch my stomach in a fit of laughter that's usually reserved for the two people closest to me. For a moment, Brooke just looks at me.

Then it happens.

Ten beautiful fucking seconds where I bathe in the warmth of her ear-to-ear smile. I can do nothing but look at her, memorizing every millimeter, every glow. I know that I will revisit this smile over and over until the next time I get to see it.

Her clear eyes are open in a way that I've yet to see, and joy radiates from her for a moment longer, until she realizes what's happened and shuts it down. The light winks out. Her face falls. She looks down at the trolley, full of our miscellaneous items, shadows now gracing her face.

"We should check out." Ice Queen, back with a vengeance, doesn't wait for me to respond as she begins walking briskly to the front of the store.

All I can do is follow.

I'm quiet at the checkout, not sure what to say. For the first time, I'm speechless. I know she had fun. I fucking *know* it. But she felt something, her walls shot up, and I'm left with a bad case of whiplash.

This can't be the end.

"What are you doing?" Ice Queen says in accusation as we reach her car, like she's only just noticed that I was following her. It's an old Honda Civic, probably close to the same age that we are. It's simple, well-kept, and *her*.

I put my hands up in surrender. "Just walking you to your car."

"It's the middle of the fucking day." She gestures to the god-awful Florida sun that never lets a day go by without torturing me. "And I can take care of myself in the dark, too."

I've never doubted it for a minute, but there is something happening in this stupid skull of mine, which prevented me from letting her walk out without doing something to prop this door open that I've cracked.

How do I win someone over who is so determined to keep me out? I've shown her how good this...*arrangement* could be. We could be friends. We could have *fun*, fully clothed and naked. Neither of us would have to worry about feelings or emotions in the other. We're the perfect pair for it. The only thing to do from here is to leave the ball in her court.

"Let me know when you're done acting like this wouldn't be fun."

I would have left it at that, but her answering scoff sends a wave of determination through me. Bracing an arm next to her head, I lean in closer, keeping just enough distance between us to avoid scaring her off, or demanding a demonstration of self-defense. My proximity sends a shiver through her body, and it takes all of my strength not to damn it all and press up against her.

"You've got my number." I pull away, backing up a few steps.

And then, because I'm nothing more than an animal, I wink.

CHAPTER THIRTEEN

Then - Brooke

Every time I've closed my eyes since seeing Lloyd, his words have haunted me. This week has been fucking hell. But Mom smiled again when I made it down the stairs this morning, and it's all I needed to convince myself this is still the right thing to do.

"Sweetie, my manager asked me to work a double shift. Do you think you can manage dinner on your own today?"

I nod. "Sure."

"That's great. We could really use the extra money."

"It's no problem, Mom."

In fact, the more time she spends away from me, the easier it is to keep up the façade. Now that I'm mobile, she's been trying to spend more time together, which usually just consists of us sitting on the couch and watching TV so as not to exert my body. It's been taking more and more to keep what haunts me at bay, but at least the TV doesn't require any interaction, besides the occasional forced chuckle.

How I spend my time doesn't matter anymore anyway. The only reason I'm still here is for her. If that means watching *Friends* repeats on free cable, then that's what I'll goddamn do. My only reprieve comes when I'm alone, meeting oblivion in the shape of a crushed-up 60mg Oxy pill.

"How are you holding up?" Mom's careful, gentle tone tells me that she remembers what happened the last time she'd asked me this.

On edge would be lightly putting how I felt after running into Lloyd. There was this constant cloud of worry, wondering and never knowing whether Lloyd would tell someone, compounded by his haunting words. Combine that with the ticket to Mom's happiness running low, and it wasn't ideal.

So when Mom offered a caring hand, I'd taken it all out on her. As usual.

Screaming at the top of my lungs to leave me alone, to get out of my room and never show her face again. A glass of water crashing against the door, leaving broken shards in the carpet, which she vacuumed up while she cried, not wanting me to hurt myself.

How am I holding up?

It reminds me of another question, playing on loop in my mind.

What if it were Genevieve?

The splintering pain starts up at the memory of hearing her name.

What if it were Genevieve?

The soul-eating guilt follows close behind, opening the gaping hole of ceaseless hell.

What if it were Genevieve?

Doesn't anyone get it? It *was* Genevieve.

Her life was taken, when it should have been mine.

And it took Lloyd—*Lloyd*—saying her name, for me to honor her with the remembrance of it.

It should have been me.

She should have been at home, studying, just like she wanted to.

It should have been me.

The corners of the room collapse on me as her last words, soft and sweet, echo within the walls of my mind.

"I'm doing better." I smile.

Everyone talks about grief, but nobody talks about guilt. Maybe because it's too hard to talk about, even if they wanted to. Admitting your responsibility in something is hard, but impossible when it's for something like the loss of a life.

I don't think I could even form the words to explain to my mom what happened that night. Why *she* got in the car. It would destroy me, and it would destroy Mom right back. So I soak up the destruction, to make sure she doesn't have to.

Mom seems pleased by my answer, so I take another bite of my cereal, while the soundtrack of squealing brakes and crunching metal continues to play in my mind.

I took a risk before, a risk which could have cost me everything I've been working so hard for. Had Lloyd developed any more of a conscience, he could have gone to my mom and revealed everything. Obviously, I would have denied it, but she would've been suspicious enough to look closer, and if anyone is capable of catching me in a lie, it's her.

After the first attempt was a bust, I needed to get smarter about this, start thinking in a way which won't get me caught. Like… a criminal.

The mistake was dealing with someone whom I had a personal connection to, however small and disconnected it seemed to me, and not doing the due diligence. Had I looked into it rather than jumping the gun, I would have known that Lloyd had gotten clean. Now I have to deal with the potential consequences of him knowing about my situation.

I won't make that mistake again.

The scary thing is how accessible and easy it will be to get what I need. All I did was come to the beach and sit on a rundown swing for a few days, with a plastic bag tied up around my cast, and simply watch. Nobody spares me a glance as I sit here for the third day, watching the unnamed kid prepare to do another deal. Whether he will have what I'm looking for I don't know, but at the very least, it will be in his best interest to help me find it.

I'm running low. Low enough that just the thought of it has my good leg bouncing uncontrollably. Looking in my backpack for the hundredth time, I'm happy to see the cash I brought hasn't gotten up and walked away. Months of working part time, on top of the strenuous study load so I could save and buy designer bags, all just to end up here.

The deal is over as quickly as it began, and the kid makes his way toward the sidewalk, heading home after a day of hard work. The moment I open my mouth, I rescind my right to be condescending.

"Hey," I say as he passes me, just a few feet away. I don't miss the spark in the kid's eye as he takes me in, hoping I'm after him, rather than the contents of his backpack. "Wondering if you could help me out."

"What makes you think I'd help anyone?"

I burn my face with a smile, like it's made from acid. "I've seen you help quite a few people today. And yesterday. And the day before that."

LAST *Stand* FOR GENEVIEVE

"And what would someone like you need help with?"

"Someone like me?" I try to keep my tone steady, nothing more than conversational. "Well, I got hurt."

The kid looks at my casts, one on my leg and the other on my arm. Intrigue (and not an ounce of empathy), shines through his expression, telling me all I need to know about him. He doesn't give a shit about my life or my well-being, which is exactly what I need.

"I'm looking for something to take the edge off."

"A girl like you? Looking to take the edge off?" His smile is like oil. "I got what you need, and I don't even need to open my backpack."

Lloyd's words raise the hair on my spine. *Are you prepared to spread your legs, open your mouth, and let someone take what they want, just for a high?*

"I'm not interested in that. I came here for one thing and one thing only, so if you can't help me, then point me in the direction of someone who will."

"Whoa, whoa, whoa. I never said I *couldn't* help, but what you're looking for will cost you. I was just offering you a special...*payment plan*."

"I have cash."

His eyes zero in on my backpack. "And what's stopping me from taking that little backpack of yours and running off with it?"

My heart starts pounding. He's right. If he made a run for it, what could I do to stop him? Nothing. Absolutely nothing. The cash would be gone, along with the oblivion I can no longer live without, and any chance I had of keeping up this façade of healing. Mom would see me fall apart, losing the only person she has left. I can't let that happen.

"It would be bad for business."

"How so?"

"Maybe you'd get away with what I brought with me today, but then you'd lose out on all I'd bring tomorrow." I'm lying through my teeth, but he can't know that there is no tomorrow, that this is the bottom of my very shallow well until I figure something else out.

Indecision weighs across his face until it's replaced by greasy laughter. "I like you."

"So you'll give me what I need?"

"Normally I only play with the fun stuff, but you're in luck. I happen to be sampling something new today." He swings his backpack around and sets it in front of him. I try not to take offense at how little a threat he deems me, not even keeping hold of his straps. "How much do you want?"

"How much does fifty bucks get me?"

He chuckles. "Not enough."

"A hundred?"

"Ehhhh"

"Two hundred?"

"That's really all a trust fund baby like you has got?"

It wouldn't be the first time someone has mistaken me for the wealthy, and honestly, despite my family never coming close to it, I'd made sure as far as appearances went, I was just like them. I worked hard to have a closet full of designer clothes, and an impressive collection of Louis-this and Gucci-that. Except where they walked in and out of luxurious stores with their parents' credit cards, I learned how to bargain and got them secondhand. Out of all the late nights between working and studying, who knew the only valuable thing I'd keep from all of it would be knowing how to bargain?

"Before I start making promises, you better show me what you have to offer because I'm starting to think it's nothing."

He unzips his backpack, kicking it toward me. My lack of experience in this area becomes clear as I take in what looks like a backpack full of demented candy of every color and size, divided up into little clear baggies. Besides the obvious marijuana, I don't recognize most of it, until I spot the little red tablets.

"Happy?"

"I'll give you three-hundred-dollars for every single one of these you have." I hold up the plastic baggy.

His lips twitch, like I've said something funny. "You even know what that is?"

He wants to treat me like I'm a child? Fine. "My boo-boo hurts pretty bad."

"Three hundred isn't nearly enough for everything I have, but I'll still throw in a little on top, as a sign of good faith in *tomorrow*."

Glancing around, I'm relieved to see that we are alone. I reach into my backpack, pulling out everything I have to my name, and trade it for the promise of oblivion.

For the promise I made to myself.

For the promise I silently made to my mom, so she doesn't lose her smile forever.

CHAPTER FOURTEEN

Now – Connor

In the wise words of Luke Combs, when it rains, it pours. Turns out my head *is* what needs to be fixed, because this gum and these patches are doing nothing for what's going on with me upstairs. I'd love nothing more than to grab my guitar, a pack of cigarettes, and head to the causeway, playing and chain smoking in the bed of my ute, or pickup, as the Americans would say, until my problems vanished.

Instead, here I am tackling my problems head-on, with a knock on a door.

For the first time since my last show, it's not Ice Queen featured at the forefront of my mind. Jayden has taken the problematic spotlight in my life, and as bloody annoying as it is, having something to get worked up over, other than Brooke, is probably healthy.

After our little Target meet up, it's been nothing but crickets as far as she is concerned. Thinking it would go differently was idiotic. She wants nothing to do with me or my tendencies, and that needs to be that.

"Mate! I know you're in there." I knock on Jayden's door again. This isn't the first, or even tenth time, I've had to show up at his flat to check for signs of life, but another round of knocks with no answer has my stomach sinking.

It's not unusual for Jayden to miss Monday rehearsals thanks to his partying, or even for him to go missing for days at a time, but he's missed Friday now, too. As much as it pisses me off, the way he puts partying before the band, I worry about him. Lives which are lived this way never last long.

LAST Stand FOR GENEVIEVE

Making my way around the side of his rundown, bottom-level apartment, I cup my hands over his bedroom window and peer inside. Sure enough, Jayden lays halfway off his single mattress, limbs sprawling where they meet the floor. The rubbish which litters every surface in the room, including the floor, confirms my suspicions. His weekend never ended, and neither did his bender. Thankfully, his chest rises and falls steadily, replacing my concern with hot anger.

Lifting my hand into a fist, I pound on the window.

Nothing.

Pound. Pound. Pound.

Nothing.

I pull back and pound as hard as I can, sending my hand through the glass with a loud shatter. "Fuck!" Shards rip through my skin, sending drops of blood to the ground.

The commotion finally rouses Jayden, head shooting up in alarm, just to fall back down to the mattress with a groan after seeing it's just me. "What the fuck, Connor!? Rehearsal isn't for another few hours."

"It's Friday, and long past rehearsal."

A pause, as if he is still finding his way back down to earth.

"Damn it." Jayden lifts his arms, running his hands down his face. "I'm sorry, man. I lost track of time."

"Losing track of time is showing up half an hour late, Jayden. The guys and I haven't heard from you in a week. We started to think you were dead."

"I don't know what to say."

"You don't have to say anything. Just open the front door."

"I'm not up for this right now."

"I don't care. Get your ass up and open the front door, or I'll tie the handle up to my hitch and rip it off its hinges." Not waiting for his answer, I stalk back around the side of his building to my ute to grab an old rag, wrapping it around my hand to stop the bleeding.

My knuckles and the back of my hand got the worst of it. Uncomfortable, yes, but nothing which would hinder my playing. Glancing at my phone, I decide to give him ten minutes before making good on my threat. This baby has pull, and I'd be happy to make use of it.

75

I fish out another piece of nicotine gum and drop the tailgate, easily taking a seat with my height. My mind wanders, trying to figure out exactly what I'm going to do when that door gets opened, one way or another.

A punch to his face would probably make me feel better, and is definitely deserved. I should probably even kick him out of the band, having given him plenty of chances. He deserves to be told off and suffer the consequences of his actions. The state of his room runs through my mind again and I know, as pissed as I am, I'm not capable of doing any of that.

With a sigh, I grab a plastic bag from the bed of my ute and toss the bloody rag into it. The truth is, Jayden is suffering. He's suffering in a way that I can't possibly understand or make sense of. Skipping out on the band is not okay, but it's becoming more and more obvious that Jayden isn't okay either.

He wasn't always this way. After meeting a few years back at an open mic, I considered him a friend. Not in the way Theo and Ara are to me, or even Ryder, but still a friend. This past year he may have shown nothing but instability and unreliability, but the years before were filled with hard work, me and Jayden side by side, building our name up to what it is now.

Over time, something started eating away at him. It started with alcohol and parties, which only became more frequent as we gathered more of a following. It wasn't long until drugs entered the mix, and took his slow decline into a full-speed nose dive.

We all have shit that weighs on us. I'm in no place to preach live-laugh-love, having my own fair share of baggage in the form of mommy and daddy issues, and that's not to mention the other shit with Lara.

Life can be a dirty, messy motherfucker, and I know what it's like to feel fucked up. But we owe it to the people whose time got cut short, who had no choice in the matter, to make the best of ours. And if I don't do something to help Jayden soon, it will be too late.

Right on cue, his front door opens, and I push past him. If I thought his room looked bad, there wouldn't even be words to describe the hellhole which is his living room. It takes all my strength not to vomit when the reek of landfill reaches my nostrils.

"You shouldn't be in here." Jayden's head hangs, embarrassed that someone is seeing how he lives. *Good.* More of a reason for him to make a change.

"Grab a trash bag." Bending down, I begin picking up the trash littered across his stained carpet.

LAST *Stand* FOR GENEVIEVE

"What are you doing?"

"What does it look like?" I'm going to help this cunt clean up his life, starting with this damn flat.

"You're not here to rip me a new asshole?" His words are still slurred, no doubt a lasting effect of whatever he was on last.

I shrug. "I could, but where would that land us?"

Jayden looks at me blankly, before moving toward his kitchen. I don't know whether he really gets what I'm trying to do here, but once he's clean, he will. A few minutes later, Jayden comes back into the living room with a trash bag in hand, making it about five steps before collapsing on the couch.

Letting out a breath, I realize I'm on my own. Jayden is in no condition for any amount of exertion right now. I gently pull the black rubbish bag from his grip and continue on my mission. Once I've gotten all the takeaway containers with leftover food and receipts from more than three weeks ago stapled to the wrapping, empty liquor bottles, beer cans, sticky red Solo cups and who knows what else from the living room into big black bags, I make my way into the next room.

Jayden's bedroom is almost just as disgusting. I haven't been inside his flat since his decline, and now I know why. This is depression to the fullest extent of the word, and Jayden needs help. This time, I find little discarded baggies and empty needles amongst the rubbish.

No matter how bleak things are, drugs are never the answer. I've been a terrible friend, allowing him to do this to himself, thinking it was another phase which would come to pass. The truth stares me in the face. I've been nothing but a coward, letting my friend go as he continued to ruin himself. Running to the toilet, I've barely made it before I start to spill my guts.

After the heaving finally subsides, I turn to the sink, splashing cold water on my face. A pamphlet, stuck to the mirror with a magnet, catches my eye. Drying my hands on my pants, I pull it down and open it up, knowing what I have to do.

Me: He's breathing.

Dane: Another bender?

Me: Yeah, but this time it was different.

Rue: Where do we draw the line?

Me: Here. Right now.

Dane: What does that mean?

Rue: Is he out?

Me: I'm gonna try to get him some help. We'll have to see from there.

Rue: You've given him so many chances already.

Me: This is the last time, I swear.

Dane: Need anything?

Me: I'm good.

I close my eyes, squeezing the bridge of my nose, absolutely dreading this next text.

Me: We have to cancel Poison Ivy.

Rue: WHAT!?

Me: If I manage to get Jayden into this program, he will be in the middle of a detox.

Dane: Can't that kid who stepped in last time help us out?

He means Ryder, and I'd rather chew off my own foot than ask him again. Not because his vocals weren't first-rate—they were—but he made sure I knew the whole thing was a pain in his ass. And I threw gasoline onto the flame when I opened my fat mouth about his workplace. We haven't spoken since.

Me: No.

Dane: Can't you do lead for one night?

Me: We either show up ready to give the crowd the night of their lives, or we don't show up at all.

Rue: This is fucked. I'm done.

Me: I'm going to fix this.

Dane: Do what you need to do. Let Rue cool off. We'll be here when you're done.

I sigh, grateful for Dane, our bassist, having my back. I'm not happy about it either.

LAST *Stand* FOR GENEVIEVE

Poison Ivy is where we started, the first venue we ever performed. It was also where the first video clip was filmed of our set that went viral, giving us our first streams. Now we're supposed to be back, for the first time in years, since gathering our small level of fame. The show sold out on the first day, thanks to the locals who've supported us from the beginning, and we've all been looking forward to it.

Making my way back to the living room, pamphlet in my back pocket, I begin taking the rubbish out, one overflowing bag at a time. The neighbors won't be happy when they find the overflowing bins, but they can bite me.

Needing to sort out the hole my fist left in his window, I rip the shower curtain from the rod and tape it up over the broken glass with some duct tape I found in one of the kitchen drawers. Not great for security, but he's got nothing to take anyway. At least it'll keep the bugs, and most of the rain, out.

Lifting Jayden's arm around my shoulder, I hoist him up with my other arm wrapped around his middle, awkwardly shuffling over the gravel drive until I get him into the passenger seat. It's clear he's still fucked up good when he barely stirs.

Taking his phone from his pocket, I walk back inside his house and toss it into the sink, where his dirty dishes now soak in soapy water. Searching his cabinets one by one, I finally find a pot which isn't covered in gunk and tuck it under my arm as I switch off all the lights and head back out. If he pukes, it won't be at the expense of my baby.

I climb into the driver's seat, tucking the pot into his lap before turning over the engine. Retrieving the pamphlet from my back pocket, I type in the address and reverse out of his driveway.

• • •

As I exit the elevator, which opens directly into our penthouse, my phone vibrates.

Dane: You sure you can't sort through whatever crap happened and get that dude from the bar to step in again?

Mentally, I groan. Ryder stepping in was supposed to be a one-time thing. I was beyond grateful, but he didn't make it easy on me. He's been my mate since we shared a sidewalk, neither of us having a place to go. Going through something like that and having each other's back bonds you.

There were weeks where he was the only one I could trust, going as far as helping me defend what I cared about most, my guitar, from a group that tried to jump us. That's when I discovered he shared a love for music. We sat together that night, nothing but the strumming of my guitar and our vocals to get us through the night.

The next morning he'd shut me out. Looking back, I don't think he ever intended to share what he did, or for me to know he's got killer vocals. It was a side effect of walking into battle together and winning, we were on a high after never-ending lows. He opened up but thought better of it the next day.

Soon after, I met Theo. Eventually Ryder found his own path, too, a path that once I knew the truth of, I'd unsuccessfully tried to convince him out of. No matter what, I know Ryder would have my back, which is why I will always consider him to be a friend. Whether I agree with his career choices or not, underneath his tough exterior is a good man, and I hate that there's been tension between us.

Me: I really don't want to ask him.

Me: He would probably say no, anyway.

Dane: I get it. But if we could somehow still do Poison Ivy, it'd mean a lot to me and Rue.

If Dane is asking, then this means something to them, and losing out on this opportunity because of my inability to come through would be irreparable. Guilt weighing in, the decision is made for me.

Me: I'll do my best to convince him.

Dane: Thanks, man. We appreciate you.

"You look like shit." Theo looks up from his laptop, where he's likely typing another best-selling story, eyes full of concern.

My brother couldn't be more my opposite. Ara and I bonded over our muddy-coloured eyes, and the unfair comparison to the piercing green of Theo's. Where my hair is a chestnut brown, wild and untameable, his near black and stupidly perfect hair always sits seamlessly put together. Where his talent is wit and words, mine is music and mischief.

Being around him always brings me instant comfort and if I sound like

I'm in love with him, it's because our bromance is one for the ages. Our friendship was forged in fire, making us family to every extent of the word, minus blood.

I groan. "I need a shower."

"Want to talk about it?"

"I just got Jayden admitted into rehab."

"Shit."

"Yeah." Leaving out the part where I spent my entire evening cleaning his flat and drowning his phone, I get straight to the part which is really eating at me. "The admittance process was so bland, there was no hope in anyone's eyes, and when I asked about his recovery, all I received were words that were full of pity."

"That's rough, man. I'm sorry."

I shake my head. "I should have done something sooner, before it got to this point."

"This isn't on you." Theo hits save and closes the laptop. "You're a good friend. The best, actually, from what I've heard."

The corner of my mouth twitches.

"You've done what you can, the rest will be up to him."

"I guess you're right." More than anything, I want Jayden to get clean and get our band back together. I want my friend and singer back. "Where's Ara?"

"She's asleep."

I nod, ready to make a clean exit to my room, not wanting to intrude on their night. My eyes trail to the two-story windows of our penthouse, providing an uninterrupted view of the bay and lit city. We never bother closing the shades, even at night. We're so high up, nobody can see into our penthouse with the bare eye anyway, and if they're so determined to see in that they grab a set of binoculars, then as far as I'm concerned, they can enjoy the view of my balls.

Living here is still surreal, even after all this time. The modern architecture and elegant furnishings never cease to impress me, with ambient lighting and neutral tones, it provides an elegant, but undeniably amazing, atmosphere.

The first night, we ran through the place whooping and yelling like two little boys, before taking shots in every room. Since it's an open concept, when it came to the living room and kitchen, we took shots in three different spots for good measure, unsure where the rooms ended and began.

We drank ourselves into unconsciousness that night in celebration of starting a new chapter. Though he never reminds me of it, I know we live here because of me. If it were up to Theo, he would've gotten far away from his abusive, piece of shit father, but he took the payoff for me, so I could pursue my music and never worry about my survival again.

Theo was a victim of domestic violence long before I entered his life, something which made me realize that being forced to live on the streets isn't the worst fate one could have. The scar on my left eye serves as a daily reminder of what Theo went through most nights, for years, something I experienced only once when his father took things too far while I was there.

As we sat in that hospital room, blood pouring from our faces, we'd found a companionship and camaraderie that would never die. Growing up with my parents as well-paid doctors, I'd learned that money doesn't buy happiness, and Theo's relationship with his father only confirmed it. But getting to live in a place like this, with people who *do* make me happy? I feel grateful every bloody day.

"Go take that shower, because I can smell you from here, but afterward I could use a Slurpee and junk food. Care to join?"

The 24-hour 7-Eleven that just opened across from our building is both the best and worst thing to ever happen to us, per Ara, with the answer to all of our cravings just a crosswalk away.

"Yeah, I'll be out in a minute." As I walk to my corner of our penthouse on the opposite end of theirs, I try to focus on the positive.

Theo's right, it's up to Jayden now, to battle his demons and get clean. He's somewhere where he can be helped, if he wishes. Whatever Jayden does from here is up to him. But that doesn't change the fact that I should have done something sooner, and that is the weight I'll carry for the rest of my life.

Suddenly I understand Ice Queen's perspective a little more. Reaching into my pocket, I grab the nicotine gum and extra patches, dumping them in the trash. Addiction is a disease just like any other, ruining and taking lives.

My life won't be one of them.

CHAPTER FIFTEEN

Then - Brooke

Out of a never-ending chain of desperate days, this may be the most desperate of them all. I have no money left, having given it all away the first time. I have nothing valuable left to sell, having sold it all within the first month after.

Asking Mom for money would not only be suspicious, but also fruitless, considering she would have none to give, with all of her money going straight to my medical bills and just regular expenses. Selling my furniture would be suspicious. Selling my TV would be even more suspicious.

I've already tried broaching the subject of getting a job, but Mom wouldn't even take the time to hear me out. Though my arm and leg are pretty much fully usable at this point, she doesn't want me exerting myself and risk lasting damage.

You have such a long life ahead of you. She said with a smile. *Let me take care of us.*

There isn't a more harrowing thought on earth, than exactly how much time I have left on it. This façade will shatter too soon, taking everything away from Mom she thought was getting back, if I don't figure something out.

I give her exactly seven to ten smiles a day, mostly small ones. Too many or too little have been cause for concern, and we can't have that. Applying my scientific mind and critical thinking to this situation is the only way I've been successful. That and ensuring I feel as close to nothing as possible, at all times.

Which is why today, right now, I have to be smarter than I've ever been. Every iota of intelligence which led to my 4.0 GPA and Ivy League acceptances, all focused toward solving this problem. Obviously, the fastest way to make money that doesn't require hours of work or weeks to be paid, is to sell something. But that lands me right back to where I started, since I have nothing to sell.

Mom has never been one to wear expensive things, either.

Wait.

Just because Mom doesn't wear them, doesn't mean she doesn't have them. In fact, she could have them, but they just wouldn't be what she considers valuable, meaning she wouldn't even notice if they were to disappear, the way things tend to do when you don't keep tabs on them. Like socks in a dryer, or that sweater you haven't seen in years.

The jitters start and indecision weighs. Realistically, there is little choice. I either steal something of relatively insignificant value, or my mom will be robbed of something far more important: the ruse, this sham of a daughter who can pretend she's okay.

As I make my way down the hallway, I let out a breath of relief. Thankfully, *her* door is closed, preventing the pastel walls and aroma of tulips from incapacitating me.

Mom's room is simple, but tidy, the way it's always been. Filled with mismatched furniture she's collected for free over the years, all in good condition, but never anything brand new. Her bedding is the same, those florals which were so popular in the nineties, sprawling across the soft, worn fabric. I make a mental note to buy her a new set, as if I have the wherewithal to do so, as if I'm not here to take something instead of gifting it.

I spot the aged jewelry box on the far dresser, solid wood and given to her by a sweet old woman having a yard sale. It lets out a loud creak, slightly nails on a chalkboard, as I flip open the top. There's nothing which looks expensive, the majority are silly things Genevieve and I made for Mom in art class. A macaroni necklace won't do a goddamn thing for me.

Spreading out the little winged storage drawers, I finally spot something of promise. Nestled in the corner is a small, navy blue jewelry box lined with gold embossing and dust. Relief washes over me, opening it to find a (probably) real pair of earrings. They've got thick, gold clip-on latches, with big bulbous pearls that dangle down to little diamonds.

This could get me somewhere.

LAST *Stand* FOR GENEVIEVE

They're a bit gaudy for my or Mom's taste, like something a great-grand-mother passes down generation after generation, for no one to think twice about wearing them. Except, Mom's never mentioned any heirlooms to me, so maybe it's left over from the woman who gave her the box. Based on the dust, it appears that's exactly what's happened here.

Perfect.

• • •

"I'll give you $25 for them."

If I wasn't so practiced at schooling my emotions into numbness, my *eyes* would bug out of my head. The thing is, if the earrings hadn't been made of real gold, pearls, and diamonds, they would've been thrown in the trash a long time ago. I snatch them back from the pawn man's greedy hand.

"That's pathetic." If he thinks he can take advantage of me because I'm young, he has another thing coming for him. "*Gold and Co* offered me $500."

It's bullshit. He knows it. I know it. But I don't give anything away.

The man laughs, saliva spraying over the glass counter where an array of jewelry and watches are already displayed. He pulls out a dirtied cloth, drag-ging it across his sweaty brow.

"What's funny?"

"I've known Randall over at *Gold and Co* for a long time, and no way would he fork out an offer like that for a pair of these." He chuckles, which turns into a fit of coughs. "But I like your hustle, kid. For that, I'll be generous and give you a hundred bucks."

The truth is, I don't know how much they're worth. If I'd been smarter, I would have researched it before leaving, but the jitters had gotten barely man-ageable, and I'd begun going out of my mind.

"My great-grandma told me they were worth more than that." I paint the picture, a granddaughter inheriting something that she'd rather sell for a pair of new jeans. "I want at least three hundred."

"Then take a walk, sweetheart, because I can assure you that my offer will be the most generous you receive. You won't find anyone eager to take your granny's old crap."

I'm desperate and he's got a point. "One fifty."

"One hundred, and that's final. Trust me, I'm doing you a favor."

"Fine."

I take the hundred and walk.

• • •

"Sweetie?"

"Yeah?"

"Has anything of yours gone missing recently?"

Trepidation fills my gut. I take another bite of corn flakes, stalling for time until I'm sure my voice won't wobble. "No. Why do you ask?"

"I'm worried someone broke in."

"Broke in?" Now I'm *too* calm. I should be alarmed at this, not relieved for not being a suspect. I widen my eyes for effect, looking around. "The house looks fine to me."

"I know. That's the only reason I'm not calling the police or losing my mind entirely. It doesn't make sense." Mom sighs. "Have you seen my grand-mother's earrings? I keep them in my jewelry box, always in the same place, but for some reason they aren't there."

My hands start to shake, but I reassure myself that she doesn't suspect me. "I'm sure they're around here somewhere. You probably misplaced them while cleaning or something."

Her beautiful face furrows into a troubled expression. I need to convince her it was no one's fault but her own.

"Mom," I say gently, in a way which would have made the old Brooke puke, laced with the kind of sweetness that makes you question your own sanity. "You've been working a lot. I know you're tired."

She looks at me then with clever, searching eyes lined with the distraught she's trying to keep a cap on for my sake, and I nearly crumble. My mom has always had a sharp mind and sixth sense for bullshit. I'm going to have to do better to undermine her mind this way. "I hope you're right. It's our family's tradition to give them to our oldest daughters to wear on their wedding day. I've been holding on to them for a long time, even though they are worth thousands."

The silence in my mind is deafening. Mom reads it as something it isn't.

LAST *Stand* FOR GENEVIEVE

"I know there's been times we could use the money, but I never wanted to take away something so meaningful from our family."

Standing, I make my way over to her and put my hand on her shoulder. "Mom, I think if you just rested, they would probably turn up."

A fraction of the tiredness that she is feeling creeps into her expression, and I know if I push it home, we'll make it out of this, I'll save her from losing her smiles. If I can just convince her to rest for a while, I can somehow get the earrings back.

"Just get some rest, Mom." Pulling her in for a soft hug, my skin begins to crawl with my betrayal, as I lay the groundwork for my cover. "I'll get the groceries and take care of things today."

I will do anything to get those earrings back, even sell my soul if I have to. *As if I'll have one left to sell after convincing my smart, loving mom to question her own mind.* Squeezing my eyes shut, I will her to agree, nearly collapsing with relief when I feel her body relax into mine.

"You're probably right." Mom puts her arms around me, pulling me close. "Thank you. I'm so grateful to have you back."

Her words crack something, but surely there's nothing left of Brooke Anderson to break.

• • •

"They're gone, little girl."

"What!? They can't be gone!" I slam my fists down on the glass counter. "I sold them to you hours ago, *and* you fucking ripped me off!"

"I didn't force you to sell shit." He points a crooked, nasty finger at me. "You took my offer on your own free will."

"You're supposed to keep the item for at least thirty days."

"And if we did things the *conventional* way here, your little mommy would have had to come down and sign the forms."

"Tell me who you sold them to." I'll steal them back.

"Now *that* would be a crime, probably like the one you committed to get your hands on those earrings in the first place."

"I didn't do anything."

He laughs, a cold wet thing. "I don't care what you did or didn't do, just what you're about to do, which is turning that skinny little ass of yours around and walking it out of my doors."

I feel sick, may just lose my stomach all over this horrible pawn shop.

"Get OUT! Before I decide to call the police."

A numbness descends over me, causing me to lose feeling of everything besides my stomach, which is churning like an angry sea. I don't remember walking out of the pawn shop or getting into my mom's car. I didn't stop and consider how I should have felt about driving again for the first time. I don't remember getting the groceries I promised to bring back, or almost hitting a bicyclist.

All I can do is replay the conversation with my mom over and over. Why didn't I say something of mine was missing too? I could have just thrown one of my belongings away and blamed it on a break-in, avoiding *all* of this.

Though, if I had done that, Mom would no longer feel safe in that house. She would have put herself out, spending money on new locks, at the very least, not knowing the criminal is the one who'd have a key. The real monster sleeps across the hall from her.

I can't do this anymore. Maybe it's because I'm weak. Every interaction feels empty, like a screen of pretend always on the precipice of shattering into irreparable pieces. But just maybe it's because there *is* still a shred left of what used to be Brooke Anderson.

A girl who loved her family, who would rage at anything that would try to pull them apart. A girl who walked the straight and narrow, who invested care and determination into everything she did. A girl who thought she understood the power of grief and believed herself immune to something as debased as addiction, just because she knew it was wrong.

My mom no longer knows the person who sits across from her at the breakfast table. She goes to work for many more hours than she sleeps, to provide and protect a stranger, an empty shell of someone who once lived.

I thought by numbing myself to the pain, my mom would be able to keep me. Now I know there is no surer way to be lost. With every escape into oblivion, I numb myself not only to what I don't want to feel, but everything I *do*.

What would I give to *feel* when my mom pulls me into her arms for a hug? When was the last time I felt a bubble of warmth underneath her love?

I can't remember.

I'm on the verge of drowning, sinking to a depth which nobody comes back from. Will I continue until there is nothing left? Will the day come when it's all too much and I go too far, becoming nothing but another sad memory? Will she blame herself for surviving, the same way I do?

Opening the ugly, heart-shaped coin purse which hides my cache, I stare at the red tablets which seem to hold my fate in their contents. Minutes pass before I've made my decision. Turning from my bathroom, my heart begins to pound as fear for what I'm about to do races through me.

The jitters begin, part from adrenaline, and part from the craving for what my body now desires above all else. I tuck the coin purse into the back waistband of my jeans and take another step, wiping my clammy palms against my thighs.

You're not strong enough!

I take another step.

You are as good as dead, anyway, why fight it?

I take another step.

She will never forgive you.

I take another step, trying to remain determined despite the vicious on-slaught.

Your mom won't love you anymore.

Almost to the door.

You're nothing but a sick, degraded monster.

One more step.

You rotten–

Even the voice quiets as I take in the sight before me, stepping into the threshold of my mom's bedroom. She sits on her bed with her back to me, hunched over something she has in her hands. I open my mouth to say something but hesitate when I see a tremor rock through her, followed by a sniffle.

My mom is crying.

I want to comfort her, to take some of the weight off her shoulders, but I don't remember how. The thought of something so real feels almost foreign to me, but knowing I'm still capable of wanting it fortifies my decision to come clean. About everything.

We can get through this together. I will get free of this, take on some of the burden which is weighing her down. We'll go somewhere new, a place which isn't full of the memories of what once was.

My mom straightens herself slightly, wiping the tears away, and that's when I see what she's holding.

A picture of Genevieve.

Her school pictures must have come in while I was under, the ones taken on the day before the accident. Genevieve had woken me up three hours early, demanding that I do her makeup so she had a chance in hell of surviving when it was framed and hung on our walls.

We had succeeded. She looks beautiful, her hair perfectly curled away from her face, the smallest touches of makeup to show off her natural beauty. Her blue eyes are kind and clear as crystals, crinkled at the corners by a smile as bright as sunshine. I can almost imagine her giggles and charm, as she surely convinced the photographer to take a few more, just in case.

Now she'll never get to see how they turned out.

My mom won't frame these so she can watch how Genevieve grows, she will frame them to remember how happy her daughter was the day before she died.

Because of *me*.

I take a silent step back as the sound of squealing brakes and crunching metal drowns out my mom's sobs.

This is *my* fault.

I have destroyed everyone I love.

I deserve to be destroyed too.

CHAPTER SIXTEEN

Now - Connor

As much as I hate what goes down behind closed doors in this bar, I gotta admit that it has character. I'm greeted by the scent of warm whiskey, as I take in the interior design which lands somewhere between hipster and old-fashioned. Plenty of seats remain open, with it only being around four in the afternoon right now.

Ryder eyes me from where he wipes a glass behind the bar. "Here to give me another lecture?"

Raising my hands in acquiescence, I prepare to weather the storm which is Ryder scorned. "Not here to lecture you."

"Then what do you want?"

"To talk."

"I'm working, so unless you're here for a drink, there's the door."

"I'll have a cider, then."

"With a side of unsolicited opinions?"

"Come on, Ryder, don't be a dick." I sigh. "I'm here to wave the white flag."

"Because you need something?"

"Listen, I know I'm a tool, but so are you. Get off your high horse and come have a chat."

Ryder's expression, caught somewhere between irritation and annoyance, doesn't budge. Just as I start to squirm, thinking he really might throw my ass out, he finally gives in, coming around the bar to take the stool next to me.

"I know you don't actually want a cider."

"Listen, man. I know I was an asshole before, but it came from a good place." That's as close as I can get to telling him that I care about him, without causing him to shut me out entirely. Ara says I'm emotionally unavailable, but Ryder is emotionally non-existent.

I'd put the pieces together.

"I have to do what I have to do." Ryde's voice is firm, but lined by an almost imperceptible layer of shame.

And that's it, the only explanation I will receive on the subject.

"I'm sorry for judging you. I'll do better." Stepping down from *my* metaphorical high horse, I offer my hand to him, and he takes it.

"Apology accepted. So, what do you need?"

That was a lot easier than I expected. "Why do I have to need something to get back on good terms?"

"Because you're one hell of a stubborn cunt." Ryder chuckles. "You must have been held at gunpoint to come here like this."

I can't help but laugh with him, the weight lifting from my stomach. He's not wrong, I *am* a stubborn cunt with a gun to my head, but it feels good to clear the tension that's been between us. I've missed this asshole.

"Guess you're right." I run my hand through my hair, and sigh. "Jayden is in rehab."

Ryder's brows shoot up. "Since when?"

"Since last week." I pause. "When I admitted him."

"Shit. Did something happen?"

"Beyond the general spiral he's been on? Not really. The nurses said he hadn't technically overdosed, but he was definitely close to it."

Ryder nods, knowing there aren't the right words, but letting me take the time to decide whether I want to say more or not.

"I'd never seen him that fucked up. It scared the shit out of me, if I'm honest."

"You found him?"

I nod. "I had to do something. If something really bad happened, I would've never forgiven myself."

"What people do…it's not on you." Shadows pass over Ryder's face, and I can't help but wonder if he's trying to convince me of that, or himself.

"Yeah, but it still wouldn't sit right." Blowing out a breath, I continue. "Anyway, the band is going to have to take some time off while he works his stuff out, obviously, but there is this one show—"

Ryder cuts me off. "And let me guess, you've been sent to convince me to step in."

"I already told them you wouldn't, but I had to try. This show… it means everything to the guys." It means everything to me. "Poison Ivy is where it took off for us. It was the people in *that* crowd who got us where we are today, and canceling on them? It's fucked up."

Ryder nods. "Why can't you step in?"

I shake my head. "Yeah, nah."

"Your voice is good. I've heard you sing."

"I don't want this show to be *good*." My voice pitches on good, as if the idea repulses me.

Understanding dawns on him. "You want it to be transcendent."

I nod. None of us have forgotten how the crowd responded to Ryder the last time he stepped in those months ago. It was surreal. Despite being at war with himself over how much to let go, at the end of the day there was no fighting the vocals which came from his soul. The thrill in his eyes when he looked more alive after our set than I'd ever seen.

We're both quiet.

That's the thing about Ryder. He can act like he's a shell, just a husk after life was too harsh and destroyed everything inside. The pretense might even fool most people, convince them that's who he is, but I know better.

"Fuck me," Ryder says as he drops his head with a groan. He's in. "Same set?"

"Pretty much. We want to add in a few things to pay homage to our first show there, but it'll be easy to pick up."

"When is rehearsal?"

"Monday, usually later in the afternoon."

"I'll have to arrange that here."

"Mate, don't bother. Just tell me when you're free and I'll get the other guys there."

"Noon would be good, then."

"Noon it is." The guys are going to be bloody stoked. Finally, some good news.

"Heyyy." The soft purr comes from my right, and I *know* what a 'hey' with three 'y's means.

Ryder rolls his eyes and stands. "That's my cue."

I smirk. "See you Monday."

Swiveling my chair to the right, I come face to face with one hell of a woman. She's absolutely stunning, and she knows it. Thick, black hair frames her golden-brown face skillfully glammed up with makeup. I don't even need to drop my eyes to know the generosity that has been gifted to her head to toe. Her sultry eyes focus on me with an openness, leaving no doubt about what she wants from me.

"G'day," I say with a smile. When she returns it with that eye flutter and a bite of the lip, I make a show out of running my eyes down her body. I wasn't wrong.

Her response is instant, melting underneath my attention. The way she dresses tells me she is successful at whatever she does, likely thanks to her confidence and ability to go for what she wants.

"Adriana." She offers her hand and I take it, with a gentle but sure grip.

"Connor." I release her hand and smile. "What do you do?"

What do you do? I sound like someone on their first date from Aussie-Match.com

Humor dances in her eyes, as if she's used to men scrambling in her vicinity. Can't say that's typical for me, no matter how impressive a woman is, but I'm not exactly scrambling either. I'd call it grasping for something to say, since it isn't coming naturally.

"I'm the Vice President of Marketing at Beauty and Beau."

Shit. They're huge. I've heard of them, and I'm not even into that shit. They're a cosmetics brand specializing in her and his products.

"You're more impressive by the second," I tell her honestly.

"And what about you, Connor?" Adrianna's eyes eat up my leather jacket and the white V-neck I wear underneath.

This is good. This is *simple*. A man and a woman, meeting in the bar as two adults who are attracted to each other and free to make their own decisions. I wait for my skin to heat, my body to come alive.

"I'm a musician."

"Interesting. I've never been with a musician." Adriana's eyebrow arches, before she drops her eyes over my body yet again. This woman is the embodiment of appeal and yet...

Any man would kill for the opportunity to share a night with this woman, and normally so would I, but something feels lacking, and it's definitely not *her*. It's me.

Fuck. My. Life.

I've been ruined by the bite of cold and cunning eyes that stare right through my bullshit. The shocking beauty that's uninterrupted by makeup. Glances of warmth which live behind icy walls.

"Who is she?" Adriana's voice, still sexy, although toned down, rips me out of my thoughts.

"Did I say all of that out loud?" Confusion and mortification climb up my neck.

Adriana laughs. "It was written all over your face."

I groan, rubbing my hands over my face and pulling my hair, as if it can free me from this hell. "It's never going to happen, though."

"Is she your brother's girl or something?"

"No, thankfully, no." I snort. "It's nothing like that."

"Then what's stopping you?"

"Imagine a metaphorical Wall of China, made of emotional ice, built specifically to keep me out."

"That's tough." She clicks her tongue. "But is she worth it in the long run?"

"Oh, I'm not *in love* with her," I explain, slightly nauseous from Adrianna's assumption. "Emotions and relationships aren't really my thing."

Adriana hides her smile with her glass as she takes a sip. "So then, what is the problem?"

Yeah, Connor, what is the fucking problem?

Since the moment Ice Queen pulled that cigarette out of my mouth, nobody has been able to get my skin buzzing, heat spreading, or have the sheer pull over me the way it happens when I'm caught in her orbit. There is no denying the infernal attraction.

"My system just needs…a reset…and I think it's only going to work with her."

Adriana snorts. "That always works out exactly how you intend."

I pretend to ignore her sarcasm. "The only issue being I have *no* idea how to get her to sleep with me."

"Hmm." Adriana slides a card across the bar with her name and number before gathering her bag. "Well, if you end up succeeding with that reset…"

"I wish we'd run into each other a few weeks ago."

"Good luck, Connor." The clever twinkle in her eye glitters, as if she's already seen the movie, and my cluelessness is simply added entertainment.

Do I know what I need to do? Fuck no. But I know with certainty I'm not fixing shit without Ice Queen. Yet my salvation depends on the one woman in the world I'm certain wants nothing to do with me.

• • •

Thankfully, neither Theo nor Ara is around when I exit the elevator into our penthouse, leaving me free to reminisce on what a good run I've had, since it's clearly coming to an end. I'd turned down a beautiful woman's advances, in favor of sitting there at the bar, blocking and deleting every single contact I'd carefully curated over the years. What's the point of having them anymore?

Only Oscar, Ara's fucked-up little cat that hates everyone but her, takes up his usual spot in the living room, where he likes to sit and glare at whoever walks by. I pass his judgy little stare and make my way to the kitchen. With no tobacco to fill the void, I decide a hot choccy is just going to have to do. Heating up the milk over the stovetop, NOT the microwave, doesn't take long, and I dump in the Lindt chocolate from the canister, giving it a little stir. Knowing there's no marshmallows around, this is as good as it's going to get.

Turning to put the spoon in the sink, I nearly dump the hot chocolate over my entire front. Oscar sits on the counter, and I swear the little shit is smirking. He never willingly gets this close to me.

"What do you want?"

His ears twitch as he rolls his eyes.

I'm losing it. Cats don't roll their eyes.

Oscar stands, flicking his tail around the way he does only for Ara, letting her know he is ready for pets. I mean, that's at least what she thinks it means, claiming he has his own language. Cautiously, I reach out, and when he doesn't immediately attack or flee, I reach a little farther and scratch his head. Fucking hell, he's so soft.

I melt. I fucking melt.

Months of the little devil barely tolerating me, giving me absolute *hell* the one time I was asked to psycho-sit and yet, with one little head bump, I think I would jump into traffic for him.

"Even you're taking pity on me, huh, little mate?"

Oscar glances at me and lets out a little grunty meow in agreement.

"Don't tell Ara about this, okay? We don't want to make her jealous."

He bumps his head against my hand again and damn it, why is that so adorable?

"You're lucky there aren't any lady-cats in here. Makes things easier for you."

Oscar seems to disagree. *I'm talking to a cat.*

"Nah, trust me. Feelings, love, emotions…you're better off without all of it. Unfortunately, I might be adding lust to that list pretty soon, too, because I'm learning that can fuck you almost as much as the others."

Oscar blinks, doing another pass so I can rub his back.

"You see, there's this woman, and I have no idea what I'm doing with her. Wooing her goes against everything I stand for, since I'm not trying to win her over for *more.*" I blow out a breath. "And maybe that makes me a tool, but I can't let go of the idea of being with her. She's gotten under my skin."

Oscar sits, looking right at me, like I'm missing something obvious.

"You think I'm trying too hard?"

Oscar blinks. *Duh, you fucking idiot.*

I read him loud and clear. "That hurts, man."

It's also exactly what I needed to hear. Ice Queen has me in knots. I've been so worried about getting untied by whatever means necessary, I haven't made peace with or taken advantage of the pleasures of being bound.

"So you're saying I should just ride it out and see what happens?"

Oscar flicks his tail in agreement.

"Okay, then, little mate. I'll ride it out." I scratch under his chin, and he juts out his head like I've found the holy grail of spots. My heart just oozed. "Don't be a stranger."

Oscar turns and walks away, heading back to his throne.

"Right." I grab my hot choccy and head down the hallway which leads to my room.

There's a contrast between how my room *should* look to match the architecture, and how it *actually* looks. The high ceilings and fancy lighting, the modern windows and stunning view call for equally elegant furniture. Except I'm not elegant, and this room is mine.

I keep the space, which is filled with various shades of brown, tidy. From the light brown cork board, holding all the handwritten music I've created over the years, to the dark oak furniture set I've carefully curated from yard sales, and the wooden stand which holds my brown leather jacket, it feels like home.

Taking a seat in my wicker chair by the windows, I set my hot choccy on the little table to my left and reach for my most prized possession of all: the acoustic guitar I was given at six years old. It's ironic really, that my dad was the one who gave it to me, having no idea he was sealing my fate as a musician.

After it started to become a passion of mine, his lack of support made me realize it had been a generic gift, given by a father who didn't know his son well enough to know that he wanted a race car set. But with the first tear of the wrapping paper on my sixth birthday, seeing the dark brown leather case which now rests on the other side of my room, race cars never crossed my mind again.

My life became filled with notes and strums and harmonies that kept me company when my parents fought. They remained by my side in the years after I turned ten, while I looked out for myself, and they pursued their careers. It's what brought me and Lara together...and what held *me* together after she was gone. Music has given me life.

Just as I strum the first note, a notification goes off on my phone. Reaching into my pocket to silence the bugger, my stomach jumps to my throat before dropping hard and fast.

Ice Kween: With so many things that can kill you, how did you manage to survive childhood?

Holy shit.

Me: Watching the Discovery Channel, are we?

Ice Kween: Honestly? I'm down the sort of rabbit hole you can only find on YouTube.

LAST Stand FOR GENEVIEVE

Me: And you've somehow ended up on a video about how scary Australia is?

Ice Kween: The exact title is *Everything In Australia Wants To Kill You.*

Sounds about right.

Me: Look something up for me?

Ice Kween: I don't know why I'm agreeing to this, but sure.

Ice Kween: If it's porn, I'm never talking to you again.

Me: Look up Ozzy Man Reviews Speedboat Crash.

Ice Kween: wtf?

Me: Just trust me.

Me: And while you're at it, let's make a wager.

Ice Kween: What's the wager?

Me: If you laugh, you have to see me again.

Ice Kween: What if I don't laugh?

Me: Then I know you're either a robot, or a serial killer, and I'd leave you alone forever.

And I know she'd be lying.

Ice Kween: You're on.

I pull up the video, watching the three minutes and twenty-four seconds for the hundredth time, and laugh as much as I did the first time. Not thirty seconds after it's finished, my phone chimes.

Ice Kween: I watched it.

Me: If you say you didn't laugh, I know you're lying.

She could say it was stupid or a waste of time and I've lost.

Ice Kween: I didn't laugh. Not even once.

A grin somewhere between shit-eating and victorious takes over my face, as something like adrenaline consumes every other part of me at what this means.

I get to see her again.

CHAPTER SEVENTEEN

Then - Brooke

"So, I was thinking…" Mom trails off, gathering the gumption to present her next idea. There's nothing worse these days than my mom getting *ideas*. "You worked so hard for so many years in school, I'd hate for it to be for nothing."

Well, it was.

"I spoke to your principal, and because of the circumstances and your previous performance, it's still a possibility for you to go back and finish your senior year. You may be a year behind, and it's slightly unorthodox, but there is still hope for you to get into medical school."

Nothing could be more of a waste of time. "I don't want to go to medical school."

Mom sighs. "I'm sure you feel that the medical field let us down–"

"I don't want to talk about it."

"You could still get your high school diploma, in case you ever change your mind."

"I already told you that I don't want to go back to school." Returning to school after all of my classmates had already graduated, seeing hundreds of people who only knew the old version of Brooke Anderson? No fucking thank you.

"Well, at the very least, you could take that test and get your GED–"

"MOM!" I shout, slamming my fists onto the table. She flinches at the loud clang of silverware against our plates. Meeting her gaze, for the first time it's suspicion I see in her eyes.

Shit, shit, shit.

"Mom, I'm sorry. That was an overreaction." I sigh, feigning guilt over my outburst. "I just really don't want to talk about my education right now. I'm not ready."

Mom doesn't drop her gaze as she takes in my expression and apology. "Okay."

My mom isn't stupid, and neither am I. She isn't placated nearly enough for this to be swept under the rug in her mind. I need to do better. "I've also been thinking."

"Oh?"

"I still want to get a job."

Her brows raise. "I thought we talked about this."

"There are a lot of bills and I want to help."

"Brooke, you don't need to feel guilty. I'm your mom and it's my job to take care of these things. Don't you dare think it's a burden."

My heart pangs. "It's not just to help you, but for me to get back out into the world a little and start my own savings for when I decide what *is* next for me."

There. Let her believe I have hope for a future.

Some of the tension leaves her shoulders. "Okay. But nothing high stress or too strenuous."

I nod. "No problem."

Little does she know, the only thing I care about funding is my ruin, which is simultaneously her salvation.

CHAPTER EIGHTEEN

Now – Connor

Connor: A deal is a deal. Don't be a coward.

Ice Kween: Fine. But I get to choose what we do and when.

Connor: Make it something fun ;)

Ice Kween: I choose right now. Shame if you can't make it on such short notice.

Connor: Wouldn't miss it.

She sends an address a moment later, which is about twenty minutes away, in an area of Tampa I can't drive through without wanting to get out of my car and offer everything I have to my name (which isn't a lot) to those less fortunate.

Ice Kween: Wear clothes you don't mind ruining.

The three little dots start up again before I can even respond.

Ice Kween: And before you get any demented ideas of what will be causing the mess, we will be painting.

I grab a black t-shirt and throw it over my head, not caring if it gets destroyed along with the gray track pants I'm already in. Taking in my reflection in the mirror resting above my oak dresser, I realize I'm probably a few weeks overdue for a haircut, not that keeping it shorter does much to tame it anyway. I drag my fingers through it a few times, fruitless as always.

The sandy brown curls topple out whichever way they decide, over my forehead and tickling the back of my neck. Definitely need to get a haircut.

LAST *Stand* FOR GENEVIEVE

Half an hour later, I'm pulling up in front of a house that has my stomach clenching, not knowing what to expect once I step inside. So much time has passed since its last paint job that there's almost no paint left on the wooden frame, sagging with rot and decay. From the few remaining spots, I think it was once blue. The sound of the driver door closing sends echoes throughout the near-empty street.

Brooke walks out onto the porch, careful to avoid a spot where the wood has given way, creating a large hole. Her hair is pulled up into a messy bun, blonde wisps coming free and framing her face. She's got overalls over a faded white tee, both covered in various shades of paint.

It's the first time I've seen her look anything but sleek. She seems relaxed in this state, content even, but the furrowed brow and *no-mucking-around* set of her shoulders tells me that I'm in for one hell of an evening.

I swallow. "Whose house is this?"

"Doesn't matter, but it's not mine, so don't come here looking for me." Her voice is the temperature of cold I've come to crave.

"Okay."

Brooke leads me past the sinking porch, and I try to understand how she thinks painting is going to be enough for this place. The door has come free from the bottom hinge, hanging at an odd angle, making the perfect entrance for whatever Florida wildlife finds itself here.

The large, open space serving as what must be a common living space isn't much better. There are a few mattresses stacked up against the wall and nausea racks my core when I realize they are smaller than a twin size, possibly belonging to children.

"Please don't make any jokes about the state of this place, I know it's bad and that's why I'm here."

Her assumption tears through me. "If you think I'd ever joke about something like this, then you've done a really good job in making sure you don't know me."

I push past her, moving into the kitchen which is much worse despite having been cleaned. The walls are stained with years of neglect, the cupboards are all doorless where they aren't falling apart further.

"A family was living here." Brooke's voice is softer now, the only apology I'll receive, as she comes to stand at my side. "When I saw the state of…everything…I decided to do what I can to make it a bit more livable here. It's just been treated for mold, which was growing up the length of almost all the walls, so now I'm giving it a new coat of paint. As a start."

"Where's the family staying now?" I'd like to know how she found this family, what made her demand to help them, but I know better than to ask.

Silence. Likely with her then.

"Painting won't be enough, you know?"

Brooke doesn't respond with a blast of ice the way I anticipate, voice coming out deflated instead. "I know, but I couldn't do *nothing*."

"I could help, you know?" Surveying the kitchen, the broken floorboards and holes in the walls where fists likely once flew. "I'm alright with a hammer and basic woodworking. I could probably even patch up these holes, along with the one on the porch, and get the door hanging straight. If you want, that is."

She blows out a breath. "Let's just start with the paint."

It's not a no.

Eyes catching on a Bluetooth speaker in the corner, a little thrill takes flight despite the circumstances, as I try to guess what she listens to. You can learn a lot about a person from their choice in music. On exactly the same train of thought, Brooke moves toward the cylinder speaker, turning it on. I'm not disappointed when she puts on a 90's and 2000's throwback playlist. There may be some fun in her after all.

The first hour is filled with no conversation aside from the brisk instructions she gave, letting my mind wander and trying to figure out the enigma that paints next to me. Behind those glacier walls of ice, she holds trauma and secrets close to her heart, secrets I may never be able to uncover. Yet below it all, there *is* a heart. That, I am sure of. This project proves it.

The way she's working, you wouldn't be able to tell there was music playing or that she had company she could pass the time with if she wanted. Each stroke is clinical, exact, and she does it all while acting as if I'm not here. The thing is, the quiet has never bothered me.

Neither has the cold.

Having done my fair share of DIYs, I do a banger job on the first wall, getting the strokes just right and leaving behind no streaks as it gets harder to fight the effect that music of any kind has on me. Whether it's Chopin or

LAST Stand FOR GENEVIEVE

Linkin Park, the melody finds its way into my soul and I can't deny what it shares with me. Right now? NSYNC is making it impossible not to sing along and time my motions with the beat.

I'm rewarded with a snort. "You like NSYNC?"

"Only a monster could resist NSYNC." A quiet pause. "Please tell me you're not one of those monsters."

"Please. As if they're not the best thing that came out of the 90s."

I smirk. "Glad to know there is a bit of human in ya."

Out of the corner of my eye, I notice her head tilt ever so slightly in my direction. My eyes remain trained on the wall in front of me, but my entire being zeroes in on her and where her eyes graze over my untamed hair, snagging on the column of my throat, bobbing with a swallow. They take their time drifting over my corded forearm, fit from years of playing and throwing a guitar around on stage.

The paint speckles over my skin as I work the roller over the wall. The room becomes a raging inferno, the heat of her gaze absolutely sweltering as it catches on the thin strip of skin, where my t-shirt rides up. Then, I'm freed, like a plunge into ice as she looks away.

"Wish I could say the same about you. You're an animal."

Oh, Ice Queen, if you only knew.

"Is that a hint of humor I detect?" In an effort not to scare her off, I pretend not to notice what her greedy eyes were doing only a moment ago, taking us back to safe ground.

"Don't bet on it."

"Speaking of bets, how did it feel to lose?"

"Almost as painful as this dialogue."

I can't help it, I throw my head back and laugh. She turns then, eyes running over me again but differently this time. Where the last time she saw my body, now it's as if she's finally letting herself see *me* for the first time. There is a quick tilt of her lip, but she turns before it can make its full impact.

God, she is beautiful. I'm not sure when this interaction with her became something I needed. Something that leaves me feeling off, until she's standing next to me, serving me my ass. Since I'm already in shark-infested waters, I might as well risk my life.

"How old are you?"

"What does it matter?"

"Just making conversation." Desperately wanting to get the bitterness out of her tone, I go on. "Telling me your age doesn't give me much to go on."

"I'm twenty-three."

"Same as my friend, Ara."

I'm pinned down by her eyes again, sending shock waves through the rest of my body. Doing my best to ignore the sensation, I reach down and get another coat on my roller.

"You don't strike me as the type to have women in your life who are just friends."

"Nah, trust me. Ara's like a sister to me and she's going to marry my best friend one day." Theo hasn't asked yet, but I know he will.

Silent deliberation. "How old are you?"

"Twenty-six."

"Practically geriatric."

Another laugh bursts out of me and I make a mental note to get my shit together. Ice Queen can't know how easily she affects me, between her brand of humor, keen eyes, and intelligent mind. Asking about her does nothing but make me more stupid and risk putting her off. So I go with another approach. "Anything else you wanna know?"

"Where are you from?"

"Sydney. Moved here a while back with my parents."

"Are you close with them?"

"No." Her answering silence tells me everything I need to know. She can relate, but where I'm full of resentment, she's full of regret. Shadows fall, but she locks them up faster than they appeared. Only a tiny crease in her brow is proof of the battle. I go on, desperate not to lose the moment. "Most people don't get to choose their family, but I did. Theo and Ara are all I need."

"How did you meet?"

"I was living on the streets–"

"You've lived on the streets?" Brooke cuts in then, disbelief and emotion in her voice, more than she's ever allowed me to see.

"Yeah, until Theo took me in." There is something buried there, under her reaction, but I choose to stay in my lane. "My parents kicked me out and there was nowhere else to go."

LAST *Stand* FOR GENEVIEVE

There are so many questions I want to ask her, but I hold back, taking a second to remind myself that knowing about someone leads to understanding, which inevitably leads to emotions and even worse…feelings. It's none of my goddamn business, anyway.

We're quiet for a while, until a wild card comes on. Not one of the poppy throwbacks like the rest, but "Use Somebody" by Kings of Leon. It's so different from what we've been listening to, I can't help but wonder if she changed the playlist when I wasn't looking.

As usual, something about the song instantly hits my soul, carrying me with it until I find myself singing along. People have always told me that I have what it takes for lead vocals, that I just need practice, having a voice which gets compared to Caleb Followill so often. But my heart has always remained with the guitar, except in these rare moments where the lyrics consume me. I'm not singing for an audience or using a little acoustic riff to win over a woman, I'm just singing.

The song comes to an end, and I turn to find Brooke staring at me. Her eyes aren't filled with her usual cold animosity, nor are they the drooly eyes of a woman I'm about to take to bed. She looks at me with a frankness nobody has, as if she sees the real me that I've shared with so few.

A pull begins to form in my belly, as if someone is weaving together threads of fate. It starts as a slight sensation, but increases force as the threads become more and more entwined, pulling me toward something unknown. I clear my throat and look away, the moment becoming something that's just too much.

Another song comes on, breaking the silence, and I make a shitty excuse to get some space. "I need some more paint."

Fuck me.

Grabbing the tray, I step out to find the supplies in the other room. Except when I get there, I set my tray aside and turn on the faucet. Cupping my hands under the cool water, I splash it on my face and neck.

Ice Queen has me acting like an idiot, like I'm some fool walking around with no rules or common sense. There is a dangerous war waging between us, and it will maim us both unless we get it out of our system. I'm convinced that's the only way.

Dumping some paint in my tray, I head back to the other room just to come up short at the threshold, as Brooke sways her hips to Beyonce. Not only is she perfectly in time, but she can *move*. Her hands are busy with the task, yet her body rolls and rolls, starting at her shoulders and carrying through to her hips.

If nothing else is accomplished today, I've learned three things tonight:

1. Brooke has a heart.
2. Brooke is twenty-three.
3. Brooke can dance.

• • •

I don't learn anything else.

Ice Queen knew she'd been caught, raising those glacier walls as she became motionless, besides the arm which rolled the paint on the wall. Each time she shuts me out, it does nothing but turn my interest into a level of maddening need I've never known. Brooke has unknowingly invaded every inch of my mind, gotten under every layer of my skin, leaving me willing to do *anything* to touch her, taste her secrets. She would only have to ask.

We've finished the room and I know that I'll be dismissed any moment now.

"Thank you for your help tonight."

"It would go much faster if I came back and helped tomorrow."

She wipes her forehead with the back of her hand, smearing a layer of paint above her brow. I can't stop myself from moving forward, dragging my thumb over the little layer of white, instantly losing myself in the feel of her soft skin. Her mouth drops open just slightly, on an inhale too low for my ears to pick up, but my eyes know it for what it is as her chest rises and falls, faster than before.

The only thing that stops me from testing her limits is the thought of the family who lives in this house, temporarily without a home until the work here is done. Pushing any further would risk her shutting me out for good, and subsequently being shut out from doing what I can to make this home a safer place. With my hands at my sides, I turn to walk away.

"Connor?"

I turn back at the sound of her voice, slightly breathless. "Yeah?"

"Can you come back tomorrow?"

I nod.

"Thank you." Brooke's voice is unsure, telling me this is rare for her, asking for help. But she chose to ask it from me.

"Anytime, Ice Queen." For some weird fucking reason, I find myself not wanting this night to end. "Do you want to get some McDonald's?"

She pauses. "Where?"

"The closest one is in Ybor."

She shakes her head. "I'm good, but thanks. See you tomorrow."

"See you tomorrow." I leave her to it, wondering if it would have changed her answer had I said something different than Ybor.

And an even better question, why do I fucking care?

CHAPTER NINETEEN

Then - Brooke

The shittiest part about my new job isn't stacking shelves. Brooke from two years ago would have looked down her nose at what I'm doing, but I don't care. That version of me died in that car and I'll never be getting her back. What really bothers me about this job is that I only get paid every two weeks.

Two. Fucking. Weeks.

I've been stacking and straightening shelves for a week already, with another whole week to go. The one problem? My supply is scary low. *Again.*

After watching my mom cry over Genevieve, I realized there's no piecing myself back together. I have no idea what I've been holding on to all this time, why I hadn't given myself over to the urges completely, much earlier. What reason is there for limiting myself?

Ever since I've given in, things have been easier. Whenever I get the need for more, I allow myself. No more holding back. No more of those punishing hours between. I've been through enough, why not permit myself this small mercy?

With that fresh in my mind, I came to the beach to ask for a loan.

"This is no charity, I'm runnin' here."

"I'm good for it, just need a little advance." My jittering hands start up, as if they think he needs more convincing.

"And what's innit for me?" That greasy smile widens as his eyes roam over my body, like he has a good idea what he'd ask for. "Why wouldn't I just go find someone who *has* money?"

"You could charge me interest. Few more dollars on the pill." This is a bad idea, but I'm desperate. If I successfully convince him, it's just kicking the can down the road, but I don't care. Consequences are for the future, not today. Warning bells go off in the back of my mind, about entering a never-ending debt spiral with someone like him, but I couldn't care less.

"Sounds okay to me then." Though he looks a little disappointed with my suggestion. "The name's Sebby, by the way. If we'll be seeing more of each other, we can be a bit more familiar."

"I'm Brooke."

He smiles, shaking his head like he's teaching me how to ride a bike without training wheels and I've nearly fallen over. "Nice to meet you, *Brooke.*"

"See you in a week, Sebby."

"I better. You don't want to know what will happen if I don't."

The slimy look on his face leaves me feeling gross the entire way home, wondering exactly what he would do to me if I didn't pay him back. I'm officially in business with the devil, willingly. Another stain on my soul which will never come out.

All thoughts of Sebby come to a screeching halt as I take a step into my room. The place is a disaster, a physical embodiment of how I've felt since I woke up in the hospital. Broken pieces of my things lay in bits across the floor, so unrecognizable I don't even remember how they once fit, as if a path of destruction passed through, leaving nothing left intact.

My eyes finally reach my bed, where my mom sits with a swollen face and a heart-shaped coin purse in her cut-up hands. Instinctively my hands fly to my empty back pocket, where the heart-shaped coin purse with my few remaining pills should have been, confirming what I already knew was true. In my haste, I'd left it behind.

And now she knows.

CHAPTER TWENTY

Now - Connor

"Why are we at Home Depot?"

"Theo is at another one of his fancy meetings and I needed back-up."

"And you thought I was the one you should bring?" Ara snorts. "That girl not only has you by the balls, but also your brain."

I open my mouth to deny it, but she's got me there. "I was hoping, rather than making me miserable, you could put a woman's touch on some shit."

"A woman's touch?"

"I told you that I was helping her paint, but I left out the what and where." I blow out a breath. "Brooke is hell bent on fixing up a home for a family in need, and you should have seen this house, Ara. It was terrible. I can't stop thinking about the little mattress I saw and the kid it probably belonged to." Or kids.

Ara turns contemplative, taking in my expression, the desperation I'm feeling. "This is bigger than a booty call, isn't it?"

I nod.

"Then let's HGTV the fuck out of that place." Ara sets her hands on her hips, looking around just enough to recognize she has no idea where to start. "Lead the way, *Chip*."

"Huh?"

"You wouldn't get it." She waves me off. Seeming to notice I don't know where to start either, Ara asks, "What's the most dire thing to be fixed?"

"The front porch. It probably needs to be rebuilt entirely, but I could start with patching a hole that's just waiting to eat up someone's leg." Once again, my thoughts stray to a kid having to maneuver around it with their little legs.

"Then we need some two-by-whatevers. Aisle eighteen!"

"If you know where the wood is, maybe you'll be useful after all."

"I read the sign, idiot."

Each of us grabbing a trolley, mine a flatbed for the wood, and Ara's deep enough to hold whatever she determines as HGTV-worthy, we head off to aisle eighteen. Finding the two-by-fours isn't too difficult, and one of the staff is nice enough to offer advice on how to treat the wood so it has a chance in hell of lasting.

"What else?" Ara asks after we've finished grabbing the supplies we need for the porch.

The memory of the sagging, dilapidated kitchen rocks me. "Cabinet doors for the kitchen."

We went with the unfinished wooden cabinet doors and basic hardware, just the necessities to get the job done.

Ara stares at them contemplatively. "You should paint them yellow."

"Is making your kitchen look like *Big Bird* all the rage on HGTV?"

Eye roll. "Yellow is a happy color. Maybe it would make it feel like more of a home."

"I'll pass the idea on to Brooke."

"Speaking of Brooke…" Ara shoots questioning eyes at me, urging me to spill my guts. I remind myself I don't do guts, therefore there is nothing to spill, nor is there any way that was a flutter I felt at the mention of her name.

"What about her?" The nonchalance I was aiming for comes out strangled.

"Come on! You're obviously into her." Ara waves her hand at our now full trollies. "Look at all this effort you're putting in."

"This is for the family, not to get laid." It's the truth. I know what it's like to go without, to have parents too proud to end their child's suffering. "Whatever happens with Brooke is completely unrelated."

"Uh-huh."

"You don't think I'm being genuine?"

"I know you're genuine about helping this family, but you have the emotional awareness of a doorknob when it comes to matters of your heart."

113

I snort. "Matters of the heart, eh?"

"I know you think you only have room for us and your band, but–"

"And you know why." It's as stern as I'd ever gotten with Ara. Everything she says and does comes from a place of love. Her best friend Lou, too. Both of them are always scouting, wanting to help me find my soulmate, but I don't believe someone can love twice, nor is the risk worth the reward.

"Don't get all defensive on me, because that would be some bullshit, but point taken. I'll drop it." She mutters lower, "For now."

Determined not to let my surliness on the subject ruin the day, I lighten the mood as we approach the checkout. "Ara, it's time you know the real reason I brought you here."

So far her trolley is only filled with the smaller tools and hardware I'll need, but I really did want her input on how to bring some life into that place.

Ara scoffs playfully. "You want me to foot the bill?"

"Try again."

Ara's eyes scan our surroundings until they land on the section just to the right of checkout, an abyss of fake greenery and colored plants, before they launch to my face for confirmation, wide with excitement.

"Go nuts," I say with a grin.

She squeals and takes off, peeling around innocent bystanders that are just trying to make it home to their families. Pulling out my phone, I snap a picture of Ara trying to choose between two plants that look the fucking same and send it to Theo.

Connor: Send help for the original help.

Theo: Ha. You're screwed.

Connor: Thanks for the reassurance, mate.

Theo: Be prepared to drag her out of there.

Connor: Pray for me.

Theo: Oh, I am.

But I have to admit, a yellow kitchen with some plants does sound pretty happy.

LAST *Stand* FOR GENEVIEVE

• • •

"What is all of this?"

Grab your jackets, ladies and gentlemen, forecast for the day shows it's overcast with brisk winds, potentially getting down to the thirties.

Shutting the driver door behind me, I get my footing, readying myself for battle.

"Supplies." I shrug. "I said I wanted to help, and I meant it."

My stomach plummets as her eyes soften a fraction. "Do you need help unloading?"

Her many facets will never cease to knock me on my ass. I'm thrown off balance by this woman yet again, and this time it's her softness which has done it. Where's my head at?

I nod. "There's a box in the back I've been directed to give to you."

Brow arch. Suspicion.

"Oh, come on, it's not rigged to spring." I roll my eyes. "My maturity level lands *just* above that."

"I'm aware. It's right below repeating dirty words as many times as you can when you're alone."

I wink. "Except I don't have to be alone to be dirty."

"Suddenly that box is calling my name." Brooke makes her way over the cracked cement driveway to the back of my ute. She slides the box toward her, not waiting to bring it inside before opening it.

Ara ended up picking out a can of yellow paint to better pitch the idea. Apparently, there's a difference between barf yellow and cute yellow, which would make all the difference in pitching the idea.

"Ara, the friend who's like my sister, went a little wild when I asked for her help. She thought this stuff could add some happiness to the place." I run my hand through my unruly curls, definitely making it worse. "The wood is for fixing the deck, and that stuff is for the kitchen."

"Thank you for this, Connor." She doesn't water down the gratitude, and that pull which has begun to form between us gets a little stronger with her gentle words and the sound of my name on her lips. I know she feels it too.

"No worries."

Brooke's hair has been pulled back into a messy bun again today, face clear of any makeup as usual, and stunning as ever. I snort when I finally notice what she's wearing: an oversized black shirt and cargo pants.

"What?"

"We're matching."

Brooke's eyes drop, taking in my black shirt and tan cargo pants. They snag on the tool belt I borrowed from a mate which is now strapped around my waist. Something sparks in her eyes at that, and a smirk pulls on her lips.

"Well, one of us is going to have to change then." Humor dances across her features, and I decide to take advantage of it before her next mood swing, see how far I can push this playful version of Brooke.

"Careful what you wish for." My voice drops an octave as my traitorous eyes land on her lips. Stepping into her space, I force her to back into the tailgate before reaching around her to grab the drill.

Brooke's eyes heat as I strap the drill into the tool belt. I subtly drag my tongue across my bottom lip, but she misses nothing, eyes flashing to the movement. My arm grazes hers as I lean impossibly forward, our chests coming together ever so softly until I set my Ice Queen free by stepping around her and heaving the two-by-fours onto my shoulder. I take a second to bask in the fucking glory of seeing her still frozen where I left her.

Another point for Connor.

I clear my throat and she launches into motion, grabbing the box and heading inside. Seeing that I genuinely care about her project has cracked something in her resistance. The jury is still out on how devastating the consequences will be.

Unsure of whether she intends to come back outside, I get to work without waiting. Thankfully today isn't too humid for a Florida afternoon, and there's a breeze gently blowing through the porch area.

Another stupid grin forces its way onto my face as I think about the fact that we're wearing the same outfit. It's always high-necked or loose-fitting clothing with her, in muted tones (if not black) and always concealing, which is fine by me. I've always had a decent imagination, and I *love* surprises.

Measuring up the jagged-edged hole, I'm pleased to see my estimate of supplies was dead on. I grab a crowbar and start ripping up the old wooden boards which are already busted, and the ones that appear to be close to it. It doesn't take too much strength to rip it up, telling me all I need to know about the dodgy structure of this thing.

Gathering up the rotten wood, I dispose of it at the edge of the street, hoping the city will be useful for something in this area. If they can't fix the streetlights, then they can at least pick up the wood scraps. I stop by the ute to grab the other tools I need, mainly the cordless circular saw. Never thought I'd be so grateful to have spent my Saturdays growing up with my mate and his tradie dad at various job sites, much of the time getting roped into helping.

My skin tingles with the awareness of being watched, and I let her do so, undisturbed. I set up the table I'll use for cutting, which could stand to be a little less flimsy. Double checking my measurements just to be safe, I pencil in the marks to guide my cuts before ripping the saw to life. Since it's only a hole I'm patching, it's not long before I've finished cutting the wood and walk away covered in sawdust, sticking to the layer of sweat which has formed on my skin.

The tingling sensation multiplies as I step onto the porch just as Brooke approaches the doorway. I pause as she does, when a tiny frown forms between her brows, as if she doesn't know how she's gotten there. She turns away without a word, clearly deciding against whatever brought her out here. For once, I'm content to let her stir, my focus on the task at hand. Thankfully, the joists aren't too bad off, and I'm able to get the new wood screwed in without any headaches.

After the last one goes in, I hang back toward my ankles, giving my knees a slight reprieve, and pull up my shirt to wipe the sawdust from my face. The shit is fucking caked to me, and I practically have to scrub it.

"I thought you might want some water." Removing the hem of my shirt from my face, I find Brooke standing there with a glass of water, letting her eyes wander over me unapologetically. She makes a grimace and puking sound before shoving the glass into my hand. "You look like you're trying to rip off a handyman calendar."

I snort. "Pretty sure they're ripping *me* off."

"Musician, painter, handyman…anything you can't do?" she says almost to herself.

"What can I say?" My smile is nothing short of animalistic. "I'm good with my hands."

Ice Queen rolls her eyes and turns to walk away, but I get this dropping sensation in my stomach at the sight of it, and I know I *need* to get her to stay. "I can't ride a bike."

She stops, slowly turning to face me once again. "You can't ride a bike?"

I shake my head. "Nope. Not one bit."

Clever as ever, she reads my expression, instantly deducing that my dad was never around to teach me. "Tragic."

"Is there anything *you* can't do?"

She considers it for less than a millisecond. "No."

I laugh. "Your modesty is overwhelming."

"Maybe I just don't want to share."

"Fair enough." I take a big gulp of water, and her eyes trace the movement of my throat, causing me to nearly swallow my tongue. To recover, I lie through my teeth. "I've already got you figured out anyway."

Brow raise. "Oh?"

"Yeah."

"Do tell me about myself."

"I'm actually a little busy at the moment." I gesture around to the menagerie of tools spread around me. "Maybe later."

Push and pull. That is the only way I'm to snare this one.

"Perfect. I'm already bored anyway." With a shrug, she walks away.

If I didn't know any better, I'd fall for her unaffected act, but I've seen enough to know that's all it is. I've felt her eyes on me, the heat that radiates before she can lock it down. I've seen the way her breathing changes and pulse flutters when I challenge her. She may be fooling herself, but she can't fool me.

Every one of her barbs is a bid for me to push in closer.

• • •

Hot, messy, and full of the kind of pleasure that makes your eyes roll back into your head. That's the only way to describe these wings, devilishly bathed in sauce on a bed of curly fucking fries. I groan for what must be the hundredth time. "Woman, where did you find these wings?"

Brooke smirks. "If I told you, I'd have to kill you."

"You're just looking for an excuse to keep me coming back."

"Hardly."

Brooke caught me off guard with a delivery of Uber Eats for the two of us, just as my stomach had begun to growl. Another sliver of evidence against her act.

"I have a thing with my band tomorrow at noon, and I'm not sure how long I'll be, but I'd like to come afterward to work on the kitchen. If you leave before I get here, do you mind leaving the back door unlocked or something?"

"I'll be here." She's quiet, but I feel her brewing. "What's up with the band?"

"I don't want to bore you with the drama."

"Come on, don't make a girl look desperate." Our eyes meet. With Brooke's attention on me, I'm suddenly conscious of making sure there's no leftover sauce on my lips. She notes the movement of my tongue, and that tinge of heat from earlier returns to her gaze.

For some, catastrophically dumb reason, I decide to open my mouth. "My lead singer is currently in recovery, so a mate of mine is stepping in for an important show of ours. Tomorrow is our first rehearsal with him."

"Recovery?"

"He suffers from addiction." I don't need to go on.

Brooke looks away before I can unpack the emotion swirling in those icy blue depths. I suddenly get the feeling that I'd walk through every ice storm and stand under every frozen look she directs at me, just to know what turns the cogs of her mind and to free her from that troubled expression. And if that doesn't make me the stupidest bloke to walk this earth, I don't know what does.

Unwilling to examine the consequences of my thoughts, I change the subject. "Guess you're going to have to kill me, with a real weapon, not just your winning personality." I hold up the receipt I snagged from the Uber Eats bag which reads *Roberta's Wings: Sauce For The Soul.*

"I already poisoned them while you weren't looking."

I scoff. "And doom yourself to miss out on *my* winning personality?"

"I'd miss the view more." Brooke's words are laced with barely contained desire.

Holy. Fuck.

The response of my body is instant, her words going straight to my dick. I slowly turn my head just in time to see her clenching her mouth shut with all her might, before losing the battle and throwing her head back into a laugh.

"You. Thought. I. Was. Being. *Serious.*" Brooke wheezes between hysterics. "That is the cringiest shit I've ever said in my life, and you *fell* for it."

My cheeks heat. *MY CHEEKS BLOODY HEAT.*

"*I'd miss the view more,*" she repeats in mocking sarcasm, another fit of laughter following close behind as she wipes her eyes. "You watch too much porn."

One point for the Ice Queen.

Two points if I admit what hearing her laugh is doing to me.

It's time to even the score. Before she has time to react, I turn, roughly placing my hands on her hips with a squeeze, easily lifting her to the top step. I force her back, back, back, until my hand reaches behind her head and stops her retreat, supporting her weight with my forearm.

Knowing she's at my mercy awakens something visceral inside of me. I can feel her heart beating from where I hold her, picking up pace as I lean in closer, leaving only a breath between us.

"You're a liar," I whisper.

Swallow. "I haven't lied."

I trace her nose with my own, tilting slightly as if I'm about to put my mouth on hers. "You *do* enjoy the view."

"You don't know anything."

I raise a finger to her pulse point, feeling the erratic palpitations. "Don't I?" Brooke's eyes clash with mine as I begin to count for sixty seconds. "I measure one-forty-five and we haven't even gotten started, baby."

"You're full of shit."

"There is no denying that you want me."

I drag my finger down her throat away from the pulse point, steering clear of the swell of her breast beneath her shirt, all the way down the center of her chest, placing my palm against the curve of her ribcage, allowing myself the immersive experience of how I affect her.

"The next time you try to act immune to me, I want you to remember the force of these desires, and that my offer still stands." I don't need to remind her of what I'd put on the table. We could have fun, no strings attached, and this is the proof. I drag my nose to her jawline and back up with a growl. "Eventually we're going to give in. It's simply a matter of science."

The moment I feel her back arch, telling me she's ready to relent, I pull away with a smirk. "I'm gonna head out. See you tomorrow."

That was definitely worth at least three points.

CHAPTER TWENTY-ONE

Then - Brooke

"I knew something was wrong, but I didn't know what." Mom sniffles, looking at the heart-shaped coin purse in her hands. "I thought I was being distrusting where it wasn't deserved. No way my girl would ever be *this* conniving, she couldn't find a way to be worse than her father." Mom looks me in the eye for the first time before continuing. "At least he was honest about his addiction. He never stole things that had meaning from me."

Far away, there is something like guilt which tries to creep in on me. A tiny little shard of Brooke Anderson urges me to feel it, but I can't. I'm too numb. The only thing at the forefront of my mind is how I can get out of this without ending up in rehab, all of my thoughts geared toward how to ensure I'm somewhere that I can get my next fix.

"Do you have anything to say at all?"

If I fight Mom on this, it's over. She will call an ambulance, or the police, or whoever is in charge of dragging teenage girls to rehab centers. Mom doesn't realize that by doing that, she would kill me, the pills are the only way I can keep going. If she forces me off of them, she will lose the only daughter she has left.

I have no choice but to play along.

"I'm sorry, Mom." There is a shake in my voice, not from regret, but from the threat of losing the only thing I care about anymore. "I need help, but I was afraid that if I asked, you would never look at me the same."

"You are my *daughter*." She swipes at her eyes, tears falling faster. "I will love you *always*. No matter *what*."

LAST *Stand* FOR GENEVIEVE

Would she love me if I told her the *truth*? Maybe Mom could forgive me for getting hooked on the pills, but she would never forgive me for what eats me alive, the sole reason I would rather feel nothing than anything at all ...

"Gen. Please tell me you're not seriously studying on a Saturday night."

I adjust the second-hand Louis Vuitton I recently scored that now rests on my shoulder. It matches my nude heels perfectly, and this outfit is absolutely slaying, if you ask me. Steven is going to lose his shit when he sees his girl arrive at the party like this. This outfit was born from my determination to make him regret not picking me up, letting me look single, and it will definitely do the trick.

"I have a feeling there is going to be a pop quiz on Monday and I want to be prepared!" Gen looks me over and rolls her eyes. "Plus, you look like you're going to be busy."

"I understand the need to study better than anyone, but Saturday nights are reserved for anything but that." My words ring true. With this being my senior year, my GPA has to be flawless if I'm going to have any shot at pursuing medicine, not to mention having to juggle my extracurricular clubs, being captain of our cheerleading squad, and volunteering to set myself ahead of the pack. If I'm awake, I'm studying, working, or searching for what will take me to the next level. Except on Saturday nights. Saturday nights are for me. "Come on, I'll take you to the party with me."

Genevieve snorts. "I'd rather peel off my fingernails."

"That's fucking foul, Gen," I say with a grimace. "But fine, I won't take you to the party. That doesn't change the fact that you need to put the textbooks away."

She does that crinkly thing with her nose before looking back to the textbook as if I'm not even standing here. Gen might as well be holding a massive sign lettered with the words, "I don't listen!"

This is going to require a drastic measure. I quietly retreat from her room, pausing down the hallway just long enough that her suspicions have likely ebbed, before running full speed into her room. Gen's eyes widen as she scrambles to save her textbooks, but she's too late. I use the strength that cheer's brought to my thighs, and launch myself into the air, diving onto Gen and her bed.

"Have you lost your mind!?" Gen screeches as I land on her bouncy mattress, the recoil sending us both flying off the bed. We land in a pile of limbs, and I can't help but laugh, even though my Louis went flying across her floor.

Gen's hair looks even messier than when I walked in, her entire face trembling with the effort of holding in her laugh. My sweet, perfect little sister isn't capable of anger, and watching her struggle to muster it might be my favorite activity in the world. She gives it her damndest, but as I let out another maniacal cackle, she loses the battle and joins in.

Genevieve is everything to me. Even if she wasn't permanently stuck with me thanks to our blood, I would have found her and made her keep me anyway. I would choose her a million times over, because she is that fucking special.

The truth is, I have a serious side. Although most people only see the fun, overachieving popular girl, the other side of me peeks through when I'm determined about something. While other people get nervous or anxious, I get as solid and cold as iron sometimes. When Dad abandoned this family, choosing addiction over his girls who loved him unconditionally, that seriousness solidified inside of me, and Gen is the one who helps me keep it from taking over completely. Every single day, she reminds me of the power a soft kindness can hold.

Wrapping my arms around Gen, I pull her close and she scoots in, wrapping hers around me in return. We stay like that for a while, staring at the ceiling covered in glow-in-the-dark stars, long enough that thoughts of Steven and a high school party seem like a distant concept.

"You're thinking about Dad, aren't you?"

Genevieve is also perceptive.

"A little. But mostly about how much I love you."

"I love you, too, Brooke." She's quiet for a second. "I don't know how you manage to do everything you do, all while being the best at it. You're my hero, you know."

Her words fill me with a kind of warmth that only pure love can bring. "If my superpower is efficient success, yours is untainted sunshine. You make everything you touch happier."

"If you could be a color, what would you be?" Genevieve asks, starting our little game we've played since we were little. The "what would you be?" game. It started as a way an older sister distracted the younger one from a household of unrest, but it's remained our thing.

"Probably brown."

Genevieve snorts. "Ewww!!!!!! That is arguably the worst color in existence."

I laugh. "If you could be a color, what would you be?"

"Yellow," she smiles. "Yellow is the happiest color of all."

"Come on." I sit up, pulling Genevieve to her feet after I make it back onto mine. "We're going."

She groans. "But I said I don't want to go to that party, I'm not cool like you are, Brooke. I'll stick out like a sore thumb."

"First of all, you are literally the coolest person I know."

Genevieve rolls her eyes.

"Second of all, forget the party. We're going out for custard."

Her eyes light up. "Rita's?"

"Rita's."

She squeals and runs in place, her version of a happy dance, before jumping over to her closet to grab her shoes

My mom blows her nose, pulling me from a reverie I'm grateful to escape, reminding me of the game of survival playing out in front of me. "I'm so sorry, Mom. Will you help me?"

Another sob escapes her, and she clasps her hand over her mouth, trying to keep it in and remain strong. Mom lost the love of her life to addiction, her youngest daughter to a terrible accident, and now her only family remaining is slipping through her fingers. "Of course, I will help you."

And just for good measure, so she doesn't, for one second, realize that this is all to mislead her, I add, "I don't want to end up like Dad."

Mom stands, pulling me close. "I won't let that happen, sweetie."

"Okay." We stand like that for a while, and I remember that there was once a time that my mom's embrace brought me comfort, unlike the bare, unfeeling emptiness I feel now. "I'm tired, Mom."

She pulls back, eyeing my backpack. My stomach drops, knowing almost everything I'd gotten from Sebby is in there, but if I don't willingly hand it over, she'll know I'm being ingenuine. So, I do, grateful to myself for having the foresight to put some of them in my front pocket, just in case.

"Get some sleep. We will clean this up in the morning and figure out what to do." My mom stands, reaching the door before turning around. "I love you, Brooke."

"I love you, too, Mom." The words are hollow, even to my own ears, I barely stop myself from cringing.

Mom hesitates at the door before quietly adding, "We owe it to Gen to survive this."

With that she leaves me, and I'm dragged back to the past.

"What are you going to order?" I ask Genevieve.

We used to have our 'regular' orders until one night we looked at the menu and saw how much we were missing out on. Now we make it a point to order something different every time.

"I got the mango gelato last time and it was sooo good. I know I'm supposed to pick something different, but how can I?" Her bottom lip juts out, pouting at the world's biggest problem.

"I think I'll get vanilla custard, covered in rainbow sprinkles."

"That sounds so yummy!!" Pause. "Actually, I'll get that too."

I shove her shoulder. "Copycat!"

"You can't have good ideas and expect me not to copy you." Gen shrugs. "I'm your little sister, it comes with the territory."

I snort, flicking on the radio of my car, which is too old for Bluetooth, or even an auxiliary cord. We'd had one in Mom's old car, the one we had to sell after our household lost its second income provider. We both cringe as the country music station that Mom loves comes on, no doubt all she listened to when she borrowed my car yesterday, while her rust bucket got a new tire.

Genevieve slaps my hand away, "I'll DJ, you watch the road."

She flips through radio station after radio station, until she squeals after one single note. I couldn't have told you what was about to play after one note of a song if someone held a gun to my head, but not my little sister. When she loves something, she loves it with her whole, entire heart. God forbid she meets a boy she isn't afraid of one day.

Genevieve's smile is a mile wide. She's not Twenty-Two, but you'd think she was with how she's singing along to Taylor Swift. The song has transformed her into a party girl in her twenties, rather than the sweet, and sometimes shy, Genevieve, who'd rather be at home reading a book. The Gen whom I love so much.

She mimes the lyrics dramatically as she sings them, as if she has to represent every single line with a motion of her body. The mostly empty road is her stage, and boy, does she give this performance her all. We're both breathless by the time the song ends, her from dancing, and me from laughing at her dancing.

The station goes to ads, and Genevieve grumbles before starting another search for a good song. One day, when I've finished medical school and I become a world-renowned doctor, I'll buy Genevieve a car that's nice enough for her to play any song she wants at any time. She can perform mini concerts in the car for me, and we will laugh like this forever.

"You know what?" Gen asks, as she continues to push buttons on the stereo.

"What?"

"I've made a really big decision."

"Oh?"

"It took a lot of thought, and it's been a very stressful event, having to come to this conclusion."

"I'm on the edge of my seat."

Gen lets out her version of a maniacal laugh. "I've decided that I'm getting both: vanilla custard covered in rainbow sprinkles AND a mango gelato!"

I laugh, ready to respond, before someone's high beams blind me, "What kind of asshole drives down Gulf to Bay with his…"

Horror hits me like a freight train. Time becomes my enemy as it slows down just enough for me to know what is about to happen, but it continues fast enough that I'm sentenced to do nothing but witness it. Those aren't high beams on the other side of the road, they are headlights pointed directly toward our car, blindingly bright because they are too close.

My head whips toward Genevieve, who looks too calm for what I know is about to happen, nothing but terror in my system at the realization that I have no idea how to protect her. Where is the superhuman strength and speed I'm supposed to gather from adrenaline when someone I love is in danger? The danger that I've put her in because I refused to let her study on a Saturday night.

I take off my seatbelt, launching myself toward the passenger side in an attempt to shield her. "GENEVIEVE!" I scream her name, pleading to God and the universe to protect her.

"It's going to be okay," she whispers, as she reaches for me, just as the unbearable squeal of brakes and crunching metal throw me through the windshield, and lay waste to what I treasure most.

Even the pills I took earlier aren't enough to keep the sounds of that night out of my head. I reach into my pocket, desperate for quiet, and swallow, before lying down to wait. Hour after hour passes, another excruciating display of time.

Mom checks on me three times.

I keep my breathing even, even when she sits on the side of my bed, quietly sobbing. A huge, impenetrable wall goes up in my mind, forever imprisoning the remains of Brooke Anderson who was once a daughter, a sister, who was destined for medical school because she wanted to save lives.

As soon as I'm certain that Mom is asleep in the other room, I pull off the covers. Grabbing a spare backpack from my closet, I stuff it with extra clothing and another pair of sneakers. I don't bother stopping in my bathroom since I'll have no running water to brush my teeth or wash my face anyway.

I'm quiet as I creep into my mom's room. Grabbing a notepad and pen from her desk, I scrawl a quick note, laying it next to the picture on her bedside table, one of me and Genevieve smiling together on her first day of high school.

This is how I want you to remember us, but she's gone,
and so is the Brooke in this picture.
Forgive me, but there is no other way I can survive.

Just as I reach the top of the stairs, I realize there is one last thing I need.

Entering Genevieve's room for the first time since the accident, pain rocks through me despite what's in my system. *Everything* hurts as I take in a room filled with nothing but *her*.

Her floral printed bedding now perfectly made, shelves still lined with her favorite romance novels, and walls still that pretty light pink. For a room that once had happiness bleed into everything it contained, there's now nothing but a debilitating sadness ready to immobilize me if I stay any longer.

Moving to the far wall, her corkboard is full of pictures of all kinds, some of our once-complete family, and some just of our parents, I find the one I'm looking for. It's the picture Mom snapped of me and Genevieve laughing at each other because of something funny I'd said. I've always thought it was so much better than the ones taken with plastered smiles.

I turn to leave when her favorite book snags my eye from where it rests on her desk. Genevieve once told me that she read it so often, there was never a reason to store it on her shelf. Mom must have put it back here after my outburst. Unsure why I even bother, I pick it up, tucking the picture into one of the pages before I take the only belongings I now have to my name, and head out onto the street.

CHAPTER TWENTY-TWO

Now - Connor

Sparring with Ice Queen yesterday, ending the final round by leaning her back against those steps and feeling her body ready to give in to its desires, ignited something in me: a burning inferno searching for an escape. Though I barely touched her, I became helpless to the rush of being so near her lavender scent, tracing her soft skin with the tip of my nose, and the feel of her heart racing just for me. Admitting that feels like a betrayal, but I can't take it back.

Regardless of the loyalty I feel toward my past, there is something in front of me that needs to run its course. I've known it from the beginning, but after feeling the way our bodies begged for each other, there is no denying there is something flammable between us.

The thing with something flammable? Unless you're careful, it eventually catches fire, and I have a feeling deep in my gut that I'll be the one getting burned.

"Connor? You with us?"

"Yep." I clear my throat. "Yeah."

"Then what do you think about Rue's suggestion?" Dane asks with a knowing smirk, bringing me back to Immoral Support's first rehearsal with Ryder.

"I think it's great."

Rue doesn't bother to hide his frustration. "Well, that's awesome, because I didn't suggest shit."

This is what I get to deal with when it comes to picking someone like Rue, who started playing the drums as a way to expel his anger. He's always angry, meaning he's also really fucking good at the drums.

"Mate, I'm sorry." I drag my hands through my messy curls. "I'm with you now, I swear."

"Have you decided on the set list for Poison Ivy?"

I've put countless hours into planning, making sure this show is nothing short of perfect. The set list is the most important factor, making or breaking the night. I'd had it roughly nailed, but with the recent swap to Ryder (who is arguably a stronger vocalist than Jayden anyway) I've decided to play with it a little more.

"Nearly there with it, I had to make some changes after the swap." At Rue's annoyed grumble, I go on. "Listen, this is the most important part of the night to figure out. I want to make sure I get it right."

I'm not arrogant enough to think the crowd will know every word to all of our original songs. We're well known, but not there yet. Part of the thrill of being in an audience is being able to sing along, voice in unison with hundreds, or thousands, of others. Nothing is worse than a crowd of crickets, having no fucking clue what's going on, or even worse, talking amongst themselves about the dipshits on the stage. Hence, why we like to throw in some covers everyone knows the words to.

The door groans as it's opened, signaling the arrival of Ryder. It's the only creaky part of this entire penthouse, and it belongs to our rehearsal space, as if the universe knows we should be in a dirty garage, a start-up band paying their dues and barely keeping the power on. The creaky door was the least it could manage to humble us.

"Hey." It's practically a sloppy kiss when it comes to a greeting from Ryder.

"It's good to see you again." Dane stands to clasp his hand. "Wish it was under better circumstances, but we're psyched to have you back."

"Thanks for stepping up, bro." Rue slaps Ryder over the shoulder and heads to his drum set in the back. Dane grabs his bass, taking up his spot on a stool across from mine, giving us as much space as the room allows.

"Thanks again for doing this, mate." I don't lay it on too thick, knowing him well enough by now.

He sighs. "What was I gonna do, say no?"

"You could have."

"I'm not *that* much of an asshole."

I grin. "Close, though, eh?"

Ryder grins back. "Close."

And just because I love the dude, I pull him in for a bro hug, his boundaries be damned. To my surprise, he doesn't stiffen or seem put off. Might have to hug the cunt more often.

"Let's start by going through our originals again with Ryder. By the time we make it through that, I should have the rest figured out." I always think best when there is music playing, even better when it's flowing from my fingertips.

We get set up, Ryder not even bothering to warm up, probably having sang in the car all the way here. I refrain from snorting, imagining him bopping along to Jordan Sparks or some shit, but if I know Ryder at all, there would have been a hell of a lot more screaming involved.

One thing I'll never take for granted is Ryder's natural ability to adopt lyrics as if they were his own, never stumbling, as smooth as the finest of whiskies. It could be a pop song or country, and he could settle into them without so much as a wobble.

Through song after song, I can't resist the excitement that begins to bubble up inside of me, finally confident that we won't let our home down at Poison Ivy. I can feel the shift in Dane and Rue's energy, too. With Ryder at the helm, we bring it all, prepared to give our souls away.

The way our vocals meld is unlike anything I've experienced outside of singing with Ryder. There is a deep richness to his voice, a smooth gravel that when combined with my own feels like brewed caramel, which makes no sense because brewed caramel doesn't exist. It's further proof that music doesn't belong in the physical universe as we know it. It's high above, somewhere only artists and the souls that music speaks to are invited.

Ryder opens up on a run, giving me fucking chills. Having written the song myself, I've heard and played it more times than I can count, yet it has never brought me full body shivers the way it just did. I try not to lean into it, to remember how it feels, knowing he will walk away after this show.

After making it through all of the originals, and feeling the energy we're bringing, I've finally decided which covers I'd like to do. "Closer" by Kings of Leon, "Believe" by Mumford & Sons, "Mr. Brightside" by Killers, and an alternative rock version of "Running Up That Hill" by Kate Bush and "Don't Stop Believin'" by Journey.

I tell the boys as much and they're all keen, the only reassurance I needed. If we're all on the same page, each of us bringing our energy and love for music, the vibe will be infectious. Paired with Ryder's voice, it's a fucking done deal.

I see Ryder's gears turning, but he keeps his mouth shut. Curiosity eats at my insides, but if he wants to share, he will. Ryder agreed to step in, but that doesn't mean he's obligated to contribute beyond that. I'm sure as hell not going to stare a vocalist in the mouth, if that's even how you use that phrase. Americans love having a go at our slang, but then they go and come up with shit like that.

We run through each cover song, several times, until our natural style begins to flow through the melodies seamlessly. Feeling satisfied with our first day of rehearsing, I tell the guys they can head off while I work out the exact order of the set list.

Ryder doesn't take off straight away, sticking around to offer his praise to Dane and Rue. Again, I try not to notice the dynamic. I can't get attached. After a while, even the guys take off, leaving me and Ryder alone.

"Got anything to drink?"

I nod, the guitar pick pressed between my lips preventing me from muttering anything discernable, as I scribble down the set list on the back of some old music paper.

"Want anything?"

I shake my head, still planning to drive over to Brooke's little project, which I've nicknamed Operation Defrost, after I wrap up here.

A few minutes later, Ryder comes back with his signature whiskey in hand, kind enough to pour it into a glass this time. He stays by the threshold, deep in thought, taking slow pulls as he mulls something over. I dutifully stay in my lane, but nearly sag with relief when he finally speaks his mind.

"What if we added in something different?"

"Like what?" I try to keep the depth of my curiosity at bay.

LAST Stand FOR GENEVIEVE

"You said you wanted to make this show *transcendent*." Ryder sits down on the stool across from me. "What if we added something people will love, but something they've never seen from Immoral Support before. A wild card."

My heartbeat double-times. "What do you suggest?"

"What if we combined our styles?"

"Alt-rock meets screamo?"

Ryder rolls his eyes. "Metal, but yeah."

"I'm intrigued." I'm more than intrigued. I'm frothing at the mouth at the idea of giving the people something unparalleled.

"It wouldn't be exactly half and half, needing to appeal to your audience."

"You're suggesting just a sprinkle of screaming?"

He nods. "Yeah, a sprinkle."

"There is only one issue I see with this." Dare I say it? Dare I risk the fallout?

"What?"

"If we do this, and we do it well, it's going to create a wildfire."

"What's the problem with that?"

"A wildfire needs to be fed." I stare at him pointedly. "If our fans come to expect, or even better, *crave* it, will you be around to give it to them?"

His face falls slightly, realizing what I'm asking and unable to give me an answer. With the high of the music falling away, we're back to the wall I always run into with him, the only truly formidable enemy Ryder will ever face: *himself.*

He knocks back the last of his whiskey without so much as a grimace. "You know where I stand."

"Then you know where I stand." I move from my stool, placing my hand on his shoulder. "Mate, I think your idea is nothing short of extraordinary, but it requires *you* to bring it to life."

He's quiet.

"Until then, I'm just grateful for you having my back. Seeing the guys' confidence today..." I shake my head, lost for words. "You need anything at all, you tell me. I owe you big, mate."

He rubs his hand across his jaw. "It's nothing."

"I gotta head off, you're welcome to stay and fuck around with whatever you want." I don't wait for a response, knowing I won't get one. Broody Ryder has made a return, and there's nothing to do but leave the guy to brood to his broody heart's content.

Plus, I can already feel the pull toward a certain enigma with a head of beautiful blonde hair, eyes the color of an iceberg, and a turtleneck up to her eyeballs that has me so twisted up, I'm going to need medical advice soon. I said I would come by today, and the world would have to end for me to not keep my word.

"Cigarette break?" Theo's amused voice calls from the couch as I make it to the living room, his ever-present laptop balanced on his lap.

"You really gotta bust my balls right now?"

He chuckles. "I'm just looking for a status update without being obvious."

"Status update?"

"Ara thinks this girl is the one."

I snort. "Tell Ara she needs to stop watching Nicholas Sparks movies."

At this moment, I'm so glad I never told Theo about the time I watched *The Notebook* after Ara kept insisting, nor that my bitch ass cried like a baby.

"Hm. I can't say I disagree with her, though." Theo tilts his head, always too clever for anyone's good. "You're headed to see her now, aren't you?"

"Like I told Ara, helping this family has nothing to do with pursuing Ice Queen. I'd be helping out even if it was a sweaty old man I was partnering up with."

"I'll take your word for it." Theo smirks. "So how goes it in the land of Arendelle?"

I snort. "I'm amazed my dick hasn't been frozen off yet."

"That good, huh?"

"Fucking splendid, mate." I groan, running my hands through my hair. "It just needs to run its course."

"You keep saying that, but what does that even mean?"

"You know, *run its course*. Like the flu. Or chickenpox."

Theo tries to hold back a grin, but I know him too well. "You're comparing this to some sort of illness?"

"She's gotten under my skin like an infection. I can't stomach smoking, or go an hour without thinking about her frosty *whatever*. What else better describes the situation other than some sort of illness?"

"I can think of one thing."

"Nah, fuck off. It's not what you're thinking." Exasperation and frustration take over and I open my mouth before I can think better of it. "And she's just too damn stubborn anyway. If she'd given in at the very beginning, I could have avoided all this misery. One and done. That's it. That's all we need."

"Uh-huh."

"You're as helpful as Ara."

"She *is* my soulmate."

Normally I love their cute shit, but when their cute shit keeps crowding into my shit, it's disturbing. "Teddy bears and heart-shaped eyes are not my thing, and don't go all shrink on me either, saying it's because I've had trauma, or I'm projecting, or using a defense mechanism, or whatever other garbage someone with a bachelor's degree in bullshit decided to blurt out."

"A little frustrated, are we?"

I blow out a breath. "Holy shit, if my balls don't explode soon, I will."

We look at each other for a moment and burst into laughter, my outburst admittedly a little entertaining.

"You better go see if something can be done about this...*illness.*"

"Pray for me," I mutter before grabbing my keys and calling the elevator, having no idea what will be waiting for me in the wake of yesterday.

CHAPTER TWENTY-THREE

Then - Brooke

Almost a full twenty-four hours and I'm still alive. During daylight it was easy. I could almost pretend I was just out for a daytrip, returning back to my bed tonight before Mom could start to worry. As night begins to fall, it's getting harder and harder. Because with the dark comes the fears.

Thankfully, having grown up not too far from here, I know which parts of the area that I should definitely avoid. I've been going back and forth on finding a spot in a neighborhood whose residents have long gone to sleep, or sticking to the more populated areas.

With the first option, if I came across the wrong person, nobody would hear my shouts or come to my rescue. On the other hand, the more populated an area, the more likely it is that I come across someone with ill intent. But surely someone would step in if I did?

Ugh. My legs ache from walking the entire day. I was worried that Mom would come looking for me after waking up to find my note, it's why I haven't stopped. While I weigh probabilities in my head, my recently healed injuries start to scream, and it becomes clear that I need rest.

My supply now being next to nothing, I haven't allowed myself another pill. The agreement I made with Sebby, and what will happen if he manages to find me, is yet another worry that has me peeking over my shoulder every few minutes, as if he's planted me with a tracker. Hopefully, if I end up running into him, I'll be in a place where I can pay him back.

The street I'm on is thankfully well-lit. A brief look at my surroundings tells me that there's nobody headed toward me, and I take a seat on a bus stop bench, setting my backpack down beside me. Closing my eyes for a moment, I try to find clarity among my racing thoughts. I just need something to ground me, to keep the worries, and withdrawals, away.

Unzipping my backpack, I take out *her* book, which is probably now my most prized possession aside from the jacket, which still remains in my backpack. I trace the worn edges of the hardcover, a special edition I was once told, with gold-foiled edges and a signature from the author. Apparently, it was one of only five in the world like this, given away to a lucky few.

Lucky. I fucking hate that word.

I'm so distracted by the details and keeping the memories at bay, I don't notice the dark figure which has approached behind me. They're utterly silent until their hand is securely wrapped around the strap of my backpack, before they snatch it and take off as fast as they can. My heart plummets, the breath getting caught in my throat, nearly choking me with terror.

"*STOP!*" I shout, taking off after the hooded figure. I'm in no shape to chase someone who is likely used to making a run for it, but I give it my everything, jamming all of my strength and determination into stride after stride.

A few blocks.

A few blocks is all I can manage before my legs turn to jelly and my lungs threaten to close in on themselves. As if the universe wants to see me suffer, as I slow to a stop, the temperature begins to drop, leaving goosebumps across my arms.

Of course, the usual suffocating Florida temperature and humidity relents on the only night where I'm without a jacket. I let out a humorless laugh, which comes out more like a gasp. Whether it's a gasp for air, or for some sign as to why I should bother remaining on this earth for another second, I don't know.

Because as it turns out, rock bottom has a basement.

Falling to my knees, I drop my head into my hands and cry. I cry for my mom, who has been nothing but wonderful to me my entire life, and I've repaid her with nothing but abandonment when she needed me most. I cry for the sister who deserved to spread her sunshine for so much longer, who could have served a far higher purpose than I've ever been capable of. I cry for the version of Brooke Anderson who died beside Genevieve in the car that night. I let myself fall apart, knowing I'll never be able to put my pieces back together.

"You good, *mija?*"

I look up, finding a plain, but beautiful, Latin American girl, probably about my age. Her eyes are so big and brown, with her puffy pink lips and round cheeks, she could walk right into a Pixar movie. Despite her innocent looks, I can see the way she's stripping me down with a competent assessment.

She wears baggy jeans, not skinny, and her shirt is too big for her by about five sizes. I don't miss the way her sneakers are still relatively clean, and despite her clothes being extremely large, her outfit somehow still appears put together, with a thick green denim jacket draped over all of it.

Her hair is cropped into a short, shaggy style, and she's asking me this question as if I'm not kneeling on a sidewalk after midnight, crying my heart out. "I don't have a backpack. I don't have a jacket. All I have is this stupid book." Which isn't a stupid book at all.

The girl looks at the only thing I own, gripped in my hands as if my very life depends on keeping it, before shrugging. "At least it has a pretty cover."

For some reason my tears stop falling.

"Where's your jacket?"

"Someone just stole it."

"And you can't just go get another one?" I feel her gaze on me. "You look like someone who would have *mucho* jackets, no?"

I like her accent, the way she says *you* like it starts with a *j*. "I don't have a home anymore either."

She raises her brows. "So, you have nowhere to go then?"

"Nowhere at all."

"Then we have something in common, *mija.*"

We're quiet, likely thinking about what led us here to this moment, both of us on a Tampa sidewalk with no home. Eventually the silence makes me uncomfortable. "My name is Brooke."

"*Ayyyyy*!!!!!" she yells, covering her ears. "No, no, no, no!! *Mija*, you're in the streets now. There are *rules.*"

"What rules?"

"First of all, don't tell *anyone* your real name. Make up a name for out here, and never tell the real one. *Entender?* You can think it over if you want."

It sounds ridiculous to me, but what would I know? "Why are you helping me?"

LAST Stand FOR GENEVIEVE

Her brow scrunches up, as if she's not even sure herself. "Well, you already got your shit stolen, which is the third rule, by the way, *always* have your shit attached to you. Nobody can take it unless you go with it. That means never put it down or let someone touch it."

"Okay."

She looks at me a moment, before grumbling a long string of what I assume are expletives in Spanish. "Come on, *mija*, I'll show you where we can sleep tonight."

We cross the street and start heading in the opposite direction of where I was headed. Smart enough to get into an Ivy League school, but God forbid I have to survive one night on my own.

"What do I call you?" I know better than to ask for her name.

"Ziggy."

Ziggy. "I like that."

Snort. "Why do you like Ziggy?"

"It's unique. Kind of fun." I shrug, trying to let the awkwardness roll off my shoulders. It's been way too long since I've socialized with anyone, but especially another girl my age. Admittedly, it's refreshing to speak to someone who isn't connected to a past where Genevieve and Brooke Anderson once lived.

"You're gonna be eaten alive out here if you keep acting like a class president."

I frown, not wanting to tell her that I *was* class president, but Ziggy doesn't miss a thing.

"You were, weren't you? Class president?"

I can't hide the sheepish look on my face and Ziggy laughs. Where I have book smarts, she has everything else smarts, the knowledge on how to survive a night on your own and read straight through people. I smile back at Ziggy, and it becomes the first time I don't put in effort to manufacture one since the accident.

"Oh, no, no, no. Don't look at me like that, *mija*. I haven't told you the second rule yet."

"Which is?"

"There are no friends out here, because having friends gets you killed."

And I thought *I* was dark. "Then what are we?"

139

"Simple. We are backup for each other, until a better option presents itself, then we drop the other like it's hot."

For someone who wanted absolutely nothing to do with this world, let alone another human less than an hour ago, I don't know why it rubs on my feelings. "That's a bit callous."

"Trust me, you can't afford to care about anyone out here." A dark look passes over her and suddenly, I'm grounded. I've been so selfish, so focused on my own pain, that I forgot that *everyone* suffers. I'm a tiny blip to this great big world out here that is full of suffering, far more gruesome than even mine. It's not enough to change how I feel, though, but it's something.

"I don't know if I'm capable of being a friend anyway. I just walked out on the only person in the world who cares about me."

"How long have you been out here?"

"Not even twenty-four hours."

She whistles. "Where did you come from? The Christian Carolinas? You look like you'd be in the choir."

I snort. "I'm not exactly worshiping anyone who affects fate at the moment."

"Don't tell me about it, *mija*, I don't want to know your story."

"I wasn't going to."

Ziggy stops suddenly, facing me. "You know what? I like that. *Carolina.*"

"Carolina?"

"Your new name. *Por las calles .*"

Since I can't think of anything better, I agree. *Carolina.*

"Well, then, Carolina, *vamos.*"

Ziggy takes us to a spot under a little bridge, nestled just outside a wealthy neighborhood. It's quiet and doesn't remind me of the past. It's as safe as it gets out here, according to Ziggy.

The same Ziggy who already violated her third rule when she lent me a spare jacket, but I don't point it out to her. I need all the help I can get to survive my first—and remaining—nights out here.

CHAPTER TWENTY—FOUR

Now Connor

*W*hiplash.

That is the only term I can think of to describe this feeling. Where is the playful, even flirty Brooke from just yesterday? I see nothing of that warmth in her today. Just a freezing ferocity, like she's trying to unload something with every rough roll of paint.

"Who took a shit in your Fruit Loops this morning?" I say, popping my head into the kitchen to alert her of my presence.

Brooke pins me with a withering glare, turning back to her task without a word. A shiver courses through me, despite the warm air. Ice Queen is in full effect tonight. In my bones, I know the mood swing has something to do with me and what went down on the stairs, but why so severe? All I've done today is exist. Is she pissed about the way I left yesterday?

Did she not understand I wanted to make sure she wasn't giving in just because of the heat in *that* moment, just to walk away full of regret? If anything were to happen between us, I want her to be in control of taking that step, to *know* she needed it.

Grabbing my tools from where they sit in the front room, I head back to the kitchen and stop short, nearly dropping my tool bag in the doorway. So wrapped up in her frostiness, I somehow overlooked the cropped crew neck and joggers she's wearing, no longer leaving her body to my imagination.

I've been with women. Never bothered to keep track of how many, but plenty. None of them have ever looked like this. Brooke is so beautiful that looking at her and not touching her could be considered a sick form of torture.

141

The crop top, though not cut low enough to display any cleavage, hugs every curve of what generously swells beneath. Her stomach is on full display, toned yet soft, leading down to joggers that on anyone else would look innocent, but with Brooke's ass, becomes nothing short of wicked.

My hands shake with the effort to keep them by my side, when all I want to do is run them over every inch of her. She has the body and face women would pay thousands for. Yet my Ice Queen usually keeps it all hidden away, as if it isn't a gift at all, but a meaningless aspect of life. What she's wearing now is so different from the lack of skin or shape she usually shows, I can't help but wonder...

Realization crashes over me, and suddenly it all makes sense; Ice Queen's frigid mood, her comfy yet agonizing outfit. This is for *me*. She wanted my attention today, and just when she knew she'd get it, she hated herself for wanting it.

I smirk.

I've begun to figure out the cold mystery in front of me, at least her very top layer. It's terrifying how deep her glacier walls must go, but I remind myself it's not my mission to uncover the depths. I only need to know and navigate enough to get us where I know we both want to be: lost in pleasure until we're both put out of our misery.

Dropping my tools on the floor with a loud clank of metal, she whips her head toward me again. "What are you doing?"

I gesture toward the drooping cabinets with missing doors. "Fixing the kitchen."

She growls in frustration. "Why do you have to pick *now* to come in here?"

"I finished the porch." *As you already know*, I refrain from saying, not wanting to sound like a moody teenager who got his porn stash taken away, but it's exactly how I feel.

"Surely you can find somewhere else to be useful, or even better, leave completely."

"Not happening. I have a task, I'll be finishing it."

"You keep acting like you give a shit, but you're only here for one reason."

I pin her with a stare. "And you keep acting like you know me *at all*."

"What's there to know besides an astronomical body count?"

LAST *Stand* FOR GENEVIEVE

A humorless laugh escapes me. "If you think that's all that's worth knowing about me, fine, but if you were smart, you'd be thinking about what all that *practice* could be doing for *you*."

"Get out."

Her rage ripples across the space between us and it ignites my own. My dick is on a short leash…and so is my bloody temper. "I'm sure the family that lives here would be really appreciative of you getting rid of the only other person who is willing to fix this place."

"I genuinely hate you."

"You hate that I'm *right*." And because I really am a tool, I rub it in. "So be a good little girl and ask me nicely for my help."

Her jaw slackens, gaping open with fury and shock.

Knowing she would rather die than ask me for my help, I don't wait for it. Telling her to ask nicely did the trick anyway. Laying out what I'll need, I work on suppressing the urge to stir the pot further. If I keep instigating, I'll likely be instigating my murder.

I steal a look at her from the corner of my eye, and she stands there with the paint roller hanging from her right hand, dripping paint onto the floor. She's so pissed, she doesn't even notice, flushed with the heat of an argument.

Can't say I'm not feeling a little warm myself, even though it's almost sunset, but I'll have to deal with it. Taking off my shirt right now would not be appreciated. I settle for rolling up my sleeves into a makeshift singlet.

Brooke drinks in my muscled arms, down to my rough, calloused hands, which deftly place a bit into the power drill, tightening it for use. She watches me like she's capable of snuffing me out with her eyes, as I screw the hardware onto each cabinet door before measuring up the frame, marking guidelines with a pencil.

Brooke lets out an animalistic growl of pure frustration, before slashing the roller through the air with all of her strength, barely holding back from throwing it at my head. Paint splatters over me, coating my hair down to my shoes in little droplets. I glance down at myself, before pinning her with a look of pure aggression.

She holds the roller out like a weapon. "Don't take a step closer."

But I'm already moving.

I wrap my hands around the roll, somehow still drenched in wet paint, and give it a squeeze. Once my hands are coated in it, I hit it out of my way, closing the distance between us. Not even a second has passed by the time I reach her, planting my paint-covered hands on her waist, branding her with my touch. The feel of her body underneath my grip has me ready to do something really stupid.

Ice Queen gasps, before shoving me away. "You bastard!"

A cruel smile spreads across my face as I take in my handiwork. If nothing else, she will be reminded where my hands held her, and as she washes it off in the shower tonight, she can think of how they felt on her bare skin.

"If you don't mind, I'll be getting back to work now." My voice comes out gruff, strained.

But before I can manage to get the first cabinet door up, I realize I'm screwed. Karma is *such* a fucking bitch. There is no way I'm going to be able to hold these cabinets level, while also screwing in the hardware. Unless I want to leave this kitchen looking worse than it already does, I'm going to have to ask for help.

Which is *fantastic*.

"I'm going to need your assistance for this."

Her laugh is cold, before she throws my words back in my face. "Then be a good little boy and ask me nicely."

"Will you stop being an icepick in my ass and help me out?"

"Hmmm." She presses a finger to those goddamn lips of hers. "*Nicer.*"

"Will you *pretty, pretty please* stop being an icepick in my ass and help me out?"

"I'll have to think about it."

"Brooke, *please.*"

She frowns at the sound of her name along with my pleading. "What do you need?"

Her. But I don't say it. "I need you to hold the cabinet door level while I screw." There's an innuendo to be made there for sure, but I pass on the opportunity.

Ice Queen grabs the door, aligning the hardware I've already screwed in with the pencil marks on the frame. I step forward with the drill and it brings our bodies close. Our chaotic breaths are the only sound, until the loud zing of the drill fills the kitchen, causing us both to flinch.

LAST *Stand* FOR GENEVIEVE

"You can let go now." I open and close the cabinet door, verifying that it's workable. "Let's do the next one."

As she aligns another door and I pull another screw from my pocket, I wonder what it is about her that draws such reactions from me. I've never been one to have a temper or obsession, usually quite the opposite. I've felt deeply for someone once, but that was a one-time thing, and even then, I didn't experience the *intensity* which is constantly pulled out by the woman in front of me.

My knuckles brush her ribcage as I raise my hand to align the screw.

The past felt like a sweet, comforting warmth which had slowly crept up on me until one day it was something I cherished. It was innocent and lovely and perfect. With Brooke, it's a cold, angry blast which burns me from the inside out. It's messy and violent and unpredictable. She challenges me to take what I want, punishing me if I don't, and surely punishing me if I do.

My eyes meet hers as the screw twists in and I find her fighting a battle of her own. For reasons which are different to mine I'm sure, she is fighting this desire with everything she has. Why? And one better, why do I care to know?

As I retreat from the cabinet door, my palm grazes her waist, over the intoxicating softness of her skin as contrasted with the scratchiness of the dried handprints on her middle. Kneeling down to retrieve more screws from my tool bag, I can't stop my eyes from lifting, looking up at her from beneath my lashes as my tongue swipes my lower lip. Her thighs press together, resisting the urge to open for me, and with that one little movement, I know she'll be mine.

Standing slowly, I keep myself only inches away as I straighten, not bothering with the screws I intended to grab. Her eyes lift from mine to my hair. I need a haircut, but she doesn't seem to mind as her fingers twitch, as if begging to sink into my unruly strands.

Ice Queen lets me watch as she takes in my strong chin and full lips, my clenched jaw. Her eyes trail my bare arms, toned from years of moving and playing music equipment and doing whatever job asked of me, then dropping to my stomach and the bulge I can no longer hide behind my jeans. I don't bother anyway. Her breath catches and she looks at me.

I nod, confirming what she already knows. She's done this to me, created a starving, yearning man who can't even remember his own name because she deigned to *look* at him. To hell with chivalry. Unable to hold myself back any longer, I push her into the wall, leaving no path for escape as I put my mouth on hers.

The cracking sound reverberates, making my ears ring before my face has even registered the impact, or the snap of my head to the right. The burning starts across my cheek, lighting my skin on fire, the only evidence I need to confirm she's slapped me. Slowly raising my eyes to hers, I find defiance and rejection of what is brewing beneath...

Lust.

My cheek stings as I drag my fingers down the handprint she's now branded *me* with. Becoming nothing but a feral animal, formed by the weight of those icy blue eyes and cruelly tantalizing lips as they slash into a scowl, I'm no longer Connor, but a hunter who has decided nothing is going to get in the way of him and his prey.

"Denying our bodies of oxygen will soon be easier than starving ourselves of this attraction."

She scoffs.

Ice Queen can play the role of unaffected all she wants, but her body gives her away. She wants this. She wants *me*. My hands wrap around her wrists, raising them above her head and trapping them against the wall.

"You want a fight?" I let my tongue drag out that last word, watching the chills spread across her skin. "I'll *give* it to you."

"You make me fucking crazy." Her voice comes out heated, laced equally with anger as it is *need*.

"Then tell me to stop." My lips trace down the column of her neck, down to her crew neck, where her breasts start to swell underneath the material. When I'm sure she won't slap me again, I release her hands.

Pulling back, a rush shoots through me as I see the last of the hesitation in her eyes burn away before she moves. She wraps her arm around my neck, using the same hand which slapped me a moment ago to pull my mouth down over hers. Kissing her is like rediscovering the reason for breathing, as freezing fire shoots through me. Our kiss is an all-consuming war, each move a battle toward curbing this starving desire which has stricken us, since the first day those cold eyes met mine. She's been fighting me at every turn, and now she fights to have more of me, as much as she can take.

LAST *Stand* FOR GENEVIEVE

As her fingers latch onto the hem of my shirt, pulling it away, she breaks the kiss to look at my body with heated eyes. "You repulse me."

I follow in time, lifting her tiny crop top and throwing it on the floor. "You infuriate me."

She reaches behind her back, and with the unclip of a bra, I'm a broken man. Her perfectly shaped breasts bob as they're released from their cupped prison, revealing everything I've been craving. The biggest fight of my goddamn life to get to this moment, soundtracked by our heavy breaths and moving bodies, and I didn't even get to undo her bra.

Irritated that she stole the honor from me, I take her breast into my mouth with a nip, my right hand brushing over the side of the swell that's decorated with a beauty mark. Ice Queen groans, sinking her hands into my hair the way I know she's been dying to. Her back arches, urging me to drop lower. My mouth trails down her ribcage, kissing and sucking as I go. How soft she is should be fucking illegal.

Growling as I finally reach the waistband of her joggers, I rip them down before she can take *that* pleasure away from me too. Part of her knew this was going to happen, *planned* for this to happen the way I did. She's perfectly smooth, just like I have two foils in the back of my pocket, as I descend onto her beautiful body once again, dropping lower.

And *lower*.

The more I move my mouth, the more I wonder who this is for. I've never been a selfish lover, but never has this kind of foreplay brought me my *own* pleasure. My dick presses harder against my jeans, so painfully that I'm certain my zipper will soon lose against the force. I groan as I continue my work, using my tongue and my fingers as if they were created just for this.

For her.

For Us.

Her hips begin to move in earnest, gasps becoming more frequent, and her hold on my hair tighter, telling me that she's on the edge. So easy for me to work her, to get her there, it's as natural as the beat of my heart. I keep the rhythm steady, right where she needs me, bringing her closer, but just before she falls over the edge, I pull back.

"What are you doing!?"

"Tell me the truth. Tell me you've wanted me since the moment you saw me."

"You *asshole.*"

Licking my lips, I continue, "I guess you need more convincing."

I capture her with my mouth again, hitting that sweet spot, until I know she's at the cusp, but yet again, I pull back.

She lets out a growl of frustration, making me smile. "Tell me you wanted me."

"I. Wanted. You."

I give her a long lick, a little reward, just enough to get her to keep going. "Since when?"

Her breathy moans leave me weak. "Since I first saw you."

"So did I, baby." My mouth and fingers are on her again, the pair perfectly synchronized until she falls over the edge with my name on her lips. Brooke falls and falls, but I keep going, tasting everything she gives me, until her body can't take anymore, dropping limply into my arms.

I hold her for a minute, just to revel in the feeling of her at my mercy, before gently lying her down on the floor and rising to stalk toward the freezer. Finding exactly what I want, I return to my Ice Queen, looking warmer than I've ever seen her.

Hovering over her, I kiss her again, long and slow to ease her back to consciousness, before putting my lips to her ear. "Have you ever felt something so cold, it burns?"

She shakes her head, eager to participate in my little game. *Perfect.*

I trail kisses down one side of her neck, as my fingers drag an ice cube down the other. "Do you feel that sting? How something that is cold enough to freeze, lights you on fire instead?"

Ice Queens gasps as the ice cube reaches her nipple, my mouth on the other. "You're a fuckboy."

"And you're colder than the fucking North Pole," I bring myself to hover at eye level, looking into those heated blue depths. "That's why we work."

Leaning down to kiss her, she raises up to meet me halfway, her calf wrapping around my low back. I take advantage of the position, giving her ass a squeeze as my eyes roam over how close our bodies are. She bucks her hips and rolls, landing me on my back and her on top. I'm finally freed as she undoes my jeans and lowers my boxers. Brooke takes me into her hand, and I can't help feeling like I'm being touched for the first time.

"You'll be the ruin of me," I whisper.

Unable to stop and think about what just escaped my mouth, I reach into my back pocket for the foil wrapper, and she rips it out of my hand, taking things into her own. *Literally.* I manage to keep my eyes open, despite the overwhelming gratification of her rolling it on, allowing me the pleasure of watching as she guides my length inside of her.

Sheer fucking euphoria. It's the only way I can describe the feel of her. Nothing can compare to this as she takes control, moving in ways that I've never known. I'd once thought myself experienced, until right now with Brooke, where it feels like the first time. I fear that this pleasure, this inferno of fire and ice, will never again be equaled.

My hands have a mind of their own, continuing to roam, as my eyes remain locked on her naked body, moving over mine, memorizing the way she looks with her head thrown back, breasts bobbing, lost in the way our bodies feel together. Her pace becomes faster, hungrier, demanding more.

I give it all to her.

Ice Queens finds her second release, and I can do nothing but follow. Our breaths haggard, I take in the state of our surroundings and our bodies: paint splattered across the wall and floor, now smeared over every inch of our skin.

We look at each other and I nearly choke, as her lips tip up into a genuine smile. "*Shit.*"

The slight warmth I felt from her earlier is nothing compared to the golden glow Brooke's emitting now, as she allows me to bask beneath her like it's a perfect summer afternoon, and she's the sun.

"Shit," I agree, before laying my head back, not allowing myself to keep looking at that smile. I should feel satiated, and more importantly, freed from her hold. Brooke should be fully expelled from my system.

Except, I'm rocked by a harrowing realization instead: I want to do it again. And again.

Maybe it'll just take a few more times for this to run its course.

CHAPTER TWENTY—FIVE

Then - Brooke

Somewhat surprisingly, I make it to the next morning. My arm is still curled around the book and picture tucked within its pages, as if the need to protect it followed me into my sleep. Ziggy lays with her eyes closed a few feet away, arms wrapped around her backpack in a similar way, still asleep.

Even though I'm still breathing, my body aches from sleeping on the hard ground. Not only that, it's now been over twenty-four hours since my last pill, and the effects are becoming even more obvious. The shakes have gone beyond my hands, affecting my entire body and mind. Unable to pause to worry about privacy, I reach into my pocket and slip one of the last pills onto my tongue before chewing through the bitter taste and swallowing.

"You just started to make a whole lot more sense."

My head whips up, Ziggy lays facing me with her eyes open, not a trace of sleepiness on her features. Adrenaline takes off in a sprint through my veins, my muscles locking up as if they expect I'll need to flee at a moment's notice.

"Are you judging me?" Or worse, she could try to take what little I have left.

The truth being that I don't know this person in front of me becomes terrifyingly clear. Of course, she didn't try to take a book while I slept, but now that she knows I have something valuable in my pockets, there is no telling what she's going to do.

Is this how she survives? Finding people in need and pretending to be their friend until she discovers that they have something worth taking? Scenarios run through my mind of her preying on the innocent, my paranoia telling me that this is how she's managed to gather so many things in that backpack of hers.

"Never going to judge you, *mija*, just my mind is thinking."

"About what?" My words come out more vicious than I intended, the tone as if she's already tried to take something of mine.

Ziggy sits up and raises her hands. "Relax, Carolina. I'm not trying to pull nothing, but I'm happy to know you've got claws after all."

I'm quiet, still assessing the situation and not taking her word for it. Nobody has leapt from the shadows in an intricate plan to take advantage of me, and she's made no move as of now. My body starts to relax as the pill takes effect, and I don't appear to be in any immediate danger.

"If you're down with *that*..." she trails off, nodding toward the rest of the pills in my pocket, "then I could give you a way to keep surviving out here."

I hate to admit it, but my interest is piqued. "What do you mean?"

"I mean that I know someone who knows someone."

"I don't speak whatever language you're speaking right now."

Ziggy laughs, but it's not completely free. She is on edge, too, perhaps because she's realized there must be something dark and rotten inside of me to turn to the life I have. "Pills, *mija*. I'm talking about pills. Like the ones you're taking."

"And what about them?"

She curses in Spanish before looking over her shoulder. "You really gonna make me spell it out for you?"

"Are you talking about dealing?"

Ziggy nods before opening her mouth, but I cut her off. "No. No fucking way."

"What, you think you're better than us just because you're the customer?"

"Do you take pills?"

Ziggy scoffs. "No, *chica tonta*, I sell them. I don't mess around with that shit."

I throw her words back in her face. "What, you think you're better than us just because you're not the customer?"

"Shit, *mija*." Ziggy smiles. "Keep those claws sharp, but you don't need them right now, *así que guárdalos*."

"Why do you keep calling me *mija*?"

151

"It means daughter. You're like a little girl, and I'm starting to think I'm stuck with you. If the sock fits, no?"

She definitely means the shoe. "And what about *chica tonta*?"

Ziggy smiles. "That one is a secret."

Whatever, I can't be bothered to press her on this one.

"So what do you think about my idea?"

A wave of nausea comes over me at the thought of enabling people like my father. What if the person I sold to has a family, and I'm providing them with the means to destroy it? But more importantly, why am I acting like I still have integrity to keep? "I'll have to think about it."

Ziggy smiles, making me realize how little I do that anymore. I used to have a smile plastered on my face at all times of the day, RBF being my sworn enemy. Oh, how the tables of life can turn and fucking turn. "You hungry, *mija*?"

My stomach growls, not waiting for me to answer. I haven't eaten since…I can't even remember, but probably coming up on forty-eight hours ago. Usually, I have to force myself to eat, but after the adrenaline of being out here, I find myself actually wanting to. "Starving, actually."

Ziggy doesn't comment on the surprise in my response; instead, she stands and begins rolling up her blanket before putting it in her backpack.

"Oh, here." I take off the jacket she lent me, but Ziggy puts her hands out.

"Keep it. I already have one, and this is Florida, I'll never need *dos*."

Fair enough. "Thank you." Since I don't have a backpack, I use the sleeves to tie it around my waist. With my book in hand, everything I own is ready to go.

"We'll get you some more supplies today, don't worry."

"But I don't have any money, and I couldn't accept–"

Ziggy cuts me off with a laugh. "I don't have money either, but you won't need any. Trust me?"

Frankly, I don't. "No."

Ziggy smiles. "Good. That's the only correct answer, *mija*."

LAST *Stand* FOR GENEVIEVE

• • •

Thankfully, today's weather is more than comfortable. It's sunny, but we've been granted a reprieve from the humidity, and a cool breeze sends shivers through the palm trees. There is not a cloud in the sky, and I couldn't feel more separate from my surroundings. The weather is definitely not a reflection of what I'm feeling.

Ziggy has been a welcome buffer. She's always rambling about never letting my guard down, having started on her lecture again after she was able to snag my book from me and run, She was gone and hiding in an instant, proving that I did not, in fact, have my "ears open and eyes listening." Her phrase doesn't make sense, but pointing that out got me another lecture.

So for the last hour I've been practicing how to listen with my eyes. Even though it's annoying, it keeps me from thinking about anything else. I've still got the jitters, and enough baggage to sink a ship, but the point is that I'm not thinking about it.

And I've never been more grateful for anything in my life.

"Okay, *mija*, even though your senses are still worse than a baby's, we need to move on to our next lesson: acting."

Guess my senses do suck, because surely I didn't just hear her correctly. "Acting?"

Ziggy rolls her eyes. "*Si, mija.* Your life will depend, more than once, on your ability to sell a story. So if you're not capable of Grammy-level shit, you're done before you start."

"You mean Oscar level?"

"Who is Oscar?"

My lip twitches. "Never mind."

"Anyway, if you can't act, you'll probably die and take me with you. So now, we practice."

That's how I ended up on an empty soccer field, giving the best dramatic performance of my life. I become character after character, between my car breaking down and twisting my ankle, the damsel in distress act definitely becomes my new specialty. I even become a mother who lost her child (that one hit a little too close to home), so I made sure I did a good job, and we could move on right away.

"You might be worth keeping around after all. Nobody is walking away from you and those *azules.*"

I sit down, feeling lightheaded.

"Since we know your role now, I won't bother teaching you *juego de manos.*" Ziggy gives me a cocky grin. "That's my specialty."

As I open my mouth to ask what that means, she reaches out and pulls one of my pills from behind my ear, before revealing the other remaining few which she holds in her hand. My hands slam into my pockets, which of course, I find empty.

Ziggy laughs at the frenzied look on my face and tosses them to me. "I told you, *mija,* I have no interest in those things. Only trying to prove my point."

"Point. Proven," I manage through gritted teeth.

"We have different strengths, meaning I'll keep you. Your only ticket to well, continuing to breathe, isn't going to dump your ass at the next bus stop. This is good news, no?"

Deadpan. "I could jump for joy."

Ziggy laughs. "*Vamos.* I want to test out our new…affiliation."

Affiliation? "Well, that's a title that's just dripping with mutual faith and affinity."

"If you ask me, we're better off without neither."

And I can't help but think, Ziggy is probably right.

• • •

"Just remember, if you start developing a conscience in there, I saw this man grope a young girl who walked into his store with my own eyes. Karma is a bitch, and we're just helping her out."

I'm quiet, still thinking this through. Getting my mind under control is key, and Ziggy is right, I can't be having second thoughts in there. Stealing has never been at the top of my to-do list, but I guess becoming an addict who lives on the street wasn't either, yet here I am. May as well round out the resume.

"Listen, *mija,* a few missing snacks isn't going to kill the guy, and like I said, he's not a good one anyway."

Does that make what we're about to do okay? What is the line of demarcation between good and evil? Right and wrong? I'm pretty sure every single person on this planet has a different definition for each. One man's sin is another man's virtue. And here I am, motion sick, right in the fucking middle of it all.

Ziggy mumbles something in Spanish I can't understand, but I know she's reached her limit of patience, which is next to nothing. It's now or never.

"Let's get this over with."

"*Ayyyyyyyy*!!!" She pumps her fist in the air and does a little swivel with her hips.

I roll my eyes, because you'd think I just surprised her with an all-expenses-paid vacation to the Maldives, not agreeing to rob a convenience store in broad daylight. Taking a deep breath, I lead the way as we cross the street. Ziggy enters first, and it's wild how easily she changes her persona. In the short time I've known her, there's never been enough space for her personality, but as she rolls her shoulders in on herself and places her head down, even I almost don't notice her.

The man behind the counter looks up, taking note of her baggy jacket with deep pockets, but in the end overlooks her to continue whatever he was doing on his computer. I blow out a breath and adjust my ponytail the way I did before taking an important exam.

Game face on, Brooke. It's just another extracurricular. You'll be stellar.

Ziggy circles back to the rolling hotdog thingy, the pre-discussed cue, and I make my entrance.

"*Waahhhhhhhh*!!!" I wail, as my toe clips the metal lip of the doorframe and I tumble to the floor, taking a spinning rack of chips down with me. There's a loud crash, and everyone in the little store turns to look at me as the man hurdles out of his chair, dashing around the counter.

"My *kneeeee*!!!" I hold my leg, rocking back and forth in pretend pain. "Ohhh, my *knneeeee*!!!" I let out a few more whines, probably enough time for my pretend adrenaline to ebb, and my pretend pain to kick in before I emit a strangled sob.

"Are you okay!?" That's not concern for me I hear in his voice. He's worried about a lawsuit, or at the very least, if what Ziggy said is true, uniforms of any kind coming around.

"Are you blliiiihhh-uhhh-nndd!?" I drag the word out with hiccupy sobs, saliva spraying from my mouth with every word. "No, I'm not OKAY!!!!

Wailing so loud, it's sensory overload? *Check.*

Convincing ugly cry? *Check.*

Causing such a scene that Ziggy can fill every pocket in her jacket and jeans without a single person noticing? *Check.*

The man's attention is still wholly on getting me to quiet down as Ziggy passes by, exiting the convenience store without even a glance over her shoulder. I take a deep breath, like I'm trying to calm myself, before looking up at the man.

As I get myself together, his eyes run down my body, and the urge to get as far away as fast as possible takes over. No longer worrying about a smooth exit, I scramble to my feet and dart out of the store. If only I could outrun my conscience.

My heart lurches before dropping a hundred feet out of my ass as someone wraps their hand around my arm and pulls. A scream climbs its way up my throat before Ziggy slaps her hand over my mouth. "Shhhhhhhh!!!! *Chica tonta,* it's just me!!"

My heart pounds and pounds, as I take in her filled pockets and proud smile. "Holy shit, we did it."

"We robbed that asshat *ciego.*"

I blame it on the strange mix of excitement, the kind you get just before taking a test that will make or break your future, and fear of what I saw in that man's eyes, but I grin. "Karma is a bitch."

"And we're just helping her out."

CHAPTER TWENTY—SIX

Now - Connor

Cheerios (half-chewed and mushy) fly by, scarcely missing me.

"What the *actual* fuck?"

Ara, not looking the least bit remorseful of her spew, shoots me a toothy grin. "You got laid, didn't you?"

"I can't even get a coffee without being *accosted* by flying food and an interrogation?" But I can't hide the proud smirk which hasn't left my face since last night.

"Oh, you *so* did. Come on, then, spill the deets."

Rolling my eyes, "A gentleman doesn't kiss and tell."

"Good thing you aren't even *remotely* close to being a gentleman."

I snort, because well, she's right, and it was witty. "Yeah, I got laid."

"Aaaaaaand?"

"And what? I got laid." I shrug. "Full stop."

Ara looks at me the way a scientist looks at one of their experiments. She measures my expression, my eyes, and by the end I feel like a mouse. "When are you taking her out next?"

"Taking her out?"

"You're telling me that there is a woman with enough power to get you to stop smoking, and leave you looking *this* smitten after *one* night, and you aren't seeing her again?"

"I didn't say I wouldn't *see* her again, I just said that I'm not taking her *out*," I scoff. "And I'm *not* smitten."

157

Understanding dawns across her features, along with an expression that's slightly too humorous for my comfort. "So this is a friends with benefits thing?"

"Exactly."

"No strings attached?"

"None whatsoever."

Ara lets out a wicked cackle, like she's some freaky witch stirring a cauldron of doom.

"What's funny?"

"Whether it's in a book or a movie, those only end one way." Ara waggles her eyebrows and mouths the word *love* like it has ten Os instead of one.

"Good thing this isn't a book or a movie. In real life they usually end with a broken heart for one, hence why I usually steer clear, but this one isn't the type to develop anything deep."

I fail to mention that I haven't managed to convince Brooke of the arrangement. *Yet.*

"She's not the one I'm worried about," Ara mutters under her breath. "Anyway, I gotta go meet a client. Do you mind feeding Oscar for me?"

"Yeah, I got it. Good luck with your client."

"Good luck with your feelings." Ara snickers all the way out the door.

I look at Oscar. "I don't have feelings."

Little mate looks pointedly at his food bowl.

"Right."

After feeding the monster, I get that haircut I've been needing for a while before heading back over to Ice Queen's little project. The barber got a bit too excited and left my hair shorter than usual, but at least I can wait a little longer in between.

Ice Queen is waiting on the porch, looking fairly pleasant, and I let out a breath I didn't realize I was holding. I wasn't sure what I'd be walking into today: Hell frozen over, or a summer day? I never bloody know, but today feels like spring.

As I step out of my ute, a little frown has her lips pouting and brow doing that adorable scrunchy thing. I dawn indifference, but honestly, there's a bubble in my stomach, as if I'm excited to see her.

"You got a haircut."

LAST Stand FOR GENEVIEVE

Brooke doesn't retreat as I approach closer, taking one porch step at a time. "I did."

"Huh." Now that I stand directly in front of her, less than a foot from where she leans against one of the support beams, I'm curious what she'll do. Walk away? Shut me out? Instead, she reaches up and runs her fingers through the much shorter strands. "I liked it better before."

A grunt of agreement is all I can manage as I focus on keeping my eyes open, despite the lulling sensation of her hands so casually in my hair. And then she's gone, my body falling after her like there's a force of gravity keeping me in her orbit, but I plant my feet and shake myself out of it.

Walking inside feels so much different than the first night I came here. The mold is gone. The walls have a fresh coat of paint, the floor has been scrubbed clean, and it feels *livable*. As I enter the kitchen, I can't help but smile. The cabinets have been painted yellow, the happy shade courtesy of Ara. Fake potted plants are placed decoratively throughout the kitchen, and a fresh white curtain has been hung over the sink's window.

It's not only cheerful, but *homey*.

Brooke steps to my side, letting me take it in before nudging me with her shoulder. "We did good, didn't we?"

"I only helped. This…" I raise my hand in a sad attempt to sum up everything she's done for this place. "This was all you."

"You should send a picture to your friend. I would've never thought of yellow, but it's perfect."

"She would love that." Pulling out my phone, I snap a quick picture and send it to Ara.

Connor: Turns out, yellow isn't disgusting.

Ara: OMGGGGGG IT'S SOOO PRETTYYYYYYY!!!!!

Ara: Stop. I'm actually so happy.

Ara: Also, tell Brooke I say hi.

My phone dings with a triple text notification.

I chuckle before tipping my phone toward Brooke, whose lips twitch before she surprises me with, "Tell her I say 'hi' back and 'thank you'."

Connor: She says hi and thank you.

Ara: Tell her she is SO welcome.

Ara: Okay, gtg. The client who thinks I'm her therapist is back.

Ara: If you don't hear from me in an hour, tell Theo to call with an emergency, byeeee!!!!

Connor: Roger that.

Brooke has moved over to the far side of the kitchen, tidying up the last remaining supplies. I can tell that she's busying herself, unsure what to do now that the project seems to be coming to an end. "So, what's left to be done here?"

She sets down the clean paint tray. "Well, I need to finish cleaning up, and then I'll probably go furniture shopping. Nothing too fancy, probably going to thrift it up or find some yard sale deals."

"Lucky for you, I'm a *master* thrifter, with a degree in yard sales."

Single brow raise. "You're not trying to stick around, are you?"

I gasp, clasping my chest dramatically to feign hurt. "I'm offended that you'd think I'm even capable of developing an attachment. Proudly, I'm as unavailable as it gets emotionally." She snorts, but I realize that now's my chance to pitch the idea. "In fact, I think we could really do this."

"Do what?"

"This. Us. Just without the *us*, you know?"

"Your eloquence is astounding."

"You know exactly what I'm saying. We could have fun, leave the complications out of it." Brooke goes to turn, but I cross the space between us and stop her with a hand on her shoulder. "I meant what I said outside of Target. We would have fun. And last night was proof of just how fun it could be."

I lift my other hand, running the backs of my knuckles over her cheekbone, before tracing that tortuous bottom lip with my thumb. She nips at it, telling me she fucking *knows*.

"Those arrangements never work."

"But that's because everyone else aren't you and me. I *don't* do feelings. My band and my family are the only things I care about." I take a breath. "And you...well, the jury is still out on whether you even have a heart."

Ice Queen punches my shoulder and I laugh.

She rolls her eyes. "I'll think about it."

With a little more time, I can convince her. I know it. "Until then, there's no harm in taking advantage of my thrifting skills and ute."

"Ute?"

"Utility vehicle." I hike a thumb over my shoulder toward the beauty out in the driveway, before putting on a thick American accent. "A pickup truck."

"Never do that again," she says with a hint of a smile.

"Only if you agree to let me drive you."

"Whatever. Let's go."

• • •

As we make our way from the parking lot, a homeless man calls from where he rests on the ground. "Carolina? Is that you?"

Brooke stiffens beside me, as if she's counting to three before she turns and looks at the man, swallowing. "I'm sorry, I think you must have me mistaken with someone else."

The old man shakes his head. "I might've lost my mind, but I haven't lost my eyesight. I know who you are."

"I'm afraid I don't know what you're talking about."

I reach into my pocket, pulling out a twenty and handing it to Brooke. "Here."

Her eyes meet mine, and I swear they warm by a few degrees.

"I'm not looking for a handout." His wrinkled face scrunches up, pointing at Brooke. "But I do know you, Miss Carolina."

Brooke walks over, crouching down to hand him the money, whispering something too low for me to hear.

The man smiles. "I'd never forget a face like yours, Carolina."

Brooke turns back in my direction, and during the split second before she can wipe her expression away, it appears like she's seen a ghost.

"Who was that?" I ask as I open the door for her.

She shrugs. "No idea. Just an old man who needed a little kindness."

The first thrift shop was a total bust, having not a single piece of furniture from the past decade, but I think we're going to have luck in this one. I can already see a little makeshift showroom set up in the very back corner near the change rooms.

We walk by a rack on the way, and as if unable to help herself, Brooke snorts and holds up a pair of men's cut-off denim shorts that are *way* too short for anyone with a dick. "I can't imagine why these have made it to the sale rack in a thrift store."

I laugh, reaching for a long, frumpy skirt that looks like my grandmother's rug vomited all over it. "It's an absolute mystery, but these two are definitely a pair."

Brooke breathes a laugh as we put them back on the rack and continue heading toward the back. It's weird to think that not even a week ago, the concept of her laughing was foreign to me. Even a smile had been a rarity. Though I know she's still closed off, unwilling to be pushed for something she isn't willing to give, I don't feel the temperature plummeting at every turn.

"This one is perfect!" Brooke runs over to the sofa closest to us as we approach. It makes sense that it's the main feature, being a nice couch which definitely came from a wealthy household. It's got a few small stains, likely from a child who spilled their drink, but it's otherwise in perfect condition. The dark nude color would look nice with the neutral walls and pop of yellow that now peeks from the kitchen. "But there's no price."

An idea strikes, utterly unable to pass up such an opportunity. "Let's make a bet."

She turns toward me with an arched brow. "A bet?"

"Too scared of losing again?"

"Oh, please, I'm not afraid."

"Good, then we'll both make a guess on the price and whoever's closest wins."

"Deal." An evil little grin spreads across her beautiful face, which is clear of makeup as usual. "If you lose, you have to wear those cut-off denim shorts to your big show coming up."

I laugh. "Deal. If *you* lose, I get to ask you any question of my choosing, and you have to answer truthfully."

She considers this. "No more than five, though."

"Fine."

Tapping on her chin, she mulls it over. "Deal."

We shake on it and make a show out of thoroughly inspecting the couch, using our observation skills to make our estimations. It's a good quality couch, but those stains really throw off its value.

"I'd say three-hundred dollars."

"You're definitely going to lose." She snorts. "That couch is easily two grand brand-new."

"Mate, those stains are super obvious."

"A good clean could get them out."

I can't let her throw me off, it could be part of her plan. "I'm locking in thice-hundred."

"My guess is six-hundred-and-fifty."

Shit. That's high. "Locking it in?"

"Locking it in." Brooke turns and spots one of the staff, raising her hand politely. "Excuse me!"

"Hi, how can I help you?" The older woman smiles, giving us a friendly greeting.

"We were interested in purchasing this couch, but we'd like to know how much it is. Do you know the price?"

"I'll have to check with the manager, I'll be right back."

As the lady walks away, we turn toward each other, getting right in each other's faces for some mad trash talking. "I'm going to win this fucking thing, so get ready to open up to ol' Connie boy."

"The only thing you're going to win is YouTube, when a video of your dick flopping out of those shorts on stage goes viral."

"Hmmm, what should I ask…maybe *your* body count? Wait, I've got it, I want to know something you've never told *anyone*."

Her finger stabs into my chest. "I'll be in the crowd making sure *everyone* has their phones opened to their cameras, ready to catch it in *full swing*."

"No need, because I'll be in full-length jeans while I mop the floor with your secrets."

"Ha! You fucking wish—"

"Thanks for waiting!" Loretta, per her name tag, says, tipping us off on her return. "That couch is amazing condition, one of the best."

"We know," we say in unison, causing us to share an unsettling glance.

"So, how much is it?" Brooke prods.

"That one is six-hundred dollars."

Brooke erupts with a cheer, which quickly turns into a high-pitched cackle. "Oh, Connor, you're going to look soooo scrumptious in those shorts."

No. Fucking *fuck* no. "Loretta, is it? Are you positive that's correct?"

She holds up a neon pink tag, with $600 written in thick Sharpie. "Positive! We were just about to hang this tag on before you got here."

Brooke takes off toward the sale rack, waving the shorts over her head like a victory flag. I can't help but laugh, because I've never seen her this happy. Those booty shorts will be fucking worth it, if only to see her little display of triumph.

"Thank you, Loretta. We'll take the couch, and those shorts she's waving around."

Loretta giggles. "I'll be at checkout when you're ready."

Brooke passes Loretta on her return, still waving the little shorts around. "Okay, the change rooms are right there. You gotta give me a little sneak peek."

"You'll have to turn up at the show if you want to get a look at me wearing these bad boys."

Brooke grabs my elbow, turning me to face a full-length mirror that's hung on the back wall of a change room, curtain open, as she holds the shorts up in front of me. With my height, I'll consider myself lucky if they even reach the tops of my thighs. She laughs again, unbelievably pleased with herself.

Pausing, I take in our reflections. She wears a white tee today, tucked into her high-waisted, wide-legged jeans. Her hair is twisted up into one of those big ass clips chicks love, that allow little tendrils to escape. I've got on a sage, casual button-up tee and cream-colored jeans. She's beautiful, cheeks flushed with delight and a golden glow emanating from that smile.

And fuck, we look *good* together.

I may have come to crave the cold, but only so I can appreciate this warmth. I'm a moth to the flame, losing myself completely in how we look standing next to each other, until the tether on my control snaps entirely.

Grabbing the back of her neck, I steer her into the change room, flicking the curtain closed behind us with my other hand. Pressing her up against the wall, I bend lower so my mouth hovers in front of hers. "Go ahead and laugh again."

Her breath catches in the back of her throat.

I kiss her anyway. She drops the shorts, slipping her hands under the hem of my shirt, running over my stomach as my muscles constrict under her touch. Brooke groans as my hand lowers and I cup her through her jeans.

"Connor." My name is both a warning and a plea.

Suddenly, the need to have her face in the crowd becomes overwhelming. If I don't see her from the stage, my mind will be wherever she is…and I can't have that. "How will you know if I followed through on my end of the bet, unless you come to Poison Ivy?"

Brooke moans, but it's not an answer.

"Say you'll be there." I kiss down her neck, pulling her shirt down the smallest bit so I can drag my teeth over her collar bone. My hand continues to move against her, providing the friction that she desires.

"I'll be there." It's breathless and everything I needed to hear.

"Good," I growl, keeping my rhythm on her front, as I dip down for another kiss. With her tongue moving against mine, I put every ounce of carefully honed skill into hitting just the right spot, despite having her jeans as a barrier. My left hand forfeits its grip on her waist, trading it for a journey up her shirt. Before I know it, her soft little moans are coming quicker as she rides against my hand, until she erupts.

A handful of minutes. Over a pair of jeans. In a thrift store change room.

With one last kiss, I pull away as her head lolls to one side and a disgusting, mushy smile pulls at my lips. "I think Loretta is waiting for us at the counter."

"Hmmm."

"Let's go get that couch."

"Don't forget the shorts."

I smirk. "I wouldn't dare."

Throwing open the change room curtain, I look around, happy that nobody seemed to overhear our little extracurricular activities.

"Connor?"

"Yeah?" I turn, and even though I had my hands on her mere seconds ago, the sight of her nearly knocks me on my ass anyway.

"We do this whenever and *wherever* we want, but just for fun."

Holy shit. "Does that mean you're taking me up on my offer?"

"If it starts to become anything else for either of us, it's done."

My grin becomes devouring. *Let the fun begin.*

CHAPTER TWENTY-SEVEN

Then - Brooke

You know that bag Mary Poppins had? It appeared somewhat normal from the outside, but somehow fit an umbrella inside? Well, those are Ziggy's pockets. I'm ninety-nine percent sure she just pulled a blanket out of her back pocket, which I hadn't even seen bulging beneath her jacket.

"For you."

She passes the blanket over to me, and something foreign happens in my chest. "Thanks."

We're back at our drama stage now, aka soccer field, and I unroll the blanket and spread it across the grass. Ziggy takes a seat and begins unloading everything else. My little display had only lasted a minute or so, but you'd think she'd spent an entire afternoon in Costco with this haul.

"Holy shit." There are no other words for the unveiling that's going down in front of me. "I don't even want to know where you just pulled that Rice Krispies Treat from."

Ziggy cackles. "Your little cry baby moment was so good, *mija*. I almost forgot I had a job to do."

"I think you did just fine, Ziggy." I nod toward the huge spread across the blanket.

"We make good backup."

Most people would say we have a sort of camaraderie, bonding over tough circumstances and letting it bring us together, a partnership and dependency. But Ziggy and I aren't normal people, and this is life on the street. She could double cross me at any moment, and I can't forget that. As she said, having friends gets you killed, and I'd add caring about someone, in general, to that list. There are more ways to die than the physical sense.

"So, about what you said earlier…I'm down."

I'd spent the brisk walk back to this field considering my options. This morning I didn't know how I'd feel about it, playing a role in delivering my same fate to others. But today I stole from someone, and not an ounce of guilt followed me as I fled.

The guy was supposedly a slimeball who deserves much worse, so is that why my conscience remained clean? Would I have felt differently if I'd found out the man I'd stolen from had been one of honor? I'd like to think I would.

We can't keep stealing from the same man, and If we *were* to keep stealing, how much time would pass before I inevitably took something from someone who *is* good? Eventually it would happen, and for some reason, that's a stain I want to keep off of my soul.

There's limited options out here. It's either stealing, selling my body (which is definitely not a fucking option), or taking Ziggy up on her offer.

Lloyd denied me, and where did that get us? I found someone else. If they aren't getting it from me, they'll get it another way. I've decided that making money off people who would be addicted with or without my help is the lesser of all evils.

The lines of demarcation between right and wrong have already begun to blur, but I vow to never be the person who sells someone their first fix. That's my line, and I'll keep it with my life.

"Then we have somewhere to be, *mija.*"

• • •

"It's like high school, which you look like you were good at, so you should be fine."

That's the only explanation I get before walking into a possibly life-threatening situation.

According to Ziggy, drug rings are like high school, just without the friends. There's the people on top, and then there's everyone else. You don't want to piss off the one's on top, otherwise your life will be hell. So, in other words, I'm supposed to keep my *chica tonta* head down (whatever the fuck that means), and shut up.

We slip in through a piece of sheet metal which sits ajar from where it covers a low-level broken window. Everything else is chained up from this side of the building, and I can't help the sweat that begins to form on my palms and brow.

Less than a year ago, I was sitting for my SAT practice test, preparing to get a minimum fifteen-hundred score, and here I am entering a dilapidated warehouse on an abandoned shipping yard, getting brought into a drug ring.

On one hand, the setup is super cliché, and just like the movies. On the other hand, it completely isn't. The entire warehouse is made from industrial metals, the walls and ceilings included. Thanks to the salty air that comes with being so close to the ocean, everything is covered by a layer of rust that varies in thickness. It's almost like it was painted in watercolor, the gradients between the metals and russet colors kind of beautifully deteriorated.

The rest of the place is a disaster. Old, busted shipping crates lay around, like they were discarded long before the current... *tenants* moved in. Decades worth of dust blanket everything else, and my nose is instantly feeling sniffly at the onslaught of must.

I shake my head, needing to focus on things other than this place needing a cleanup, like the group of men we're approaching. Everything about them looks average, until you spot the firearms they all hold. They're not the shotguns dads keep in their closet to threaten teenage boys, we're talking hard core artillery.

My heart takes off in a sprint and I swallow, the danger of the situation becoming abundantly clear, proving exactly how far from fucking high school I really am. As we approach, my thoughts inexplicably drift to my mom, hoping she never gets to see what I've become. I reassure myself that she's safe, tucked away at work or home, not about to follow me inside this place.

"Where's Marty?"

"Hey there, little *señoritaaaa*." One of the men pushes off the shipping container he's leaning against, licking his lips at Ziggy. He's missing more teeth than he has, and I can smell the rot from here. "Sure you're not looking for me?"

"Honestly? If I found my eyes straying in your direction on their own, Gilly, I would cut them out." Ziggy puts her hands on her hips and rolls her eyes, like his grip on the AK-something-or-other didn't just tighten at her attitude. "Now, where is Marty? I have someone for him to meet."

That's when their eyes fall on me, and in this moment I realize something that is impossible to deny: I'm a coward. There's only been one other time that I've felt as scared as I am right now, coming face to face with these dirty men and their weapons, and I ended up losing the most important person in my life that night. My eyes dart back to Ziggy.

A few of the men snicker as they take me in, while others become consumed by a hunger I would give anything not to see in their eyes. The jitters start in my hands, and I tuck them into my pockets so they don't take it as a weakness. These men would eat me alive at the first sign of submission.

"You could leave the little gift with us, Zigs." A nameless man sneers.

Ziggy catches my eye, and though she doesn't say a word, I know what she's thinking. *Show them your claws, mija.*

Right. I summon everything I have into filling my voice with acid. "Take a step closer, and I'll eat your balls for breakfast."

Ziggy lets out a maniacal laugh, "Please, boys, do come closer, because I'd *loooove* to see what she'd do."

I take a step forward, even though my mind is screaming at me to run the other direction, my heart racing with fear. "Now, where the fuck is Marty?"

A little bit of motherly pride makes an appearance on Ziggy's features, before disappearing faster than it came. "You don't want to make her ask twice."

Gilly spits on the ground, before shuffling a foot. "He's with Victor, but he'll be back soon."

Everyone looks off into the distance at the same moment, as if to hide the alarm and sheer fear that comes with the mention of that name. Nobody asks if Victor is coming as well, but I assume that's because asking about Victor's comings and goings is a no-no.

Lovely. Gilly isn't the worst of it then.

Ziggy motions for me to follow her with a jerk of her head. "Tell Marty we're out back."

We duck through a space between a huge roller door, which looks like it's been peeled back by a giant monster, and the wall to get outside. Once we're far enough away that Ziggy deems it safe, she slaps me on the back. "You did good, *mija.*"

Although I'm one peg away from hyperventilating, my head feels suspiciously clear. "Just like high school," I repeat, not because it's true, but the fact that it was her sole advice for *THAT* is just fucking comical. Deathly comical. "Ziggy, did you ever *go* to high school?"

"No, but I've seen *Mean Girls*."

"You've seen *Mean Girls*." I nod slowly. "My life was hanging in the balance of advice you're giving based on Regina fucking George?"

"*Sí.*"

I can't help it, but I fucking laugh. "You're actually insane."

"Nobody told you different," Ziggy says with a shrug before walking over to the edge of the water.

I join her, looking at the ripples on its surface, similar to the way it is with life. Perhaps someone dropped a stone into the water in Mexico, and the little waves have just made it all the way to Tampa. A tiny little moment, which I feel the effects of, all the way over here.

Like taking your little sister to get custard on a Saturday night.

"So how does this usually work?"

Ziggy shrugs. "Like you'd expect. He gives you some *stuff*, threatens you a bit, and then Pop's your uncle."

Uh– "You mean Bob?"

"Who is Bob?"

"The uncle…"

"Who's uncle? *Mija*, you're not making sense."

"You compared dealing with criminals to fictional popular girls, but sure, I'm the one who's not making sense."

"You're self-aware, that's a good *calidad*."

"Ziggy, have you ever heard of sarcasm?"

"No."

"Figures." I roll my eyes.

"*I* was being sarcastic, *chica tonta. Dios mio…*" Ziggy goes off on one of her little rants I have no hope in understanding, and though I know whatever she's saying is extremely offensive, it's become my favorite thing of hers.

"Anyway, *mija*, don't underestimate Marty. He acts dumb so people do exactly that, but he's as smart as they come, and he's got a sixth sense for sniffing out double-crosses and discrepancies," Ziggy tells me. "Never let your guard down around him, and never show an *onza* of weakness, or you'll be eaten. Don't try to lie because he will catch you in it like a *rata* in a trap. You will not outsmart him, because all the ones who tried before are dead."

LAST *Stand* FOR GENEVIEVE

I nod, absorbing everything like I'll be pop-quizzed later. In a way, I will, but rather than a grade point average, I'll either keep my life or I won't. Weirdly, at some point in the last twenty-four hours, I started caring that I do.

"Never allow yourself to be alone with Gilly." Ziggy can't stop the full body rejection of whatever memory passed through her mind. "He's scared of Marty, but Marty doesn't give a shit about your feelings. He won't punish Gilly, because according to him, we should be smart enough to not let something happen in the first place."

Nausea rocks me, but I listen as she continues.

"The rest aren't worth learning the names of because well...they change a lot."

She doesn't need to spell it out for me. If they fuck up, they die, and it sounds like they fuck up a lot.

"Just be on your guard. Watch out for the ones who are bad to you, but even worse is someone who's trying to be a hero. They're either a cop who's about to put you away for good, or they're a dumbass with a heart that's going to get you killed. Either way, stay far away, *mija*."

"And trust no one."

"Not even me." Ziggy nods. "Because between you and me, if it comes down to it, I will always choose myself."

Something sharp happens in my chest, but I can't be angry with her for being honest. She's keeping it real, giving me the truth of the matter, rather than leading me on just to stab me in the back one day. At least this way I'll have the opportunity to dodge the knife, or go down with grace.

"And you keep those claws sharp at all times."

"Claws sharp at all times," I repeat her words back, etching them into my memory and my very soul.

Then, a booming male voice breaks the moment in half. "Ziggy!"

She flinches, me and the water the only witnesses, before she plasters on a hot-shot smile and turns around with all the confidence in the world. It's a tiny look inside what's really happening in that head of hers, and I know the feeling.

It's like forcing your feet into shoes that are two sizes too small, or wearing a pair of jeans that are too tight. Similar to forcing a puzzle piece that looks like a match, into fitting despite the truth that it *never* will. It's a feeling between being trapped and suffocation, a vise around who you really are, squeezing your life force into nothingness.

It's everything I've been feeling, and she feels it too.

"Marty!" Ziggy's act is good, she'd sell the story to me, too, if I hadn't been living the same one since the accident. "It's been too long, but what can I say? Business has been *bueno*!"

Marty isn't necessarily what I'd expect of someone in a position of power in this *industry* (for lack of a better word). He looks like an average, middle-aged man, sporting New Balances and khakis of all things.

With a dopey grin and cheeks that are too red, he would be the opposite of intimidating if I didn't know what he gets up to with his time. Now I understand why people underestimate him, his demeanor being calculated toward exactly that.

The intimidation comes from behind him, where a tall and built European-looking man is emanating a "I'd love it if someone would try and fuck with me because I'm bored as hell" vibe.

Note to self: Definitely don't fuck with him.

"Marty, I want you to meet someone." Ziggy moves to the side, and I step forward, shoulders squared. "This is Carolina."

"Carolina." Marty tilts his head and chuckles like he's being silly. "It's nice to meet you, Carolina. What brought you to this area?"

In other words, why is a preppy blonde trying to get accepted into his circle? I haven't gotten a chance to drill my Marty flashcards, and it's already time for that quiz, the life or death one. My palms begin to sweat. Ziggy doesn't even glance in my direction, but picks at her nail as if this is the most boring interaction in the world.

Don't try to lie because he will catch you in it like a rata in a trap.

"My other life started not to…*fit*." It tells him enough, without telling him a thing. Not a lie, but not a truth per se.

He laughs a big, booming laugh designed to put people like me at ease, but Ziggy's warnings remain at the forefront of my mind. My guard doesn't drop a millimeter. "I think we've all been there before, Carolina. Sounds like you'll fit right in."

As words, they seem innocent enough. Yet there's a warning laced inside, threatening what stands to happen if I *don't* fit in, if I don't follow whatever rules exist in this world which I've yet to learn.

LAST *Stand* FOR GENEVIEVE

"Gilly will get you set up with what you need." Marty gives me a once over, top to bottom before looking back to Ziggy. "Good find, *bonita*."

The way these men use Ziggy's words against her grates on my nerves. I try to keep it off my face, but I know my eyes have turned to shards of ice. Ziggy is a pro, giving him a smile before thickening her accent and pretending not to speak the language as well as she can, "I am how do you say...the star child, *no?*"

Marty laughs and walks away, leaving us in the hands of Gilly.

These men think they're smarter than her, but Ziggy is the smartest of us all.

Everything else happens in a blur. Product is handed over to me with threats. I wonder what the fuck I'm doing and how I got here. Before I can think twice about it, I've entered a drug ring, and just like that, I'm working side by side with criminals who have done much worse than hand over a little baggy.

As we exit the warehouse, I take a breath. The salty air, which was once a comfort, is now associated with a certain degree of fear. The unknown hangs over me, reminding me that this decision will have a far-reaching ripple, just like my others. There's just no telling what it'll be this time.

Ziggy stops, putting a hand on my shoulder before looking me in the eye. "How are those claws, *mija?*"

I nod, feeling a little bit blank, but present. "Sharp."

Whatever she sees convinces her enough. "Good. Now let's go do what we do."

CHAPTER TWENTY-EIGHT

Now – Connor

The energy is already buzzing, filling myself and the guys with a current only achievable in moments like this, where you're about to walk out onto a stage to meet a crowd that is already losing its mind. For *you*.

It brings a smile to my face as I meet the eyes of my bassist, Dane. His gratitude shines through, telling me how much being here means to him. Even Rue, normally pissed at anything he can find, hasn't found a single excuse to get angry. Ryder stands with us, running his hand over his jaw, which I've learned is his only tell.

Despite everything, we've made it here. I'd called the rehabilitation center where I'd taken Jayden, but they legally couldn't give me an update since I'm not a relative, patient privacy and all. But tonight, I can't let my worries over him taint this out-of-body experience, where we've returned to our roots and have a sold-out show.

Poison Ivy is made up of exactly what you'd expect: a stage, a generously sized bar, and a massive empty space in the middle for moshing or dancing (depending on the crowd), with a bathroom on the very other side, slick with a floor that is permanently wet from who knows what. There's a second-floor balcony which juts out over the empty floor, allowing more room for the sweating attendees.

The walls and ceiling are painted all black, the only color being the bright green molding shaped like ivy, which climbs up and down, swirling around the entire space. It's as if the poisoned vines came in, wrapping and squeezing, before sucking all the color out of the rest of the space.

It was the video taken here, in this venue, which set our success into motion. We owe everything to Poison Ivy—the least we can do is give them one *hell* of a show tonight.

A waitress walks by, eyeing my super short-shorts and laughs. I'd been right, they hardly reached the tops of my thighs, leaving me looking almost naked behind my guitar. I'd had to borrow some of Theo's briefs (folded up and under the tiny little shorts) to make sure my favorite part didn't make his debut tonight.

Ryder looks at my shorts. "I actually can't believe you're wearing those."

I shrug. "I never back down from a bet."

Hesitation marks his features, as he gives his jaw another rub. "Listen, I was thinking–"

Before he can get the words out, the emcee announces over the already screaming crowd, "Please welcome back to our stage *Immoral Support*, with special guest Ryder Cassidy!"

Glancing at the entrance to the stage, my heartbeat picks up before looking back to Ryder. "Later?"

He nods and I wrap my arm around his shoulder, and with that, I lead the guys into the lights. Though I didn't think it was possible, the crowd manages to erupt even louder, and I can't help the ear-splitting grin that takes over.

Dane and Rue find their usual places, as if it's just another afternoon rehearsal, but I see the gleam in their eyes. Ryder looks more comfortable than the last time, even at ease, as he grabs the mic at the very center of the stage. This show is everything I've imagined and more, being here with the guys and the fans we treasure.

I lean into my mic with my usual greeting, "G'day."

The crowd goes feral. In moments like this, I marvel at how every moment in my life has led to me being here, how Theo's sacrifice in taking his father's payoff allows me to do what I love. The screaming only intensifies, deepening the moment.

Squinting my eyes against the light, I make out the faces of the screaming fans in the crowd, and as they collide with a certain pair of icy blue eyes staring back at me from directly in front of where I stand on the stage, my knees go weak.

I'd know those eyes anywhere, even if I were blind.

Everything else disappears as I zero in on her beautiful features, the high cheekbones and pert little nose, her soft lips that now live in a memory against my own. Brooke's face is clear of makeup as I've come to expect, and she wears a light brown turtleneck, paired with none other than the unsightly skirt from the thrift shop.

I can't help my genuine laugh, wrapped with surprise and elation. She must have gone back for it, wearing it just for me, in front of all of these people. Something happens in my chest, it feels like someone is squeezing their fist around my heart to crush it. She smiles back at me, beaming brighter than the brightest stage light.

My mind captures the sight, knowing it will be embedded into my memory forever. It'll be what I think about when I've had a shit day, or when I can't get my father's cruel words out of my head. A beautiful girl in a hideous skirt, looking at me like I'm not wearing cut-off denim shorts that are so short my dick could peek out, surrounded by a crowd who loves my music.

I will live in this moment for eternity.

Ryder coughs into the mic, reminding me that I'm on a stage in front of nearly a thousand people. "Our guitarist lost a bet, obviously. I apologize in advance for any uh, *slips*."

The crowd screams, as if they wouldn't mind at all, so I turn around and give them a little wiggle of my ass, and their response is deafening, making me laugh. Facing the crowd again, I struggle to keep my eyes on anything other than the beauty right up front, but I try. "Let's get started, yeah?"

As the crowd goes wild, hundreds of phones lighting up with a flash, Rue starts us off with a little beat, and we jump right into our very first song, "Living or Dying." It's the first full song I ever wrote, during a time I'd lost the one source of happiness in my life, and I wasn't sure which one of us had actually died that day.

The melody instantly carries us away, and we become lost in how the crowd chants the lyrics along with Ryder. With me joining in at the right moments, our harmonized vocals are unlike anything we've attained, even in rehearsals.

Ryder has gone gravelly, a lower range than what we'd practiced. He looks to me, and I push myself into a higher range and fucking nail it, letting my voice out of its cage. Ryder fucking *smiles*, eyes full of excitement, and we do

LAST Stand FOR GENEVIEVE

it again on the next run. It's the slightest of changes, but it transforms every song on the set list. With the contrast of harmonized notes, his low growls and my honeyed whines, we create something which has never been done before.

Song after song, the chemistry between our vocals sets fire to the crowd. I've never felt the kind of energy that is flowing within these walls, reaching an aesthetic height I'd never known. It's as easy as breathing, but it changes me, creating the kind of magic I've only dreamed possible.

Finally, we come to the end, but the crowd refuses to accept it. Cheering and chanting us into doing another song. So we give it to them.

Sweat runs down my forehead, Ryder's shirt absolutely soaked in it. We stand, shoulder to shoulder, guzzling water and laughing. The only thing that keeps me grounded, keeps me from floating away forever, are those amazing eyes and a smile I've worked so hard to earn.

Tonight was *transcendent*.

I lean into my mic and give my thanks, telling the crowd how much they mean to us, and what Poison Ivy has done for our trajectory, before walking off from my place on the stage. For the first time, I spare no thought to who I hand my guitar to, it could have been Arnold fucking Schwarzenegger for all I know.

Not breaking eye contact as I leap over an amp, landing on the ground, I close the few steps that remain, and kiss the hell out of her. This thing between us is only for fun, whenever and wherever we want, and I want it here and now. The crowd could be screaming for us, but I have no idea because I'm not paying attention to anything besides her lips on mine.

Only breaking away to drag her toward the hidden side door behind a curtain, I pull her into the alley which is empty except a parked van waiting to cart our music gear away. Pushing her back against the door, I make sure nobody can slip out and disturb us.

We say nothing as our hunger becomes too intense to ignore. I take hold of that hideous skirt and pull it up, just as she reaches around to pull out the foil she knew would be in my back pocket.

"Cute shorts, by the way." Brooke reaches for the button of my jean shorts, undoing it easily. "Be sure to send my regards to your stylist."

"I'll let her know you liked them." I drop my lips to kiss her neck and groan when my lips are met with knitted material instead of her soft skin. "I hate these fucking turtlenecks."

She giggles, making quick work of what's in the foiled wrapper, and putting her hand under my chin to bring my lips back to her mouth. I reach down to move her underwear out of the way and find her softness.

"Fuck me, woman." Breathy, deep, and hoarse, I say it as a prayer, but she takes it as a command.

"I'm about to."

I easily lift her, keeping her back against the door, and with one push I'm exactly where I want to be. The sensation is all consuming, being lost in the feel of each other's bodies and sounds. This arrangement is the best fucking idea I've ever had.

CHAPTER TWENTY—NINE

Then - Brooke

"So what do we do now?"

"Well, we don't hold up sign like we're a *limonada* stand." Ziggy shrugs. "We just wait."

Ziggy has taken us to an area in Tampa called Ybor, there's a bunch of clubs, and per Ziggy, these people like to get fucked up. Turns out, it's Saturday, which was news to me. Since it's only about ten, the night hasn't gotten into full swing yet, and we have some time to kill.

It's not awkward with Ziggy, but it's weird because how do you kill time without talking? But what do you talk about if you're not meant to become friends? The past is off the table even for me, but if we talk about anything else, we will inevitably agree on something, and it'll make me like her even more than I already do.

But as usual, Ziggy is prepared for anything. "*Mija*, would you rather have the power to read minds or fly?"

I snort. "Fly. Definitely."

"Same."

"Okay, let me think of one." The kids in my class used to play a drinking version of this at parties. "Would you rather be in jail for five years, or a coma for seven?"

"*Ayyyyy, mija*, this is supposed to be fun! You're dark." Ziggy laughs. "But probably jail."

"Same." Shit. We already agree on something.

"Would you rather puke on a guy you like, or have him puke on you?"

I groan, because fucking neither. "I guess…get puked on."

"What!? For *real*!?"

"Yes! Can you imagine the embarrassment of puking on a boy following you around forEVER!?"

Ziggy tsk-tsks, "No man is worth getting puked on. I would puke on him. Easily. Never think about it again."

"Of course, you wouldn't." I roll my eyes. Other questions pop up in my head, but to some degree they'd reveal too much.

Would you rather have a forward or backward button on your life?

Would you rather be able to change the past or predict the future?

Would you rather betray someone or be betrayed?

I already know the answer to the last one anyway.

"Okay, Ziggy, would you rather lay by the pool or on the beach?"

"Neither. I hate bathing suits."

I look over at her. "What do you mean, you hate bathing suits?"

"They don't make baggy bathing suits, and I don't like feeling tight." Ziggy shivers like the thought alone bothers her.

"Okay, would you rather lay by the pool or beach, fully clothed?"

"The pool. For sure. Fuck sand."

We laugh at our agreement, and I hate that there is so much of it.

"Okay, would *mija* rather have four nipples or twelve toes?"

"Twelve toes!" I howl and smack Ziggy playfully. "Would you rather wear the same underwear for a week, or the same socks for a month?"

"*Eres asquerosa.*" Ziggy shakes her head. "The socks, I guess. I wear mine inside out because I don't like the threads touching my toes."

How am I supposed to *not* be her friend when she tells me stupid things like that? Though I once considered myself one who had many friends, this feeling with Ziggy is unique. I resist the urge to share an inconsequential detail about myself in return.

"Your turn, *mija.*"

I think it over, wanting to make this one good. "Would you rather find a roach or a spider in your bed?"

"*Noooooooooooo. Joder, no, absolutamente no.*" Ziggy gets up and starts pacing. "*No puedo elegir ambos no son.*"

"Ziggy, I have no idea what you're saying," I say with a giggle.

"I don't do bugs."

"You stare criminals in the eye and probably risk your life regularly, but you can't face down a little bug?"

"Go ahead and laugh, but the answer is *hellll tooo thee nooooo.*"

"Okay, fine, I'll let you off the hook this one time." I tap my chin, then think of another. "Would you rather never eat watermelon again, or have to eat strawberries with every meal for the rest of your life?"

"I'd give up watermelon, it's not my favorite anyway."

I frown. "That was too easy."

"Well, you already put images in my head of bugs crawling on me, which will keep me up all night tonight–"

"Okay! Okay! I'm sorry, I won't bring up bugs again."

"It's my turn." Ziggy is quiet for a tad longer, and I can't help but start to dread whatever she comes up with. "Would you rather never know when you'd lose someone you love, or live your life knowing exactly when it would happen, but not be able to change it?"

"Ask me something else."

"Too deep for you, *mija?*"

I nod. "Too deep."

"Okay, then, would you rather order Coke or Pepsi?'

Honestly, I like both, but since I have to choose, "Pepsi."

Ziggy frowns. "Shit."

"What?"

"*Nosotras somos demasiado similares.*"

"Huh?"

"Nothing. It's showtime."

Looking beyond our little spot, I realize that she's right. Tons of people are now roaming the streets, grabbing pizza before going into the clubs. One person is stuffing a bottle of something into their jeans, the other guys with him laughing and taking photos as it starts to look like a huge erection. I roll my eyes.

Someone spots Ziggy from across the street and lifts a hand in a subtle wave. She nods, and the guy says something to his friend before crossing the street.

"How are those claws, *mija?*"

"Sharp."

"*Bueno.*"

"Is he a regular?"

Ziggy nods. "*Sí.*"

It's surprisingly easy, doing what we're doing, though I still feel that now familiar black ink, spreading through my soul with every exchange. I peer over at Ziggy, and she's stone cold. There's not a trace of guilt or regret, not a glimpse of the vivacious, swaggering (and sometimes sweet) Ziggy I've come to know. It's like she manages to turn everything off, so I try to do the same.

It makes it a little easier, but far away, I know what we're doing is wrong.

• • •

Since this is my first time, I don't know what's considered normal, but I feel like we moved a lot. Ziggy seems pleased, having gone through almost everything we had. Guess Saturdays in Ybor are where it's at. It was successful enough that my pockets weigh heavy with cash, enough that I'm extra worried about walking around tonight.

We've finally made the trek back to our little bridge, just outside of the nice neighborhood and I loose a breath. Never thought a bridge in the middle of the night could give me a sense of security, but I guess you can't knock it till you've tried it.

Speaking of feeling safe, there's a question I've been too afraid to ask, which haunted me the entire night. It had me looking over my shoulder, not just for thieves. "Do you know someone named Sebby? He does what we're doing."

Ziggy shakes her head. "He must be part of another crew. Victor has St. Pete and Tampa, owning the trade to the rich kids who have money to spend."

I nod, hoping this is good news. Realistically, Tampa Bay isn't all that big. Running into him at a Publix on a Wednesday afternoon is still a likely possibility.

"You owe him money or something?"

I nod.

"Well, if Sebby is part of another crew I wouldn't worry, it means they'd be much smaller. They all stay out of Victor's hair."

He could still go to Publix. "I plan to pay him back with some of this, anyway." I've finally just reclined with my ass on the ground and arms braced behind me, hoping we can pass out, when Ziggy opens her mouth.

"I have somewhere I have to be, but you need to stay here."

My eyebrows shoot up, though admittedly, it's not like we agreed to do everything together. I'm sure she has things she doesn't want to share with me, just like I have things I don't want to share with her. Except this is the first time she's walking away from me and… it's weird.

She's told me over and over again that we aren't friends, but we *are* back-up, and I don't like the idea of not being able to watch her back. "What do you mean, I have to stay here?"

"It means no following me. *Entender?*"

No. No *entender*. But I nod anyway, knowing there's no way I'll persuade her to take me along.

"*Gracias.*" Ziggy's shoulders sag, as if relieved that I didn't fight her. Guess she knows I can be just as stubborn as her, which is exactly why I'm going to follow without her knowledge.

"I'll see you in the morning, Ziggy." I take out my jacket, fluffing it up as close to a pillow as I come these days.

"Be safe, *mija*." With that she turns and leaves, as I watch her walk to the end of the street and turn the corner.

I'm on my feet in an instant, knowing I need to make it to the end of this street by the time she makes it to the end of the next one, that way I can pop my head around the corner and see which way she goes. Double-checking I have all of my belongings with me, I take off in a light jog, slowing as I finally reach the end of the street. An ache starts up in my bad leg, but not enough to stop me from continuing.

There's one of those fancy mailboxes on the corner that's half the size of a house, giving me the perfect hiding spot. Positioning myself behind the monstrosity, I peek my head around to see Ziggy hanging left. Before she goes, as if she feels my eyes on her, she whips her head back in my direction. I shrink behind the mailbox, hoping the dark concealed the small of my head which had emerged.

I count to two hundred, plenty of time for her to find me if she'd decided to come back my way, meaning I'm in the clear. I pop out of my hiding spot, picking up a jog again down the next street. There's nothing on this corner, meaning I have to risk stepping into the open to see which way she goes. This time she takes a right, and thankfully she doesn't look back.

We continue to move in the same way, Ziggy none the wiser with me as her shadow, long past the point I'd began wishing she would stop. I mean seriously, it feels like we should be halfway to California by now. Everything aches, my knees and ankles and soul, but especially my eyes. My body isn't used to dealing with the kind of adrenaline rush I had today, but especially not when I'm living off of pills and Rice Krispies Treats.

God, I would kill for a caramel iced macchiato about now. Sometimes I feel myself missing the little things like coffee, or having a long hot shower. My body trembles at the desire to have one now, just to relax my muscles before drifting off into a peaceful sleep.

But that's not my life anymore. Walking into my old home means walking into my past, straight into the nightmare with no end. I'd take the aches and pains that come with sleeping on the ground any day over the emotional agony I face in that house.

Finally, hours later (not an exaggeration), Ziggy pauses, a quiet whimper of relief escaping at the sight. I duck behind a trash can, carefully peeking around the side, as Ziggy scans the surroundings, checking to make sure she hasn't been followed. With the caution she's taken, I realize there's a much bigger danger than the preppy white girl she's taken under her wing that could be lurking. Wherever she's going, it needs protection.

Ziggy deems it clear and approaches a house. I lose her for a second, but squint my eyes, and thankfully, my eyes adjust quickly. I can't make out much of the details, this area of the street being almost entirely concealed by darkness thanks to a bunch of busted streetlights.

Part of me wonders if Ziggy spent an entire night doing just that, as an extra security precaution. Because even if she was followed, it'd be hard to tell where she went after she disappears into the shadows as I'm struggling to do now.

The only thing I can glean from the shadows is that this house has seen much better days, the whole street has honestly. I didn't grow up wealthy, though I did my damndest to make it look like I did. Never would I presume to know what the people who live on this street go through, but my heart squeezes at the thought of it.

Guess I may still have one after all?

LAST *Stand* FOR GENEVIEVE

I shake my head, reminding myself that I don't. Walking out on my own mother, my beautiful and loving mother who's never done me wrong, how dare I consider that I still have a heart if I couldn't give it to her.

Ziggy approaches the porch, kneeling down to look at something. Again, I can see almost nothing, but I do see the shadow of her arm reach down to yank a piece of wood away. She does it again and again, before the outline of her head drops into her hands with a shake.

Is she crying?

That foreign feeling returns, the desire to comfort her, but I'm not even supposed to be here right now, let alone console her in an emotional moment the way a friend would. Ziggy stands, wiping her face, and retrieves something from the yard. In the dark, I can't see what it is, but she positions it over the spot where she threw the wood from.

A hole then. The porch is starting to collapse.

Ziggy takes a few moments, trying to steady the makeshift blockade, and then shakes out her arms. She paces back and forth a few times, gathering her emotions. I see the exact moment the strong Ziggy I've come to know snaps back. It's weird. I've known her for a few days, yet I can read her like it's broad daylight, and she's narrating her actions to me via radio.

She glances in my direction again, definitely feeling my eyes, but I duck behind a car just in time. Ziggy opens one of the windows on the left of the front door, before reaching into her backpack and dropping the wad of cash inside. She closes the window and checks over her shoulder again before moving to the other side of the house.

Again, she opens a window, but this time she rests her arms against the frame and stares inside for a moment. Lost in the moment from afar, I step out from behind the car, unable to stop myself from wanting to see more of the moment. She stands there, gazing in through the window for uncountable minutes.

Just as the light of morning begins to creep up on us, Ziggy reaches into her backpack and pulls out a small stuffed animal. Though I know it's clean and utterly brand new, she dusts it off, as if to make it perfect before gently tossing it in through the window. As if being broken from a trance, Ziggy stiffens before wiping her tears and closing the window.

I am so enraptured that as Ziggy turns, I forget to dive back behind the car. With the sun starting to peek through, there's no shadows to conceal me or the expression that consumes Ziggy the second she spots me. It's shock, followed by fear and rage.

Ziggy stalks toward me, intent in her eyes, but my legs are locked. I stand there gaping at her, unable to move. She grabs me by my shirt and throws me into the car I'd been hiding behind. My back screams, as she pulls me forward just to shove me back into it.

"I swear to God, Carolina. If you tell a soul about what you just saw, I won't hesitate to end your life, and the life of anyone you ratted to."

I see it in her eyes, Ziggy means it, she wouldn't think twice about killing me to protect whoever is inside that house. Except, I would *never* tell anyone, and Ziggy must see it written all over my face. She closes her eyes before releasing my shirt and smoothing it back down.

"I'm sorry, *mija*. You don't work with the people we do if you have something they can use as leverage. Hear me? I wouldn't want to, but if something happens to them, I will end you with no questions asked."

I nod.

That's when I know without a doubt, Ziggy's family lives inside that house, and she lives this life so they can live theirs. She is not only one of the smartest and most resourceful people I've ever met, but she has a heart big enough to rival someone who once reminded me of spring and tulips.

CHAPTER THIRTY

Now – Connor

Over the years, I'd expected someone with connections stumbling over our music online and thinking, "Hey, I should give these guys a chance." I'd even imagined the right person being at the place at the right time and seeing our music live.

Me, wearing denim booty shorts on stage after losing a bet, resulting in a doubling of our online following? Hadn't crossed my mind. Poison Ivy is really where it all happens for us, one way or another.

My phone vibrates, and I pull it out to find Ryder finally answering the text I sent him the day after Poison Ivy.

Connor: Last night was... incredible. Thank you again, mate.

Connor: What were you going to say before the show? I didn't get to catch up with you after.

Ryder: Don't worry about it. It was stupid.

Meaning he'd had an idea. I roll my eyes, not letting his typical broodiness ruin my mood.

As I walk up the steps and enter the reception area of the drug rehabilitation center, I mentally run through all the good news from the last few weeks since the show at Poison Ivy, excited to share it with Jayden, hopefully giving him something to look forward to when he gets out. I'd hate for him to be in here without his phone, feeling terrible about leaving us high and dry.

What Ryder had done with his vocals was insane, and although Jayden and I don't meld in quite the same way, I think we still have a shot at imitating it together. With practice. Luckily there are tons of videos going around online as examples, and our views on YouTube have spiked again.

"Good afternoon," the receptionist greets me with a smile. "How can I help you?"

Her expression is friendly enough, but her eyes are tired. I can only imagine how strong this woman has to be, seeing what she does on a daily basis. The fact that she can still muster a welcoming persona is beyond admirable.

"Hello, I'm hoping that I can visit a friend who is staying here." I give her my most charming smile. "I know immediate relatives are the only ones typically allowed for visitation, but I'm the one who helped get him here, so I was hoping you could make an exception? I just want to make sure he's doing okay."

"Ah, I understand perfectly." She gives me a wink, "And what was your *brother's* name again?"

I smile. "Jayden White."

"Let me see here." The receptionist types his name into the system and a little bit of hope trickles into my chest, until her brow furrows. "White as in W-h-i-t-e?"

"Yes, exactly."

She looks at me, her eyes softening with a tinge of sadness. "I'm really sorry, but we don't have a patient here under that name."

"How is that possible? It's only been a few weeks and I checked him in myself." This doesn't make sense. "How could he have finished the program that quickly?"

"Our facility doesn't keep involuntary patients, meaning your friend could have checked himself out." The receptionist looks around, making sure nobody is close enough to overhear, before scrolling a little more on the computer. "Per the records, he was only here for... two days."

That tiny little bit of hope I had for my friend, my fellow musician and the person I thought I'd build a musical empire with, shrivels up and dies behind my ribs. Was he already too far gone? Is it because I waited too long to bring him in? It actually hurts, the guilt that comes crashing in.

"Sir," the receptionist's voice softens, "I see many loved ones have the same realization you are having now, but please know that this is not your fault. You did the right thing, bringing him here, but no matter how hard you try, if someone doesn't want to be helped, there is nothing you'll be able to do."

LAST *Stand* FOR GENEVIEVE

"I just…" I shake my head, realizing this woman has enough on her plate as it is. "Thank you for the information and for doing what you do here. Have a good day."

With that I walk away, not getting farther than the seat of my ute, resting my forehead on the steering wheel. This entire time, I imagined I was giving Jayden space, without a reminder of his monsters. I'd wanted to give him as much time as he needed to rehabilitate, to rediscover the Jayden I used to know who's been buried beneath substances for far too long.

I slam my hands against the steering wheel, raging against this feeling of helplessness that comes with watching someone you care about get taken away by a form of sickness. I swore I'd never feel this again, but here I am with my stupid fucking heart, bleeding out.

So, where does this leave him? Will Jayden never again set aside the drugs and alcohol in favor of feeling something which isn't synthetic?

Not only tormented about what this means for him, but this changes *everything*. It affects the fate of not only me, but the band. Our lives and success were riding on him giving it his all and getting clean. With that no longer being the case, we will need to find another lead singer, and being at such a pivotal moment in our career, it could break us. All of our hard work and years developing what we have, completely gone to waste.

I have no idea what to do or how to make this better. I'm truly at a loss, and for the first time, turning to my music won't serve as an escape, but only a reminder of the worst of it. Pulling my hair, I throw my head against the headrest in frustration.

My phone goes off a moment later, and my stomach sinks when I see the message.

Ice Kween: Did you make it in?

I regret telling her where I was going today. Unable to bring myself to answer, I set my phone in the cup holder and return to my self-loathing. I'll add ignoring her message to the list of things I hate about today. The silence doesn't last, as if my mind can't help but fill it with something.

See you when you fail, Son.

My dear ol' dad may not be seeing me, but that's equivalent to failure. I've always dreamed of making it to newsstands on the cover of *Rolling Stone* and the online news pages he reads every morning, so my success could be shoved down his throat without me having to lift a finger.

More time passes, marked only by the amount of times my father's voice echoes through my head, before my phone alerts me for the second time.

Ice Kween: He wasn't there, was he?

I don't know how she knows, but she does. Yet another clue that someone in her life has struggled with substance abuse. It's the only thing I can come up with to explain her ferocity toward any form of substance, even caffeine.

Although things have continued between us over these past few weeks, she hasn't opened up even a crack more to me, and honestly, the less I know, the better. We don't share because everyone knows sharing is caring. And fuck caring.

Jayden is a prime example of why I have my rules. With my heart not behaving these days with someone I'm *not* sleeping with, I need to keep it on an even tighter leash with the person I am.

Thankfully, there's been no hint at her developing feelings for me beyond the explosive attraction we share. I'm grateful for it because my attraction to her has reached a level I don't think my dick would survive me walking away from. Aside from the moments where I'm buried inside of her, we keep it simple, nothing more than an easy surface-level friendship whenever we make a late night Walmart run and find ourselves laughing down the aisles. We never talked about our arrangement being exclusive, but it's happened naturally on my end.

Ara thinks it's because we have something "more," but I think it's because after you've tasted gourmet, artisan chocolate truffles, you don't go back to Hershey's unless you're drunk by a fire and in need of a sloppy s'more.

I groan as another alert comes through.

Ice Kween: Let's pretend you didn't leave me on read just now. Are you free?

Connor: Yeah.

Ice Kween: Then meet me at our fixer up, Chip.

I don't bother asking who Chip is, just put my ute in drive and head over to Operation Defrost. Since we've finished the project, I'd be lying if I said my curiosity isn't poking its head out behind the cloud of self-loathing.

As usual, the drive goes by quickly with the relatively low traffic in Tampa. The residents who complain about the traffic here have no bloody clue what traffic is until they've tried to get somewhere during rush hour in Sydney.

LAST *Stand* FOR GENEVIEVE

I pull up along the curb across from our little project. The streetlights closest to where I've parked are all out, allowing me to be engulfed in darkness as my headlights go out. It feels fitting considering my mood. That is, until a glowing light from the house grabs my attention. Brooke's silhouette, a shape I'd know anywhere, approaches my door at that exact moment, backlit by the scene playing out behind her.

Stepping out of the driver's side, I lean against the cab of my ute to the right of where she's propped herself. Feeling guilty about not answering her messages, I allow my arm to brush hers, letting her know in the only way I know how that my mood has nothing to do with her. Brooke remains silent, but comfortable, and I'm relieved to know she hasn't taken it personally.

My attention returns to the scene playing out at the glowing house, where Brooke gazes with an unreadable expression on her face. Two kids are playing on the porch, racing toy cars across the fresh wood where the huge hole once was. One of them looks to be several years older than the other, but just as content being able to play with the younger one.

A woman moves around in the kitchen, attending to the stove and oven with perfectly timed motions. That's when the delicious smell reaches all the way to where we stand, and I deeply inhale, catching authentic spices of something South American. The woman retrieves a dish from the oven and turns all of the appliances off, before approaching the screen door.

"*Ven acqui*, my loves!" She calls to who I assume are her children, based on the motherly tone her voice takes.

"Okay, *Mama*!" The eldest child responds before dipping down to gather his younger brother and the toys. They race inside, the younger boy doing a little hop of excitement.

The boys take their seats at the small dining table we'd placed where the bed used to be, between the window we're looking through and the kitchen, while their mother brings out the food. The eldest smacks the hand of the younger child as he reaches for the hot dish, after his mother retreats to the kitchen for the rest of the dinner.

I chuckle. "Are they family of yours?"

Brooke shakes her head, a sadness taking over her expression. She shares a somber look that I've never seen, and a peek into what caused her to construct her defenses. Despite the day I've had, which was the *perfect* reminder of why I don't do feelings, I can't help the idiotic desire to know more.

"Who are they to you?"

Brooke is quiet for a moment. "I owed someone. This was the least I could do."

My idiocy turns to lunacy with the sudden urge to pry, to beg for more, but I know she'd never give it to me. "Whatever you owed them, I'm sure what you've done for their family has repaid them tenfold."

"It doesn't even come close." It's a devastating truth, and I don't miss the swipe of her hand across the side of her face which is farthest from me, no matter how much she wishes that I don't see.

"Want to go out? Get some gelato or something?"

Pain flicks across her features, even more raw, and I can't help but wonder what it was that I said. "Maybe next time."

Guess I'm not the only one having a shitty day.

"But maybe I can stop by after I finish up here…" she continues, the hopeful intonation at the end of her sentence before she trails off nearly brings me to my knees.

"Of course."

I don't know if it was her obvious vulnerability in that moment, or the fact that today of all days we need a form of release to chase away the shadows that are haunting us both, but I forget all about my rule on never bringing a woman into my home until I'm halfway there and my stomach is flipping at the idea.

• • •

The elevator dings and I pretend like I haven't been sitting here for over an hour, waiting for that sound. Theo and Ara are long asleep, leaving only four eyes to land on Brooke as she exits the elevator, mine and the ones belonging to the judgy little feline sitting just out of reach.

I stand a little too quickly, Brooke's brow lifting as she takes in our place. Part of never bringing a woman here has been because I don't want to give them the wrong idea. I'm not rich, and wouldn't have much to offer them outside of music gear.

Ice Queen takes in the floor-to-ceiling windows and view of the city. "Nice place."

"Technically, it's Theo's, but he lets me stay here." The shadows from earlier still follow her, but she's doing a better job of hiding it. "Have you eaten yet?"

My appetite had vanished with today's events, and with my stomach tied up over the idea of her coming over, I wouldn't have been able to keep anything down until now. But now that she's here, in my home, I'm starving.

"Yeah, I already ate."

Shit. "Mind if I scarf something down real quick?"

She shakes her head. "Go for it."

I lead her to the kitchen, which is probably my favorite thing about this place besides the view, having huge windows and enough natural light allowed for black to be the prominent color. The countertops, or benchtops as I'd say back home, are made out of wood of the finest quality, matching a few of the cabinet doors, that are artistically placed to tie it all in. The ambient lighting that's featured throughout the entire penthouse is also found here, lining the bottoms of every surface, always taking it to the next level of luxury.

I rummage through the cabinets, finally finding what I'm looking for. Ara has many strong points, but cabinet organization is not one of them. I won't bother her over it, seeing as though I'm currently thieving her of her second favorite cuisine.

Brooke snorts as I place my findings on the bench and look for a little pot. "Seriously? Mac & Cheese?"

I turn back, pointing my spatula at her. "Don't tell a soul, either. It would ruin my reputation."

"Your reputation?"

"Yeah. I'm not supposed to like this fake, powdered cheese, and disgusting American food. I'm losing touch, but I deserve to be miserable about it without my people knowing the truth."

She snorts.

The water comes to a boil, and I dump in the little noodles. "You sure you don't want any?"

"I'm stuffed, but I'd take you up on it any other day."

"Fair enough." Moving to the fridge, I grab my other supplies: milk, butter, and shredded cheddar cheese. I don't stop there, grabbing the garlic powder and smoked paprika from the spice cabinet before putting everything (including the powdered crap they provide) into a smaller pan, melting and mixing it into a cheese sauce from heaven. The noodles are ready just in time, and I add them into my concoction. It's not my first time robbing Ara blind of this orangey goodness.

I take a little bite to make sure it's ready.

Fucking masterpiece.

"And you've never shown your little recipe to anyone else?"

"Absolutely not. It's part of my culture, shitting on you Americans. I can't go falling in love with things like fake cheese." Or anything else, for that matter.

"Okay, hand it over. I need to try this."

I pin her with a look. "I asked if you wanted any and you said no."

"I just want a *bite*." She rounds the island, coming up close.

Everything in my mind quiets down as her hand comes up to my chest, running down my front and grabbing the waistband of my jeans to yank me closer. I'm so distracted by the prospect of what's about to unfold, I completely miss her reaching around me to snag my bowl of cheesy heaven. It only registers as she quickly backs away, sporting a victorious smile before stuffing a spoonful of Mac & Cheese into the mouth I was just getting ready for.

Brooke's eyes roll back into her head, letting out a groan which should be illegal, and definitely not for Mac & Cheese. "This is fucked-up good."

"I know, so give it back."

She shakes her head before putting another spoonful into her mouth. "Mm-mmm."

"Don't make me come and get it."

Her eyebrow lifts with challenge, but lowers as she thinks better of it, piling another mound into her mouth before handing the bowl over. "Fine. Here."

"Thank you." That's a relief because those chasing games only result in adorable shit.

I take a bite and my soul is instantly soothed, then another one, before passing the bowl back to Brooke and sliding down to the floor with my back against the island. Indecision marks her features for a moment before she takes another bite, slides down next to me, and passes the bowl back. We sit there quietly, passing it back and forth until the spoon scrapes the bottom of the empty bowl. I insisted on Brooke having the last bite because I'm not all bad.

LAST *Stand* FOR GENEVIEVE

Closing my eyes, I tip my head back against the wall of the island and run my fingers through my hair. My Ice Queen stays quiet, as if this sort of interaction is foreign to her. I won't lie, it's a little foreign to me too. Not the comfort or having someone be there for me, but having an interaction with a woman I'm sleeping with, that doesn't require being in the nude.

It's been this way between us since the beginning, but I'm only acknowledging it now. Whether we're playing *Home Improvement* or trying to make each other miserable, I genuinely enjoy having her around. Even if we're just sitting in silence, like right now. Maybe I was purposely trying not to notice, or maybe it was because it's never been more clear than right now. With my emotions so raw from the day, I've lost control of them all.

Brooke reaches over and pulls my hand from my hair, lacing her fingers through mine. It's perhaps the most innocent touch we've shared, but looking at the way her fingers wrap around mine has me drifting away.

This goes beyond the touch. It's not just her fingers she's lacing me up with, it's the knowledge that she's choosing to hold me. Brooke is choosing to be here when she doesn't have to be, *outside* of our arrangement. She's choosing to touch me, not for gratification, but because she knows I've had a shit day.

Brooke may never be the woman who wants to spill her secrets or discover my depths. I may never be the man who buys her flowers just because it's Tuesday, but *this*? This is enough. This is all either of us can give, and it's all I could want.

We sit there for a while, lost in our own thoughts, sharing space instead of words. At first only our hands touch, but as the minutes tick by, our shoulders become pressed together, her knee draped over mine. Every point of contact is a beacon of relief, never erasing what I lost in Jayden today, but something that reminds me there's still hope out there.

I *will* figure out what to tell the guys, and I'll sell my soul if that's what it takes to find another lead singer whom our fans will love just as much as they once loved Jayden, if not more. We can survive this. *I* can survive this.

And maybe one day I'll have it in me to forgive Jayden for giving up on himself.

Peering at the enigma beside me, I'm surprised to find her eyes already on me. The icy depths send me into a freezing plunge, so cold that I feel like I'm on fire. Suddenly the places where our bodies touch are not just a beacon of relief, but a promise for what's about to transpire.

We move in sync, our lips finding each other in the dim lighting like they could do it anywhere, as if one day when we weren't paying attention, we became ingrained into each other's cellular makeup. I lift her up, carrying her through the hallway to my room.

Her arm wraps around my neck, pulling me down as she leans back onto my bed and I oblige, letting her feel my entire body as I come over her. The way her curves feel against mine never feels repetitive, as if I could spend every single night discovering the different ways she moves. Every different sound she makes. Every different way she breathes.

I've been captured by her spell, landing somewhere between the twilight zone and Stockholm syndrome. Ice Queen has captured me against my will, yet instead of raging against it, I'm a man who's lost his mind. Nothing more than a rabbit caught in a snare, except I *never* fucking want to get free, *praying* that I remain a captive of her soft skin, sharp tongue, clever mind, and mood swings.

As our bodies move together, we become a song that never dulls, no matter how many times you play it. Touching her is lyrical genius, a perfect melody sent from the stars. Tonight is different, deliberately unhurried, sharing everything we couldn't bring ourselves to voice with our bodies instead. Our rhythm ebbs and flows, we take and we give, until we combust into a crescendo that supersedes anything that has previously existed in this universe.

Brooke doesn't pull out of my arms straight away. We aren't cuddling, but we aren't *not* cuddling as she lays on her stomach beside me, her face laid against her arm as she gazes up at me. Much like the rest of the night, it feels unusually intimate.

Something captures my attention, derailing my thoughts before they inevitably reach the warning bells. "What's this?"

I trace my fingers over the tattoo between her shoulder blades that I hadn't noticed until now. Two quarters of the tattoo are beautiful, anatomically correct wings. The other two quarters are shaped the same, but made of beautiful tiny flowers, tulips if I were to guess. When I look closely, I swear the top left has an almost imperceptible outline of the letter *G* in the same way that the bottom right has an *M*.

After freezing for a moment too long, my Ice Queen shrugs. "I woke up with it one morning, after getting black-out drunk the night before."

With the detail and artistic perfection, it's much more than a drunken tattoo, but I leave it at that, intending to descend back into a comfortable silence, still coming down from such a tremendous high.

"The family we helped…they belonged to someone I once knew. A friend."

Her admission leaves me dazed. Although, I had already assumed as much, I know this moment is tender. She is offering me a piece of her soul, *willingly,* a tiny clue into the secrets that have made her into the woman she is today.

And I didn't know how much I needed it.

Something tiny, yet monumental, shifts between us before she gets out of my bed and sees herself out.

CHAPTER THIRTY-ONE

Then - Brooke

It's too late to sleep now, or early, depending on how you look at it. My guess is it's coming up to about 6:30 in the morning at this point. Just as I'm about to beg Ziggy not to walk us all the way back to that bridge, she takes a turn in the opposite direction.

We haven't been talking, not a single word.

She threatened me, but for some reason I'm not holding it against her. If someone had threatened what I cared about most, I would have done the exact same thing. So why are we being quiet? Because witnessing that made me know her, and now she knows that I know her.

Where does that leave us?

Still just backup until we find something better?

Between the thoughts plaguing the walls of my mind, and the exhaustion from walking all night, the rest of our walk is nothing but a blur until all of a sudden, I realize Ziggy is picking a lock. She must have been working at it for a while too (before I snapped out of the fog), because there's a little click before she celebrates in words I don't understand.

Peering at our surroundings for the first time, I realize we're at a high school. Thankfully, it's not mine, but a rival of the one I went to, so I'm familiar with it having come here many times as the cheerleading captain.

"Bringing back the golden days?" Ziggy jokes, but her tone is hollow, lacking the typical spice she sprinkles atop her words.

"Who said they were ever gold?"

"Ohhhh, come on, *mija*. You probably owned halls like these."

LAST *Stand* FOR GENEVIEVE

She isn't wrong, but looking back, it meant a whole lot of fucking nothing. "And it was plastic and terrible. The mask I wore was suffocating, I'd just never realized it."

There. A tiny little shred of me, so the footing is a tad more even.

We walk inside, the only light being that which creeps in through the various small windows along the hallway. Trophies and pictures line the walls, filling the glass cases with team spirit in the physical form. This team was always especially…*proud.* For shits and giggles, I walk up to one of the cases that sports the trophies from a much more recent year.

My senior year.

Our football team had lost the championship to theirs by an extra point. It was absolutely brutal. We had all been so upset that night, having been in the lead until the very end before the win got ripped away from us. I snort, remembering how destroyed I was over something so trivial.

"Hate to be the one to tell you this, but you definitely peaked in high school." Ziggy leans in closer, as if to get a better look.

"Huh?"

"Look who I found looking like a *loro gritando.*"

I take a step over to where she is, and sure-fucking-enough, there I am. I'd forgotten all about this part of the night.

"Is it even legal to win by an extra point!? Surely they have to make a goal."

I roll my eyes. "Wrong sport, Gen."

"Whatever, you know what I mean."

"Whether it was by one point or ten, they won." I shrug, attempting to put on a good face even though I'm fucking pissed about it. This night has meant everything to the team, to my squad, and our school. I don't know how we'll ever recover from such a blow to our spirits.

The worst part? Our spirits are my entire responsibility as cheer captain.

"I think you guys will find a way to come out of it! You always do."

I sigh. Gen is always there for me, the sunshine to my shade. I'm so obsessed with being the best, sometimes it gets a little dark in here. But every time it does, she's always there, turning on a flashlight and grabbing my hand.

"I mean it, Brooke, you'll be fine."

She can tell I'm not convinced, and she does that adorable little nose scrunch she does when she's anything but at rest. Gen's nose scrunches when she's stumped, feeling awkward, curious, embarrassed, the whole gamut really, except pissed because I've never seen her mad since the day she was born. She came out like spring, all tulips and life, and nothing and nobody has ever been able to turn her cold.

"Just add some extra twerking to your routine, I'm sure the boys will perk right up."

I snort, because well, she's probably right. For someone who claims to be allergic to socializing, Gen has figured out more about human behavior than all of us. She sits on the outside and watches, learning. Without being wrapped up in being the center of it all (my greatest weakness), she's far above any of the rest of us. While we climb the ladder, she's the one who's watching from the rooftop, the key to the game being not to play.

My walls start to crack a little and she smiles, victorious as usual. Gen always gets me to crack, banishing my seriousness with a giggle and sprinkle of her magic. "I guess I could talk to my co-captain—"

"Ooooooo!!! And you should change the music to something circa 2000s, with the lyrics involving drops, floors, and popping."

I smile. "You're a true mastermind, Gen."

She dusts off her shoulders. "It's no big deal."

I wrap my arm around her shoulder to lead us away, but she locks up in place.

"Gen? What is it? What's wrong?"

"You have a split second to decide whether or not you think I'm insane. If you do, walk away; otherwise, get next to me and strike the most horrific pose you can think of."

I step closer to her. "You're definitely insane, but it's on brand."

She points, and I realize the winning team has gathered all together, holding the trophy in the air. Their school photographer has finally set up the camera just right, and is counting down toward the click, with me and Gen (sheer luck) standing behind them, but just off to the side. We're definitely still in frame, but not enough to be noticeable right away.

4, 3, 2...1

I stick out my tongue and launch two middle fingers in the air.

Flash.

They didn't choose the one of me with my middle fingers up, but the aftermath of me spotting the pose Gen had chosen. She'd bent over, ass facing the camera with her hands on her butt. It'd sent me straight into hysterics because it was so unlike her. I'd expected a goofy grin, but she'd wholeheartedly

LAST *Stand* FOR GENEVIEVE

committed.

They must have continued to snap photos, because in this one, Genevieve is on the ground, trying not to pee her pants while I'm uncontrollably laughing, a second away from dropping down beside her.

"Who's that with you?"

I shrug, shoving everything down. "Some random I met at the game who happened to have the same idea."

We continue to look at the picture. It's extremely painful, but the memory is so fond that for a second it blocks out the pain. For just a second, I remember what it was like to exist without agony and feel the warmth Gen brought everywhere with her.

After a moment, Ziggy meets my eyes, reading what I don't say aloud.

She was the person who was everything to me, until she became everything I lost and everything I'll never recover from.

Ziggy nods, letting me know she understands while giving me her blessing to keep it locked up tight. "Well, this is boring. Let's find the showers. You fucking stink, *mija*."

Ziggy is terrible at *just* being backup.

• • •

She's also terrible at singing.

I mean, the acoustics of a high school shower room aren't great to begin with, but holy hell, I'll be lucky to still have the ability to use my ears after this.

"Hey, Ziggy?"

"Yes, *mija*?"

"Don't quit your day job."

"*Ayyyyy*, give me a break. I was only a little off-key."

"For you to be off-key, it would mean that whatever that was had the other ingredients of singing. That was…a shitty impersonation of a donkey, *if* I'm being generous."

Ziggy scoffs. "Like you could do any better."

I laugh. "I couldn't, hence why I keep my mouth shut."

"You're just jealous because I'm the next Shakira."

I snort. "Of course, you are."

201

"Crazier things can happen, *mjia*."

Cheers to that.

We descend back into quiet as I relish in the feel of the water gliding down my body. I *really* needed this shower. We're trying to preserve the hot water, so it's only warm, but what it lacks in degrees, it makes up for in solace. Although this week has stained my soul in irreparable ways, this shower feels cleansing.

Showers have always been my reset button. When Dad left, it allowed me to cry without leaving the evidence or having to wipe my tears and stifle my sobs. In high school, it was the part of the day that I finally got to wash away my mask and be the real me. Perhaps this shower could erase some of the marks on my soul too.

We'd managed to find a stray bottle of body wash in the boy's shower room, the girls likely spending way too much on their regimen to risk leaving it behind, so icy douchebag scent it is. At least it's better than body odor.

"Ziggy, heads up!"

I toss the bottle over the shower wall that separates us, and she catches it on the other side before it slips through her fingers and crashes against the ground. Whatever it is about showers, everything feels louder when it falls.

Drop the shampoo bottle? People in the next country heard it.

Ziggy lets out a string of curses. "We should go, just in case someone heard that."

"Okay."

We take a moment longer, Ziggy washing and me just…standing here. With my eyes closed and head tipped back, the warm water flowing over me, I can almost pretend that when I step out, I'll be stepping into my own bathroom, in my old home. I'd walk downstairs with a towel wrapped around my head and join Gen for breakfast.

I can pretend.

And I do.

Until the water cuts off, breaking the spell.

• • •

"Ziggy, this is a bad idea."

LAST *Stand* FOR GENEVIEVE

"You're not hungry?"

"I *am*, but can't we just sneak into the cafeteria? You're going to hurt your arm." Ziggy bends her arm into an even worse angle, giving the impression that it's about to snap. I turn my back, not able to watch as she gets close to dislocating something. "I don't know how to pop anything back into place, so be prepared to be left in misery."

"*Mija*, I've done this many times before. Just stand there and be a pretty little lookout."

I roll my eyes, even though she doesn't see it, before swiveling my head around to make sure we're alone. Either security sucks in this place, or we really are alone. After a few more minutes of grunting and torture to her poor elbow, Ziggy manages to dislodge a snack from the bottom row on the vending machine.

"*Ayayayayayaya*!!"

"Ziggyy!!! Shhhh!!!!"

"I got the Oreos! It's worth celebrating."

"Okay. Great." Something is spooking me, and I don't like the feeling. Maybe the empty halls are just getting in my head, or paranoia (my new bestie) is back. Either way, I want to get out of here. "Let's go."

"No way, I'm having good luck today. I'm going back for the Doritos."

Staring bullets through the back of her head, I realize trying to dissuade her is completely futile. Once Ziggy decides on something, she's doing it, but I flinch at the sound of a door closing somewhere, followed by the loud echo that comes with an empty school. Not paranoia then.

"Ziggy. We need to go."

"Just…gimme one more *segunda*…"

"We need to go *now*."

Another door closes, the sound bouncing off the floors and lockers, making it seem like it's coming from every direction. Either Klaus Mikaelson is about to hold us prisoner in a classroom to lure the Salvatore brothers, or security is finally making an appearance and they know that someone is inside.

"Ziggy! *Now*!"

The crinkle of wrapping tells me the vending machine has finally lost the battle, and Ziggy will get to snack on Doritos while we run for our lives.

"Happy now!?"

"Okay, okay, *mija*. I'm coming."

Another door opens and closes, this time much closer. Whoever it is, is nearly to us now.

"Uh…small *problema*…" Ziggy trails off.

"Hey!!!!"

Adrenaline shoots through me as a booming voice nearly knocks me on my ass from the very far end of the hallway. Fortunately, he's about as far away as he can be despite having eyes on us, but unfortunately, he's not old, and he's not out of shape.

"ZIGGY!!"

"*Mija*, I'm stuck." She goes to pull back, and swears. "*Oh, mieda.*"

"*WHAT!?*" I rip my gaze away from the security guard who's making his way to us. The long, baggy sleeve of her t-shirt is caught around the metal claws, and it's not giving way. With her angle, she doesn't have the strength to tear it or lift it enough to unhook it.

"Fuck!!!"

Ziggy looks back toward the security guard who's neared the middle of the hallway now. "*Mija*, you need to go, I'll catch up with you, but right now you need to *go*."

My eyes widen at what she's saying. She wants me to leave her, and if I don't make a decision now, we'll both be grabbed. Do people go to juvie for breaking into a school without vandalism? Didn't the guy in *Step Up* just get community service? Am I about to have a dance battle? I'm panicking. I need to move. But I can't.

"*Run, mija!!!!!!*" Ziggy screams, breaking me out of my stupor. I take off in the opposite direction of the security guard, knowing immediately that I'm probably going to regret this for the rest of my life. My stomach sinks with the weight of it, but it's not like shit can get any worse.

Skidding to a stop in front of a closet I'd spotted earlier, I throw open the door and know that the guardian angel who watches over delinquent children is on our side today. Grabbing the empty metal hanger, I run back around the corner.

Ziggy is still struggling, and the security guard is nearly upon her. My heart pounds as I squat down, bending the metal hanger in a way that will hopefully allow me to reach Ziggy's sleeve. I push it up through the flap, and it

LAST *Stand* FOR GENEVIEVE

reaches her sleeve, but does that weird bendy thing, and falls out of my hands.

"Fuck!!" I grab it from where it's fallen like a snack, but it's too late. The security guard puts his hands on Ziggy's backpack, and I know that if he pulls hard enough, he could really hurt her without even meaning to. Ziggy starts to struggle, and I'm back on my feet.

"*Quitate de encima, animal*!!"

"Get your hands off of her!" I shout, as I kick the security guard right in the shin.

Maybe I'm not a blackbelt, but everyone has a shin, and every man has a nut sac. Just as I expect, his grip loosens on Ziggy's backpack, and he bends over just slightly as the pain lashes through his leg. It's just enough for me to have the perfect angle…

My foot meets his groin, and I hope the poor dude already knocked up his girl, because I'm not sure how much of a chance he'll have after that bullseye of a kick, his face purpling as he falls to the ground.

"Fuck yeah, *mija*!!" Ziggy cheers, though I can tell by the sweat dripping down her forehead that she is far from celebrating yet. Her arm is still stuck, and I only have seconds before he's back on his feet.

Picking up the hanger, I bend it a little better and stick it up the vending machine once more. I take a deep breath, banishing the thoughts of the blondes in the movies who can't get their key in the door, because this blonde is going to save the fucking day. With my heart pounding, I measure my movements to the sound, keeping my hand steady.

I push up, and up, and up, until Ziggy hoots in triumph as her sleeve comes free. I drop the hanger, reach in and grab the Oreos and Doritos, stuffing them into her gigantic pockets before pulling her to her feet.

We take off down the next hallway, taking turn after turn until I see a halo of light up ahead, meaning a door to the outside. We burst through it, setting the alarm off, and leaving it blaring in our wake.

A fire exit. *Naturally.*

"Don't look back, *mija*!! Badasses never look back at the explosions!!"

I try to laugh, but I'm too out of breath. We run and we run until it must have been over a mile, and our lungs and legs threaten to give out. Coming to a stop, we wheeze and wheeze, until I bend over and start puking, as the adrenaline crashes down from the high. It's definitely minutes before either of us can even look at each other.

"*You came back for me*," Ziggy says with her eyes.

"*Don't fucking mention it*," I say with mine.

"How are those claws, *mija*?"

"Sharp."

Ziggy grins, and it's nothing short of hellish. "Sure as fuck they are."

Neither of us says the truth aloud, but now we both know I'd never leave a friend behind.

CHAPTER THIRTY—TWO

Now — Connor

Unsure if it's closure or confirmation that I'm after, I step out of my ute, shutting the door behind me. If anyone is home and conscious, they'll know I've arrived. Taking a deep breath, I summon the courage to do whatever it is I came here to do.

From the outside, Jayden's place looks like it's been fixed up a bit. The yard has been trimmed, the rubbish removed from where it was scattered on the porch. A dumb part of me perks up at the thought, thinking maybe he left the center because he'd decided to get his shit together on his own.

Met by nothing but silence after a couple knocks on the door, I sigh, the feeling all too familiar. Leaves crunch as I step off his porch, making my way around the side of the house to Jayden's window. It's been fixed since my last visit, and after a peek inside, understanding dawns.

The room is clean, obviously having been repainted and now completely empty. I check the other rooms, and it's all the same, a hollow reminder of the man who was once my friend, a fellow dreamer. I rest my hand against the rough, cement wall, the aftermath of my realization hitting me hard.

Jayden no longer lives here.

With one decision, Jayden could have gotten clean, come back to the band and lived the dream that we'd always talked about. Instead, he chose substances over all else; friendship, success, fame, it meant nothing to him if he couldn't find it at the bottom of a bottle or the inside of a bag.

No matter how hard I try, I just can't understand it. There is nothing in this world I wouldn't give up if I had to choose between *it* and the people who care about me. But that's the difference, isn't it? I don't understand because I've never had to fight that kind of sickness.

So all I have left is anger. Anger that he didn't choose me, that he didn't choose music, and he didn't choose our dream. He made his choice, and I can do nothing but try to let go of my guilt, my resentment, and accept it.

The truth is, if someone is on a path toward destruction, no matter how bad you want to save them, only *they* have the power to decide to change their trajectory. Sometimes the only thing left for you to do is to get out of their way, so you're not taken down with them.

I shake my head, taking one last look behind me before getting back into my ute and pulling out of the driveway. In a way, it feels like the end of a chapter, for both me and *Immoral Support*. Jayden will be a page in our origin story one day, but for me, I'll never forget the bricks he helped me lay. I can only hope that he doesn't forget it either.

It's been a rough few weeks for *Immoral Support*, mostly because the guys and I just aren't whole unless we're working on preparing for another set, but I haven't wanted to commit to anything until we sorted ourselves out. Not to mention, I've had to hold off on writing any new music since I have no idea *who* would be singing it. Not writing music is like trying to suppress my heartbeat.

I had been holding out on finding someone new, hoping that after Poison Ivy, Ryder would come around after seeing the reaction to what we pulled on the stage that night, but nah. He hasn't, and he won't, and it's time for me to let go of the hope of that too.

Today is supposed to put an end to this fuckaround. We've got about five guys coming at various times today to play with us, and I'm banking on the fact that at least one of them will be a good match. A mate of mine agreed to let us use his studio, so I could avoid letting strangers into my home, and that's where I'm headed now.

The studio is over in Clearwater, on the other side of the Courtney Campbell Causeway. I don't mind because this drive has always felt therapeutic to me. Getting to roll down the windows and turn up the music, taking in the sparkling water and palm trees swaying in the breeze, it's a form of healing.

Most people hate Florida, but I like it, especially Clearwater. Sure, some days are borderline unbearable, but nobody can change my mind about it being my favorite place in the world. There's a contentedness about it that I've never experienced anywhere else, not even Tampa, even though it's only a half an hour away. I'm sure there's a beach town somewhere in Australia that'd give it a run for its money, but I haven't been there yet.

I make a mental note to visit this side of the water more often, maybe even take Ice Queen to the beach, see if she melts when I toss her in the water.

Pulling up to the studio, I park and make my way in.

Dane and Rue are already here, getting set up. We'd sent over the lyrics to the guys to get familiar with before coming, but we still have a stand set up for them to read off of.

Dane nods in my direction as I walk through the doorway to the part of the studio we've commandeered. "Hey, man, everything good?"

I do my best to put on a smile. "I have a good feeling about today."

"Good for you guys, I can't find a fucking drum stick worth anything around here. I'm gonna get my own from the car."

I smirk at Rue, always irritated about something.

Dane watches him leave and then quietly, "Jayden?"

I shake my head. "He's gone, Dane. I don't think he's ever coming back."

A somber look crosses his features. "Connor, you did everything you could. This is on *him*."

"I know." And I do…I know it in the way where something *shouldn't* bother you, but it does. Perhaps my biggest weakness of all is wanting to help. Some say it's a strength, but at times like these, it feels like the chink in my armor that's going to get me killed. Regardless of the fact that I'm not the one who started him on that path, nor am I the one who chose for him to stay on it, I can't shake the feeling of responsibility.

Rue comes back a second later, pumping a better set of drumsticks in the air. "Wanna fuck around a little before they get here?"

Dane meets my eyes, and we nod simultaneously. We both need it. When things have gotten tough in the past, or if one of us needed to blow off some steam, we'd get together and just play music for fun, just to remind ourselves why we do this. Today, we decide to play a little game of Russian roulette, karaoke style.

Essentially, I put my some twenty-five-thousand saved songs on shuffle, and we have to cover the first one that comes on, no matter *what* it is.

"You guys ready?" They nod, so I choose *All Songs* and hit the little shuffle button. A laugh bursts out of me, knowing that Rue is just going to *love* this. Pushing pause before the first note can play out, I let the anticipation build with my smirk. "'Girls Just Want to Have Fun' by Cyndi Lauper."

Rue sputters, "Dude! Why do you even have that song saved!?"

Dane laughs. "Worried about your manhood, Rue?"

Shaking his head, Rue goes, "We need to use someone else's music. I'm sick of Connor's ridiculous fucking songs. Never once have we gotten Linkin Park, Our Last Night, or *anything* good. It's always shit like this."

"That's what makes it so interesting," I say with a laugh. What can I say, I love all music. In every song, I can find something to appreciate. An artist put their heart and soul into it, and a lot of work, so why not give them a save?

But also, I secretly fucking love Cyndi Lauper.

We listen to the song once through, just to get a bit of familiarity, and I watch the lyrics as Apple Music rolls them up the screen. I already know the words by heart, but the guys don't need to know that. The song plays out and we get into our spots.

Rue takes his place at his drum set, Dane puts the shoulder strap over his head and does a little strum on the bass. I pick up my guitar, doing the same before clearing my throat. One thing I know? I'll always be able to rely on these two.

"I'm glad I have you guys." With the emotion clear in my voice, Dane gives me a knowing nod.

Rue snorts. "The music in your saves is starting to make more sense."

"What do you mean?"

"The Disney songs? Fergalicious? Whitney Houston the time before that? I'm starting to think you're hiding a vagina down there, Connor."

I laugh, unable to help it. "Shut the fuck up and start us off."

The performance is dog shit, I'm singing off key, the guys are completely off with their notes, but that's not what this is about. We're laughing our asses off, stepping outside of our comfort zone and having fun with our music. The seriousness of today is left at the doorstep, and we're ready to take this on with the right headspace: we do this because it makes us happy. Full stop.

The first guy comes in shortly after we finish our little karaoke session. Unfortunately, he's a definite no because our voices just don't complement each other, and sorry, mate, but I was here first. The second guy is good, and honestly, it's a little bit of a relief to know I have someone to fall back on, should the rest go terribly. The third isn't better than the second, so we move onto the fourth who is probably so nervous, it could have gone a lot better if he wasn't, but I can't have someone with nerves that high.

The fifth and final guy, named Dylan, comes in with an easy air about him. Never been in a band or performed outside of his own four walls, but he figured he'd take a shot at it since people have told him he's got a good voice. Turns out, Dylan's been a fan of *Immoral Support* since the early days, but he seems as relaxed as anyone could be standing here with us.

Rue starts us off, me and Dane following his lead with the bass and guitar. Dylan steps up to the mic, his foot tapping to the beat before opening his mouth to sing the first line of the song. Thankfully, I have a shoulder strap on because I'm pretty sure I would have dropped my guitar otherwise.

Dylan is good. Really fucking good. Almost as good as Jayden. Nobody has a voice like Ryder's, so I don't let myself compare the two because it'd be completely unfair to Dylan here. And unlike Ryder, Dylan wants to be here.

We finish the song, and I glance back at the guys. Dane looks pleased, and Rue looks less annoyed than he has all day.

"Thanks, mate, that was great." I reach over, bumping knuckles with Dylan to show my appreciation.

"All good. Even if nothing comes from it, it was a dream to play with you guys. I know you'll be big one day, and it'll be a cool story to tell."

Dylan can sing, and he seems like a cool guy too. A massive weight lifts from my shoulders, knowing things could definitely work out. It would take a little effort, teaching him the ropes of live vocals and keeping the crowd entertained, but he has what it takes.

"We'll be in touch. Have a good night, Dylan."

"See you, man."

"Later."

We wait for Dylan to close the door behind him, before turning to each other.

"He was good. Really good," Dane offers.

"I agree. Think we could make something work with that kid." Rue pitches in.

Relief floods through me. "Then I'll call him tomorrow, let him know he's got a place with us."

A weight lifts from my chest as they nod their support. Pleased that I'm not the only one feeling like this could work, I pull out my phone.

Connor: I'm almost done here. I could swing by after.

Ice Kween: Swing by where?

Connor: Your place...?

Connor: I still haven't seen it, and you could just be catfishing me this whole time.

Ice Kween: You know what I look like...

Connor: But I don't know what your place looks like.

Ice Kween: And you're not missing much. I'll come by yours after work.

I sigh. Outside of fixing that home and learning the family inside once belonged to someone she knew, I haven't gotten a single glimpse into her life since. Where she lives, what she does for work, and everything else is just a big fat question mark. Sure, she did trash duty for Joe at least once, but I have no idea if it's a regular thing.

At this point, I'm practically convinced that she's a spy, with her never being home or letting anyone get close.

Connor: You're a spy, aren't you?

Ice Kween: No, but you ARE a fucking idiot.

Connor: That's what a spy would say.

Ice Kween: I'll see you tonight.

Ice Kween: At YOUR place.

The most intimidating part about her life being mostly hidden from me? Is that I know that I'll take what I can get.

• • •

As it's been for the last few weeks, she comes over late, past the time anyone else in this house is awake, even Oscar. The elevator dings, and my stomach drops.

LAST Stand FOR GENEVIEVE

Ice Queen comes in wearing a short black skirt, tight around her thighs and hips. An oversized cream sweater is tucked into the low waist of her skirt, and a white collared shirt appears from the neckline, paired with her usual, squeaky clean, white sneakers.

And I'm a dead man.

She walks in completely nonchalant, tossing her little bag onto the island and kicking off her shoes, as if she isn't the most irresistible, mental-haze-inducing fucking woman. Brooke is completely unaware of the absolute chokehold she has on me any time she enters the room. The centrifugal force that has me trapped.

Brooke takes her place at the bar stool, like she's done almost every night these few weeks. I take out the little pot, the way I do as soon as she's sat down. We do this little "Honey, I'm home!" ritual every night, and although we pretend it's nothing more than a late-night snack, in reality it's an excuse to talk. It's the only time we do, and if I end up putting on a bunch of kilos because of it, it'll still be worth it.

As I bring the water to a boil, I dump in the Mac & Cheese noodles.

"How did today go?"

I shake my head. Even though it's a little sweet that she asked about my day, a side she rarely shows, tonight I'm determined to learn a little more about her. "Nah, it's your turn tonight. At least tell me what you do for work?"

She groans, as if she knew this was coming. "Another game of twenty questions?"

I point my cooking spoon at her. "You'd have to actually answer for it to be considered playing a game."

Eye roll. "I'm a bit of a nomad. I used to work really hard at everything I did, but at the end of the day it got me nowhere. Now I just do a little bit of here and there, but it's all completely legal, and not under the jurisdiction of a single agency, national or foreign. Until I start my own thing one day, I'm content."

"What would you do if you could?"

Shrug. "Not sure."

"You never had a dream growing up?"

"I didn't say that, but things change."

"Okay." Point taken, moving on in conversation and giving the noodles a bit of a stir. "Why don't you have social media?"

213

"There's better things to do with my time, and I'm not exactly a sharer, in case you hadn't noticed."

I whip back around, shock across my features, tone oozing with sarcasm. "Nooo!? That is definitely news to me."

Brooke snorts, and I turn back to drain the noodles and mix in the other ingredients.

"Besides, I think it's a bit of a trap. Nothing is worse than having a bad day, then going on there to see someone who seemingly has it all together, making whatever is going on in your head a hundred times worse."

"Are you saying that from personal experience?"

"I guess. It's how I felt in high school when I had it. But I deleted it a few years ago and just never downloaded it again. Felt more peaceful without it."

"Why did you delete it originally?" A cold draft drags across my back as I dump my mixture into the noodles, meaning I've pushed my limits for tonight. "Food is ready."

"How was it today?" She ignores the question she doesn't want to answer entirely.

I sigh, filling up our bowl and grabbing a spoon. We make our way to the side of the island, both of us sliding down to the floor with our legs extended in front of us. Don't ask me why we do this, but we do. There's plenty of sit-worthy surfaces in this penthouse, but this spot feels like ours.

"Started out pretty shit. I went to Jayden's old flat, but he was gone. All of his things too. He completely ghosted, without even a word."

"I'm sorry." And I can tell she really means it. There's emotion and regret in her eyes, cementing my theory that someone she loved struggled with an addiction.

"It's time I accepted that we weren't enough for him."

Brooke hesitates, debating her next words and choosing them carefully. "I don't think he felt that *you* weren't enough. At the root of his problem are all the ways he feels like *he* isn't enough. Jayden left because he knew you wouldn't give up on him, and he didn't want to keep hurting you." She hands our bowl back to me even though neither of us have taken a bite yet, and pauses with her fingers grazing mine. "But you were enough for him. That, I know."

Control is completely taken away from me as I set the bowl aside and lean forward, capturing her lips in mine. We kiss all the time, but it's never *just*

LAST *Stand* FOR GENEVIEVE

kissing. It's never paired with a tender moment, and it never stops at our lips. Where it's usually an all-consuming war and freezing fire traveling through my entire body, this kiss fires a direct, powerful blow to my chest. It feels like I've been crushed, my ribs have been shattered, and it's hard to breathe.

Her soft, pillowy lips have become ingrained into my makeup, like a vicious disease your immune system can't fight because it thinks it's part of your own body. Her comforting words have unlocked an unfamiliar feeling inside of me, a fervor that goes far beyond physical limits.

We remember ourselves in the same moment, the kiss coming to a jarring halt, yet we both hesitate before pulling away, as if it was the hardest thing we've ever done. Brooke doesn't meet my eyes, just picks the bowl up from where I'd placed it a moment ago and takes a bite.

"How did the audition part go?"

It hurts a little, the way she can move on as if nothing just happened, while I'm still failing to gather my bearings. I clear my throat. "Well, we needed a cheer up, so before we started, we had a little round of Russian roulette karaoke–"

"A round of *what*?"

I smirk. "A little game the guys and I came up with a while back after a shitty show and we were convinced we couldn't play a damn thing. We shuffled my music and forced ourselves to learn and play whatever song came on, regardless of the drama. It's usually bloody awful, and that's what makes it so fun."

Brooke abruptly gets on her feet before sticking a hand out to pull me up after her. "Come on, I think we both need some cheering up."

CHAPTER THIRTY-THREE

Then - Brooke

"You're cute," I say with a smile, letting my eyes wander enough that I know I'll have to bleach them later.

The cashier smiles. "Yeah? You're not so bad yourself."

Not so bad? I'm way out of this dude's league.

I grab a piece of hair and begin twirling it around my finger, tipping my head down so I can look up at him through my eyelashes. "You really think so?"

He shifts uncomfortably in his chair, putting his hand in his pocket. It takes a lot not to vomit on the plastic window that separates us across the counter, but I manage to bat my eyes a little more. "Yeahhh."

Ziggy coughs somewhere behind me, nearly failing to keep her shit together. If she doesn't hurry up, I'm going to kill her the moment we get out of here. Strangulation is looking better and better.

"What's your name?" he asks me, hand moving around in his pocket.

"Carolina."

"Carolina?"

"Uh-huh." Not sure why he had to repeat it back to me. "What's your name, cutie?"

Ziggy coughs again and the cashier's eyes catch on something behind me. Shoving her into traffic could also be an option. I need to get his attention back and fast.

"I asked for your name, cutie." I let out a giggle, featuring a little throw up in the back of my mouth.

216

LAST *Stand* FOR GENEVIEVE

His eyes are back on me. "Conan."

"It's soooo nice to meet you, Conan."

A can of Pringles hits the floor, rolling all the way down one of the aisles, toward where I stand at the checkout. I bite my cheek to keep myself from grimacing. Ziggy's head pokes out a second later.

"Can't you see we're in the middle of talking?" I growl.

She puts her hands up in acquiescence, but it's one of those moments where because you can't laugh, you lose all control, even if something isn't that funny. Like when you're presenting something to the class that's worth half your grade, and a face in the back that you've seen every day since you were seven suddenly becomes the most hilarious thing you've ever seen? You skip laughter entirely and go straight to those horrific, squealing pig sounds, and tears start pouring down your face?

Yeah. Like that.

Ziggy's the first to lose it, and I clamp my jaw tight, looking away from Conan the cashier in an effort to not give myself away as I summon the strength not to laugh. Just as I think I'm in the clear, I make eye contact with Ziggy and I burst the farting balloon that's trying to hold back as Ziggy squeals like a piglet.

Then we're moving, but you can't move very fast when you're laughing.

"Kyyyeewwww-TEEEEEEE!!!" Ziggy wails, and I nearly hit the ground as I grab her arm, dragging her away.

The belled glass door crashes against the outer wall behind us, slack-jawed Conan throwing it open to watch our graceless escape, just as a bag of Doritos falls out of Ziggy's pants.

"HEY!!!" he yells, pointing at us.

I snatch the bag off the ground and we take off running. We're still howling and I definitely just peed a little, but we keep going until we get far enough away that we can stop. Somehow we always end up back at this godforsaken field.

"I'm. Always. Running. Because. Of. You." I pant, but I can't sound angry because we're still going in and out of hysterical laughter.

"Kyeww-teeee!!" Ziggy is still laughing, wiping her eyes. "Ah, I'll never forget that for as long as I die."

Wheeze. Gasp. "For as long as you live?"

"*Si.*" Wheeze. Cough.

I hold my hand out like a claw, which in the language of breathless Brooke means "Gimme." Ziggy reaches into one of her deep jacket pockets and pulls out a yellow Gatorade.

"Are you fucking kidding me!? I did all of that for the lemon-lime flavor!?

Ziggy frowns. "What's wrong with *lima limon*?"

"Everyone knows that's the worst flavor!"

"I didn't realize you would be so *quisquillosa*!"

"I save your ass, seriously risking my own, TWICE, and you give me a lemon-lime Gatorade!?" I nod slowly, pointing at her. "I'll remember this."

"*Ayyyyyy*, mija, relax, okay? I'll make it up to you. Just drink the fucking Gatorade, you look like you're about to pass out."

The plastic lid cracks open, and I gulp down several sips before grimacing. It's not doing revolutionary things for my taste buds, but it's helping with the dizziness. I'm definitely dehydrated, and severely lacking in the food and sleep departments. If one could feel pale, that's how I'd describe it.

"We need to keep going," Ziggy says eventually.

I groan, but she grabs my arm and starts pulling me to the edge of the field, shoving me under a tree for some shade.

"You had your candy today?"

I shake my head, knowing what she means.

She frowns. "Take one now."

"What?" My brows shoot up.

"Your body is going into panic mode, and we can't have that."

Reaching into my jeans, I do as she says, but for some reason, I feel weird about it. I hadn't necessarily been feeling the need, but she's right. As the adrenaline recedes, my body is about to shut down, and we don't have the resources for that.

I plop a pill onto my tongue, and she hands me a Twix bar to wash it down and get some sugar pumping along with it. Ziggy holds her Gatorade against my forehead, mine having already been guzzled back. Did I do that? I don't even remember.

"Why is Florida so fucking hot?"

Ziggy shrugs. "I like the weather here."

"You're genuinely the only person who has said those words out loud."

LAST *Stand* FOR GENEVIEVE

"How's the head?"

"Better. Less spinny."

"Good. Then we gotta keep moving."

I groan, but Ziggy hoists me up. Have I been sitting down?

We're walking toward the nicer part of Tampa again, sort of on the way to our little bridge. For some reason, even though I'm an actual criminal now, I always feel safer when we cross that invisible threshold, like the other bad guys can't get me here.

"Where are we going?"

"Just wait here." Ziggy plops me on a bench, it's a weird angle with my backpack still on, but I'm not going to take it off. I need to stay alert, watching her back, but my eyes are threatening to close.

At some point, they do because suddenly I'm being shaken awake. My eyes fly open, but thankfully it's just Ziggy. She's got water, orange Gatorade, a banana, and protein bars in her hands. They're not stuffed into her pockets, and we aren't running.

"Did you pay for those?"

"*Si.*"

"Oh."

She opens the banana and shoves it in my mouth, right as I open my mouth to make a joke about it.

"God is on our side today."

My grumbled disagreement is muffled by the banana, but Ziggy points her eyes at me.

"He is." Ziggy cracks open the Gatorade and puts it in my hand. "We need supplies, and you need...rest. I've figured out how to get both."

"How?"

Ziggy takes a seat next to me as a beautiful blonde woman comes out of the gas station. Her hair is perfectly in place, makeup expertly done in a way it isn't too much. Her clothes are neutral, but you can tell that the leisure set is expensive.

She's talking on the phone as she makes her way over to the passenger side of her specced-out BMW SUV that would probably take five years of my mom's yearly salary to purchase. Her husband (I presume) is still pumping the gas, and there's a small kid in the back who's rolling the window up and down.

"Did you see that woman?"

I nod. Who wouldn't notice her? She was absolutely beautiful, living the kind of life that every low-income household would dream of.

"Well, I couldn't help but overhear her conversation with the security company." Ziggy opens one of the protein bars and passes it to me. "Their alarm isn't working, which is very concerning because she's driving up to her in-law's place for the weekend."

"And what does that have to do with anything?"

"Well, she was very frustrated to find out that there's been county-wide issues, and the security company won't be able to send a technician until Tuesday, meaning the house will be empty for the next three to four days. With no alarm system."

"Wow. That sucks."

"For her it does, but for us, it's a *mina de oro*."

"Huh?"

"She had to give the address connected to her account for them to pull up the record." Ziggy smiles at me. "Meaning there's an unoccupied mansion, with no alarm, and I know exactly how to find it."

CHAPTER THIRTY—FOUR

Now – Connor

"What are we doing in my rehearsal room?"

Brooke looks at me pointedly. "Russian roulette karaoke. Obviously."

I can't help but laugh, and hand over my phone.

She lifts a brow. "So willing to hand over something that would give me an unobstructed view into your life?"

I shrug, realizing that I'm not opposed to her examining every single aspect of me, whether that be in the real world, or through whatever that device holds of mine. I've never hidden who I am from her, but for some reason right now, I kind of like the idea of her discovering more. "Passcode is 6969."

She snorts, "Of course it is."

I laugh. "I'm just kidding. It's 1225."

"Christmas?"

"Theo's birthday, but yeah, also Christmas."

"If I didn't know any better, I'd think you were in love with him."

"Oh, I am. He's the greatest love of my life." I shrug. "So far, at least."

Her eyes dart up, hanging on mine for a second too long. I have no idea where that last line came from, my full intention having been to never love anyone else again, but the words snuck out, and now I have no idea how to take them back. Or if I should.

She finally looks away and I nearly sag with relief. Had she taken it as some sort of implication that I'd meant her, she'd be out of here faster than I could chase her. The weird thing is that I know I would, because in a way I haven't stopped chasing her since she ripped that cigarette out of my mouth.

Brooke doesn't need to look hard for the music app, since it's pinned at the bottom with the other three of my VIP apps, as I like to call them. Her little thumb taps on it, and I can tell when she reaches the list of all my saved songs, because her eyes widen a little.

"You have so many songs."

"And that's after having to rebuild it. My *family sharing* account with Theo crashed once and I lost all of my music." I shake my head at the memory, it'd destroyed me trying to piece together everything I had lost.

She does a little swipe, scrolling down a ways before smiling. "This is going to be interesting. You have a lot of good stuff in here."

I'm certain what she considers *good* is what would likely be the most embarrassing thing for me to sing, but I have no shame, and even less remorse. "Go ahead and click shuffle. As soon as the song comes up, hit pause in case I need the lyrics."

"Ready?" Brooke says with a mushy grin. It nearly sends me to my knees. I've only seen her this buoyant when she picked out the denim short-shorts.

"Ready."

Brooke hits shuffle and quickly pauses it, her grin getting even mushier, borderlining on goofy. It's a side of her I've never seen, and it's instantly my favorite. She turns the phone in my direction as a giggle escapes her lips.

Cyndi Lauper really is my girl today. "Play it."

Her brows lift in surprise, and with her pert nose and puffy lips, she looks a little too good to be true. "You don't need the lyrics?"

"Fuck no."

She grins, pushing play, and the melody plays out, instantly bringing a smile to my face. Only a monster could resist Cyndi fucking Lauper. My head swivels back and forth, effectively leaving my masculinity in the dust, and I don't mind even a little. I pop my knees and sway my hips side to side. Think Jimmy Fallon lip sync battle performance of the best kind, and double it. I'm putting everything I have into these lyrics and interpretive, pop-sensation moves.

And the way Brooke is looking at me? Fuck.

She's got this glow in her eyes that I've never seen before. Those crystal blue depths are shining with a warmth that reaches into my chest, setting it on fire. They're the color of crystal blue, Caribbean waters warming you at the height of summer. They're the Florida sky on a cloudless afternoon, as the palm trees sway in the breeze. The frost of winter has melted away, making me wonder how I'd ever compared them to ice as I become powerless under her light.

I'd seen the glimmer of potential that day in Target, and that night when I was on stage in front of hundreds and she stood there wearing that horrible skirt just for me, and I'd been the only one she was looking at. Even on the night she comforted me, and I made her Mac & Cheese for the first time, there had been warmth even then.

Those moments had all felt huge, but standing here underneath tonight's gaze and giggles, I know the truth. Those moments had only been microscopic advances, only a tiny peek at the impact of *this* moment.

I keep singing and I keep dancing, making the rehearsal room my stage. Brooke giggles and keeps her eyes pinned on me as I continue to move and sway until the song comes to a close, and with it, a blanket of tension.

Tonight has been different.

This *whole* night, start to fucking finish, has been *different*.

That pull which began to form that night in the kitchen of Operation Defrost, as if someone had started weaving together threads of fate, had only been an inkling. It's become the kind of force that holds an entire galaxy together, as if whoever has been weaving our fates together has finally finished their project, and we are irrevocably entwined.

Neither of us can breathe, and this time, neither of us look away.

Instead, we move in tandem.

Her lips come against mine, no longer frosty but full of heat. I'm burned from the inside out, as everything we'd been fighting against bursts from where we've kept it locked away. I press her against the wall and cradle the front of her throat, tipping her chin back with my thumb so I can taste her deeper.

She moans against my mouth, wrapping her arms around my neck to pull me closer. We aren't close enough, not by a long shot. My hand trails down her front, feeling everything that has been my most grueling torture and generous reward, until I bend and scoop her into my arms.

After that tiny confession about what the family in that house had meant to her, we've never gone back to my room, as if sharing my bed in any way would make this into something too personal. It's been the kitchen, living room, or loft ever since, depending how far we could make it. But tonight, in yet *another* way, will be different.

Brooke doesn't protest as I continue to cradle her, kissing her neck and whispering things in her ear, as I bring us to my room. Setting her down just on the other side of the threshold, she takes it in as if it's the first time I've brought her here.

In a way, it is. We'd been so wrapped up in one another the last time, I don't even remember if I'd gotten the lights on before I laid her down on my bed. Now, she takes her time running her eyes and hands over everything I own. It feels more sensual, more personal than some of the moments I've spent buried inside of her.

Her delicate hands trace over my wooden furniture, the little pictures of me, Theo, and Ara which are stuck to the mirror that sits atop my oak dresser. There's even a few with Ara's best friend Lou smiling brightly, and Ryder's sour face, our perfectly dysfunctional little family.

She makes her way to where my handwritten music hangs, pinned to the cork board on my wall, a peek into my soul waiting at her very fingertips. My brown leather jacket hangs close by, and she surprises me by slipping it on and inhaling deeply, as if she wants my scent to surround her completely.

I snap, crossing the distance between us like an animal, remembering just in time that I will be holding something delicate and more valuable than any precious gem between my palms. So slowly, I slide the leather jacket from her shoulders, hanging it back where she found it and never taking my mouth off of hers.

My fingers find the hem of her cream sweater, lifting it over her beautiful face, before finding the zip on this agony-inducing mini-skirt. She stands there in her stockings and lacy black bra, and it becomes clear how effectively she's ruined me with her body and her soul.

As I reach for the seam of her stockings, my hands start to shake. Something about it makes her swallow, before she peers up at me with those beautiful goddamn eyes, still warm as a summer's day. Relief flows through me, knowing the moment hasn't slipped away from us.

LAST *Stand* FOR GENEVIEVE

I kneel down, pausing to ensure her eyes are locked onto mine as I lazily pull her stockings down her legs. Goosebumps lift across her skin with the movement, and I can't help but lick my lips at the promise of what's to come. With painstaking attention, I remove every bit of lace that remains on her mostly naked body, almost losing myself in my pants before even getting to touch her.

She may think she's at my mercy, but I'm certain that it's the other way around. My reverent touch travels to her breasts, to the soft spot between her legs, as I become certain with my lips and tongue that she's ready for me.

Standing back up to my full height, she moves for my shirt, and I let her pull it off of me, before she reaches up and runs her hands through my hair, as if she can't help herself. I know that she's always loved my hair and strong chin, being the first places her hands go. Even now, her hands move from my hair to trace the line of my jaw, right to the edge of my chin.

Brooke guides my lips back onto hers, as she reaches for my belt and undoes my jeans. Before she can remove them fully, I reach for my back pocket, but she stops my hand with a little shake of her head.

"I got on the pill."

Oh, bloody fucking mercy. I'm a dead man standing.

Her voice is nothing but a whisper. "Have you been with–"

"No." I don't wait for her to finish her question. "Nobody since, well, *you.*"

My words do something to her, the way that word *you* becomes all-encompassing, holding more meaning than perhaps any words we've previously exchanged. She pulls my jeans the rest of the way down, freeing me in a way I've never been freed. I lie her back on the bed, worshiping every inch of her with my mouth and my hands, ensuring that every cell in her body knows that I exist just for them.

I find my way inside of her and it's a pleasure I have *never* known, getting to feel every bit of her warmth and the smallest of movements, it's a closeness with no comparison. With the look in her summer eyes and my name on her lips as she falls over the edge again and again, I find a release that knows no rival, past or future, unless it's with her.

I'm in uncharted territory, terrified for the moment she pulls away and walks out my door, as if this night was completely insignificant to her. My heart tightens at the thought, reminding me exactly why I have rules against this very fucking thing, but instead of following them, I've cut out my heart and offered it up.

We're teetering on the edge of a knife, and it's unnerving to know that whichever way we fall, I will be in dangerous territory. We lie next to each other, motionless besides the rough rise and fall of our breathing, until Brooke rolls on her side to rest her face on my chest. Her index finger traces across my face as she gazes up at me, the only sun which now exists.

We tip, falling in a way that sends your stomach flipping, to the side of the knife that could prove to be the most fatal of the two.

• • •

When my eyes first open, a lazy smile follows at the memory of last night and how comfortable my bed feels. It's warmer than usual, and her lavender scent still wraps around me and the sheets, amazing it's lasted until morning. I could lie here forever.

A soft hand glides down my chest before halting with a jerk. She stiffens next to me, and I stiffen in response, before we both jump out of bed in utter shock as if someone has dropped a bucket of water on us.

Brooke takes the sheet with her, covering herself as if I didn't have my hands and mouth on every inch of her last night. Our eyes dart to the bed and back to each other, enough times that we probably look like we fell out of a cartoon.

Brooke points an accusing finger at me. "This cuddling thing can never happen again."

My jaw drops, offended that she thinks it's *my* fault. "Never fucking ever. I had assumed you'd sneak out!"

"I mean it, Connor," she sputters, "this is…bad."

"Absolutely terrible," I say, concealing my sarcasm well enough.

We nod, still looking at each other with the bed between us, until the moment becomes too comical (even for the once-reigning Ice Queen), and we both crack a smile. My face heats and I look down, feeling unusually bashful. Running my hand through my hair, I glance back up to find her gaze still on me. Her eyes drop all the way down my chest and abs to the part of me that's happiest she's still here.

LAST *Stand* FOR GENEVIEVE

She clears her throat and looks away. "I should probably get going."

"Yeah, no worries." I lock my mouth up, knowing there is an embarrassed ramble trying to escape. Where is the charm? The infallible Connor who made women sigh and gave them wild stories to tell over a glass of wine at girls' night?

Oh, that's right. He went and broke his rules like a fucking idiot.

Brooke gathers up her things, letting the sheet fall away as she gets dressed. I've never done the gentlemanly thing and offered to walk her out, but we've also never woken up snuggling. More important to me than my feelings are hers. Does she want to pretend like nothing has changed? Or would it crush her the way I can no longer deny it would crush me?

Thankfully, I don't have much time to go in circles as she dresses quickly and efficiently, no nonsense as usual. She steps in front of my mirror, and I watch as she combs through her beautiful blonde strands with her fingertips, before pulling it all into a low bun.

Last night blew everything I thought I knew to bits, and I've been reduced to a brainless rubble, stuck with a pair of eyes that follow her every move.

"Connor?"

I'm jarred from my whatever-the-fuck-that-was and come back to reality. Although she's more reserved than last night, as if she woke up this morning and remembered herself, I'm grateful to see her glacier walls haven't slammed me out again. It may not be a summer's day, but thankfully we haven't plunged back into the cold.

"Yeah?"

"I gotta go."

"Right." With a split second to decide, I make my choice. I don't let myself marvel at the fact that Brooke can bring me such peace, her presence seeming to poke holes in the part of me that is sometimes convinced there is no purpose to life. "I'll, uh, see you out."

I lead Brooke down the hallway toward the kitchen (and the only path of escape), sending up a prayer that Theo and Ara aren't up yet. The thing about prayers?

They're not always answered.

As we emerge from the hallway, I immediately wish I'd made a rope from my clothes so Brooke could leave through the window.

"Late mor–" Ara's jaw drops mid word as she spots Brooke, before closing it for a second, just to drop it open again and follow it up with dropping a plate.

Theo, with his back to us, jumps in alarm as the plate shatters on the tile floor. "Ara! What the *fu*–"

His eyes lock on Brooke, his face slackens, and he drops his pan right behind his girlfriend, creating a fucking symphony of the worst kind, and a gruesome murder scene of where my dignity died along with it. Eggs fly everywhere. Pretty sure the food on the stove lights on fire. Someone starts screaming.

Oh wait, that's just Oscar.

"This is NOT what it looks like," I explain with my hands up, as if I'm facing down two wild animals. "We are JUST having sex."

Ara coughs, before becoming the first to get their shit together. "Of course. Right. Just sex. We'd expect nothing else." Then her eyes dart to Theo's in that we-are-definitely-talking-about-this-later way.

Brooke conceals a small smile, before reaching her hand out to Ara. "I'm Brooke."

"I'm Ara!" She wipes her palms across the pajama pants I got her last Christmas, which have Theo's face printed all over them. "It's really nice to meet you. I've heard a lot about–" (I send her a threatening glare, making sure she doesn't finish that sentence the way she wants to) "—lots of random things! About nothing in particular!"

Ara laughs nervously, before turning to tap Theo into the ring.

"I'm Theo." He takes Brooke's hand in his, giving it a gentle shake. "It's nice to meet you, Brooke."

"Nice to meet you guys. I've heard a lot about you both."

Ara giggles hysterically. "Cool."

This whole interchange is going to haunt us all. I know it.

"You can stay for breakfast if you'd like," Theo offers with a welcoming grin, a hell of a lot smoother than the woman by his side. "I promise not to give you anything off the floor."

"Oh, thank you, but I've got to get going anyway," Brooke says, the way I knew she would.

"Right." I clear my throat. "Well, Brooke is leaving now, so uh, feel free to go back to whatever you were just doing."

"Bye!" Ara waves the spatula, sending eggs splattering against the backsplash, and Theo groaning as he reaches for a paper towel.

The downside of an open concept? There's nowhere to bloody hide, but even the universe takes pity on me. Someone must have recently taken the elevator to a floor right below ours, because by some miracle, it doesn't take more than a handful of seconds to arrive.

I follow Brooke into the elevator, not ready to confront the interrogation that is waiting for me in the kitchen, and also because I can't stand the trainwreck that just occurred being the last thought on her mind. It's quiet at first, besides the elevator music which seems to be laughing at me.

"I'm really sorr–"

"Well, that was–"

I smile. "You go first."

"That was *interesting*."

"I'm really sorry about them. I mean, Ara is usually a social invalid, but Theo…" I blow out a breath. "That was uncharacteristically awkward."

"They're not used to you bringing women home?"

Considering what it would reveal, telling her that she's the only woman I've ever brought home, I take a page from her playbook and keep quiet. The little ding rings out, letting us know we've reached the ground floor. As she steps toward the front of the elevator, I capture her hand in mine, pulling her against me.

With her mouth on mine, the embarrassment from moments ago vanishes, replaced with the fire unique to only her touch. Her arms circle my neck, pulling me close, and I squeeze her waist, not allowing her to take another step since it means parting from me. Someone clears their throat, but I'm incapable of pulling away. The way her tongue moves against mine, just before she gives me a little nip…

Another throat clear, followed by a stern, "*Mr. Connor.*"

Brooke pulls away with a triumphant grin before stepping around me to walk out of the elevator, leaving me gaping after her. If it were up to me, I'd drag her back into my bed and not let her leave for a week, but she obviously has other plans.

The elevator doors close, and I find myself alone, the only thing on my mind being when I can see her again. I spent an entire night and morning curled up with her, but I want nothing more than to spend the rest of the day with her?

Since I'm well and truly fucked already, I might as well damn us straight to the lowest depths.

I shove my palm against the "Open Door" button and tear out of the elevator. I race through the lobby, nearly taking someone out before throwing open the door, giving my poor doorman Clive a heart attack. My head thrashes back and forth, eyes scanning every direction for her.

"She went that way, sir!"

"Thank you, Clive!" I yell over my shoulder, as I take off to my right. The streets aren't too busy, and I quickly spot her now that I know where to look. "Brooke!!"

She doesn't turn.

"Brooke!!" I yell a little louder, and it does the trick, her little bun whipping around as she turns to face me. I'm nearly breathless as I jog up to her with a smile. "Hey."

"What? Did I forget something?"

"No, I, uh…" *I…what!? What am I fucking doing here?!* "I wanted to ask you to brunch."

"To brunch?"

"To brunch."

Her eyes shutter, and my stomach sinks. "We don't do brunch, Connor."

"We do whatever we want, whenever we want, as long as it's for fun." I shrug, reciting the terms of our arrangement. "Brunch is fun."

"But we woke up *cuddling*, Connor, and now you're asking me to brunch." Her eyes search my face, finding something that has her taking a step back and looking away. "You know the rules, so if something has changed…then you know what we need to do."

I'm speechless.

Genuinely not a single thing crosses my mind as something to say to that.

"I'm sorry, but I really do have to go."

And with that, Brooke walks away, leaving me to deal with the consequences of broken rules.

CHAPTER THIRTY—FIVE

Then - Brooke

Calling this a house would be such an understatement that it borders on inaccurate. I think a residence like this may be referred to as an estate? A resort, maybe? Ziggy is quiet, like me, as we take in the full magnitude of what's in front of us.

As far as typical goes, it's painted in the trademarked creamy color of every newly manufactured house in Florida with white trim and a terracotta roof. Beyond that, it's something unlike any home I've seen before, not even in a magazine. If I had to figure how to describe it, I'd probably go with a combination of Italian architecture and a sprawling villa from Mexico, with a billion dollars thrown at it.

The landscaping alone is…just…wow. I'd bet they paid someone to fly all over the world to find the prettiest, most symmetrical, eye-pleasing palm trees and put them in this yard.

Yard? Is this even a yard? Can I call it that?

Every tree and awe-inspiring plant has its own light underneath it, as if they spent enough money on each one they'd want you to notice every fucking leaf. The lawn itself is a masterpiece, definitely not meant to be walked on.

What I originally thought was a driveway, isn't a driveway at all. It's a courtyard, beautifully paved to tie in with the terracotta roof, with a stunning white fountain in the middle. The *actual* driveway goes around to an entirely different building I'd assume is dedicated for cars.

Ziggy lets out a low whistle.

"I don't know if this is a good idea. They probably have a ton of staff, just to keep this place looking put together. I mean, they've probably got a guy who scrubs this fountain with a toothbrush every day, because look how clean–"

"*Mija.* She said it was going to be empty."

"She was probably just saying that to get them to do something faster!"

"Maybe she gave the staff the weekend off too."

"Ziggy. There's no way we can spend an entire weekend here without getting caught."

"What about one night?"

"Ziggy–"

"Come on! Wouldn't you love to eat something you can't get at a gas station?"

"We can splurge on some diner pancakes after another good night in Ybor."

"What about a hot shower?"

I sigh. "Already had one of those, and look how well that worked out."

"You could use another." Ziggy pretends to sniff me and grimace. I don't laugh, so she shoves me playfully. "What about a bubble bath?"

She knows that I'm starting to waver and takes advantage, using the momentum and throwing out things that were once normalities, but are now extraordinary after being out here.

"How about sleeping on a mattress that's worth more than a car? Curling up under a fluffy blanket and not having to move at first light?"

Admittedly, that sounds fucking amazing, but I keep my mouth shut.

"We could watch movie after movie, and if you're really nice to me, I'll let you pick one for us to watch."

"How generous of you. One whole movie."

"Well, I have a list, and when else am I going to have such an opportunity? How often do you find yourself doing a movie marathon when you don't even have a house?"

Ziggy wants this, I realize. For me, watching movies and sleeping in a bed were things that happened on an average day. Sure, a hot shower is special for even me now, but for Ziggy, maybe they were never average things.

LAST Stand FOR GENEVIEVE

For all I know, she's spent her entire life worrying about taking care of others, never letting herself have something for herself. Ziggy's dark brown eyes brighten at the possibility, just one night spent in luxury, and for whatever reason I can't take that away from her.

"Fine."

Ziggy does her little *aaaayyyyayayayayaya* thing, and I plant my hand over her mouth, looking around to make sure nobody heard that. "But we don't go in until this evening, *after* work hours just in case there are any lingering staff."

"Yes, *mija*." She frowns a little. "Until then, let's find you a bench to nap on. I can't take this cranky Carolina any longer."

I roll my eyes, but end up falling asleep on a bench in less than ten minutes. After napping like the dead, Ziggy finally wakes me up well past dark. My body clock is so fucked, when I open my eyes I expect to see the sun, but find the moon instead. The nap did wonders anyway, regardless.

"You ready to walk a mile in expensive shoes, *mija*?"

"If we're actually walking a mile, I'm not coming."

"Relax, the promised land is just around the corner." Ziggy snorts. "How are those claws?"

"Sharp," I grunt, hoping I don't live to regret this.

Ziggy claps. "*Perfecto.*"

We're still shocked into silence as we walk up to the stunning property, but rather than standing on the road with open mouths, we slip around the side of the fence where there's lots of tree coverage. Ziggy gives me a boost so I can hop over the fence, and then throws her backpack over to me, lightening her load as she spider monkeys up the pretty metal bars.

I shake my head. "Not even a zoo could keep you in."

"Zoos keep animals. I'm a jalapeño." She lands on her feet, blows me a kiss, and grabs her backpack, walking up to the side of the house like she owns the place. As usual, I follow her lead and hope we make it out alive. I keep an eye out for anyone who might see us, but it's too private to be noticed easily, someone would have to *really* be looking. It's only slightly reassuring.

Ziggy finds a door on the side of the house, likely a staff entrance because can you imagine using the same front door as the cook? Okay, that's probably too harsh. The house is so big that it's probably more convenient for the cook to come in this way, but still. I'm going to be salty about it and no one will stop me.

I keep my eyes on the surroundings, as the familiar clinking and tinkering fills the quiet evening air. It's not too warm tonight, kind of nice, unlike the day from heatstroke hell. A few minutes later, Ziggy woots as the lock clicks to the right, unlocking our retreat for the night. I'm proven completely correct as the door opens to reveal the kitchen.

"The chef has *arrrivveeddddd*!!!" Ziggy does a little earthworm dance, I'm talking lots of gyrations. "Let's get cookin' *mijaaa*!!!"

Ziggy's excitement and smile warms my insides in a way I didn't know I was still capable of. It's quite bizarre, actually. I haven't escaped my problems or recovered from the bone-crushing loss and guilt I've been fighting since the accident, but somehow, she lightens the load. I'm not sure it's healthy that I depend on her for that, but I do.

For some reason, Ziggy's rules echo back to me:

1. *Don't tell anyone your real name.*
2. *Always have your shit attached to you.*
3. *There are no friends out here, because having friends gets you killed.*

Ziggy was hurt by someone, that is clear. But tonight, she tossed me her backpack without a blink of an eye. Sure, it probably wouldn't be a big deal for anyone else, but for Ziggy, that was huge. And even though she will likely lead me to my demise one day, I'd follow this tiny jalapeño in baggy clothes to the end of the earth. Even though I say that jovially, I know I really will go out by her side, because I'm never going to leave it.

"What are the chances of rich white people having some tortillas?"

I snort. "Pretty high based on the size of this pantry, it's a fucking Publix over here." The pantry is bigger than my old bedroom. Glancing at the door handle I used to open it, I realize quickly that we need to set some ground rules. "We're leaving fingerprints everywhere."

"You're thinking like a serial killer." Ziggy smiles. "I like it."

I roll my eyes. "I meant that we need to avoid doing anything that would make them feel the need to *check* for fingerprints."

"Easy." Ziggy shrugs.

"That means no messes and no stealing."

"Who do you think you're talking to? I'm as tidy and honest as they come."

"Ziggy. I'm serious."

LAST Stand FOR GENEVIEVE

"And what will happen when they find our fingerprints? Connect it to all of the crime scenes we've been at? Show up to our homes where we spend all of our time?"

That's kind of a good point. "Well–"

"This isn't *Law & Order, mija*. But anyway, I wasn't planning to take anything, even if my fingers start feeling a little sticky. This is a slumber party, meaning no hustling and only wholesome."

I eye her, but take her word for it before moving fully into the pantry, finding some tortillas relatively easily. It's on a shelf with everything else I'd assume she would need, and I gather up the supplies for her, bringing them over to the kitchen continent (calling it an island doesn't do it justice).

"*Santa mierda.*"

"What?"

"*Por donde empiezo?*" Ziggy puts her hands on her hips. "There's like seven ovens!"

"I count eight."

"*Exactemente*!! Which one do I use?"

"Ever heard of eeny, meeny, miny, moe?"

"*Esta perra….*" Ziggy starts messing with the ovens and I head off onto my own little side quest, getting out a tub of ice cream.

It's the expensive stuff, too, so you don't get those awful chunks of ice that ruin the experience. Rummaging through the pantries (yes, plural, because I discovered another one), I gather together all the things for toppings. Fudge syrup. Oreos. Gummy worms. I even find some cookie dough and whipped cream in the fridge.

Suddenly it's like fucking Coldstone over here, and I'm mixing the toppings in with spatulas like my life depends on making this into perfection. Ziggy is cooking something that smells delicious, full of spices and cheese and whatever it is, I know it will blow my mind.

We eat dessert first while Ziggy's creation bakes in the oven, then we destroy what I find out are enchiladas, moaning over what is definitely the best meal I've ever had. There's something about a hot meal that just warms your very fucking soul. Then we eat even more dessert, and once our stomachs are too full to fit anything else, we start to explore floor after floor, discovering everything this place has to offer.

Ziggy quickly figures out that there's a surround sound system installed throughout every room, and puts on some spicy music from the controls closet. I don't know the name or the genre or what any of the lyrics mean, but damn, I can tell that it's spicy. And for the first time in a while, my hips start to move, and I start to laugh.

We turn off the lights and turn on some flashlights we find nearby, pretending like we're at a club, just two girls enjoying a night out. I would say that I'm an exceptional dancer, or at least I was when I was doing it often, but Ziggy's hips aren't even attached to her body. Even in her baggy clothes, the way she moves should be illegal.

There's a loft area just above the first flight of stairs with hardwood floors that are so smooth, it's a safety hazard. So naturally, we kick off our shoes and see who can slide for the longest. Ziggy can shake it, but her balance is *not* it. Cheerleading captain and school president takes the win on this activity.

Up the second flight of stairs, we find a closet from my dreams. It's like the one from *Hannah Montana*, but even better because it isn't filled with clothing from the 2000s. There's designer everything, no matter which way I turn. Labels that meant everything to me to own at one point, the only things that I once desired from life.

Ironic that I'm now surrounded by them, and yet what makes the moment special is the weirdo standing next to me who just asked "Who is Louis Vuitton" and didn't say it as a joke, because she's genuinely never fucking heard of the brand.

I snort, dragging her out of the closet, and we run up the next flight of stairs. This floor is FULL of more bedrooms and bathrooms. We laugh about which of the relatives are the least favorite to get banned to the third floor, and in honor of the rejects of the world, Ziggy and I deem this to be our favorite floor.

We drag one of the mattresses to the very top of the stairs, and I shove while Ziggy slides down atop the mattress. Admittedly, this is a horrible idea because neither of us can afford a broken arm, but fuck me, the smile on Ziggy's face is worth the risk. I've never seen her this carefree.

Ziggy lets me pick *High School Musical* as my movie selection. It was my comfort movie once upon a time. The movie I'd put on when I needed something to make me smile, and it hasn't lost its touch. Nostalgia washes over me, along with a little sadness at the memory of who used to watch this by my side. I glance at Ziggy, who's smiling up at Troy Bolton despite herself, and I breathe through the moment. We dance some more. We go swimming.

And I can't help but think that in another life, Ziggy would be my very best friend.

CHAPTER THIRTY–SIX

Now – Connor

stepped into this elevator feeling ten-feet tall (with an Australian-sized portion of mortification), and now I'm stepping out of it feeling like roadkill (with an American-sized portion of mortification). Did I read the last twenty-four hours completely wrong?

Frankly, I'm wondering if they happened at all.

The elevator dings and Ara's head shoots up from the other side of the counter like a Whac-A-Mole. "Did Brooke leave?"

"Yeah…she did."

Ara observes my face. "…I thought we knew Brooke was leaving?"

"We did."

Theo comes out of the bathroom then, takes one look at me, and says, "What happened?"

Ara shushes him. "That's what I'm trying to find out."

"I asked her to brunch."

Their eyes dart to each other before locking back on me. Ara regards me like a small toddler. "You…asked…her…to…*brunch*?"

I nod.

"Why aren't you getting ready?"

I shrug. "She said no."

"I like her even more now," Ara says with a snort. "You need someone who makes you work for it and doesn't take your shit."

"Well, she said no, so now *no one* is taking/not taking my shit." And why does that bother me? That's been my intention. I mean, I've taken pains to ensure that very thing.

Ara smacks Theo on the back. "I'll leave this one to you. Seems like one of those cute little bro-mance moments." Just as she reaches the hallway, she turns back, smiling. "Your trope just went from friends-with-benefits to he-fell-first. I love when I'm right."

Theo chuckles. "Want me to translate?"

"Nah. I know that was a *bookie* version of 'I told you so.'"

"You mean *bookish*, but yeah, pretty much." Theo pauses, giving me a moment to prepare for what I know he's about to ask. "So, uh, Brooke spent the night? And then bailed on brunch?"

"The first part of that technically wasn't intentional."

"Which explains why she turned down brunch, then?"

"Yes and no." I move to the coffee machine, needing to be able to think clearly, process the messed-up shit in my head. "She's been coming over for weeks, actually, but usually the moment we're, uh, *done*, she gets up and leaves. So no, staying over wasn't on purpose, but she *did* choose to stay in my bed long enough that she fell asleep."

Theo nods. "Which is why you thought you had a shot at brunch?"

I shake my head. "I didn't think it through. If I had, I wouldn't have asked."

"Why not?"

I give him a look, before sliding his mug of coffee toward him and starting on mine. "You really gonna make me spell it out, mate?"

"Yep." He takes a sip.

I groan. "We made a very specific arrangement, and the past twenty-four hours were…not what we'd agreed on. She was never going to say yes."

"And did you want her to say yes to brunch?"

"No," I say it too quickly, and he hides his amusement with his mug.

"You sure about that?"

I much prefer the Theo who gets drunk and plays Mario Kart with me when I'm upset. This relaxed, wise version of him who asks questions my heart starts wanting to answer is aggravating. Regardless, I take my mug and sit next to him, willing to suffer through it since it's Theo we're talking about.

"No, I'm not sure." I give him a look, kind of like the ones toddlers give their mom's when they're being faced with something they obviously did, but plan on taking it to the grave.

Theo laughs. "Don't be one of those people who deny their feelings for months even though you're inevitably going to get together."

"You mean like you and Ara?" I say with a wink.

"Ara had just lost the most important person in her life. *WE* had a good reason. But still, I don't recommend it. My balls are still recovering."

Even I laugh at that. I can't imagine knowing and spending time with Brooke for six months and not laying a hand on her. Not even in a sexual way, but just being near her and never feeling close enough? Sounds like hell.

I run my hand through my hair. "I've spent the past ten years making sure I didn't get close to a woman. What happened with Lara, I can't ever imagine going through something like that again."

"I know."

"I was doing bloody fine with my rules and my routine, and then Brooke walks into my life, fucking it all up with her mood swings and infuriating silence and those…eyes…and screws with my head." Frustration I hadn't realized was buried finds its way to the surface. "One minute I'm thinking we need to get it out of our systems, then as soon as we do, I can't fucking stop. I mean, I can't even *think* about anyone else. I *tried*, man. I *tried* to take a woman home, and it felt like I was about to take a cheese grater to my dick."

Theo winces at the visual.

"I fucking *can't*, and I wish I could, because she's…she's got me feeling sick, and I mean literally sick. And the worst part? It goes far beyond not being able to sleep with anyone else. It doesn't stop there. My stomach is in this constant state of turmoil, rising and falling whenever she's around.

"I can't do *anything* without wondering how it would make her feel, and ensuring that whatever I do, I'm doing right by her. I can't go to the shops without thinking about her. I can't write music without thinking about her. I can't do fucking anything without thinking about her. She invades my every waking breath and thought."

Theo opens his mouth to respond, but I cut him off, needing to get this out.

LAST Stand FOR GENEVIEVE

"Then I went and got even more stupid, thinking maybe, *just maybe* she feels the same way about me. So I take a fucking leap of faith and end up belly flopping onto a bed of nails, because she walks away without even a glance over her shoulder. Meaning, this disease she's stricken me with, is *excruciatingly* one-sided. What am I supposed to do!?"

"Well, I'll tell you one thing."

"What?" I'm panting, as if saying that aloud required physical fight.

"It's not one-sided, but I think you've just managed to find the one person worse at dealing with their feelings than you."

I frown at him.

"But I also believe that she has a good reason for being that way. You just need to uncover why, walk her through it, show her that it would be different with you."

And here is where I get stumped, the part that holds me back from giving myself over fully, regardless of the consequences to my own heart. "*Would* it be different though? I'm an emotionally unavailable asshole."

Theo rests his hand on my shoulder. "Anyone who knows you, and I mean *really* knows you, knows that *that* couldn't be further from the truth. You have the biggest heart of anyone I've ever met."

I look at Theo, emotion swirling in both of our eyes, needing to lighten the mood before we start crying into our coffee. "Should we make out?"

Theo laughs, rubbing his nose. "It'd probably be easier than trying to navigate the minds of women."

"Amen to that, brother."

Theo starts again. "With Brooke it's never going to be easy. It won't be the typical '*Harry Met Sally*' and they lived happily ever after'. So the question you need to ask yourself is this: is she worth the fight it's going to take?"

"*Yes.*" Without a doubt in my mind, I know that she is. She's worth that and more.

"Then keep fighting and never take no for an answer."

If I can set aside my fears and self-doubt for a second, I can see that I've found a woman who has brought something inside of me to life, which has never before been given sentience. Brooke is the oxygen which feeds the fire in my veins and my soul. I never wanted to feel anything for her, but I do.

At some point there was a breach in my chest, and although I've battled gallantly, it's time to surrender. There is no more room in this war to use my strength to deny it, the way I've done for too long. Whatever tenacity I have left, I will use it to invade her heart the way she has invaded mine.

I pull out my phone.

Connor: I have an idea.

Ice Kween: No, thanks.

I roll my eyes.

Connor: You don't even know what it is.

Ice Kween: Doesn't matter. Not interested.

Theo stands then, taking his mug with him, face saturated in amusement. "Good luck, brother. Hope it's as painless as possible."

I snort before looking back down at my phone and grumble, knowing I won't be so lucky.

Connor: What are your favorite flowers?

Ice Kween: The invisible kind.

Ha. I can't help it. That was funny. Guess we're doing this again.

Connor: Favorite chocolates?

Ice Kween: The kind I buy for myself, now leave me alone.

Connor: I wish I could.

I delete that one before I'm stupid enough to send it, and type *cute date ideas* into Google instead.

Fuck me. Couples go hard these days when it comes to romance. Theo and Ara aren't this fancy, but maybe it's because they're so naturally perfect for each other, they could be sitting in front of a TV or climbing a skyscraper, and as long as the other was there, they'd be happy. But I guess before they got there, they had to fight tooth and claw for it.

I sigh, dreading my own impending action sequence that is likely to get a lot more bloody.

Connor: What about a morning in a hot air balloon?

Ice Kween: Sure. As long as I can push you out of the basket once we reach maximum altitude.

Yeahr, I didn't think that one through.

LAST Stand FOR GENEVIEVE

Connor: We could take a cooking class.

Ice Kween: I'd rather cook with Gordon Ramsay.

Connor: We could go on a hike.

Ice Kween: I've been begging you to take a hike all morning.

Ice Kween: But also, we live in Florida. No, thanks.

Connor: Aquarium?

Ice Kween: I'll throw you in with the sharks.

Connor: Strawberry pickling?

Ice Kween: They're not in season.

Connor: What about a museum?

Ice Kween: I hate that one the least, because it wouldn't involve talking, but it's still a no.

At this point, I'm desperate.

Connor: How about an archery range? Or ax throwing?

Connor: There will be weapons.

Ice Kween: No, Connor.

Ice Kween: And don't ask me again.

Connor: Why not?

Ice Kween: Because you know the rules and you're wanting to break them.

Connor: You know what they say, rules are meant to be broken...

Ice Kween: Not these ones. So stop asking me!

Ice Kween: I don't know why you keep pushing this!?

Because I have no fucking choice, that's why.

I've gone through everything Google (and Pinterest, for fuck's sake) has to offer, trying to come up with grandiose gestures to win Brooke over. Flowers and holding up a jukebox outside her window, a picnic outdoors with red wine and more, but now I realize that was never going to be how our story goes.

Connor: I'll let it go if you come over tonight. Usual time.

Brooke: K.

The only way it's going to happen, the only way anything has *ever* happened with us, is with a fucking battle of wills.

• • •

The elevator door opens, this time I don't try to hide the fact that I've been standing here, waiting. I stalk up to her, not even giving her the time to toss her things onto the counter before I shove the bowl of Mac & Cheese into her hands.

"We need to talk."

Ice Queen tosses her bag onto the couch before sending an accusatory finger in my direction, as the temperature of the room plummets. "You said you would let this go!"

"Yep. I *misled* you."

She growls and shoves the bowl back into my hands, before angrily grabbing her bag and turning back toward the elevator. Thankfully, it's been called back to the bottom, meaning I have a few more minutes to get through to her before she can escape.

I slam the bowl down on a side table, probably cracking them both before following her to stand in front of the elevator. "I lied, just like you're lying to me and to yourself!"

Her head whips around, murder in her eyes as she repeatedly slams her fingers into the down button behind her.

"You can blame this all on me, and claim that staying over last night was an accident, but the truth is that you *craved* me. You wanted my closeness and my warmth, and you couldn't bring yourself to pull away!"

"That is *bullshit!*"

"No! It's bullshit that you're being such a coward!"

"How dare you!? You know *nothing* about me!"

"Exactly!!! And I'm standing here, begging for you to let me in, to show me *everything*, and you just shut me out every time I get close!"

"We have RULES, Connor!!"

"Then why didn't you immediately write me off?" I lower my voice, taking a slow step toward her. "Why did you show up tonight?"

Another step. She swallows.

LAST Stand FOR GENEVIEVE

"I caught *feelings*, Brooke." My voice is that of a broken man, a man who has used up every drop of strength fighting a battle he was never going to win. Agony steals across her features at my admission. "Whether I'm waking up or going to sleep, you're the first and last thing on my mind."

I take another step. "When I look at other women, I feel nothing. But when I look at you? It's like I've reached the end of a fuse, erupting into a fiery explosion, and it makes me *burn*."

Her breath becomes strangulated in her throat as I take another step.

"When my heart beats, it's beating for *you*."

Brooke's head whips side to side, unchecked fear and pain on her face. "You can't feel *any* of that, Connor. We promised each other that it wouldn't come to this."

"Then end it."

Her eyes widen.

"End our arrangement. Just like we agreed we would."

"But—"

"Why are you hesitating, Brooke?" I take another step, voice full of animosity and frustration as I continue to push her, needing her to fall over that edge of control. "You didn't hesitate this morning when you walked away from me. Why are you hesitating now?"

"Because—"

"Go ahead and turn your back on me, but just know that you'll be taking my heart with you because unfortunately, it's yours. Despite my best fucking efforts, it belongs to you now."

She shakes her head, her skin becoming red and splotchy, as if the emotions that are brewing beneath her skin are searching for an outlet her mouth just won't give them. "Connor, *no—*"

"*Do* it, Brooke! Shatter me into a *million* pieces. You have the power to." Only a foot between us now and she remains silent. "It's because you can't, can you? You're fighting it with everything you have, but you don't have the strength to turn your back on me, just like I don't have the strength to turn mine on you."

Brooke shakes her head, one last vicious attempt at fighting this inferno that has built between us, capable of reducing this high-rise to rubble. I'm upon her now, crowding her into the wall so she has nowhere to go as she trembles with the anger, fear, and desire she tries not to show.

245

I run my fingers down the side of her cheek as she clenches her jaw hard enough that I know it hurts. She can battle this with every cell in her body, but at the end of the day, I know that she's as weak as I am.

My fingers trail over the feathering muscles and down the front of her throat as I lean in, whispering against her ear, "Tell me the truth. It's more than just my body you've wanted since you pulled that cigarette out of my mouth."

"You're wrong."

I tsk. "Don't lie—"

Brooke's hands hit my chest, and I barely have time to catch myself as she shoves me with a force that is entirely too impressive for her size. "You're wrong because that wasn't the first time I saw you! It wasn't the first time I *wanted* you!"

Everything goes silent. "What?"

"It was earlier, you insufferable, stubborn asshole! *Before* the show! You were one of the first people there and you walked over to our staff area, greeting *everyone* by name, offering to help out. I thought you were part of the crew until they started taking selfies with you."

Her voice drips with contempt, making my appreciation to the people who make the event what it is sound like a grotesque transgression, the most upsetting thing in the world. And how could I possibly have missed her, standing in that tent? So many thoughts take off in my head that I'm speechless, but Brooke *finally* isn't.

"I'd been careful not to feel a fucking thing, successfully shutting out people I've known and loved my *entire life*, but then one little thoughtful moment from you and..." She trails off, covering her face like it hurts, before yanking them away in resentment. "It was the first time I'd felt something in YEARS. I didn't even know your name, and you had me feeling things I'd thought had *died* inside of me. It ruined *everything*, because the fear came right behind it! I've lost every single person I care about, and I don't want to curse you to the same fate." She starts dry sobbing, like she forbade tears when she forbade her heart from hurting. "But you just wouldn't leave me alone!!"

"Because I *can't*!!! I didn't want this either!!! I never wanted feelings or love or any of it!!! You think you're the only one who has ever lost someone!? I lost my high school sweetheart before she ever got to graduate, and I didn't even know, until it was too late to give her the kind of memories she deserved

LAST *Stand* FOR GENEVIEVE

to take with her." My hands plunge into my hair, running through the wild strands and pulling the ends with a growl. "I NEVER wanted to care about anyone again!"

"Then take back those words and LET. ME. GO!"

"I. Fucking. Can't." I laugh, a dry raspy thing. "Don't you get it? Every single fucking day when I wake up, nothing feels complete unless I've felt you, unless I'm covered in your lavender scent and playing white water rapids with your moods, trying not to break my neck with your waves of animosity!"

"This whole thing is so unhealthy, Connor! You make me fucking *sick*!"

"Then come be sick with *me*." The words come out soft, pleading, as if I would get down on my knees right now and beg. I probably would if it meant that she would stop fighting this. "Because I don't think I can do healthy if it's with anyone else."

The weight of my words descends over us, realization falling down like acid rain.

My truth. Her Truth. *Our* truth.

We are irrevocably intertwined.

For a moment everything is silent as we take each other in under a new light, then the elevator dings like a starting pistol, launching us into motion. As my mouth comes down over hers, I grab her wrists and secure them to the wall above her head, not giving her the chance to try anything fucking smart this time.

She pulls back, a slight smirk on her lips. "You disgust me."

"And you infuriate me," I say back, reciting my rebuttal from the night we first gave in to this burning desire racing through our veins, just the way it does now. Once I'm sure she won't fight me off, I release her wrists and reach for her shirt, a beautiful, pale blue satin blouse with these delicate buttons all down the front.

It's too bad they now scatter across the floor.

She gasps as I pull the rest of her shirt away, revealing one of those lacy bras that are designed in fucking heaven. It's the same pale blue as her blouse, with little flowers lining the lace, but so graciously showing what lies beneath.

Brooke's hands dive into my hair, as wild as what I feel for this vexatious woman. My hands, followed by my lips and tongue, trail down the rest of her, softer than the world's finest satins.

As her back arches, I slip my hand down the front of her white slacks, groaning at how ready she is for me. It's always this way with us, a growing, insatiable need for the other. As if mirroring my thoughts, she reaches for the hem of my shirt and rips it over my head.

We work each other into a frenzy, until our mouths and hands just aren't enough. The rest of our garments come off, discarded somewhere on the way to the stairs. I push her back, so she's sprawled across several steps and holding onto the banister for support, completely bare. My hungry eyes take a moment to devour every inch of her naked body, how the moonlight coming in from our floor-to-ceiling windows alight her every curve, before getting on my knees to worship.

I had once feared this pleasure, this inferno of fire and ice that could never again be equaled, but not anymore. With her hands in my hair and my name on her lips, I *prove* to her what we are.

Irrevocably intertwined.

It's gone far beyond sex for a while, but with our feelings now in the open, our physical need feels more powerful than ever before. Nothing, and no one, will ever be able to compare to Brooke. It's her special brand of freezing fire, the kind that consumes my every waking thought and breath. I feared she would be my destruction, and in a way, she is. She destroyed my rules, and my plans, and my ability to pretend that I no longer had a heart.

Every moment of push and pull has led up to this moment.

This final battle.

I take a moment to gaze into her eyes. Tonight they're the color of warm Caribbean water on a summer's day. The fear and the anger from earlier are long gone. I'm not stupid enough to think it will ever be easy with this woman who lies below me, but for now I smile, basking in her sunlight.

If there was a shred of me left that didn't belong to her before, as her lips spread into the most beautiful fucking smile I've ever seen, I lose myself completely to her. Our bodies move together as if that's what they were created to do, until our angry confessions are erased with our soft touches, and we fall over the edge in the way I hope we do everything from now on.

Together.

CHAPTER THIRTY—SEVEN

Then - Brooke

Our bellies, bones, and backs woke up happy, and so did we. We woke up later than we planned, tearing through the house like a tornado to get everything tidied up and looking exactly as we'd found it. This weird bubble has followed us since we left, as if our joy is untouchable.

As we pass by a homeless man sitting in front of a store just outside the neighborhood, Ziggy comes to a stop in front of him, handing over a leftover protein bar she has in her pocket. "*Hola*, Abe. How's life treating you?"

"Can't complain." He smiles a toothless smile, and it's so genuine I find myself returning it. "Who's your friend?"

Ziggy doesn't correct him on his word choice. "This is Carolina."

"Nice to meet you, Abe." I shake his hand that isn't holding the protein bar.

He gives me a once over, but it's purely observative, nothing salacious crossing his features. "What's a girl like you doing on the street?"

Ziggy snorts. "Oh, now I'm offended. She doesn't belong, but I do?"

Abe rolls his eyes. "Nobody could stuff you into a normal life and you know it, Ziggy. Just like me, you were born a nomad. But this one looks like she belongs somewhere."

"Now *I'm* offended." I kid with him.

Abe rolls his eyes. "*Women.*"

"*Adios anciano!*"

"Thank you for the treat, Ziggy."

"Any time."

"It was nice to meet you, Abe!" I call as she leads me away, since we're operating off of a somewhat loose schedule today. We'll go to Ybor and move some more product tonight. Is that even what they say? I'm still learning the lingo, but mostly nobody says anything at all. It's just *known*.

It's not a short walk to the abandoned warehouse, but my body has gotten used to the daily trekking. I've started building muscles in my legs again, and the aches from the bones that were broken in the accident ache less and less, as they strengthen every day.

Before long, we're approaching the shipyard. I briefly wonder if this place is always this packed, or if there's business hours just like any typical establishment. Sounds like a question I'd get shot for if I was stupid enough to ask, so I keep my mouth shut.

The scent of saltwater and mustiness invade my senses, accompanied by the sound of water lapping against the sea wall, and someone blaring a boat's horn. It's warm out today, but not as hot as yesterday, a perfect day for boating. Judging by the placement of the sun, it's early afternoon, meaning we made pretty good time getting here.

A distinct feeling of danger slips over us, thoroughly bursting the little bubble of joy that's been floating around us until now. Our smiles recede behind our masks, our carefree attitude disappearing at the sight of the first gun, and we step a little farther away from each other. We've gotten closer than the last time we came around, but they can't know that.

Gilly notices us first, coating us in the slime that comes with his revolting gaze. It takes all of my self-control not to step in front of Ziggy, shielding her from it entirely, but that would give us away. A glance to my left tells me she can fight her own battles anyway, as she reaches into her pocket, pulling out a middle finger as her opening statement.

I can't help but snort, and Gilly's face falls into a set of annoyance.

"Where's Marty?" Ziggy asks.

"In a meeting." Gilly sneers.

"Then I guess you'll have to do. We'll take the usual."

"And what if I don't feel like helping?"

Ziggy smiles, but it's a mean thing. "Then I'll make sure Marty knows you're bad for business, and you know how he feels about things that are bad for business."

"Find somewhere else to be until he's ready." Gilly spits on the ground, a little too close to Ziggy's shoe for my liking.

"Thanks, *princesa*."

Ziggy turns to lead me toward the water's edge, as I grumble, "He's such a fucking prick."

"You're saying to me." Out of nowhere, Ziggy gasps, and I rush to her, just to realize she's still looking out over the water, and it's a look of awe rather than alarm. At first I don't understand, until finally a fin breaks the water, and another one. Dolphins. "I've never seen them before, *mija*."

We sit on the ground, our legs folded in front of us. Moments like this are the ones that easily pass us by, without recognition of how special they really are. So I memorize it all, Ziggy's childlike wonder, and the blue of the sky, and how the breeze feels as it stirs my hair. We sit and watch the fins as they appear and disappear, across the bay, a quiet moment, before that distinct sense of danger creeps over us again.

Ziggy glances behind us and stiffens. "Follow my lead, *mija,* and try your best not to be noticed."

Marty is walking out of the abandoned warehouse with a man I've never seen before, but somehow I know it's Victor without Ziggy having to tell me. The boss's boss. Their security trail behind them, far enough to give the illusion of privacy.

Where Marty is unassuming in khakis and those New Balance sneakers, Victor is the opposite, exuding danger through his every pore. And not the kind of danger that makes you want to get a little closer, but the kind that repels anything that has a desire to live.

Somewhere in his late thirties or early forties, you can tell Victor has seen and done things that would make your skin crawl. He walks with the fearlessness that comes with knowing your soul cannot be tainted more than it already is. Although he's clean, hair neatly styled and wearing a suit that is perfectly tailored, you know without a doubt that he is a dirty man.

My gut sinks as I see Ziggy set her shoulders back even farther, meaning Victor is an even greater danger than any we've already faced. As if having felt our gaze, Victor's eyes immediately lift to Ziggy's, and then mine, where they stay.

Ziggy's mouth doesn't move, but I hear the intake of breath. Victor stops, Marty immediately coming to a halt by his side, like a well-trained dog. We're too far away to hear the words, but I read the question from his lips.

Who is that?

How Marty responds, I'll never know, but whatever he says has Victor changing his trajectory toward us. To all other eyes, Ziggy remains perfectly relaxed, but I know the truth: she's terrified. Whether it's a general fear for our safety, or something more specific…I'll have to wait and find out. Until then, I follow her lead and try not to get noticed, just like she said.

"How are those claws, mija?" Ziggy whispers.

"Sharp."

As Victor walks up with his eyes wholly focused on me, I realize it's too late. I've already been noticed.

"I don't believe we've met before." His voice is deep, edged in a rage that he hides well, but is ever present. Victor is a man who was obviously born evil.

"I believe you'd be right."

Victor smiles. It doesn't have a reassuring effect; in fact, it does quite the opposite. "What's your name?"

"Carolina." I don't miss a beat, speaking as blandly as possible.

"You're quite pretty, Carolina."

Ziggy tenses, and this time, everyone notices.

"Thank you." *Fuck. This is not good.*

"Pretty enough to be very, *very* useful."

My stomach roils as my mind jumps to every possible conclusion at what this lawless man could mean by that. None of them are good.

"Ever thought of being a bartender?"

Well, that was not what I was expecting. Not nearly as bad as sex slave, boner garage, or anything else I'd just imagined. I relax a fraction of an inch, until Ziggy's eyes finally meet mine, full of alarm. She can't speak up without the risk of getting us both killed, but I read her loud and clear. I am *not* to let my guard down.

"I haven't."

"Would you think about it? If I offered you a position?"

I'm trapped. Utterly fucked if I say yes because it opens the door, but if I say no and offend him, what's to stop him from putting a bullet between my eyes right now? Or worse, Ziggy's?

LAST Stand FOR GENEVIEVE

"I'm not old enough to be a bartender." This man breaks the law for a living, and that's the best excuse I could come up with? Sweat trickles down my back as I realize something worse, I've given away a personal detail. My age.

Victor takes a step toward me, close enough now that I can smell his cologne. It's exactly what you'd expect: alcohol and murder, if it had an essence. "You look old enough for plenty."

My stomach sinks, and I place my hands in my pockets to hide the shakes. "I really appreciate the offer, but I'm not looking for work at the moment."

Victor chuckles. "I'm not used to someone saying no to me."

"I don't mean to offend you." But I fear I already have.

Victor looks at Ziggy, and I remember what true fear is, that feeling of time moving so slow that it's nearly still, yet you're frozen with it, unable to stop the pieces that the universe deems must fall into place. Understanding, cold and grim, dawns behind his black eyes before they meet mine again. "Your friend can come too."

My jaw slackens the tiniest bit, open and ready to deny our friendship, but it's futile. Victor knows we're a unit, and what he does with that knowledge won't change with an attempt to deny it. If he used Ziggy against me, I know in my bones that I would do anything he asked of me. I'll never lose someone I love again, especially if I'm given a chance to keep them safe, no matter how fucked up it is.

"You simply can't decline until you see the place. It's beautiful." His eyes drag down my frame. "Irresistible, even."

His double-edged words aren't just referring to the bar. "I'll have to take your word for it because we have somewhere to be."

Victor smiles at Ziggy, like a lion gazes at a gazelle before a hunt. "Ybor doesn't wake up until ten tonight. We both know that."

His off-the-cuff knowledge of our usual whereabouts startles Ziggy, but she remains silent.

Stay strong, I tell her with my eyes. *We got this.*

Do we? She asks with hers.

Victor spares a glance at his gold and diamond-encrusted Rolex. "I think we have just enough time for what I'm planning."

Men appear behind us with a snap of his fingers, and we're being pushed toward a blacked-out SUV. There's no use fighting or screaming, nobody would come to our aid, and we would lose the battle anyway.

Ziggy is lifted into the backseat first, and just before I follow in behind her, a different presence appears behind me. The cologne gives him away as his body presses up against mine.

"You'll soon learn that I always get what I want."

CHAPTER THIRTY-EIGHT

Now - Connor

Everything feels different this morning. The way the early morning sun bleeds in through the windows to warm my sheets. While I normally don't spend long in bed, I feel torturously content, like I could stay here all day. And with the woman beside me? Maybe all fucking week.

"So, your high school sweetheart, huh?"

"What a way to start off the first morning you're not running from my bed." I chuckle, pulling her closer.

She sighs. "I'm sorry, but it's been eating away at me since last night. Not in the way you might think, but because it was completely self-absorbed of me not to consider you were struggling as much as I was."

"I get it. Loss is…an all-consuming kind of thing."

It's something Ara and I bonded over early on. Theo, too, in his own way of having never experienced something good enough to lose. His father was horrible, and he never knew his mother.

"Her name was Lara. We were friends as kids, and the older we grew, the more it blossomed into something more. She was sweet, full of kindness, and wore her feelings on her sleeve. Although we had known each other for years, she had never told me that she struggled with an autoimmune disease. Lara didn't want me to worry, since she had it under control. But then one day she didn't."

Brooke finds my hand and laces her fingers through mine, giving it a little squeeze.

"I have regrets over it. Because by that point, her decline was so swift that we spent all of the time we had left in her hospital room. I'd never treated her poorly, but I feel she deserved to have every single one of her dreams come true first, and I was robbed of the opportunity to give them to her."

"I'm sorry." Her other hand soothingly strokes my hair, down my face to stop at my chin. "You should give yourself more credit, though. She was extremely lucky to have known love from someone like you."

"Thank you. I just, never want to go through anything like that again. Getting blindsided is something you can't ever prepare yourself for." I'm quiet for a moment. "So if there's anything I should know about you...please tell me. I don't think I can survive more secrets."

Brooke's hand slides away, as she sinks into quiet, before rolling away. My heart seizes with fear and expectation of her leaving, running from my question the way she always has.

Instead, she sits up, holding the blanket around her as if she needs the comfort and safety it provides, while she looks out my window and speaks. "My dad was addicted to Oxycodone. At first it was just a habit, something to take the edge off, until it became the reason he abandoned my mom, my sister, and me."

I remain quiet, giving her as long as she needs to continue.

"A couple years later, my little sister Genevieve died in a car accident."

My heart breaks. I feel it physically splinter, stabbing my lungs and taking away my ability to breathe. She told me that she lost everyone she had ever cared about, and I realize now, it was in the worst ways.

A man who was supposed to be her protector, choosing to abandon his children in favor of something that would likely kill him one day. I know Brooke would have stepped up, wanting to become the protector of her little sister, just for her to be ripped away so suddenly? I can't fucking imagine it, the sheer weight of that pain.

"The laws of the land determined that I was not at fault for the accident, but I was the driver, and I have to live with the responsibility of that. Phone records showed that the other driver, another teenager, had been texting their friends while driving, causing her to swerve over the yellow lines and directly into us. I'd taken off my seatbelt in hopes that I could shield my sister, but I was thrown from the windshield before the car crunched into a telephone pole, killing her on impact. If I'd kept my seatbelt on, they think I would have been killed too."

There are no words, nothing fucking exists to acknowledge the fucking tragedy that Brooke has known. She is the strongest person I've ever met, somehow finding a way to survive that kind of pain, to find it in herself to care again.

"I don't even have someone to hate because the other girl died too. Her family lost a child and a sibling that night, just like we did."

"Is that the meaning behind your tattoo? Your sister?"

Nod. "Mostly. All I had left of her was a favorite book and one single picture, which I almost lost once. I decided to get something in her memory that no one could take, unless I went with it."

"What happened to your mom? Are you still close with her?"

She stiffens, before forcing her body to relax, breathing through the memories this conversation pulls forth. I hate that I'm the one forcing her to relive this, but I need to understand. I need to *know* her.

"No. I didn't handle my grief well. I was terrible to her, and we haven't spoken in a few years."

"She would forgive you. Whatever you did wrong, she would." I may not have a good track record with my own blood, but I know what I say is true. Her mom would understand. And hearing her story, I decide to put in more effort to repair what broke with my own. "Thank you for sharing all of that with me.

Brooke shakes her head. "I'm not innocent, Connor. I don't want you painting me as a victim in this story."

In other words, she sees herself as the villain.

"I've painted you as neither the victim nor the villain, but a survivor. Someone who's experienced hardship, and found it in themself to keep going." Like Theo. Like Ara.

Brooke remains silent, meaning what she's shared is all I'll get out of her. I know there's something she still isn't sharing, something that runs even deeper, but I choose to let it go. As long as the secrets are ones of the past, I can only hope they won't affect our future.

I walk around the side of the bed, sitting beside her and pulling her close. "Want some coffee?"

"Only if it's decaf." She pulls herself out of whatever reverie she sank into, before turning to me with a grin. It's troubled, as if she squeezed it out just for me, but it's still beautiful. "And I might need to borrow some clothes."

• • •

As we walk down the hallway toward the kitchen, the smell of already (poorly) brewed coffee greets me, and I don't bother praying to avoid another run-in. It's inevitable. And this time, as I step into the kitchen with my girl a short distance behind me, it's exactly what it looks like.

Ara is the first one to spot me.

"Oh, thank God. So it *wasn't* a murder scene I cleaned up this morning, just the pregame to what was probably a sex marathon." Ara passes me the stack of our clothes that she must have gathered off the floor with a roll of her eyes. I smile, noticing she sewed all of Brooke's buttons back into place. "*What?* That blouse was way too cute to throw away. Make sure you get it back to her."

"Why don't you give it to her yourself?"

Just as the words leave my mouth, Brooke emerges from the hallway behind me, looking fucking delicious in my sweats and matching hoodie. Ara blanches, eyes pinballing between us.

Here we go again.

All aboard the train to Awkward Station.

Ara recovers a little quicker this time, a wide grin spreading across her face. She pushes right past me and envelops Brooke into a hug. "I'm so happy you came back even though we did our best to scare you away."

Brooke stiffens for the slightest of seconds, before taking a deep breath and wrapping her hands around Ara. "The only scary part was when Connor chased me down the street like he was going to snatch my bag. Turns out he'd left his dignity in my pocket."

I open my mouth to get offended, but Ara cuts me off with a cackle. "I knew I was going to like you."

Brooke smiles, hesitantly, but it's there. "Thank you for the yellow paint, by the way. It was perfect. So were the plants."

LAST *Stand* FOR GENEVIEVE

I know her well enough now to see that Brooke likes Ara, too, and that's scary for her, but she's pushing through the fear.

Ara waves her hand through the air, a lighthearted dismissal. "Psh. Don't even mention it. Artificial plants are my specialty, and I'd jump at any excuse to buy them."

If I leave these girls to chat any longer, it's going to be a morning of girl power, and I'll find myself on the curb. I'm going to need my brother to help me even out the ratio here. "Where's Theo this morning?"

"He went down to the publishing house to sign the ARCs they're giving away for his next release, but he should be back any minute now." Ara's smile slowly turns to a frown as she looks toward the stove. "I was assigned to breakfast duty and…it's not going great."

"And we're acting surprised?" I ask, earning me a spatula smack that leaves a chunk of black goo on the sleeve of my shirt. "*Oiiii*!!!"

Brooke giggles. "Are those…*pancakes*?"

Ara sighs. "They were supposed to be, but I think in their final state, they're closer to the asphalt family."

Brooke laughs, a genuine one. "Let me help you. I'm kind of a pancake master."

Ara's eyes fill with excitement at this news. "Connor. You might have done something right for once."

Brooke giggles again and I smile, knowing I'll never get used to the sound, even if it means letting these two team up against me forever. She takes the pan and spatula from Ara, deeming them too far gone to be used before a thorough scrub. "Mind if I start with a fresh slate?"

"Yeah. Everything you need will be in the drawers under the stove."

Brooke starts to make herself comfortable, pulling out her supplies and finding her way around the kitchen. She even finds a cute little apron that was probably hung up to make the place feel "lived in" before it was handed over to us. It's definitely never been used.

"So what do you do, Ara?"

"I'm a clothing designer. I do a lot of commission pieces, but also full clothing lines. It's a somewhat recent thing, doing it as a profession, but I'm really enjoying it so far."

"That's amazing. What's the name of your label?" Brooke asks as she begins whisking the fresh mixture.

"AraDesigns."

Brooke whips around. "Shut up! You're Ara of THE AraDesigns?"

"Ha. Yep. That's me." A blush forms across Ara's face, still not used to the following she's amassed in such a short amount of time. I think if it weren't for seeing how happy her clients are, she wouldn't do it at all. She's not made for fame, but she *is* made for making things that make people happy, so she deals with the rest.

"I love your designs. I've always wanted an outfit from you, but it's never been the right time or place, and you always sell out in like thirty seconds after launching something new."

Brooke pours the first batch of batter into the pan.

"I know, it's so weird." Ara chuckles nervously. "Well, you know where to come once it is the right time and place. I'll make you whatever you want."

"This is crazy." Brooke shakes her head. "I've followed you on Pinterest since that first, *insanely* beautiful dress went viral. I can't believe I didn't recognize you immediately."

Ara groans. "I'm not offended. In fact, I wish nobody recognized me *ever*. I mean, I can't even fix a wedgie in public anymore."

Brooke laughs, flipping the pancake. "That's terrible."

"I mean, can you imagine walking through IKEA with your underwear fully up your ass, but everywhere you turn, there's teenage girls snapping pictures?" Ara shakes her head. "Don't get me wrong, I'd much rather this than everyone throwing up at what I make like I had expected, but damn, a girl needs a moment to pick a wedgie now and then, you know?"

"It's basic wedgie rights." Brooke nods along in agreement as she reaches for a plate, placing the pancake carefully in the middle of it. She grabs a few of the toppings Ara had laid out, toying with them a little before sporting a triumphant grin and presenting the plate to Ara.

Ara looks down at the plate, staring silently, for *way* too long. I almost laugh when I realize why. Brooke made the pancake in the shape of Mickey Mouse, using the toppings to give it a little face.

Then, completely deadpan, Ara turns her face toward me. "You better not fuck this up, because if you do, I'm keeping her instead of you."

I laugh. "A Mickey Mouse pancake and all loyalty just flies out the window."

I glance at Brooke, whose eyes are focused on Ara, the temperature of Caribbean waters and warm summer days. A part of me (one I wasn't aware of) relaxes, seeing them meld so effortlessly. Theo and Ara are my family, and witnessing one of them accepting Brooke as their own so easily, it has me feeling things I can't put into words.

Theo walks in at the exact moment that Ara pulls out her phone to snap a picture of her pancake, and takes in the scene: the pile of asphalt, the perfectly decorated pancake on Ara's plate, Brooke in a cute little apron, and me, probably looking like a lovesick school girl.

Theo smiles knowingly. "What do I have to do to get one of those?"

"Swear all loyalty to the Ice Queen, apparently," I mumble as Theo smacks his hand against mine, pulling me into one of those dude hugs.

"I'm happy for you, man," Theo says, only loud enough for me to hear, before pulling away and wrapping Ara in his arms. He reaches to snag one of her berries and she smacks his hand.

"You're eventually going to have to eat it," Theo says with a chuckle.

"Yeah, but I'm not ready yet," Ara says, indignant.

Brooke smiles, returning to her task of making pancakes as we all continue to talk about nothing and everything. Turns out, the Mickey Mouse specialty was only for Ara, forming a special little camaraderie between her and Brooke as Theo and I are smacked with ordinary ones.

"Tomorrow is actually my birthday dinner," Ara says to Brooke. "It'll be here, we're going to have a table-long spread of nachos and other Mexican food. It'll be a smaller thing, but I'd love for you to come."

"I'll be there," Brooke says with a grin, less hesitant than before.

I watch her every move, as we volunteer for clean-up duty and dance around the kitchen, afraid that she's going to open her mouth any second to tell me that she has to go, when all I want is to spend the rest of the day with her.

Eventually, I get brave enough to take fate into my own hands. "I want to take you somewhere."

She glances up with a smile. "Okay."

Huh. "*Okay?*"

"Yeah, okay."

I shake my head in disbelief. "Fuck, that's weird."

"What's weird?"

"Just going to have to get used to doing things without waging a war first."

She arches a brow. "I mean, I don't *have* to make things easy on you."

Closing the distance between us, I wrap my arms around her waist, appreciating the fact that I can do it whenever I want. "I'm not convinced that you would know *easy* if it smacked you in the face."

She smirks, before rising to her tiptoes and kissing me softly. "Are you sure about that?"

"I'd say I'm open to gathering further evidence." My hands move up to hold either side of her face as I kiss her again and she giggles against my lips. "Come on. Let's go."

• • •

Hanging hammocks is a lot fucking harder than it looks. The fact that these palm trees are so skinny and smooth probably has something to do with it, but being a hammock amateur, I couldn't tell you for sure.

The only thing keeping me sane is the beautiful blonde sitting on the bed of my ute, watching on as I make a fool of myself. Brooke must be in an extra good mood, having kept her mouth shut the entire time, decorated with a sweet smile.

Her blonde hair isn't pulled back, the breeze running through her strands like a soft caress. As usual, she doesn't have an ounce of makeup, the sun glancing across her face, illuminating her smooth skin. I was wrong before, the cloudless Florida sky has *nothing* on her eyes. Even with the blue backdrop, they stand out. One day I'll have to take her to the Caribbean just to see whether the water does them any justice as a comparison.

It's the most relaxed I've ever seen her, likely because she's no longer fighting herself at every turn, but a little part of me marvels at the fact that it may have a little bit to do with me.

"I think I've finally got these fuckers secured." I wipe the back of my hand across my forehead.

LAST *Stand* FOR GENEVIEVE

"Yeah? You sure this isn't just a carefully laid trap to get me to fall?"

"Pretty sure you *fell* all on your own." I tip my head in her direction, with a little wink because I'm an animal, and that's one thing that will never change.

Brooke rolls her eyes before walking over to one of the hammocks, pulling on the ropes and testing it with some weight. "Looks good. Guess we can add hammock hanging to your list of expertise."

There's an innuendo there, but I keep my mouth shut, not wanting to ruin the moment. "Not bad to have around, yeah?"

"How did you learn how to fix all of the things in that house?" Her little brow furrows in contemplation. "And how did you learn to play the guitar? How or why do you do anything?"

"So many questions, so much curiosity." I chuckle. "I'll tell you everything, but you have to get in the hammock and answer one question of mine first."

Brooke wobbles a little, trying to balance as she hands over control. She's putting all of her trust in something I've built, and the significance of this moment isn't beyond me. Finally finding her way despite the gravity and forces that pull her in other directions, she lies back, cocooned by the soft rope. Safe. With me.

Grabbing the acoustic guitar that I keep in the backseat of the ute, I head back over to join her, lying opposite so we can face each other. I mindlessly strum the guitar, playing something simple and sweet, perfect for this moment before asking my one question. "Where do you live?"

Brooke snorts. "I told you, I'm a bit of a nomad. Every couple weeks I move to another Airbnb."

Huh. "And which Airbnb are you at now?"

"You said one question." She gives me a cheeky smile. "It's my turn now."

I roll my eyes. "What do you want to know first?"

She takes a second to weigh her thoughts. "Tell me how you learned all the handyman stuff."

"That's easy. My mate growing up had a tradie for a father and he took us on jobs with him."

"Tradie?"

"Right. A tradesman. The guy who builds you a deck, or a kitchen, or whatever else you need." I smirk, loving the chance to teach her a little Aussie

263

slang. "My parents worked a lot, being doctors. So I was often at my mate's house, and his dad made sure I earned my keep. I picked up a lot of skills throughout the time I was with him."

"And when did you start to love music?"

I blow out a breath. "My first memory is of music. I was all by myself in my crib and someone had gifted my mother one of those things that play music over a baby? What's it called?"

"A mobile?"

"Yeah! A mobile. I remember wanting to sit there and listen to it forever. Eventually my mother came in and found me awake, just lying there, listening to music." I pause my strumming. "My dad gifted me a guitar when I was a child, not realizing it would become my passion in life, and the rest you know."

"They eventually kicked you out and you met Theo, then Ara."

"Yeah. Lou and Ryder too." I pick up the strumming again. "I'll introduce you properly tomorrow. Lou'll get to you before I even have the chance."

"You're lucky to have them and to have music."

"I know."

"I wonder if things would have been different for me, if I'd had something like music to pour myself into."

"Music saved my life. Writing saved Theo's. Designing clothes saved Ara's." I'm quiet for a second, observing the emotion swirl in her eyes. "Imagine how alone we'd feel in this world if there were no artists. I think creativity is the stuff of life itself, it's why we exist at all. People say that if you have an imagination, you're delusional. If they can't see what we see, then it's not *real*. But how would any of us have a future if we didn't imagine it? If we don't take the things we invent in our heads and bring them to life? If we don't take our trauma and find a way to turn it into something beautiful?"

"You have a lot of layers, Connor." Brooke brushes away a stray tear. "And you're right. All we have are our dreams."

"So, tell me one of yours."

Brooke opens her mouth, ready to shut it down or make less of whatever she is about to share with me, but thinks better of it. "I want to save the world." She pauses, looking down at her hands. "I want people to be happy again. I want to help them find their way, not leave them to be lost in their suffering. It's probably too late, but I have an idea of how I'd start."

Fuck me. I understand her perhaps better than ever. Brooke carries the weight of the world on her shoulders, wanting to help every single person on it. Every failure feels like her failure. When someone suffers, it's her suffering too.

"How would you start?"

"By spreading the truth about addiction, to prevent it if I can, and to help those who struggle with it. Give them a safe place or *something* to turn to besides substance abuse." She looks up at me. "Like music."

Brooke's always been beautiful, in a way that brings fire to my veins, burning me from the inside here. But sitting here, listening to her dreams that she's held so close to heart, she's bringing fire to my *soul.* Living my life by the side of a woman doing what she can to help those in need? Helping her bring art to the people who need it most?

I could think of no greater fucking purpose.

"Count me in."

Brooke looks up at me with a shy smile. "You don't think I'm crazy?"

"Oh, you're definitely crazy, but I think us crazy people are the only ones who have a chance at saving this place."

Something brightens in her eyes at my words. "If I do this, I'm probably going to need to learn how one turns to creativity. Maybe even learn an instrument myself."

I smile, deviously. "If only you knew someone with a guitar and a band."

Brooke takes my challenge for what it is, nearly knocking us both into the sand as the hammock shifts and twists, before she finally finds her place, leaning back into my chest. I place the guitar in her lap, wrapping my arms around her body to place her hands where they're supposed to go. I pull her close and decide to start with the basics.

Brushing my lips against the hollow of her throat, I breathe in her scent, eliciting a little shiver from her. "This is the neck." I move our hands up and down the neck of the guitar.

With our other hands, I press down on the body of the guitar, pressing her more against me in turn. I can feel her heart beating against the front of my chest. "This is the body."

I drag her hands over the strings, creating the smallest of vibrations as our hands glide over them. "These are the strings."

Brooke swallows. "I knew that one."

I smile against her hair, guiding her fingers over the bridge next. "Do you know what this one is called?"

She shakes her head.

"The bridge." Sort of like this moment.

As I continue to teach her the basics, my heart warms as it quickly becomes obvious that she's a natural. It could be her intelligent mind, which would set her ahead with anything she does, but there's a degree of innate talent here. The music speaks to her too.

After a few hours, she starts strumming the beginning notes to "Free Fallin'" by Tom Petty. It's then that I realize that I would do anything to make sure this never changes, that I get to spend my days with this woman, whether that means sitting back and listening to her play simple songs on the guitar, or following her into a den of dragons.

CHAPTER THIRTY-NINE

Then - Brooke

We remain silent, the windows of the backseat tinted too dark to even enjoy the scenery as we drive over the bridge from Tampa to St. Pete. I don't know what waits for us on the other side of this drive. It could be a bar, just like he said, but I hardly believe he will show us around celebrity-house-tour-style and then let us go.

It's too early for the bar to be open, but we walk right in. It takes a minute or two before my eyes adjust from the darkness of the car, to the bright sunlight outside, and now the dim lighting we find ourselves in.

One thing was true, the bar is beautiful. It's old fashioned, a little bit hipster-looking, but modern somehow. Like it was built from old money and has been kept beautiful by new money (or blood money, if we're being frank).

There's a bartender, whose eyes widen as we enter the bar. Within a second, those clever eyes have deduced that Ziggy and I aren't here on our own will, based on the hands which are wrapped around each of our arms. The men bark something at him about a button, but he hesitates, looking between me and Ziggy.

Dragging young girls here against their will must not be a common occurrence then, increasing our probabilities that it's *not* a sex dungeon back there. It's a bit of a relief, but who knows, this could be the bartender's first day. A moment too long has passed and someone barks at him again, louder this time.

If I weren't being dragged to my potential death—or torture—I'd take a minute to appreciate the fact that he's second-guessing this. Meaning he's not a monster, but the type of guy who stops if someone looks like they need help, despite himself, because there's some morals buried under that dark hair and tattooed skin. Maybe he's who I'm supposed to be replacing, thanks to those morals he's exhibiting right now.

There's no point. I want to tell him. *Save yourself.*

Almost as if I said the words aloud, defeat washes over his expression, proving that to whatever degree his hands are dirty too. The bartender reaches under the bar, pressing what should be a panic button, but is actually the button that unlocks a secret door along the back wall.

Victor tells everyone but his bodyguard to remain at the front of the bar as he leads me and Ziggy through the secret door. It leads to a lounge of sorts, the kind of place where some seriously shady shit goes down. Everything is black and red, no light is being let in, even during the day. The only visibility is provided by the red LEDs that give the place a bloody glow. The stages and poles don't surprise me, nor does the bar at the back until I realize they're displaying more than alcohol.

It's like a fucking narcotic candy store. Big clear cylinders (just like in a candy store), except with a solid gold dispenser at the bottom, line the far wall, holding pills of every shape and color. "Surely the cops would bust you too easily, with everything on display like that?"

Victor laughs. "It's adorable that you think cops actually work for the innocent."

I'm not sure why I even said it out loud; of course, he would have someone under his thumb to keep the trail unfollowed. And even if someone who *wasn't* crooked wandered in, from the outside it looks like a normal bar. You'd never know this was here.

"The city pays too little to keep men from going to the dark side. Eventually someone's kid gets sick, and they need money they can't seem to get their hands on in the daylight." Victor shrugs. "Even I'm charitable at times."

I keep my remark to myself, but I'd hardly call taking advantage of a good man, caught in a desperate time charitable, but okay. Victor gestures for me to take a seat and I do, picking a luxurious lounge that allows me to have eyes on the door we came through, also the only exit from what I can tell. I try not to think about the sort of things that likely happen exactly where I'm sitting.

LAST *Stand* FOR GENEVIEVE

Ziggy is still on edge, well past the point of trying to hide it. She sits on one of the lounge couches across from me, her right knee bouncing up and down. I've never seen her so…uncollected.

Does she think there's no use hiding how she feels, because there is no way out of this for us? I refuse to believe that. I will get us out of here, some *how* or some *way*. And if it can't be both of us, I'll make sure it's her.

"So you see, Carolina. I've put a lot of work and a lot of money into this bar, especially for the facilities dedicated to our most-valued parishioners."

"Cool." I can't think of anything else to say. Why is he telling me this?

"We take care of our bartenders, compensate them for the risk they believe they're taking for being at the front of such a place. As I said earlier, there's no *real* danger. Police are friends, not foes, for the right dime. Regardless, we'd make sure you feel compensated appropriately."

"Why are you offering this to me?"

"Because you've caught my eye."

Ziggy flinches across from me and I hate it, seeing her afraid. Why is it like that when you care for someone? Their suffering becomes your suffering, and all you want to do is absorb it all so it never bothers them again. I've never had much success with protecting someone, but as she sits there, eyes pinballing around, I vow to do a better job.

"The bar and this…club…are impressive, to say the least. But I'm content with what I'm doing now."

"Imagine what it would be like, having enough money to support your family."

"I don't have a family." My mask is on tight, I don't give a single thing away except for that tidbit.

"Then imagine being able to support hers." He sticks his jaw out toward Ziggy, and there's horror on her face.

Lucky guess? Or does he know more about the two of us than we imagined?

"She doesn't have one either."

He laughs again.

I hate that sound, especially when I'm not trying to be funny.

"Then imagine being rich enough to have a mansion of your own and anything else in the world you desire. Diamonds, private jets, designer things…

warm meals. Live a life where you don't have to hustle in the dark, putting yourself in danger every night."

Ziggy's eyes flash to mine, full of worry. Does she think I would consider getting into business with this man? More than I already am, that is. There's a large difference between being a worker bee off pollinating some distant flower, and being right in the hive.

Or I'd like to think there is.

"You make it sound very tempting, but I have to respectfully decline."

Victor looks at me then, before glancing over at Ziggy. She straightens her shoulders, forcing herself to find that bottomless bravado of hers I've become accustomed to, but it falls flat.

Victor snorts, and I feel like killing him. "I'd even make room for your… little friend over there, but only if it'd sweeten the deal."

I open my mouth, knowing full well what I'm about to say is going to get me in trouble, when one of his henchmen cuts me off. "Boss, there's an urgent matter you're needed for."

Snapping my mouth shut, my annoyance ripples off me instead.

"Feel like that was good timing for you." Victor doesn't miss a thing, and it irritates me further. He glances at the cell phone handed to him by one of the guys. "Make sure you get these two to wherever they want to go."

Getting out of here is that easy? Doesn't make sense. "And what's to stop me from going and blabbing my mouth about being kidnapped and taken to an all-you-can-pop pill lounge?"

Ziggy stiffens. I can feel her screaming at the side of my skull, *Are you fucking crazy, mija!? Why would you put that idea in his head!?*

Victor laughs. "Probably the fact that you're chock full of pills yourself. I go down, you go down, sweetheart."

There's a threat laced in there, I'm just not sure exactly where.

"Well, I wouldn't say anything anyway."

"I know. I'm not dumb enough to bring a rat into my own kitchen." Victor does a few silent signals with his hands, and his men move into action, besides the one designated to see us out. If I didn't want him to die on the spot, I'd probably think it was badass. "And keep an eye on the blonde one for me. Anything that happens with her, I want to know about it."

My stomach churns.

LAST Stand FOR GENEVIEVE

As Victor reaches the secret door, he pauses, turning back. "*Everyone* has a family if you look hard enough. Whoever you two have left, if you ever try to fuck me over, I'll find them."

• • •

"I should have shaved your fucking head."

Ziggy hasn't calmed down since we walked out of the bar, got shoved into the back of one of Victor's SUVs again, just to be dumped out on the side of the road as soon as we were within the Tampa limits.

"What are you talking about?" I tighten the straps on my backpack, just something to do with my hands.

"We need to go. We need to get out."

"Ziggy, you're not making sense."

"What don't you get? We need to go straight to the bus station and get as far as fuck away as we can."

Away? Away from her family?

"Ziggy, we can't do that. What about–" I shut my mouth, not wanting to continue, feeling the paranoia of imaginary eyes. I lower my voice. "You know who."

"There's a postal system."

"A postal system?" I scoff. "Sure! To send things! But what about seeing them?"

"We can visit."

"Ziggy. I feel like you're overreacting."

She spins on me, getting right up in my face. This is a side of her I have never seen, completely undone, utterly unraveled. "Overreacting!? You think I'm overreacting!?"

Ziggy pulls her hair and walks away with a yell. She kicks the air, punches through oxygen like she can defeat the phantom of whatever has been following us around since Victor first spotted me. I sigh, covering my face with my hands, not knowing how to calm her down.

"He knows that I have a *family*!!!!"

"It was a lucky guess; he doesn't know for sure." I hope. I *plead*.

"Doesn't matter! Even if it was a lucky guess, now he has a reason to look!"

"We haven't given him one, and we *won't*." All we have to do is not fuck him over, it shouldn't be too hard.

Ziggy laughs, but it's hopeless and defeated. "Were you not listening to a thing he said? He *wants* you. And he'll do anything to get you."

A haunting trickle drifts down my spine as I remember Victor's whispered words.

You'll soon learn that I always get what I want.

How far would he really go? Looking into the brown eyes of my best friend, wide and worried, I can see she thinks there's no line he wouldn't cross. And when has she ever steered me wrong? A sinking feeling hits my stomach as the scope of danger finally dawns on me, too late.

"Victor has decided he wants you, and unless you manage to get out from underneath his gaze, there will be no other outcome." She pauses, looking away for a moment. "He is evil, Carolina. He will use me and anyone else he can find against you. The only thing we can do is leave."

"Ziggy...I'm sorry. If you need to...go away...from me...to protect yourself... you should." And my mom? How would I ever protect her?

"*Chica estupida, estupida.*" She goes on and on, raging around the sidewalk saying things she knows I don't understand. Eventually, her breathing starts to slow. She runs her hands through her cropped hair, stops to look through her backpack like it's her version of hitting factory reset, making sure her supplies are accounted for and everything is in order. Ziggy nods, content with what she finds, and then turns toward me, recalibration complete.

"Here's the plan. We go back to the shipyard, see Marty and get what we originally went for. We unload it all tonight, give Marty the money he's owed, take only what we need, and drop everything else off." She meets my eyes and I understand everything she doesn't say aloud. We leave some for her family. We even leave some for my mom. "Then we take a bus somewhere far away, until Victor forgets all about the pretty blonde named Carolina."

"Ziggy, you shouldn't be forced to leave because of me. I should be the one to go."

She rolls her eyes. "If I wanted to be free from you, I'd get free. Yeah?"

My chest squeezes. "Yeah."

LAST *Stand* FOR GENEVIEVE

Something like fondness brushes across her face, there and gone so quickly I wonder if I imagine it. "How are those claws, mija?"

"Sharp."

"*Bueno.*"

We just need to get through tonight.

• • •

"I'm not going to miss this humidity."

I chuckle, relieved to have a little more of my friend back. The walk from the shipyard to just outside of Ybor has been relatively quiet, not something we do often. "Me neither. Maybe we can go somewhere where the leaves turn orange."

Fall was one of the things I used to love most, even the Florida version which barely qualifies. The moment it was deemed fall, I'd feel lighter, like my worries were falling away with the leaves. I'd be at Starbucks for my pumpkin spice latte, wearing a cardigan and boots even though it was too warm to do so. Imagine if it looked and felt like fall too?

A tentative feeling overtakes my chest, something a little like excitement. It's a cautious and timid thing, but it's there, leaving me to wonder whether I might still find joy in such simple things, despite what I've lost?

"What would you do with a fresh start, *mija*?"

A place where nobody knows who I am or who I was? It doesn't seem so bad. Far away from everything which has haunted me, everything that reminds me of what once was, maybe I could learn to walk again, without my tiny red crutches. Maybe it's not too late to get a little of myself back, for me and my mom to find our way back to each other one day.

"Someone I knew once loved books. She said that reading could save any day if you let it whisk you away to a world where your problems didn't exist. Being able to escape them sometimes helped her solve them." I shrug, a sharp fondness for her piercing my heart. "So maybe I'd work in a library, or a bookstore."

Ziggy nods, giving me a second in my feelings before throwing me a buoy. "I'm going to be a singer."

I laugh, knowing it's a joke. I'd never put her down if it wasn't, but the acoustics in that shower room told me all I needed to know. "You'd better think of something else."

"*Honestemente*, I don't know what I'd do. I've never allowed myself to imagine another life for me. This wasn't the life I would have chosen, *eso es seguro*, but it's all I could figure out with what I had and who I had to care for."

"Well, if you did let yourself imagine it, what would you do?"

Ziggy mulls this over, but shakes her head. "*No se, mija*. Thinking about that is new for me, not sure I know how."

"Fair enough."

"Well, there is *one* thing I'd like to do."

"What's that?"

Ziggy sighs, as if she shouldn't share this with me, but has officially thrown her rules out the window. "I want to watch the sun come up."

"You've never watched the sunrise?" Now that I think about it, I'm not sure if I have either. I've seen it happening in the background, but I've never slowed down to appreciate it as the forefront of the scene.

"I never wanted to ruin seeing it for the first time. My neighborhood... didn't have the best view for that. Since it's the one thing I *could* choose, when and where and how, I've been saving it for a day that I could wake up early and *buy* a coffee. Real honest, you know? Go somewhere with a nice view, and watch the sunrise." Ziggy shrugs. "It sounds *estupida*, but I don't care."

It doesn't sound stupid at all.

"Then that's what we'll do. Wherever we end up, we'll make sure it's got one hell of a view and a coffee shop."

"What do you think that's like, *mija*? Getting to do whatever you want?"

"I don't... I don't really know." When I was in school, my academics and everything I felt I had to prove owned me. Working so I could have the designer things while never feeling good enough, buried under the weight of my father's choices. I let it dictate everything I did. And even that doesn't hold a candle to the power my grief has had over me. Or the pills.

As we turn the corner on the home stretch, both of us begin to taste the freedom that's nearly ours. It's a life where we get to start over and choose for ourselves.

A life where we can be best friends.

My quiet contentment is split down the middle by Ziggy's scream. Time begins moving too quickly, leaving me behind to suffocate in its dust as I'm trapped in slow motion.

My head turns toward her, taking in the arm wrapped around her throat and the other arm creating a vise around her torso and arms. She's fighting them, but the arm tightens around her throat, forcing her to emit this horrible choking sound from her mouth and silencing her screams.

Ziggy can't breathe.

I use every bit of strength I have to battle the slow motion so I can get to her, free her, but I'm not fast enough. With a crack to the back of my head, everything goes black, trapping me in the antechamber of unconsciousness, where I can feel everything that's happening to me, but lose all control over my body. Sounds are muted as if I'm under water, my limbs remaining motionless as boots slam into my stomach, over and over.

I know this isn't death. I've been trapped here before.

Far away, Ziggy is screaming, but then she goes silent.

And as her cries disappear, so does my hope.

CHAPTER FORTY

Now - Connor

Rolling over, I take a deep inhale and grin. Brooke had to wake up early for work this morning, but my bed still smells like her, meaning that yesterday wasn't a dream. I spent the entire day with her, basking in her presence and soaking up the sun, as we took turns strumming on the guitar and trading pieces of ourselves. And yet, I still don't know what she does for work. Making a mental note to ask her about it when she's back, I focus on the parts of herself she *did* share.

What she revealed to me yesterday has opened my eyes to the kind of person Brooke really is. Not only is she beautiful, but she is brilliant, funny, and above all else, she is strong. She loves as fiercely as she fights. Brooke pushes me, she makes me question *everything*, and she ignites the passion that was slumbering within me.

Thanks to her, I'm becoming a better version of myself.

From the moment I met her, I should have known it would be different, the way she invaded my thoughts and warped my status quo. With one step into my life, she had me throwing away cigarettes and meaningless nights with women, in favor of something that gave me a future.

And that is exactly what I see in her.

A future.

I shake my head, the full weight of how much of an idiot I was, trying to deny my feelings for her, descending over me. What I feel for her is something far greater than just love, because love can come and go, but our fates have

LAST *Stand* FOR GENEVIEVE

been weaved together in a way that can never be undone. We are irrevocably intertwined for a reason that had never made sense until now.

Beyond love and even a future, she has given me a *purpose*.

I've always wanted to make people happier. Through music and creativity, I'd always aimed to leave people feeling better than when I found them. But Brooke? She wants to save the fucking world, and damnit, I'll do anything I can to help her do it. I'll use whatever following I amass to bring awareness to her cause, so people like Jayden know they're not alone, and they have something or someone to turn to before it's too late.

I open my phone, hoping to have something from the woman who brought a wrecking ball to my rules, and I'm not disappointed. She sent an anatomically correct heart emoji with the loud effect, seemingly giving it a heartbeat at the sight of me. I smack my face with a pillow, trying to wipe off the embarrassing amount of glee at her creativity, before returning the favor.

Then I notice a text from Ara.

Ara: I just saw your lady friend going into the courthouse.

Ara: I tried to say hi, but her power walk was a lot more impressive than mine, and I couldn't catch up.

Huh. The time stamp is around the time Brooke said she'd be going to work.

Connor: I'm a fellow victim of that power walk.

Connor: We should start a support group.

Ara: Ha. I LOL'd at that.

Ara: Like, actually LOLd.

Ara: She's still coming tonight, right?

Connor: I think so. She didn't say she wasn't coming.

Ara: Yay!

I can't help but feel slightly odd that Brooke didn't mention stopping by the courthouse. I mean, it's not really any of my business what she's doing at every hour of the day, but she had made such a big deal about getting to work at "nine on the dot" when I'd tried to tempt her to stay in bed instead, and per Ara's text, that's when she was arriving at the courthouse.

Brooke did say she's a nomad when it comes to work, so for all I know, she could be working at the courthouse today. She's never given me reason not to trust her, and thus, this suspicion is not deserved. There will be a reasonable explanation.

Connor: What are you up to?

Brooke doesn't answer immediately. Or even after a few minutes. Or fifteen.

I toss my phone and force myself to expel the mistrust and sinking feeling that's entered my gut, the way it does when someone isn't telling you the full truth. Running my hands through my hair, I chalk it up to the scars from my past doing their worst in an attempt to prevent further injury. Brooke will be at Ara's dinner, and I can ask her about it then. We'll probably laugh about how silly this was, my jumping to conclusions.

I'd called a meeting with the band today and they'll be arriving here soon, so I need to get my ass out of bed. They should keep me occupied enough. I'm in and out of the shower in ten minutes flat, before moving to the kitchen to get the coffees ready.

With a ding from the elevator, Rue and Dane are the first to arrive.

"Why the *fuck* are we meeting before noon?" Rue says as he does a zombie walk toward the mug of coffee I placed on the island.

I chuckle, having learned a long time ago that Rue could not be further from a morning person. He's barely a noon person. "Sorry, guys, this couldn't wait, but Ara's birthday dinner is tonight, and she'll be setting up all afternoon. So unless you want Lou roping you into–"

Rue raises his hand, cutting me off. "This morning is great, actually."

Dane smirks. "What is so urgent that you wanted us to meet now?"

With incredibly perfect timing, the elevator dings again, Dylan stepping out with a funny look on his face, as if he's just landed in an alternate dimension. "Holy…" He trails off, taking in the architecture and interior design of the penthouse. "…shit."

The floor-to-ceiling windows that look out over the water is where everyone looks first, followed by the kitchen. His gaze drifts toward every corner of the room, and I let him take his time. It's not every day people get to hang out in a place like this. When his eyes land on the spiral stairs I'd had Brooke on the other night, I claim his attention back and away, as if the evidence of what we did might be pressed into the wood.

"In case you're wondering, I'm not actually rich, mate. I'm just lucky to live here and have a rehearsal space."

LAST *Stand* FOR GENEVIEVE

Dylan whistles, still in shock, and I decide to keep going anyway. "I want to take our band to the next level."

"What are you suggesting?"

"I want to write more music, record *everything*, and start submitting our work to anyone who could give us a leg up. I'm talking labels, other bands that have connections, fucking everyone. I want to shoot our shot for real." I glance at Dylan, who's done ogling the flat and back with us. "I'm also considering finding a manager for the band, someone who can take our marketing and publicity to the next level.

Rue raises his brows, "What's brought this about? You've always stood by letting things happen naturally. Making a go of it on our own."

"And we've done well for ourselves starting out that way, but if we want to be bigger, we aren't going to get there unless we *hustle*."

The guys nod.

"Beyond all that, I want to make our sound more unique, but still *us*. I'm going to start to work on strengthening my own vocals, see if Dylan and I can't get close to what Ryder and I did at Poison Ivy that night. The response was insane." I take a second, meeting the eyes of every single guy. "Are you guys in?"

Dane and Dylan are the first to agree, so I set my sights back on Rue. "Rue? You in, mate? You know we can't do this without you."

Rue rolls his eyes. "Yeah, whatever. I'm in."

"Sweet as." I smile. "But tone down the enthusiasm, it's kinda disgusting."

Rue tosses me a middle finger and walks off in the direction of the rehearsal room.

"Connor, can I catch up with you for a second?" Dylan hasn't asked to speak alone with me before, and I get that awful feeling of trepidation for the second time today. Maybe I have food poisoning. That would explain the nonstop flipping of my stomach. I glance at Dane who nods before heading after Rue, giving me and Dylan some privacy.

"What's up, Dylan?"

"Listen, man, I just found out that my girlfriend is pregnant."

There's a weird stage of life where suddenly you don't know whether to say "Oh shit" or "Congratulations" when someone drops that kind of news on you. Guess it happens somewhere in our twenties, because I'm a deer in the headlights as I try to read his face and decide which route to go with.

Dylan laughs at my expression. "We're excited about it."

I release an embarrassed breath. "Then I'm happy for you, mate." But I still can't figure out why he's pulled me aside to tell me this.

"This sucks, so I'm just gonna come out and say it." A troubled look passes over his features as he grabs the back of his neck. "You've got me for the next seven to eight months, maybe a few more than that if you haven't found someone else, but after that I'm going to need to make being a dad my priority. I feel like shit because this opportunity is a *dream,* and I really believe in *Immoral Support.* And I don't want to mess you guys around—"

"Dylan…" I cut him off, placing a hand on his shoulder. "I completely understand, and I appreciate you giving me a heads up."

"Thanks, man, it's been eating me alive since I found out, but I want to give my kid the best life I can. Missing their first steps because I'm on tour? It would get to me."

"Then you're going to be a great dad." I smile, meaning it down to my bones.

He sighs. "Thanks, man."

"Head in and I'll be right behind you."

Dylan heads after the other guys, and I walk to the windows, needing some space. I'd been right about Dylan, but I hope I'm wrong about Brooke.

My phone pings, and I reach for it, a little too desperate.

Brooke: At work. Can't talk.

Right.

Connor: All good.

Running my hands through my hair for what feels like the hundredth time today, I try to brush off the mystery, keep my head in the game of taking my band to the next level while having no idea who will be the lead singer anymore. The hunt for another one starts anew, but at least I have six to eight months to figure it out.

• • •

Pretty soon, they're going to have to come up with a name for a new weather system, one that's a force to be reckoned with, capable of leveling environmental structures. It'll have to be something terrifying. Dashes of blues and golden curls whip through the space, more vicious than a tornado and as intimidating as a tsunami.

Lou, the one and only, tears around the penthouse, ensuring everything is perfect for her best friend's birthday dinner. Ara has been banished from helping set up her own party, and sits awkwardly on the couch as she's forced to watch everything come together.

Lou sends a finger stabbing through the air at me, and I glance behind me just to confirm it's me she wants. "Yes, *you*, you idiot."

I muster a smirk, but it's half-assed.

Her eyes narrow, "What's wrong with you?"

"He's lovesick!!" Ara yells from the couch.

Theo laughs from where he hangs decorations from the ceiling. "Be nice, girls. Connor is at a pivotal time, probably the first major moment in his life since he discovered boobs."

I gape at Theo. "What happened to bro code!?"

Lou snorts. "Who's the poor girl sentenced to being the object of his affections?"

"Don't be a douche," I tell Lou while sending a middle finger at Theo for teaming up against me. "Her name is Brooke and she's coming tonight, so don't make it weird."

Ara claps her hands together. "I'm so glad we can finally talk about this all together! Connor is absolutely *smitten*."

Lou pauses her assault on the party decorations. "As if you haven't already been sharing every single detail with me along the way."

I shoot Ara a pointed look.

"What? You never told me not to tell anyone, and even if you did, best friends don't count. And besides, who is Lou going to tell? I'm literally her only friend."

"Okay, fuck you for that." Lou mocks hurt.

Ara snorts, "I mean, am I wrong?"

"No, but you're still an asshole."

"A *right* asshole..."

The elevator dings and in comes someone who usually manages to get more shit for existing than even me, and I sigh with relief. It takes a millisecond for Ryder to notice the girls' expressions and the way I'm looking at him like he's my personal savior. His steps pause, like he might turn around. "The fuck did I just walk into?"

Lou and Ara both grin, before loping over to excitedly greet him with a hug. Ryder is still extremely awkward at their shows of affection, but he accepts it every time. I think he's got a soft spot for those two, and I don't blame him. They're too genuine to deserve the cold shoulder he specializes in for the rest of humanity.

"You're going to crush your gift," Ryder says into Ara's hair.

Ara pulls back, "You got me a gift!?"

Ryder rolls his eyes. "Yes."

Lou gives him one more squeeze, before snagging the gift out of his hands and taking it over to the present table.

I clap Ryder on the back before hanging my arm around his shoulders. "Thank God you showed up when you did, mate. I was getting triple-teamed. Theo's gone to the dark side."

"What'd you do to get shit this time?" Ryder's lips twitch, the only indication he finds something amusing. "Did you bring flavored condoms as a gift again?"

I can't help but grin. "That was a bloody great gift."

Ara scoffs. "You'll be lucky if I don't ban you from the Christmas Potluck this year for poor conduct."

"Who ended up taking them home, anyway?" I ask, genuinely curious about where they'd disappeared to.

Theo comes down off the ladder, joining us where we stand. "If it wasn't you, and it wasn't us…"

"We know it wasn't me." Lou rolls her eyes.

Ryder, straight faced and dry as ale, comments, "It was probably Dave."

We all burst into laughter, Ryder's lips twitching on both sides. Dave is what you'd consider a family friend, but also the most jolly man in the postal service. Over the year he spent delivering letters left by Ara's dad to her, they bonded, and he's got a standing invitation to all major holidays.

As soon as our laughter dies down, Ara doesn't give me an ounce of space. "And to answer your question from a second ago, Ryder, Connor went and fell in love."

Ryder looks at me, genuine shock splayed across his face. "Seriously?"

I nod.

"Holy shit." He shakes his head in disbelief. "You really had to go and leave me out here in the cold?"

"I'm still single too," Lou grumbles from where she's stuffing party favors.

"Sorry, mate. And actually, I'm the one who got caught in the cold–" My sentence is cut off by the ding of the elevator, and I know exactly who it is stepping through those elevator doors. That familiar tug in my stomach pulls me around to face her, and I lose my breath.

She has makeup on today, the first time I've ever seen her wear it. And fuck me, she's an artist. I won't even try to explain what she's done, because I'm a dude and I would butcher it, but she's all glowy dew atop the right amount of colors and shadows. Brooke's facial structure is stunning without a drop of whatever she's using, but with the effort she's put in to highlight every feature, she's something out of my dreams. Her blouse is a high neck, soft satin in ballet pink without a single crease, paired with high-waisted trousers in a deep red, and of course, her spotless white sneakers.

All in all, I'm a bloody goner.

There's nothing new about *that*, but the audience that's raptly watching me lose my shit *is* new. There's no way to conceal everything that I'm feeling, so I let myself write it across my face for them to see. I let every single person witness how wrecked I am for this woman as my stomach finally settles for the first time today, and I stalk across the room to claim her mouth with mine.

There could be an entire city watching, or nobody at all as we lose ourselves in each other. It's crazy how you can spend a handful of days with someone, and your existence becomes so altered that you feel off-centered in their absence. She pulls back first, her smile and eyes the temperature of a balmy summer breeze, and everything feels right in the world.

"I fucking get it now," Lou whisper-yells too loudly to Ara.

"Right!? She's fucking stunning."

"Not just that, but she's whipped his ass already." Lou pauses. "That came out wrong."

Brooke giggles and I smile, before she turns toward Lou. "You must be Lou. I'm Brooke."

"Oh, I know." Lou shakes her head. "You just brought about fifty more hottie points to this friend group. I mean, *damn* girl."

Brooke blanches for a second before recovering smoothly, as if she's slowly trying to remember what it's like to socialize and trade affections so freely. "Is that on top of the hundred you brought?"

Lou smiles. "Okay. I love you."

"Just wait until you try her pancakes." Ara moves forward to hug Brooke, then directs her attention to Ryder. "This is Ryder, by the way, our resident sourpuss, but he'll warm up to you eventually."

Ryder rolls his eyes and sticks out his hand. "I'm not that bad."

Brooke takes his hand and cocks her head. "You look familiar for some reason."

"Do you like to go bar hopping through St. Pete?"

She shakes her head, even though I see recognition strike in her eyes a second before it strikes in his. With her dad's background, she must know a thing or two about where druggies like to hang around. Would she be able to connect the dots that fast about Ryder's side hustle? In an attempt to steer the conversation away from that shoal, I remind her, "Ryder stepped in as lead at Poison Ivy. That's probably why you recognize him."

"Yeah, that must be it." Her grin is a little ingenuine this time, and I swear, I see Ryder's walls go up in the exact moment. As if they're both too clever not to connect the dots, as they watch the other do the same.

Ara glances between them, eyes widening at the tension that begins to permeate the room. She figured out on her own what happens behind closed doors where Ryder bartends.

"I'll make some drinks." Ryder makes his exit and Lou follows after him, their little camaraderie usually being the thing that gets him to chill the fuck out. Lou trades a glance with Ara as she walks away, and I know she'll fill her in later. Theo passes us two sodas from the giant bowl filled with ice, and we drink it quietly.

The tension recedes after a few minutes, Brooke getting her game face back on. I can tell that she's determined to make this a success. She and Ryder don't interact much after that, but everything is back in full swing as the others show up, mostly Ara's friends from the industry.

Ivy is the only one whom I've met. She was the first person to ask for a commissioned piece from Ara, and she just so happened to be a social media influencer with a massive following. Like, in the millions, across them all. Ivy

LAST *Stand* FOR GENEVIEVE

took Ara under her content-creation wing and helped her build AraDesigns to what it is, becoming friends in the process. She's rarely around, with all of her influencer travels, but it's cool when she is.

Everyone begins to make their way to the table, but before we sit, I just have to get this out of the way so we can fully enjoy the night. I gently tug Brooke toward the windows, far enough that nobody can overhear us. "You know you can tell me anything, right?"

Her brows lift in alarm. "What do you mean?"

I decide to take the indirect approach. "I'm just saying, if you were in trouble or if something happened, you could tell me."

"Uh…yeah. Of course." Full stop.

Okay. Direct approach then. "Why were you at the courthouse this morning?"

Her eyes flatten the smallest bit, taking up the defensive. "Were you following me or something?"

"What? No, of course not! Ara happened to be passing by and she tried to catch up to say hi, but you were too far ahead. She mentioned that she'd run into you, but I thought you were going to be at work."

She relaxes the tiniest bit, but I can tell there's something else there. "I had to pay a parking ticket before work, I didn't think it was a big deal."

"It's not a big deal, and you don't owe me an explanation for everything you do. I just…" Ugh, how do I even say this without sounding like a psycho? "Just know that if you ever got arrested, I want to be your phone call to bail you out. I'd be pissed that I wasn't deep in shit with you, but I mean it. If you need help to bury a body, I want to be your first call."

She swallows, before opening her mouth to respond, but I continue.

"I understand that you may never share everything there is to know about your past, and I have accepted that, but you have to swear to me that those are the *only* secrets between us. Never secrets about your present or our future."

My stomach plummets as I risk a glance up from where I clasp her hands in mine, finding the answer written all over her face. *Guilt.* She *is* keeping something from me, and whatever she was doing at the courthouse wasn't over a parking ticket. I could let it go, but unless I get the truth, we won't have a chance. "Why didn't you tell me you had to pay a ticket?"

She glances away, not making eye contact with me. "I was embarrassed."

For the first time, ice fills my veins, encasing my heart in cold as Brooke lies to my face. The dangerous thing about ice, it makes something that much easier to shatter, especially hearts. Giving her one last chance, I ask her a question which has the power to break us.

"Do you promise that you're telling me the truth?"

My question seems to torture her, but I refuse to back down.

Brooke closes her eyes, taking a deep breath. "Connor, I–"

She's cut off by the ding of the elevator, and based on the horror plastered on her face, which matches the rest of ours, she must have figured out exactly who's stepping out of the elevator.

Bill Carter.

Bulldog defense attorney. Terrible father. All around piece of shit.

Why *the fuck* is Theo's dad here?

CHAPTER FORTY—ONE

Then - Brooke

My face and head throb with enough ferocity, I'm eventually dragged from the depths of unconsciousness. One of my eyes barely opens, and everything looks blurry out the other. I groan as I close them again, wriggling my fingers and toes, and testing my arms and legs. Everything hurts, but it works. I force my eyes open again and all I see is the night sky.

Where am I?

My brain feels like thick slime as it struggles for an answer to my question.

How did I get here?

I'd been walking with Ziggy and then…her screams echo through my mind, followed by the terrifyingly loud silence that came after. Adrenaline shoots through my body, and I launch into an upright position too quickly, sending myself into a fit of vomiting. Doesn't seem like a great sign, but I don't care about myself right now.

Wiping my mouth on my sleeve, I spot Ziggy through my swollen eyes, where she lays in a heap just a few feet away. My stomach screams in protest as I force myself to crawl over to her motionless body. Small, raspy sobs break loose as I start to shake her and receive no response. My eyes are too blurry to see if her chest is moving or not, the ringing in my ears too loud to try and hear a heartbeat.

"Ziggy?"

No response.

"Ziggy, please."

This can't be happening.

"Ziggy, wake up!" I give her a shake, not gentle at all.

Nothing.

I shake her again. This time, she lets out a low groan. I can do nothing but rest my forehead on her chest and cry. So close to losing another person I love. Too close.

"*Mija*, if there is a drop of snot on my shirt, you're stealing me a new one." Her throat is raw from screaming, but I can still hear the sarcasm.

I laugh, but it comes out as another sob. "I thought you were…"

Ziggy slowly lifts one of her arms, wrapping it around me as I squeeze her closer. We sit there for a minute soaking it in, as if we both need the reassurance that it's real, that we both made it.

At some point I finally stop crying, and help lift Ziggy into a sitting position. Her face is heavily bruised from the hit that must have knocked her out, and her neck has a dark purple bruise in the shape of a forearm. The look on her face as she'd lost oxygen crowds my vision, but I force myself to look past it. We take in the surroundings, finding ourselves fully clothed, backpacks still here.

Ziggy's brow creases as she reaches into her backpack to account for her supplies. "Everything is how I left it. You?"

"Same." My stuff is all still inside, a weight lifting off my chest as I run my hand over Genevieve's favorite book, safe and sound.

A mix of realization and horror dawns on her face before Ziggy reaches into one of her pockets that descends all the way to Narnia and closes her eyes in defeat.

"*What*!? What is it, Ziggy?"

She pulls her hand out of her pocket, horribly empty. "They took all of it."

"*What*!?"

"I know you heard me, *mija*." Her voice is barely a whisper. "And you know exactly what they took."

"But…but…we can't have lost it." My mind rejects what she so clearly means. "That would mean…"

"It was Victor."

"How do you know that?"

"This was planned by someone who knew my route, knew exactly where to find us."

"But why would he…."

Ziggy looks up at me, sad and angry, hopelessness swirling in her big brown eyes. "Because he wants you. And now we *owe* him."

The words settle over me as dread finds a way out of the abstract part of the universe where thoughts and feelings usually live and takes on a physical form. It's a blanket, cool and terrifying, sending goosebumps and adrenaline through me. It's fear and despair in that all-encompassing way. "Then we have to leave now."

"We can't."

"Why? Just a few hours ago you said we could leave!"

"A few hours ago we hadn't lost an entire night's worth of product." Ziggy runs her hands through her cropped hair. "There's a difference between leaving when we owe Victor nothing, and leaving after royally fucking him over."

"He won't find us."

"As long as he lives, we would have a target on our backs. We could *never* come back here. I could never see my family, and you could never see your mom, and that's *if* he doesn't use them to draw us back. Or worse, kill them."

"Let's bring our families with us. We can outrun the targets on our back."

"Too risky. They won't be safe."

I cover my face, hoping the darkness provides clarity, but I see no way out. All because of my stupid hair and my stupid face, and because I was too weak to fight the darkness within me on my own, getting wrapped up in something that is way out of my league.

"We need to figure out some way to fix this, *mija*."

"We just have to get the money for what we took, right?"

"Yes, but unless we figure out how to do that tonight…" Ziggy groans as she lifts herself onto her feet. "It won't go unnoticed if we don't turn up tonight. There will be consequences."

She starts to pace, limping slightly as she does. The situation may seem lost, but that clever look is back in Ziggy's eye. With every painful step she takes, back and forth, I see her raising her shield of bravado.

"We go to Marty." Ziggy begins thinking out loud. "We tell him that we lost it, *temporarily*, but we have a way to pay him back. We just need an extension."

"When I had a job, it would have taken me months to make that kind of money. Would he make an allowance for that long?"

"I don't know!" Ziggy yells in frustration.

But she does know, and so do I. The answer is no. He wouldn't.

We would have days, not months.

We *have* to figure this out. It's nothing more than an equation. My mind starts to race, running through different scenarios and possible ways out of this, playing with the variables. When I needed to make a quick buck before, I'd sold my mom's earrings. Although I'd been gullible enough to be taken advantage of, it had still worked.

The issue now is that we don't have anything to sell. We're not professional thieves. Petty theft? Stuffing a candy bar in my pants? Sure. But candy bars won't be getting us the kind of money we need. There's only two of us, and neither of us have experience planning a *heist*. It'd have to be somewhere private, with little to no security, and lots of valuables.

Lightbulb.

Even though it's my idea, my soul flinches a little, but I won't let Ziggy's life become forfeit because I don't have the stomach to do what's necessary. "We can break back into that mansion we had our sleepover at, steal something and sell it."

Ziggy whips toward me, where I still sit on the ground. "I thought you didn't like my sticky fingers."

"I don't like the idea of someone else suffering because of our mistake, but I'm sure we could find something that they wouldn't miss too much."

"I'm sure even *they* would agree that one little bracelet isn't worth losing our lives."

"Remind me of that when my conscience starts rearing its head."

"You're a genius, *mija*." Ziggy grabs my hand, pulling me to my feet, and kisses me on the cheek. "We're going to survive this."

• • •

Evening has long since descended by the time we approach the shipyard. There's no cars out front besides Marty's, not even the crappy ones that I didn't realize belonged to anyone, and thankfully, none of those black-tinted SUVs

LAST *Stand* FOR GENEVIEVE

either. Ziggy said there couldn't be an audience, otherwise Marty would have to deny our extension, just to avoid setting a precedence of leniency.

Ziggy has spent the entire walk explaining how many powers are in play at a single moment within this ring. Marty must live his life, constantly looking over his shoulder to catch who is about to stab him in the back next. It sounds terrifying. And lonely.

A cool ocean breeze brushes over us as the little waves lap against the sea wall. It must be the effect of being here at night, but fear trickles down my spine, sending my gut flipping over itself. Looking over my shoulder, I find nothing and no one. Ziggy grabs my hand, giving it a little squeeze.

Even the warehouse is empty.

"Is this normal?" I whisper.

"I've never been here at this time. Everyone must be out doing what they do best." Ziggy shrugs. "It's a good sign, *mija*. I can handle Marty as long as nobody else knows. If the others were here, we wouldn't have a chance. Now we do."

Taking a deep breath, I use Ziggy's confidence to try and steady myself, but I can't shake the wariness. I glance over my shoulder one more time, finding nothing but empty shadows. Ziggy says they're out, but I can't help the feeling that they were *commanded* away, leaving behind a tangible eeriness similar to that of an empty town, evacuated before a storm.

Ziggy slows and drops my hand as we approach rusted metal stairs that don't do much for instilling confidence in their fortitude. "How are those claws, *mija*?"

"Sharp."

"Then let's get this show on the street."

A small smile graces my lips at her phrasing, as we take the stairs one by one, finding ourselves outside a door propped open with a paint can. Marty's office is just like the rest of this place, dilapidated and musty, the only difference being that his space is tidy. As Ziggy steps forward, Marty's bodyguard steps into the doorway, blocking our way inside.

"Let them in," Marty calls.

The monstrous man takes a step to the side, letting us pass. Marty's brow is furrowed, mouth drawn tight as he takes in our appearance. If I didn't know better, I'd mistake it for concern. "What happened?"

Ziggy squares her shoulders. "It doesn't matter what happened, we're here to tell you how we're going to fix it."

Marty's brow lifts.

"Everything you gave us today is gone."

"How did this happen?" A little bit of the danger that hides behind khakis and New Balance sneakers creeps through those words.

"We were jumped, knocked out from behind, and when we woke up, everything was gone."

Marty's eyes trail over our battered bodies. "That explains why you look like shit, but are you stupid enough to forget that this isn't a charity I'm running?"

Ziggy rolls her eyes. "Of course, I didn't, which is why we're here to tell you what's going to happen."

Marty opens his mouth, not loving the implied command from Ziggy, but I quickly jump in. "The way we see it, you have two options. You can shoot us, or enslave us, or whatever it is that you do with people who mess up. We may be dealt with, but at the end of the day, you'd still be missing product and money. You can pass the problem up to Victor, but from what I gather, that wouldn't be pleasant. As you so cleverly pointed out, this isn't a charity."

Marty narrows his eyes on me. "The second option?"

"You give us three extra days and we'll pay you back in full."

Marty laughs, but it's more like a scoff. "And how would two little girls get their hands on that kind of money? It'd be tough finding men who'd pay that much for your...services, looking as roughed up as you do."

My stomach roils at the implication, but I don't back down. "You know firsthand how dangerous it is to underestimate someone, because your enemies do it all the time." Marty's brow lifts with a hint of respect, and I use it to get another leg up. "You don't need to know how we'll get it, just know that we're good for it."

I catch Ziggy's eyes, feeling the kind of trust and camaraderie you only find in someone who has traveled by your side as you ascended from the pits of hell. It's that irreversible and unmatchable bond that goes beyond love, blood, and time, unique to staring death in the face and living to tell the story. Her eyes shine with it, and a little pride too. I'm a far cry from that broken, drugged girl she found sobbing on the sidewalk. I may still be drugged, and a little broken, but it's not all I am anymore.

"You have twenty-four hours." It's gruff, and dissatisfied, and simultaneously everything we needed to hear.

Ziggy and I try not to sag with relief, but it permeates the space between us. An extra day. It's not a lot of time, but it'll have to be enough.

"And you won't be paying me back in full, you'll be paying me back double-and-a-half as a little reminder to watch your fucking backs."

"My broken ribs and crushed trachea beat you to your little lesson, *hombre*." Ziggy rasps. "Make it double and you have a deal."

"You think you're in any sort of position to bargain?" A tiny bit of amusement dances across Marty's features. "I could just as easily take your lives instead."

"Okay, then." Ziggy shrugs. "Have fun balancing the books so Victor doesn't find out that product went missing under *your* eyes."

Marty laughs. "Double it is. And if you're late, I'll let Gilly choose what happens with you both, and he'd make it… regrettable."

Ziggy and I glance at each other.

"And not a word about the bone I've thrown you to anyone, or I'll make Victor look like a bully at recess. Am I understood?"

"*Si.*"

Marty looks at his wrist, wrapped with one of those ugly Velcro watches. He pushes a button, sending the god-awful beep reverberating through his bare office. "Your timer starts now, so I'd get the fuck out of here."

We don't have to be told twice, Ziggy and I nearly tripping over each other's feet as we back toward the door. We fucking did it. We have a chance to fix this. We're getting out of here.

Just as we reach the threshold, we're halted by a lazy, yet ear-splitting applause that starts up from behind us, echoing throughout the warehouse as if it's coming from all directions. Maybe it's the effect of the setting, but it's too loud and too menacing to mean anything good.

A cold, raw fear descends over me. I don't have to turn around, already knowing who's downstairs. Confusion, followed by fear, passes over Marty's face as he comes to the same conclusion as I do. With a flick of his hand, Marty has his bodyguard pulling a gun and pushing past us, down the stairs.

My paranoia wasn't paranoia. We were being watched as he laid out the cheese and we scurried right into the trap. There's a quiet zing, followed by the sound of a body dropping to the ground, just before it tumbles down the stairs.

I close my eyes, briefly wondering if he has a family that will miss him. No matter if you spend your life in triumph or suffering, it's so fleeting, taken from you faster than you can blink an eye.

Ziggy stands at my side, where she's supposed to stay forever, and we turn around together, meeting the stare of Victor as he strides across the ground floor. My first instinct is to run and hide, but I'm not a child, and this isn't a game. His gaze is unflinching as his hands return to his side, and a slow smile spreads across his face.

"Well, well, well. What do we have here?"

I almost snort, his line being less than original. Though Victor has only one guard with him, I feel dreadfully outnumbered.

Marty is the first to speak. "I wasn't expecting you back tonight."

It's an explanation, and accusation, all in one, but by the pitch of his voice, I can tell he's no longer at ease. Guess a dead bodyguard will do that to you.

"Is that why you thought it a good idea to let two thieves off scot-free?"

"*We're* the thieves?!" Ziggy scoffs, utterly outraged, but I silence her with an arm over her chest.

The less attention we draw to ourselves, the better. I peek over my shoulder to Marty's office. If things go really bad, we could break through one of the brittle windows and hope the jump from the second floor doesn't cause injuries that would prevent us from running.

"Come down here, *now*, the three of you."

There goes my window plan.

Marty surprises me by stepping in front of us to lead the way down the rusted steps. Does he have a sense of decency after all? Maybe, it never fully goes away even when we wish it to. But as I step over the dead bodyguard, I remember that isn't true for Victor.

"Ziggy has proven to be good on her word. I gave them twenty-four hours of leeway, and they know what happens if they don't follow through with it." Marty's voice is even, as if he's trying to reason with a wild animal.

"And you know what that says about you?" There's a pause, but Marty doesn't bother trying to answer. It's a good thing, too, because he wouldn't have had time. Victor pulls his gun and shoots him in the head, because that's what a shred of decency gets you in *this* world. "It says that your usefulness has expired."

A minute ago, I'd tell you it'd be impossible for my heart to beat faster than it already was, but it takes off again in another sprint. I'm on the verge of a panic attack, but I force myself to take measured breaths, knowing my life (and Ziggy's) depends on me keeping my shit together. Victor is speaking quietly to his bodyguard, and I use his distraction to look at Ziggy.

What do we do? I ask with my eyes.

I don't know. Ziggy's eyes are wide with fear, bouncing around the warehouse as if she can find us a way out of here if she looks hard enough. But neither of us can outrun a bullet, and with no weapons, we're at Victor's disposal.

The worst part? He knows it.

"So, ladies? Will it be cash or card?"

His bodyguard laughs, as if part of his job description includes making Victor feel clever.

"We have a plan," I reiterate pointlessly. "We only need a little extra time."

"We'll pay back what you stole from us and *then* some," Ziggy growls from beside me.

"You're right. I'm the one who sent those men to jump you." Victor smiles, not caring if we know the truth. "And since I didn't actually lose *any-thing*, you don't technically owe me money. Therefore, I'm only accepting *alternate methods* to make it up to me, for failing to protect what was mine."

My stomach sinks through my toes.

Ziggy's shoulders sag, but she takes a step forward. "It was *my* fault."

"As much as it was mine." I follow her with a step of my own, evening out our positions with a glare at her for trying to take the brunt of this herself. "So what do you want?" I snap.

Victor flicks his fingers, and with one giant stride, his bodyguard shoves Ziggy away from me. She hits the floor, nearly ten feet away, before rolling into a stack of crates with a loud thud.

"*Ziggy!*"

Thankfully, she scrambles to her feet, but the bodyguard holds up a gun and she stops where she is. Every cell in my body screams for me to look away, to close my eyes, but I refuse to cower.

"I want *you*, Carolina." Victor takes a step toward me. "Well, mostly just your mouth."

"No." I steel myself. "You don't get to touch me."

"Fighting, are we?" Victor tsks. "Had you been a willing participant, that may have been enough. But now that I'll obviously have to work for it…it's not really a fair exchange, is it?"

"DON'T YOU FUCKING TOUCH HER, YOU PERV!" Ziggy yells from her spot, but she quiets down as the bodyguard's finger plays on the trigger. A fraction more, and a bullet will be lodged in my best friend's brain.

Victor's gaze lands on Ziggy. "The only reason you're still alive is for leverage, so don't fucking push me."

As he takes another step toward me, eyes full of hungry intent, I begin to talk myself through it, because what else can I do?

I've survived a lot. Though I didn't do it the right way, I fucking survived.

I will find a way to survive this. Whatever sort of intrusion I'm about to face, I will get up and walk away from it.

This will *not* own me. Victor will *not* own me.

Nobody and nothing will ever own me again.

Victor takes a measured step as his eyes drag down my body, but I don't give him the satisfaction of looking scared or cowed.

Ziggy lets out a feral scream as he takes another step.

It's okay. I tell her with my eyes.

No, it's not. She tells me with hers, and I know it's from personal experience.

Look away. But I know she won't. She'll wear the scars of this night with me.

"I know you're jealous, *amiga*, but you can only watch." Victor jeers at Ziggy, making me sick.

"*Voy a sacarte de aquí, mija. El no te tocará,*" Ziggy whispers. She's speaking to me, but I don't know what it means, and I don't have time to wonder.

The warehouse, void of the usual crowd, felt like an omen earlier, and while I wasn't wrong, I'm grateful for the emptiness now. Victor's bodyguard watches on with rapt eyes, barely keeping the drool inside his mouth. Realizing there could have been countless more witnesses makes this feel like a small mercy.

LAST *Stand* FOR GENEVIEVE

Victor licks his lips as he takes that final, revolting step. I swear to myself not to cry, not to scream, or give this man an ounce of the power he wants to have over me. As his hands drift up my stomach, I bite down on my tongue as the reality of it sinks in.

And then I scream.

Blood splatters across my face, and before I have time to figure out where the gunshot came from, Victor falls to the ground. My ears scream with the echo of the unsilenced bang, ringing loud enough that I don't hear the quiet zing from where the bodyguard stands.

All I see is blood. I'm covered by it. But none of it is mine.

My head whips toward Ziggy, the entire world tilting on its axis as I watch her clutch her chest and sway on her feet. Time slows down, just enough so I can watch, but not slow enough for me to stop it. Trapped as its witness yet again, I pray for the superhuman strength and speed I'm supposed to gather from someone I love being in danger.

But it doesn't come.

"NOOOOOOOO!!!" I scream.

Ziggy's free wrist flicks up with a gun I didn't know she had, just before she hits the ground. Another loud shot rings out, and the bodyguard hits the floor. I'm surrounded by bodies, and I pray they're all well and truly dead, as I run to my best friend, my partner in crime.

No. Not again. Please not again.

"Ziggy!" I fall to my knees beside her, barely getting oxygen down. "Ziggy!"

She groans as I lift her shirt to find where the blood is coming out, pressing my hand over the wound. I feel around her back, but there's no exit hole. Ziggy has a gunshot wound to the chest, the bullet is still inside, and she's bleeding too much, too fast.

A small sob escapes me because the version of Brooke that planned to go to medical school knows what this means. We have three to five minutes before she bleeds out, and the average response time is seven. I launch over to Victor's dead body, gagging as I feel through his clothing and find a phone to make the call anyway.

"911 what's your emergency?"

I sniffle. "I've been shot in the chest. There's no exit wound. I'm bleeding out."

"Ma'am, what is your name?"

Tears run down my face, but I stifle my cries. This part is important. "I'm at an abandoned warehouse off the Port of Tampa Dock, the one directly on the water. It's a light green building, covered in rust and broken windows. There's a silver sedan parked outside. Please hurry."

Ziggy coughs and I crawl over to her, moving her into my lap as I rip away half of my shirt, balling it up and applying pressure to the wound.

"If your stubborn *culo* looks that worried, this can't be good for me."

Another sob escapes because I'm not capable of laughing right now.

"If…I don't make it…please make sure *mi familia* is okay." Her words are less than a whisper.

I nod furiously, because of course I will. "I promise."

Ziggy smiles, her face pale. Though her bleeding has slowed, there's still too much seeping through the cloth onto my fingers.

"Can I tell you something?" Ziggy doesn't wait for me to answer. "My real name is Melinda."

Melinda.

"It suits you." I run my fingers through her cropped hair, praying that help is almost here. "Brooke and Melinda."

"Brooke and Melinda." She smiles at that. "*Mi mejor amiga.*"

And then I lose it. I'm sobbing and sobbing because I don't understand most of her Spanish phrases, but somehow I know what this means. "Please don't leave me."

"Don't let it own you this time." Ziggy's eyes close, as if she's too tired to keep them open for any longer. I can't imagine a world without her big brown eyes. "I'll miss you, *mija.*"

I lean down, hugging my best friend tight, wishing and praying there was anything I could do to keep her here with me. "Please don't go. Please don't go yet."

"*Nos volveremos a encontrar.*"

"Please…we…we didn't get to watch the sunrise."

"*Prometo estar ahí cuando lo hagas.*"

"You shouldn't have to die for me!"

"*Lo haría de nuevo, chica tonta. En un instante.*"

Melinda takes her last shallow breath, and I hold mine, praying that another one of hers comes, but it never does.

CHAPTER FORTY-TWO

Now - Conner

ill has deteriorated even more than the last time I saw him, his skin a deeper red and skin a tougher leather, as if he's slowly withering away from the continued abuse of alcohol, and the festering rot of his soul.

At first the room is frozen, and it pleases the hell out of him, having this effect on people. I see the anger explode within Ara first, but seconds before she tries to launch toward him, Theo grabs her arm to hold her back. It does nothing to keep her words in, though. "Get OUT!"

"You must forget that I own the place, and therefore reserve the right to stop by any time I like." Bill's eyes drag across the room, hanging on Brooke for a second too long, and for whatever odd, instinctive reason, I gently push her behind me, as if I can shield her from his poison. "Heard there was a party I wasn't invited to, so I figured I'd drop by and let you know that my feelings are hurt."

"*Good.* I hope they're fucking hurt." Ara is physically vibrating with the urge to claw his eyes out, and I can't blame her.

"What do you want?" Theo's voice is hard as granite, and despite the years of abuse this man put him through, he stands strong. My chest fills with pride at my brother's steadiness.

"Like I said, I felt like going to a party."

"Well, you've gone to one, and now it's time to leave."

Bill's eyes drift back to Brooke from where she peeks around my shoulder, a strange look on his face before going back to Theo and Ara once again. Even sunshiny Lou has murder written in her eyes. Ryder's got his hand on her shoulder, holding her put as the other guests whisper between each other, trying to figure out what the fuck is going on.

Then the scariest thing in the world happens, Bill smiles, nice and slow before pinning his gaze on Brooke. "Wait, don't I know you?"

My stomach sinks.

"Aren't you the disaster of a girl who showed up at my office with some pathetic sob story, asking for pro bono representation?" The way he says pro bono makes helping another person sound revolting, and to him it probably is.

"I don't know what you're talking about." Brooke's voice is nothing but a husk of a whisper.

"Saying that does nothing but prove that you know *exactly* what I'm talking about, you just don't want *them* to know." Bill laughs, the sound is something from my nightmares. "Would anyone else like to know her little secret?"

Nobody says a word, but it won't deter him from sharing it anyway.

"Or maybe you all already know and don't care, and *that* would be a direct breach of our little living agreement here, resulting in eviction. If you recall, one of my only stipulations for providing this place to you for free, was *no* criminals." Bill takes a few slow steps toward the table of snacks, in what he believes is a power move before popping a pretzel in his mouth. "And that little blonde over there is a convicted criminal."

Brooke steps out from behind me, and this time I don't stop her, my world falling off its newly found axis. "I'm in the middle of an appeal hearing to be exonerated from that conviction."

"Regardless of what the courts say, underneath that pretty little face is nothing but a worthless drug addict."

"HA! All that coming from a deadbeat alcoholic who likes to beat on kids when he's not getting rich off the guilty!" Ara pitches in, not letting her new friend take it on her own. I'm glad she does because I'm useless, standing here in this frozen horror, too shattered to get my shit together and help.

"I'm not denying that I was once an addict, but when I was charged, I was clean. I plead not guilty because I truly wasn't." Brooke steels herself. "There was evidence that would have exonerated me. I've petitioned for a re-trial of my case to clear my name, to get the fresh start I'd nearly killed myself to get, before the justice system took it away."

Everything else goes quiet as the sound of rushing water encompasses my mind. Thoughts, just small moments in time that once seemed unrelated, race by, caught in the furious current.

It explains why she's so against anything that has an addictive quality, the walls she's built around her past, and her poor handling of grief which estranged her from her mother. When I'd told her I'd lived on the streets, and her begrudging acceptance of me after learning that, as if she understood me *better* because of it.

It's why she takes on strange jobs and moves from Airbnb to Airbnb, if that was even the truth. Why she turned down a trip to McDonald's after finding out which location it was, Ybor is crawling with druggies, and if she's on parole, that would certainly risk violating it. It's how the homeless man recognized her outside of the thrift store. It's why she seemed to have so much certainty on how Jayden was feeling.

It's why she was at the courthouse today.

Understanding comes crashing together like one life-threatening wave, finally allowing me to make sense of the enigma which has always been Ice Queen. It steals my oxygen and drags me across the floor, leaving me feeling battered and broken. How many times has she lied to me? How many secrets has she kept, even though she knew it was the only way she could really hurt me?

Somewhere far away, Bill swipes a finger through Ara's birthday cake, sampling the frosting. If my heart wasn't getting trampled, I'd find it nauseating, probably even get a good punch in. But I *am* getting trampled.

The voices are muted as they continue to go back and forth around me, as I watch on, useless and disconnected.

"The danger with reopening cases is that more evidence can come to light, not just what you want to be seen. Imagine what would happen if someone moved that you should've been tried as an adult, with a few more years getting tacked on."

I should be protecting the girl who has my heart, calling his bluff on his empty threats, but I'm lost. Brooke's secrets have broken that heart, and I'm stuck, utterly motionless outside of the cacophony that's happening between my ribs.

Brooke's shoulders cave in, sending Theo stepping forward in my absence. "While we're imagining things, let's say a son came forward with piles of evidence, proving years of abuse. What would happen to the father and his position?"

Bill laughs. "So you've finally found your balls, son."

Sound rushes back in as I finally hit the surface, ripped out from underneath the wave by Bill's hateful words.

Three strides. That's all it takes for me to get to him. Using every bit of lean muscle, I throw my arm back to gather the momentum needed to smash this motherfucker's face. But a soft, small hand hooks around my elbow before I can let it fly. I meet her eyes, the anger still brimming within me.

"Don't give him what he wants." Brooke gives her head a little shake, a strength and gentle promise of retribution in her eyes. "Don't."

And as usual, as if she's got a universal remote to my emotions, I ease back into a quiet anger. Without the explosive heat of rage, I'm left to feel the sharp stabs in my chest, the reminder that I can no longer trust the promises in her clear blue depths.

Bill laughs, clapping his hands. "Oh, isn't this just delicious? This party is turning out to be even more fun than I expected!"

I gently pull my arm from Brooke's grasp, grateful for her interception, but her touch reminding me that I can no longer depend on it. Making my way over to Theo, I get ready to weather whatever storm Bill decides to throw at us next.

"You know what's even more dangerous than getting thrown in jail? Tik-Tok." All of our heads turn as Ivy stomps toward Bill in her purple stilettos, pointing to her phone. "I just recorded this entire little display of yours. I hit one little button and my five-million followers, not to mention the *billions* of other users, will get to watch your toxic little power play. And if you've never heard of cancel culture, let me educate you. You will be ridiculed. Your career will be over in an instant. You won't be able to leave your house, until someone gets your address and decides to burn it down. So unless you want the world to know exactly who Bill the Bulldog *really* is, you're going to walk your ass out of this penthouse and leave my friends alone."

Bill looks Ivy up and down, assessing his adversary. He smiles, but it's less confident than before as he meets Theo's eyes. "Always letting the little girls fight your battles. See you *soon*, son."

LAST Stand FOR GENEVIEVE

As Bill pivots to make an exit, Lou rips her shoulder out of Ryder's grasp, sprinting toward the table and grabbing Ara's cake. "Hey, Billy Bob! You forgot something, you piece of shit!" And with that, she launches the small, chocolate buttercream cake through the air. It's cartoon-worthy perfection, as it hits its mark just as Bill turns around, smacking him in the face before sliding down the front of his expensive clothes.

Everyone howls, as Bill raises his finger in the air and points at Lou. "I'll find you."

"Relax, *Liam Neeson*." Lou snorts, rolling her eyes. "I'd be more worried about that pretty little shirt of yours. You got some frosting on it."

Ara squeals and wraps her arms around Lou and Ivy.

Bill turns and storms toward the elevator, slamming the button over and over in fury as he's forced to stand there in all his chocolate glory, waiting for the elevator to finish its ascent through forty-something floors.

"We really have to get a fucking door." Theo chuckles.

"No doubt," I agree, shaking my head and putting my hand on his shoulder. "You good?"

Theo nods. "Thanks to you guys, I came out of that relatively unscathed."

There's finally a ding, and with it, Bill is gone, all of us releasing a breath.

"Now let's get this fucking party started again!" Lou rushes back into action, enlisting the help of the rest of Ara's fashion friends. "Who wants to help me Uber a new cake!?"

Ryder makes his way over, having already poured an entire serving tray worth of shots. They're in mismatched cups, from plastic tumblers to crystal wine glasses and coffee mugs, but it'll do the trick. His only contribution to the battle, but goddamn, is it perfect timing.

We all knock one back. Even Brooke.

Theo looks between the two of us, before grabbing Ara's hand. "We'll give you two some privacy."

I stalk toward my room, knowing Brooke will follow. Facing the windows, my room no longer feels like my own. It's full of her, covered in her scent and memories. This morning it felt like a sanctuary, but that was before she took my trust and used it as a doormat.

"Connor, I'm *so* sorry."

"You lied to me." I pause, turning to look at her.

303

She's so beautiful, and it makes this so much more painful, not being able to pull her into my arms, but this is something that can't be fixed with her skin against mine.

"You were going to *keep* lying to me." My voice cracks, just like my heart did.

Brooke shakes her head. "I was going to tell you, I *swear* that I was. I just didn't know how–"

"You didn't know *how*!? I gave you *so* many opportunities!" My voice is unintentionally getting louder, so I take a breath, running my hands through my hair until I feel my soul go quiet. "I *begged* for you to share everything with me."

"I know, but I was just…so afraid."

"Afraid!? Afraid of *what*?"

"This!!" She motions between us, as if there is something tangible there. "You turning your back on me!"

"You've forced my hand!"

"Can't you understand? The thought of you walking away from me is terrifying! And I knew that's exactly what would happen if I told you everything!"

"Then you still don't know me at all." I scoff.

"You say that, yet you're walking away from me right now!" Brooke puts her hands over her mouth, holding back a dry sob. "I can already feel it, the distance between us, as if you've already severed what tied us together. I've lost you, haven't I?"

"I have nothing to say to that, other than I guess when you start to wonder where all this went wrong, take a look in the fucking mirror." I know I'm being too harsh, but it's like the scars from the wounds of my past have been meticulously sliced open by a scalpel, and I'm bleeding out where I stand.

"Connor, please. I don't blame you for rejecting this, because what kind of life could you have with someone like me, but I've *changed*. I have made… so many mistakes. More than anyone should be allowed to make in a lifetime. I will *never* make up for what has been lost, but I swear, I *have* changed–"

"Do you think this is because you struggled with addiction? Or have a criminal record?"

She pauses. "Isn't it?"

My laugh is lifeless, a dead husk of a thing.

LAST *Stand* FOR GENEVIEVE

"How many times must I say this?" I ask the sky, before taking a few steps toward her, just to come to a stop again, reminding myself that although she's here physically, what we had is now too far out of reach. "Brooke. I need you to hear me. To really fucking listen to what I'm about to say."

She nods.

"I don't care if you have a fucking record. I don't even care if you get fucking arrested *tomorrow*, as long as when they put you in the back of the cop car, I'm right there next to you!" My chest feels raw, so painful. "This has never been about your past, or judging you for mistakes that you've made. I would *never* hold that against you. I'm standing here in front of you, as a broken man, because you had no problem keeping it a secret from me when it spilled into your present. *Our* present." I shake my head. "And that was the *one* thing I begged you never to do."

There's a silence, something has shifted. A pressure descends over us, like a cloud pushing and pulling as if it's trying to force the atmosphere into action.

And then, she starts to cry.

Fuck me does it hurt not to be able to wipe it away, to pull her into my arms and tell her everything will be okay.

It'd be an empty promise. Just like hers.

Brooke touches her face, as if in shock, as more tears begin to fall. It's a foreign feeling, but her fingertips glisten with the truth of it. Caught in a moment of disbelief, Brooke rubs them together before looking up to me.

"I'm glad to see you're finally letting yourself feel." I shove my hands into the pockets of my jeans. "I just wish it wasn't too late."

And with that, I walk away from the center of my orbit.

The sit-down dinner idea has been thrown to the wolves as I take in the state of the living room, which looks more like a rager than anything else. Everyone is already on their way to drunk, partying away what the start of the night had brought. I locate the birthday girl fairly quickly and make my way over.

"Connorrrrrrrr!!!!!" Ara tipsy dances her way over to me, but her face starts to fall as she reads the expression on my face.

"I need to go get some air." I lean in, giving her a quick kiss on the cheek. "Happy birthday, bestie. Let's have a do-over sometime, yeah?"

Ara nods, concern in her eyes. I know she wants to ask what happened between me and Brooke, but I'm not ready for that yet. It's too raw. She gives me a reassuring smile, with a knuckle bump to my shoulder, and lets me go.

Right now, I just need to be alone.

CHAPTER FORTY-THREE

Now - Brooke

There's a knock at the door, even though it's open, meaning whoever is standing there has already seen me slumped over, bawling my fucking eyes out over a pile of tissues. They're just being kind enough to give me the opportunity to not acknowledge them and pretend like nobody found me like this.

But I know exactly who's standing there.

"Come on in, birthday girl." I blow a disgusting amount of snot into another tissue, following it up with a second one, just in case.

Ara stumbles into the room, plopping down next to me on Connor's bed with the grace of a chimpanzee. "*Ooof.* Sorry 'bout the crash landing. I'm a little tipsy, and I'm bad in heels as it is."

I push my pile of tissues to the side and grimace. "I'm not exactly in a position to judge."

"True," she agrees merrily. "So, you went to jail?"

"Yeah. I did."

"What was it like?"

"For the most part, I was left alone. Scary shit happened, but it wasn't every day, and a lot of the time it was because of the guards, not the other inmates."

Ara shudders, but keeps the pity off her face.

"Nothing ever happened to me. I was enough of an emotional zombie that nobody took much notice, and my cell mate watched my back when they did. If I'd been in a better place, we probably could have been friends. She was terrifying, but...ultimately good."

"How long were you there?"

"Two years."

Ara gasps. "Two years!?"

"It went by faster than you'd think. And besides, I sort of needed that time to...decompress."

"What did you do when you got out?"

"What most people do when they're on probation. I've been bouncing between crappy apartments and crappy jobs, accepting whatever I'm offered by those willing to hire a criminal."

"That's awful."

"The messed-up part? When I got 'caught', I wasn't even—" I sigh, can't help it really. "It's a long story and I fucking hate crying. And emotions."

"You don't say?" Ara manages to keep her smile to a two out of ten, but her amusement is impossible to conceal.

"I fucked up, didn't I?"

"Yeah, you did." Ara shrugs. "But you can fix it."

"How can you be sure?"

"Well, I know Connor...and as much as he wishes he didn't, he has a huge heart. I've never seen him care about anyone the way he cares about you, which means you're one of the few lucky ones who's earned a spot inside. You just have to show him that it's safe to have you there."

"You make it sound so easy."

"You're the one making it complicated." She pauses, before smacking her hand over her mouth and mumbling, "Oh God, that was *way* too honest."

"Honest, but not wrong." I shake my head as more tears begin to fall, as if every single one that I've denied for the last few years has returned with a vengeance. "I've lost too many people, and it was the fear of losing another which made the possibility into a certainty."

My admission drags me back to the night I lost someone else.

Each second is excruciating as I sit here, holding her limp body, crying and crying. All it took was a handful of minutes to lose everything I've started to treasure. I could rip the universe to shreds for this. The sound of a distant siren rends me from my misery.

Looking around the warehouse bathed in blood and dust, desperation flows through my veins. It's wrong to leave her here. I know that. But knowing that I'd get caught up with the police and possible drug lord revenge, Ziggy would tell me that it's wrong to stay.

What would Melinda want? I'd like nothing more than to be able to ask her, but since I can't, I'm forced to honor what I know Ziggy would want.

Picking up the cell phone, I wipe off my prints, using what remains of my t-shirt and place it in Ziggy's still-warm hand. A sob escapes me as I imagine her rolling her eyes and saying something snarky in Spanish that I couldn't understand.

I'll miss her personality that was too big to fit in a room.

I'll miss her teasing.

I'll just miss her.

Grabbing the gun from where she dropped it, I wipe off her prints and slide it across the floor so it lands somewhere in the middle of the mayhem and murder. The sirens are closer now, I have to hurry.

I hate it. I hate everything about this world.

This world where my dad walked out.

This world that stole my sister away.

This world that took my best friend before I ever got to tell her what she meant to me.

The sirens are louder now. They'll be here any second.

Falling to my knees for the second time tonight, I lean down, kissing her on the forehead.

"I'm going to try to be grateful that you saved me. I'm going to try to be worth it."

The sirens are right outside now. I grab my backpack off the floor and find a broken window that's just wide enough for me to squeeze through. Tires screech and doors open, followed by shouts and running footsteps.

I allow one final sob to escape before I shove it all down and swear never to cry again. With that, I duck out the window, leaving my best friend in the world to become nothing but another Jane Doe in the morgue.

What does Genevieve think of me now? She told me I was her hero once.

The paramedics are rushing around as if they still have a chance, but I felt my friend stop breathing. I felt her last heartbeat. And that feeling will haunt me for as long as I live.

When I lost Gen, she was just... gone. Seeing death is different. Watching it creep in and steal someone away, leaving you with a shell of what they were, it breaks you a little harder than the concept of it.

The paramedics carry her out on a stretcher, shouting as they rush her to the ambulance. A small bubble of hope creeps up in my chest, until one of them yells, "Still no heartbeat. We're out of time!"

Always out of time.

They lift her into the back of the ambulance, and with the slam of the double doors, this short chapter of my life comes to a close. My head falls into my hands. In one way or another, I have lost every single person I have ever cared about. After so much experience with it, I know that there are two ways to respond.

You can let it consume you bit by bit every day, losing yourself and losing your connection to them. With it, you lose the joy you once felt in their presence, because when you think of them now, all you see is pain. You don't remember their smile or the moments you should treasure because it's overshadowed by what it was like to lose them.

Or you can make a stand.

You can feel it, but you don't let it consume you. You can fight for your freedom to continue to love them, and never let the grief take that away. You don't let the loss taint the joy you once felt by their side. You force yourself through the pain so you can remember their smile and smell, because the good times are fucking worth it.

And then one day, the love and gratitude for getting to share whatever time you got with them will eventually outweigh the pain.

When I lost Gen, I let it consume me.

I lost my connection to her.

I lost myself.

I lost my mom.

And then, I lost my best friend.

If I keep living my life this way, letting tragedy own me, I will continue to lose everyone.

This time, I'm going to fight. I'm going to fight for the life Gen never got to live. I'm going to fight for the freedom Melinda never got to taste. And because I can't live with the thought of Genevieve watching over me, seeing what I've become, it's time I make a stand.

LAST Stand FOR GENEVIEVE

I stop at the first gas station I find, using the coins left in my backpack to buy five bottles of water. My legs ache as I walk all the way back to the bridge, which has been like a home to me out here. The shakes have already started, but this time I embrace them.

No pain I feel will compare to the pain Genevieve felt, the pain Melinda felt. I will be stronger than it. I won't give in.

Cold turkey is life threatening, I know that, but if I survive this, I'll honor their lives by truly living mine. And if I don't, then maybe I'll get to see them again.

Ara gives my shoulder a gentle shake. "Brooke? You still with me?"

"Yeah." Except I wasn't.

"I asked you if you love him."

Fuck. "Oh."

Do I love him?

I think of the way Connor's shaggy hair falls over his face when it's grown out too long. The feel of his calloused hands as they drag across my skin. The look of determination he sports when he's trying to get something right. The infinite amount of care he shows for his friends, how he shows up for them even when they're at their worst. The sheer euphoria on his face when he's on stage and the music has claimed his soul. I think of his patience. His tender looks.

Connor challenges me. He infuriates me. He ignites me.

He makes me laugh on days that seem the darkest.

And fuck me, does he make the world's best Mac & Cheese.

I've known the love of a mother, of a sister, and of a best friend, but never the kind that I see in Connor's eyes when he's looking at me. The connection I feel to him is the all-encompassing kind, one of the body, mind, and soul.

My heart constricts with the truth.

And I believe with every cell in my body that I will never find a love like his again.

"I do." And for some reason, the tears finally stop.

Ara smiles. "Then I'm going to help you fix this."

CHAPTER FORTY—FOUR

Now – Connor

When the person who once gave you strength to stand against crashing waves becomes the one to pull you under, it's worse than drowning on your own.

I don't know where I'm headed, but I walk down a random sidewalk, gasping for air and never getting quite enough oxygen. Maybe dying of heartbreak is a real thing, and the scientists just call it cardiac arrest.

All I want in the world is to sit on my kitchen floor and share a bowl of Mac & Cheese with the woman who holds my heart, as she sits there with me, tucked between my legs.

That's the fucked-up part about getting hurt by the person who was once your solace: they've smashed you to bits, and all you want is to gather enough strength to crawl back to them in hopes that they'll put the rest of you back together.

I shake my head. This is my fault. I'd had rules for a reason, to avoid this *exact* feeling. They'd been working for me too. Nearly ten years had gone by without my heart getting tossed into a meat grinder.

Spent almost a decade never straying from the path that those rules had forged for me, but then I went and stepped off of it, like a fucking idiot, got caught in the cold, and now I'm fighting a case of frostbite that I'll never recover from. I'd brought *everything* this time, gave my trust away with the hope that it wasn't misplaced.

Like I said, a fucking idiot.

LAST *Stand* FOR GENEVIEVE

At some point I need to stop walking. Taking a second to glance around at my surroundings, I huff a laugh. I've somehow ended up on a familiar sidewalk that I walked the last time I found myself with nowhere to go. I plop down, shrugging off the sense of déjà vu.

When someone betrays your trust, once they've lost it, it's nearly impossible to give again. With the violation, they take away your choice. Even though it's what *they* chose to do with it, you get stuck with the consequences and no say, as the aftermath wreaks havoc on you.

And the truth of that drags me back to the past.

Who ghosts someone after years of friendship, and years after that spent being in love? I wouldn't think that's what was happening, except it's exactly what's happening.

It's bizarre.

If Lara doesn't call me back soon to let me know she's alive, or at least show up to school, I'm going to show up at her house. She didn't want me to catch the sickness she came down with, but surely she's better now. It's been weeks.

And goddamnit, I miss her.

As I get closer and closer to graduating, the pressures from my parents are getting worse and worse. Lara has always been the buffer between me and them. Not in the physical sense, but she lets me talk about my feelings, and every time it prevents me from exploding on them.

And explosions have never built anything, according to Lara.

After the breakfast I just had with them, I need her more than ever before. I'm going to flatten the entirety of Sydney the next time I open my mouth, and my father is at the receiving end.

Hopping off the bus, I run my hands through my hair, trying and failing to keep my shit together until I see her. I manage to cool off a little in the last bit of the walk to school, but I start to get a little worried now that I see Lara isn't here. Again.

If she was, she'd be sitting at our favorite table under the tree, giving me a warm smile as I walked up. Lara is everything sweet, good, and kind in this world.

Whatever nasty bug she's caught, it's been giving her hell. I'd noticed her being a little more sleepy than usual, and not as perky, then it hit her a lot harder. She said she's been to the doctor and they're managing it, but I haven't been allowed to visit. Whatever she has, it's contagious apparently.

I still brought her soup and left it with her mother, who'd also been looking quite tired recently. She smiled kindly and told me she'd get it to her.

Lara had loved the soup. She texted me so, sent a cute selfie with her red little nose and puffy eyes and baby pink sheets.

Man, I really fucking miss her.

The school bell rings and still no Lara. Glancing in the direction of my class, it takes a split second for the decision to be made, and I'm walking back toward the bus stop.

Her house isn't too far from our school, so I'm there pretty quickly.

I knock on the door and wait.

And wait.

Seconds? Minutes? Hours? Time feels weird without her.

I peer inside and it's empty.

Not empty like they moved, but empty of life.

I frown.

If Lara's sick, her mother wouldn't leave her side. So what the fuck's going on?

Walking around the side of the house, peering into windows, I find that every room is the same. The lights are off, everything is tidy but looking untouched, as if they're on an extended holiday. Which they're not, because Lara would have told me.

I try ringing Lara. Straight to voicemail. Lara used my phone to call her mother once when her phone died, maybe I can find it.

This weird feeling starts to happen in my stomach, close to nausea but not quite. Lara would know how to describe it, she's always reading and knows way more words than I do. But I know this feeling well enough, it appears when you think something bad might happen.

I take a seat on the steps of her porch, scrolling through months of phone calls. They're almost all to and from Lara, aside from the good ol' spammers and parents, both of which I never answer.

Ha. Got it. I touch the number and call, but it rings out before going to voicemail.

"They're not home, probably won't be for a while."

I look up, finding Lara's neighbor looking at me a bit sympathetically.

"You're the boy who's always following Lara around."

It's true enough. "Do you know where they are? I'm starting to get worried."

The older woman gives me a sad smile. "They're staying at the hospital."

I shoot up from where I sit. "The hospital??"

She nods. "Lara is sick. Has been for a while."

"I knew that! But I...I brought her soup...and..." My thoughts are everywhere. "I'm sorry, do you know which hospital they're at?"

"Sydney Children's Hospital."

The ground feels like it's disappeared. I know the neighbor is still talking to me, but I don't hear any of it. I'm too focused on trying to breathe and keep my breakfast down.

Seconds? Minutes? Hours? All of them or none of them pass, until there's a hand on my shoulder, squeezing hard enough to pull me back. Then there's a glass of water in my hands and I'm gulping it down.

"Connor, is it?"

I nod, wondering briefly how she knows my name.

Then there's a phone being placed in my hand and guided up to my ear.

"Connor?" I've known her long enough that I recognize her voice immediately. It's Lara's mother on the other line. "Are you there?"

"Yeah." It sounds like I've been yelling. Have I?

She sniffles. "I'm so sorry you have to find out like this, but Lara...she wouldn't let us tell you."

I'm quiet, discovering for the first time what it's like to trust someone completely and realize that although you told them everything, they kept everything from you.

"Lara has struggled with an autoimmune disease her entire life. We always knew this was a possibility, but we'd hoped it would never come to this." Her mom sniffles, pulls the phone away for a second. "No matter how many times I asked her to, Lara refused to tell you. She said that you treated her like she was invincible, the only person who never hovered out of fear, and she never wanted that to change."

"Can I come see her?"

Her mom pauses. "I'm not sure if that's best, Connor. She's really tired, and if she wakes up and finds out that you know, she might get upset."

I ignore the fifth word in her second sentence, because I fucking hate that word now.

"Please." My voice cracks, the desperation loud and clear.

"Okay." I can tell she doesn't really think that it's okay, but I don't think she could really deny me.

Wordlessly, I pass the phone back to the neighbor. She hands me a ham and cheese toastie. She's a kind woman. Just like Lara's mom. And Lara.

The urgency I expect doesn't hit me. I'm not racing to the hospital. Everything feels slightly far away, kind of numb at best. Is this what going into shock feels like?

"Can I give you a piece of advice?"

I nod, not capable of words yet.

"I would go to her and make every moment as special as possible."

• • •

Lara's mom is waiting for me at reception, letting them know that I'm family. As we navigate through the hospital toward Lara's room, she goes into detail about her sickness, the science of it, how quickly she worsened. Some of it I hear, and the parts I do make things start to make sense.

But most of it I don't hear because all I can do is stare at the sleeping girl whom I love, who should be running into my arms after so much time apart, but instead I'm stuck in this alternate reality where I'll be lucky if she wakes up.

Why does this universe have to be the one that's real?

With one look I can see how exhausted Lara's body has become. While I've been fighting with my parents, she's been fighting for her life. And I wasn't even here.

The paper in my back pocket feels like it's been lit on fire, burning me from the outside. On the bus ride over, I'd made a list of things we could do to prepare for the worst, so we could smile when the best happened.

I'd thought we could do Mad Libs the way we did as kids, talk about dreams and our future so she has something to look forward to...you know, bucket list things. I'd thought maybe I could marry her, even, if she wanted to. Even though I'm only seventeen, I've always known that she would be part of my life forever.

My plans were stupid. Lara is too sick to do any of that. She can only sleep. So I talk to her, just in case she's not too tired to listen. And I throw my list away because holding her hand will have to be special enough.

Hours? Days? Weeks? Months?

She doesn't wake up.

And horribly soon, her body becomes too tired to breathe.

I'll have to live with the guilt of knowing I couldn't make the time leading up to it special, but I owe it to her to live anyway, because she didn't get to.

The scuff of footsteps on a sidewalk pull me from the reverie. Can't say I give much of a fuck about getting out of their way, but I guess whoever is walking by did me a solid by pulling me out of that depression cloud. The least I can do is bend my knees, so they don't have to step over me.

When did it get dark outside?

The black chucks stop a few feet away, and I tip my head back, the silhouette set aglow by the streetlamp behind them. "You look like an angel."

Snort. "Can't say I've ever gotten *that*."

"How'd you find me?"

"Followed the poignant scent of self-pity."

I roll my eyes as Ryder pulls out a small bottle of whiskey from his back pocket, like he carries one around like an ID.

"Kidding. I had a feeling you'd come to this particular stretch of sidewalk."

Where I went the last time I had nowhere to go. "And you came to have a heart to heart?"

He sits down next to me, right where we first met. "Fuck no. I came to get drunk."

Ryder passes the little bottle in my direction, and I take a tiny wee sip. This bottle isn't enough to get him drunk even if he *wasn't* sharing with me, but I don't point that out. Admittedly, I'm not one of those hardcore blokes who can drink much of the strong stuff straight anyway. Ryder, on the other hand, drinks whiskey like it's lemonade on a hot day. He's got a smug look on his face, and in an attempt to wipe it off, I take a bigger swig before passing it back to him.

"So, that was intense. With Brooke."

I nod, breathing through the burn in my throat. "It was."

"Lou and I were eavesdropping on your conversation the entire time."

"Come on, mate." I run my hands through my hair.

"Listen, I only followed so I could drag her ass back, but then it was like watching TV, except in real life. I couldn't bring myself to leave. I mean, the shit that left your mouth…" He takes another swig. "That was some serious shit."

"Glad my world crumbling around me was so entertaining."

"Don't be so dramatic. Nothing has crumbled." Ryder passes the bottle back to me. At this rate we're going to need another one. And soon.

I swig. "Easy for you to say."

"It was pretty fucking romantic."

I snort. "Are you kidding me right now?"

"I'm just saying." He shrugs. "Had me feeling like doing something epic."

"Like what? Planting one on an unsuspecting Lou?"

Ryder's lips twitch into a half smile, a rarity for him. "I'd like to keep my dick attached to my body, thank you very much."

I laugh, and we descend into a sort of comfortable quiet for a few minutes, letting our minds wander.

"You ever love someone before?" I finally ask.

Ryder frowns, before tipping his head into a shallow nod. "Yeah. Once."

"And it didn't work out?"

He grabs the bottle back from me. "I made sure it didn't."

Oof. That's a can of worms I think I'll skirt right on by. I snag the bottle back and take another swig, the buzz finally easing some of the pressure in my chest. But I know as quickly as the relief comes, it will go.

"I saw the tension between you and Brooke tonight." Saying her name hurts, but my curiosity is getting the best of me. "Did you know her in her other life?

Ryder shakes his head. "Nah, I didn't know her. Our paths crossed once. Briefly. I never saw her again after that."

"Small world," I marvel.

"Too small," he agrees. Then a moment later, almost too quiet for me to hear, "Yet sometimes, not small enough."

"You'd give Brooke a run for her money on secrets, you cryptic fuck."

Ryder coughs. "You really love her, don't you?"

"Yeah. I do."

He passes me the bottle and I take the last swig, shaking the remaining droplets onto my tongue, earning me an amused snort.

"Then what are you doing *here*?"

"I don't fucking know." I shake my head. "She hurt me. She broke my trust. I said things that were…too fucking far…and I don't know how either of us can take *any* of that back."

"Just go and fix it."

I scoff. "If it's so easy, why don't you go fix your shit?"

"My situation is different."

"Different how?"

"Just. Different." Full stop. That's all I'll be getting on *that* subject then. "*Brooke* is within reach. You know exactly where to find her, and she's probably there, just waiting for you to come back. All you have to do is show up."

"And what about all the years of trauma that just got blown up in our faces?"

Shrug. "Alcohol helps. You just gotta drink the hard stuff. And more of it."

"God forbid you ever become a therapist," I mutter.

"I'm a bartender. I'm the one people see when they're *avoiding* their therapist."

I can't help but smile, grateful to bear witness to the side of Ryder he shares with people so rarely. "I'll sort my shit out with her."

"I know. You just have to be a stubborn arse first."

I laugh. "Speaking of an arse, mine's getting sore."

"Been a while since we've slept on concrete."

"Can't say I miss it."

He shakes his head. "Me neither. There's some things I do, though."

"How about the bizarre sense of freedom that comes with having nothing?"

Ryder grunts his agreement. "And not being owned by anyone or anything," he tacks on a tad wistfully.

Fuck. "We're gonna need more alcohol."

• • •

My body aches and my head is slamming as I step into the living room the next morning. Ryder and I were out the whole night. We got plastered, ran a foot race down the Courtney Campbell Causeway, and I think we even climbed a huge ass oak tree. It was nothing special, but I fucking needed it.

Theo looks up and nods from where he types on his laptop. "Didn't sleep?"

I shake my head.

"Brooke either."

My stomach drops. "She's still here?"

"No, but she stayed up all night on this couch, hoping you'd come home." Theo's voice isn't disapproving, just matter of fact, and perhaps a little curious about where I went. "Did you sort your head out?"

The way it's pounding, it doesn't feel like it. "I did."

"Good." Theo looks at his watch, closes his laptop. "Because Brooke's final hearing starts in an hour."

CHAPTER FORTY—FIVE

Now - Brooke

"**W**ell, Ms. Anderson, this will be the last of these hearings." The prosecutor clears his throat. "And while even I can admit that you have a very moving story, I have yet to see why your conviction for dealing should be expunged."

Glancing around the courthouse, I swallow, not finding any of the faces I'd hoped to see here today. Not for their support, but so that they can hear my story and decide if the person underneath is worth a second chance.

Despite not sleeping a wink last night, I've managed to pull myself together for today. I'm wearing a light purple top, decorated with white embroidered flowers on the collar. I chose it because they look like tulips and make me think of spring. My hair is styled neatly, but I wear it down today. I've added touches of makeup, mostly to conceal the sleepless night, but I no longer need the carefully curated mask of makeup that I once relied on.

A door at the back of the courtroom opens, the hope in my heart beginning to soar like the first glance of dawn after an endless, horrible night. The first thing I see is a head of sandy brown hair, too shaggy for a courtroom, and the most perfect thing I've ever seen. Ara and Theo follow behind, coming through the door hand in hand. I don't stop to wonder how they made it in when the doors should probably be locked.

"Hi!" Ara mouths with a smile. Theo puts a hand on her shoulder before shuffling her over to the defense side, right up front.

My eyes remain glued to Connor as he takes his time finding a seat next to them. I wait and wait for his eyes to meet my own, and slowly they rise. I nearly crumple in relief when they finally find mine, reflecting everything I myself feel: remorse, forgiveness, and most importantly, love.

"Ms. Anderson? Time is of the essence."

"My apologies." I clear my throat, steeling myself and squaring my shoulders. "I was only trying to remember where I'd left off."

"You had mentioned going cold turkey."

Right. Connor gives me a reassuring nod, my eyes remaining locked on his, as I tell him the remainder of my story.

It's quite amazing what the human body can survive. Once I read a story about a man surviving a rod going through his brain, and another who walked away after falling from the sky without a parachute, all because he managed to land on a blackberry bush. Never believed them really.

But then I was certain I was going to die and didn't.

The second and third days of coming off were hell on earth.

My battered body felt like every nerve ending had been put on high alert, sentenced to feel the excruciating sensory overload, mentally and physically. Old injuries had been awakened from the beating, the concussion caused by the crack in the head, my ribs which were likely fractured, screamed with pain.

The line between nightmares and real life began to blur. I'd dreamt of being covered in my friend's blood, just to wake up and discover my clothes stained in it. Even when I was conscious, I'd see the slump of bodies, the blinding headlights that were much too close, the sound of crunching metal. It all rushed in at once, giving me every reason to break.

I tracked the days by scratching a line into the concrete with a rock, every time I noticed it was dark outside. By my count, it was four days of agony before I could finally manage to get myself on my feet long enough to find more water, and I'm not proud of where I found it. It was a few more days after that before I started to clear the haze.

Walking became a form of therapy for me, seeing people and places which were new, not layered in memories. Every day I'd walk, working through the pain and pushing myself until I finally felt like my body was mine again. I got my job back at the grocery store, stocking shelves, and stopped living off what I could fit in my pockets.

Every day, I put one foot in front of the other.

It's been several weeks of this, being alone.

This morning I realized that I don't have to be.

Mom should be working a shift at the diner this afternoon, and the lunchtime rush is finished by now. Taking a seat on a bench across the road, I wait. It's not more than a couple minutes before I see her breezing through the aisle between booths that are closest to the window with a smile on her face. She stops to refill someone's mug of coffee, and they must say something funny because she tips her head back and laughs.

My eyes burn, but I don't let the tears come out.

We've only been apart for a few months, so I guess I shouldn't expect her to look much different, and she doesn't. Mom is in the diner, looking happy, despite the agony I put her through, and having no guarantee of a happy ending. I don't know how I've never seen it before, where Genevieve got her sunshine, but sitting here across the road while my mom still has the strength to laugh, it becomes clear as day.

Suddenly, I can't wait until after her shift, I need to feel her comforting arms around me and tell her that I'm sorry. For everything. Hurrying to my feet, I manage a few steps toward the crosswalk before something across the street catches my eye. My pulse picks up as I recognize the figure moving toward the corner.

Sebby.

Shit. Things must have already drastically changed in that world if he's over in Tampa. Sebby stops on the corner, leaning on the building, waiting. Part of me wants to keep walking and hope he doesn't notice me, but if I take that route, I'll always worry about the day he does. My ties to that life need to be completely severed.

I follow Sebby's gaze, which is focused on a young kid, diagonal to me, waiting to cross. Even with his hood pulled over his head, I can tell he isn't more than fourteen or fifteen years old. He looks nervous as he finally darts across the road and approaches Sebby. My stomach sinks as I put together what's about to happen.

I won't let it.

Looking both ways quickly, I jog across the street without a walk signal, right up to the kid, blocking the last few steps between him and Sebby. "Hey. You don't need to do this."

The kid glances up at me, wide-eyed and stammering, not getting any words out.

"Don't listen to that whore, I don't know who she is, putting her nose in—" Sebby's words come to a halt on his tongue as he realizes exactly which whore is putting her nose into his business.

"New turf?" I ask with my brows raised.

Sebby smiles in delight, giving off his usual slime effect. "Just visiting for the day, testing out the warmer waters."

"I don't recommend making it your regular." I reach into my backpack, grabbing one of the envelopes of cash I've been saving before slamming it into Sebby's chest. "That's enough to cover what I owe you, and whatever this kid was about to take. Now, do us a favor and get the fuck out of here."

The kid's eyes are even wider now, pinballing between me and Sebby.

"You don't want to get wrapped up in this world. Whatever you're trying to escape from, you won't." Blowing out a breath I try to force my expression into something a little kinder. "It'll still haunt you, and you'll lose the fraction of good that's left in your life."

Sebby snorts. "What are you, a missionary now?"

I ignore his jab, desperately needing this kid to understand. "Someone warned me, too, and I decided not to listen. You don't want to know what I've seen…what I've lost…because I didn't heed their warning. Just please, don't make the same mistake I did."

The kid looks over at Sebby who smiles, clenching product in his fist, waiting for the kid to reach out his hand. The kid's eyes come back to mine, and I see the indecision weighing there.

"You can still walk away," I urge.

The kid opens his mouth to say something, but snaps it shut as a car door slams behind me and someone yells, "Freeze!!"

Weirdly, when someone yells at you to freeze, you naturally do. Even if you shouldn't, and even if it's only for a second. Sebby, on the other hand, likely having lots of practice fleeing, takes off without a second thought, sprinting down the street too quickly for anyone to catch him.

My eyes drop to where a small baggy lays on the ground, just waiting to be scooped up as evidence. I should run, too, but I can't leave this kid to get grabbed before he ever gets a second chance. Goddamnit.

I launch forward, shoving the kid out of his stupor. "RUN!!! Get out of here!!!!!"

A strong hand grips my forearm, squeezing tight enough that it hurts, preventing me from going any farther. The kid is like a deer in headlights as he watches me struggle against my captor. I manage to break free just long enough to shove him one more time. "GO!! It's not too late!!!"

Finally, he snaps out of it and takes off.

"Don't choose this life!!" I call after him before my eyes trail up to meet ones that are full of accusation. The police officer knows what he saw. All the evidence he needs lays right in front of my shoe. The three of us were making a deal, and I took the fall out of loyalty. No justice system on planet earth is going to believe a teenage girl's story about trying to intercept some random kid from going down the wrong path.

Cold metal tightens around my wrist.

"You are under arrest for possession with intent to sell. You have the right to remain silent. Anything you say can and will be used against you in a court of law." Cold metal pinches around my other wrist before I'm pushed toward a black sedan. "You have the right to an attorney. If you cannot afford an attorney, one will be provided for you."

I say the words along with him in my head, having seen my fair share of Law & Order. The door is opened for me, and just before my head is shoved inside, my eyes catch on ones as crystal blue as my own, but where mine are full of regret, hers are full of sorrow. She places a hand over her mouth to conceal a sob as she watches through the window, while her only living daughter gets thrown into the back of a police car.

And then something I'd never expect in the world happens.

My mom drops her hand to her side, squares her shoulders, and turns her back on me.

CHAPTER FORTY—SIX

Now – Connor

The defense attorney stands, buttoning his suit jacket.

"Ms. Anderson's story proves that she has seen the worst of where abuse of illegal substances can land your life. She saw it in her father, who abandoned their family for it. In a moment of weakness, after a great loss, she fell victim to the force of addiction herself. And as if that wasn't enough, she lost her very best friend to the world that supplied it soon after."

Although I missed the start of her story, with the attorney's recap I can fill in the blanks. Part of me hopes that one day she'll tell me the story from the beginning, but even if she never does, hearing the end of it was enough to punch me straight in the gut.

"While a baggy of Adderall *was* found at the time of arrest," her attorney continues, "it was *not* found on Brooke's person, nor were her prints recovered from it. Additionally, her drug test taken at the time of arrest ran clean. All details which were withheld in the original trial due to an 'administrative oversight'. The arresting officer did stumble upon a deal that afternoon, but the only thing Ms. Anderson is guilty of is preventing another young life from being ruined by substance abuse."

Brooke looks beautiful, but I see the pain written all over her. The scars of what she went through to get clean, what she had to lose in order to gather the strength to do so. Being penalized for a crime she didn't commit, right as she had started to turn her life around.

"The defense rests, Your Honor." The attorney unbuttons his jacket before taking a seat.

LAST *Stand* FOR GENEVIEVE

The judge nods. "You are excused, Ms. Anderson."

Brooke extends her thanks before returning to her seat, facing the judge.

Ara wipes away tears which have run onto her freckled cheeks as Theo places his hand on her knee for comfort. Brooke has seen the world in a way that the three of us will never be able to understand, even if we wish too. All we can give her is our acceptance and our love.

The judge shuffles some papers around before speaking. "The court is prepared to proceed with its ruling. Will the defendant please rise?"

My stomach drops as Brooke stands, waiting for the outcome. I remind myself that regardless of what happens here today, I can still hold her in my arms tonight. Whether she walks out of here with a criminal record or not, I'll proudly stand by her side.

"The court finds that there is a factual basis for the expungement, as the evidence which was excluded in the first trial proves beyond reasonable doubt that the defendant is not guilty on all counts."

Brooke sways on her feet. The judge continues to go on about what happens from here, but I don't hear it. My eyes and ears and soul are locked on this beautiful girl who is officially free of her past, at least in the legal sense. She has been gifted a blank slate, and where she chooses to go from here will be nothing short of incredible.

The gavel sounds. "Court is adjourned."

Brooke hugs her attorney who looks stunned, but gives her a pat on the back. She pushes through the swivel gate and finds her place in my arms. Ara and Theo circle their arms around us. Ara is still crying, and as we pull back, I notice that Brooke is, too, tears flow freely as she wraps Ara in her arms.

"You're my hero," Ara says through her sobs, and Brooke cries even harder.

Theo and I find comfort in each other, letting them be the ones to have snot dripping out of their noses while we try to keep our composure. The truth? We're some of the softest blokes around, and if we let it happen, we'd be drowning in tears too. But the girls need us. So we let them have their moment before pulling them to our chests when they finally break apart.

"Want to get out of here?" I whisper into Brooke's ear.

I feel her nod against my chest, so I place my hand on her lower back and steer her out of the courtroom. We're quiet until we make it through the metal detectors and out onto the steps, as Brooke takes a deep breath. I follow suit, grateful for the fresh air.

Theo places his hand on my shoulder and gives it a squeeze, before giving Brooke an embrace of his own. "Your story is incredible. It could save lives if you ever wanted to tell it."

"I think someday I will," Brooke says with a watery smile. "Right after I finally share it with the people who deserve to hear it the most."

Theo smiles before pulling away, and giving Ara an insistent tug on one of her hands.

"See you tonight," Ara says to Brooke with a wink before looking at me with a half-hearted point. "You better not fuck this up."

I roll my eyes. "I won't."

With that, my friends walk away, and I turn toward my girl. My girl with eyes the color of warm Caribbean waters, hair so blonde it's almost white, soft skin, and pillowy lips. The most beautiful and challenging woman on the planet, and she's mine. Or she could be.

"There's so much to say, I don't know where the fuck to start," I admit, pulling at the shaggy strands of my hair as too many things run through my head at once.

"Well, you basically know everything now." She smiles a shy smile before glancing down. "Does it change anything?"

"Yes," I say honestly, because it does. I place my hand under her chin, guiding her eyes back to mine as I slide my palm to her cheek. "I've fallen so deeply in love with you. More so than even before."

Brooke's eyes fill with more tears, and she swipes at them quickly before chuckling. "I'm sorry, they just haven't stopped since they started."

I smile. "It's okay to feel things, Brooke."

"I feel *so* many things." Her hand slides up my forearm to cover my hand with her own, as she presses it snugly against her cheek. "At first it was terrifying, but I'm not scared anymore."

Brooke's eyes bore into mine, and I can't help but feel as if those threads of fate which were being weaved together these past few months have finally completed their masterpiece.

"I'm so in love with you too." She shakes her head. "It's irreversible."

"Irrevocably intertwined," I murmur almost to myself, before slipping my fingers into her hair and pulling her mouth against mine. It's slow. It's fast. It's hard. It's soft. The kiss is everything we've felt, and never been brave enough to share out loud.

We fall and fall and fall.

Then we fall a little more, before finally pulling away.

I trace her face with my eyes, brush her cheek with the back of my hand, letting her feel how much I treasure this moment in the same way that I'll treasure her for the rest of our lives.

I rest my forehead against hers with a smile on my face. "You're just in this for the Mac & Cheese, aren't you?"

Brooke laughs, tipping her head back as she does, her smile brighter than the entire sky. "How did you know?

CHAPTER FORTY-SEVEN

One Year (and a bit) Later - Brooke

It's early in the morning, still cool enough to need a sweater. The book I brought feels heavy in my hands. So do the tulips. The grass is damp with dew, adding to the lushness underfoot as I make my way across the beautiful lawn. It's taken me far too long to come here. I was too injured after the accident to come for the service, and although it would have been a small one, I wouldn't have had the strength to face it anyway. Which makes me a horrible coward, and why I've worked so hard to become worthy of this moment before visiting her for the first time. Getting clean wasn't enough for what I'd done. There are more amends to be made, but I couldn't miss another birthday even if it has to be celebrated here.

At her grave.

It's beautiful, what Mom chose for her. A black obsidian color, so it isn't ruined by time and growth. There is a beautiful pink tulip with a green stem engraved at the top, above the dedication.

In Loving Memory of
Genevieve Anderson
Spread love and sunshine wherever you go.

Mom didn't confine her to the years she lived on this earth, because it would be impossible to define pure light in that way. I drop down to my knees, gently placing the tulips and her favorite book in front of her headstone.

"I'm sorry it took me so long to visit." I sniffle. "I had to, uh, work through some things. And trust me, you wouldn't have wanted to see me, though maybe you were forced to from wherever you are. If you did, you know it got pretty bad. Then it got even worse."

Tears begin flowing freely down my face.

"And then…eventually it got better. I've built something you'd love. It became a mission of mine, inspired by how we felt when Dad walked out, what I went through myself, and what I need to make up for. But mostly, it was inspired by a friend." I smile a little, adding a tad wistfully, "Maybe you've met her already."

A quiet, comforting breeze pulls through my hair.

"There is a library inside because you taught me the power of books. The windows are big enough to let in the sunlight, with plush seats you could spend the entire day reading on. It's the place where people can escape this world for a little while, and I named the library after you. And it's opening today, on your birthday."

I pause, reaching over to fiddle with her favorite book. "I believe that one day the good that comes from the center will outshine the bad that I was part of. The decisions I made and allowing my weakness to corrupt what good there was left in life, I *can* make up for that.

"But…" The tears start running faster, and I cover my face with my hands. "I'm trying to figure out how to forgive myself for what happened to *you*. I haven't worked out how I ever will, but I've decided to start by asking for yours first. I'm sorry I convinced you to get custard with me that night, for putting you in danger. If you were here, you'd say it wasn't my fault, but it was. You wanted to stay home, and I begged you to come with me. I put you in that car and then…"

There is a quantifiable, physical weight to emotion, and for the first time I'm allowing myself to be freed from it. I let it all out, the years of pain and grief and regret that I've forced so deep inside me. It comes exploding out of me with a velocity so strong it would overwhelm any instrument.

Finally, I find my breaths again. "Do you forgive me?"

In less than a heartbeat, the warm morning sun peeks its head over a nearby oak tree, casting its sunshine over the flowers I brought, then the book, and then me. I close my eyes, tipping my face up, basking in its light. More tears escape as I understand what this is: forgiveness. For minutes I sit there, soaking up the sun and sentiment, feeling more whole than I've felt in a long time.

A throat clears from behind me, and I shoot up, nearly losing my balance as I see my mom standing there, holding tulips.

"Oh." I wipe my face. "I'm sorry, I didn't mean to…"

I could swear the sunlight giggles from behind me.

My mom reaches up, tucking some hair behind her ear. "I got your letter."

"Good, I'm…I'm glad." I came out of this woman's vagina, spent my entire life being raised by her, and I'm standing here awkwardly like a fucking idiot.

"But you didn't leave any way for me to contact you afterward."

Didn't I? Now that I think about it, maybe I didn't. Shit.

"You're not on Facebook or Instagram or that TikTok thing. You don't work at the grocery store anymore. None of your friends from school have heard from you in years. I didn't know how to find you."

"Oh."

She smiles a little before looking down, sad. "I'm sorry I turned my back on you."

"*You're* sorry!?" Sentences, Brooke, come on…you need to say some fucking sentences. "But you have… nothing to be sorry for. *I'm* the one who walked out on you when you needed me the most."

"It's not your job to take care of me. You were in pain. It was my job to take care of you… and I failed."

"Don't *ever* say that." I cross the space between us, gripping her shoulders, needing her to know what I'm saying is true. Her choices didn't lead me down the path I went, mine did. "You did everything right. I was just so rotten inside…and I…well, you read my letter."

Ara had suggested it to me.

After what my mom saw, I wanted to explain myself for so long, but I knew I'd never be able to get the words out properly. So I took Ara's advice and wrote her a letter. Connor was by my side, reading as I wrote, comforting me when it became too much, but I've found that the more I talk about it, the easier it gets.

LAST *Stand* FOR GENEVIEVE

I wrote down every single detail of what happened before I became hooked, how it happened, and everything that followed: meeting Ziggy and saving her from the security guard at that high school, our slumber party, and how she became my best friend just before she saved my life.

Then I told her what I planned to do, to make up for everything that I had done so that I could change the world. I left the letter for her at the diner, waiting across the street to make sure it got to her, and then apparently, didn't leave a way for her to contact me.

My mom wraps her arms around me.

The space inside me that has been filled with shame and regret has hollowed out. As I stand here in my mom's arms, feeling her undying love and forgiveness, warmed by Genevieve's sunshine, that hollowness begins to fill. Happiness pours in, accompanied by hope and gratitude, burning away the darkness and rot that I let fester inside me for too long.

Pulling back, I smile at my mom. "Can I take you somewhere?"

• • •

Everything is perfect. That's the only way to describe it.

My mom and I walk up, the first people aside from the event crew to arrive. We take in the beautiful decorations, pastel blues and pinks and purples. At one glance, you know this is a celebration.

I planned to hire an event agency for the grand opening of Ziggy's Kids, wanting it to be as special as it could possibly be, but I'd gotten a few quotes, and they'd been astronomical. I'd settled with me, Ara, and Lou tackling it ourselves when Marcy, the event coordinator with *Elegant Events*, found out what this opening would mean for the community. She spoke to her boss, and they gave me a huge discount, making all of this possible.

Activities have been set up everywhere. Games and challenges, all free of charge. Tables are being set up with all sorts of cuisines and beverages. There's even a cotton candy machine. I smile at Lloyd, the first staff volunteer to sign up, as we pass by where he's speaking with Marcy, the event coordinator. He returns my smile and nods before Marcy directs his attention back to her clipboard.

"This is incredible." My mom looks around in wonder.

"It is," I agree, equally amazed. "But this isn't what I brought you to see."

Hooking my arm through my mom's, I lead her inside, giving her a brief little tour of everything as we pass through: the tutoring room, the recreational room, the music room, a hall of designated rooms for private counseling, and more.

When I open the doors to *The Genevieve Room,* my mom gasps, before whispering, "It's the most beautiful place I've ever seen."

She takes in the windows and plush chairs, the walls which are lined with shelves full of books and one of those rolling ladders. Her eyes fill with tears as she reads the quote along the far wall.

A book can save any day if you let it whisk you away.
-Genevieve Anderson

"She would love it here."

I smile. "I know."

"And she would be *so* proud of you, just like I am." My mom pulls me into an embrace, and we stay there for a while. "I always knew you were going to do amazing things."

We spend the rest of the morning in *The Genevieve Room,* catching up and swapping stories. I tell her more about Ziggy, the kind of person she was, and how she inspired me. We talk about Connor, Theo, Ara, Lou, and even Ryder, and what they've come to mean to me.

Mom tells me that she's officially and legally separated herself from my dad, that she went on a date with a man, and that he's really nice. We laugh about how dorky she was, not knowing how *that* world works anymore.

And for the first time, we talk about Genevieve, and what we miss about her the most.

We cry. We cry a little more. We heal. Together.

Eventually, Connor wanders in, knowing exactly where to find me. He stops short when he sees me with my mom (our resemblance telling him exactly who she is), warring with leaving us be, or coming to introduce himself to the woman he's heard so much about.

Mom recognizes him immediately from the pictures I've shown her today, not hesitating as she stands and pulls him in for a hug.

Connor responds in kind, sending me a tender look over her shoulder. "I'm so sorry to interrupt, and it is *really* good to finally meet you, but, uh, Brooke's got a ribbon to cut."

"Shit!" I look at my phone, realizing the entire morning has passed by, and it's five minutes away from ribbon cutting. "Mom, we have to go!"

Grabbing their hands, I pull them down the hallway toward a side door, which gives us access to a sidewalk that wraps around to the front of the building. My heart seizes as we take in the hundreds of people who have come today. News channels and media groups have crowded around, setting up their cameras for the big reveal. I'm not sure who gave them the heads up, but having them here will result in a massive amount of exposure to the community, letting them know they have somewhere to go.

It's everything I've hoped for. And more.

Giving my mom a quick hug and Connor a chaste kiss, I step on stage, pulling the speech that Theo helped me write from my pocket. Pride glows from my mom's face, and there isn't a cloud in the sky to block the sun from shining down over this perfect moment.

I make it through my speech without stumbling, telling the crowd about the friend who inspired it, a little of our story, and most importantly, what I hope this becomes for *them*. Everyone cheers as I cut the ribbon and open the doors.

After almost everyone has shuffled inside, Connor wraps his arms around my waist, kissing my cheek from behind. "I'm so proud of you."

I revel in his never-ending warmth, his scent, his everything. "Thank you."

"You're going to change the world."

"Maybe." I turn, facing him. "But only with my hot, musician boyfriend by my side."

"You couldn't get rid of me even when you tried."

I smile, knowing it's true. Taking his hand, we turn to look for the rest of our friends.

"Who is that with Ryder?" Connor asks, curiosity coloring his tone.

Knowing exactly where to look after seeing Ryder moping around the back of the crowd while I was giving my speech, I spot him instantly. The girl he's standing with is beautiful. I'm talking fell-out-of-a-fairytale stunning. "I don't know. She could be someone from the community."

"I don't know…she's got that air about her, like she lives and breathes this place." He pauses. "She's not from the events company?"

"I was working with someone named Marcy, and that's not her. Maybe she's from one of the media agencies?"

"Maybe. They seem…close." Connor shakes his head, more intrigued than usual about Ryder's business. "I want to know who she is."

I give his hand a tug, pulling him toward the rest of our friends gathered around the window of a food truck. "Guess we're just going to have to wait and find out."

EPILOGUE

Three Years Later

I drove to the other coast of Florida this morning. Sunrise is better from over here, according to Google. Found this cute little Airbnb that provides wristbands which get you into a private beach. There's a cute, retro-looking lifeguard tower, and this little wooden bench, right in the sand.

Although there's still no sign of the sun, the sky has started to lighten, telling me it'll make its grand entrance any moment, just as I feel a presence next to me. Risking a glance, tears fill my eyes, and my heart squeezes to the point of pain.

She's changed. Her hair is long now, thick and shiny even in the dimness of early morning light. Her big brown eyes are shining brighter than I've ever seen, and calm, not darting around or looking over her shoulder. Even her face has filled out into that of a healthy woman, no longer belonging to a slim, scrappy adolescent.

But her clothes are still baggy.

"Miss me, *mija*?"

Have you ever been so happy that it's painful? I stand from the bench and wrap her into my arms, a few heavy sobs escaping from me. The years had felt long as they passed, but as I squeeze her now, in a way it feels as though time never moved. "I missed you more than you know."

We pull away, and she wipes one of my cheeks with her knuckles. "So we're doing that crying thing again, *ay*?"

I laugh, taking one of the two coffees she holds. "Why didn't you contact me earlier?"

"The dust needed to fall."

I hide my smile at her special brand of custom phrasing.

"Our old, uh—*community* doesn't take well to people walking away from shootouts without explaining themselves." Melinda shrugs. "I saw my chance to walk away from that world and I took it. Everyone thought I died."

"*I* thought you died." It had nearly broken me completely.

"And, technically, I *was* dead for almost seven minutes, but one of the paramedics didn't give up. I was given a second chance."

"I wouldn't have told a soul."

"It wasn't about trust, *mija*. I didn't want to accidentally lead anyone your way either. My death got you out too. And you needed an ice water dump to snap you out of your wannabe baddie phase, to learn to walk on your own two feet."

She's right, so I just squeeze her again before pulling her down onto the bench next to me. We take a sip of our coffees, paid for real honestly.

"Besides, you know I love me some soap opera. *Me encanta el drama*. I've been planning my entrance back into your life for three years."

"You're such an asshole." I laugh, shaking my head. "So... where have you been?"

Melinda mindlessly takes my hand, reassuring me that she's really here. "After that paramedic revived me, I was taken to a hospital and went into surgery. Miraculously, they retrieved the bullet and stopped the bleeding. When I woke up, some detectives had questions for me, but I told them I went into the warehouse looking for a place to stay and stumbled upon men with guns. They didn't have proof of anything else, so they left me alone."

"Just like that?"

She shrugs. "Just like that, *mija*."

"Guess this means I have to get your half of the memorial tattoo removed."

Melinda snorts. "Don't be dramatic."

I smile. "So, where did you go from there?"

"After leaving the hospital, I got on the first bus, which took me to Connecticut. You ever been there?"

"No."

"Well, it's boring. And perfect."

I smile. "What do you do there?"

"I heard from someone who heard from someone else that reading doesn't suck. Turns out they were right, so I got a job in a bookstore." She takes a sip of her coffee. "I saw what you started. *Ziggy's Kids*. It's beautiful."

"I wanted to make a change." I shrug. "Well, that's what it eventually became, and what I tell people, but really I needed to prove to myself that I was still capable of something good."

"And? Are you?"

"I am," I say with a smile, knowing it's true.

Melinda is quiet for a heartbeat, before asking what she's been dying to know. "How's *mi familia*?"

"Good. Really good, actually. I've been keeping an eye on them, just like you asked. Why don't you see them?"

Melinda shakes her head. "I don't want to risk being seen. Their safety is *más importante*."

"I brought you something, just in case you said that." I hand over the envelope, which she takes with a look of confusion.

"What's in here?" She opens it, answering her own question by sliding out the pictures I've gathered of her family over the last few years.

There's one of her mamá in the yellow kitchen, smiling in an apron, the day they moved back in after I'd revealed what Connor and I had done to it. There's one of me and Connor at the dinner table with the kids from the same night that her mamá insisted on taking. There's another one of them sitting on the porch one morning, which I took just before breakfast.

Melinda looks through photo after photo, then starts at the beginning and looks through them again. "Their house…it looks…"

"I fixed it up with a little help."

Melinda's eyes drop to the ring on my finger, and she rolls her eyes. "*Amor cachorro enferma.*"

"*No seas mala.*" I shoot back with a smug little smile.

Melinda's brows shoot up in surprise.

"Your family taught me a little."

"Well, they need to do a better job on your accent." Melinda rolls her eyes, mocking the words in my accent.

We both laugh, and just as a retort reaches the edge of my tongue, the sun pokes its head over the horizon. We quiet down, taking sips of our honest coffees, staying quiet as we watch the sun rise and rise, until light casts over the entire area and the town behind us starts to stir. Shops are opening, cars and pedestrians hurrying about their business. The world is awake, and I have my best friend by my side finally. Resting my head on her shoulder, we stay like that for hours.

The scent of the salty ocean used to remind me of how much I lost in an abandoned warehouse one night, completely surrounded by it. Now the salty air tells me a different story.

One of survival.

Look Out for Book Three: *Last Home for Evelyn*

**Ryder would do *anything,* if it meant Evie
could have everything she desires.
What happens when *anything* becomes that
which puts her in danger?**

Both orphaned and without a home, Evie and Ryder meet as young children the day they find themselves sharing a foster home. Their bond becomes one born from survival, only to be torn apart as it begins to transform into something tender.

Adopted into a well-off family, Evie's fought tooth and claw to succeed in a world which is convinced she doesn't belong: the cut-throat upper class.

Ever since Ryder was forced to watch Evie walk away, he has been preparing for the unlikely day that their paths cross again, even if it required staining his soul.

If Evie lets Ryder back into her life after living worlds apart, she stands to lose everything she's built. And potentially her life.

Last Home for Evelyn is a dual point-of-view romance novel with an alternating timeline that will have your heart squeezing and stomach twisting.

With its own happily ever after, it can be read as a standalone novel or as *Book Three* in *The Last Series*, following *Last Stand for Genevieve.*

www.kaymiewuerfel.com

Follow Me On Socials For More Updates
Instagram: @kaymiewuerfelwrites
TikTok: @kayywuerf

ACKNOWLEDGMENTS

Thank you to my readers, for loving *Last Letters to Ara* and sticking around for Connor's story. Sharing these characters with you is my greatest joy. There will be many more adventures to come.

I want to thank my husband for not only supporting my reading habits, but also my writing habits, which I've learned are so much more expensive. Thank you for believing in me, and keeping yourself entertained while I spend time with my characters.

Thank you to my family, who have supported my storytelling since I was a toddler in the back of the car, talking about monsters and faraway worlds.

Thank you to my brother, who was always such an inspiration when it came to music, and for being the first person to show me that music genres outside of Pop existed.

To my friends. My soul mates. My found family. I'll never know how I got so lucky, but thank the fucking stars you looked at me and thought, "I'll keep this one." Out of all the planets and universes, I'm fortunate enough to walk this one with you.

Thank you to my friend Rachel, who not only introduced me to *Our Last Night*, but for also making a devastatingly clever pun which became the name of the unnamable band, *Immoral Support*. Thank you for loving Connor and Ryder the way I do, for being my sounding board and helping me bring this story to life.

Thank you to Arielle, for taking a chance on a debut author's ARC and becoming a close friend. I'll never forget the day I opened my phone to your feedback and started to believe that I could do this. I'm so happy that in this great big world, I managed to find you.

Thank you to Elaine at *Allusion Publishing*, for being so much more than just an editor, and helping me find my footing as an author every step of the way. The care you take in your work is so inspiring, adding beauty into every manuscript you touch. I'm so thankful that our paths crossed.

Thank you to Jules at *Covers by Jules* for the beautiful cover art.

Thank you to my girlies on Bookstagram (*@thesparklinglibrary, @haleighs.bookshelf, @emsbookcase_, @perlas.readingspace, @_ellieslibrary, @demis.library, @bookish_farrah, @book.greed, @twins.reading.books, @najatbookshelf*) who believed in my debut series <3

And lastly, I want to thank *Our Last Night,* my inspiration for Connor and Ryder. Although I created Connor and Ryder's characters before I knew they existed, I nearly shat myself when I found them. Trevor and Matthew are the only two vocalists I've found with the chemistry and relationship that took what was inside my head and brought it to life. I could listen to them all day, except walking around drooling all the time just wouldn't do. So thank you for the many hours of inspiration you've contributed to this writer, having no idea I existed.

ABOUT THE AUTHOR

Originally from the United States, Kaymie Wuerfel now lives in Sydney, Australia, with her husband and two fur-babies.

She's a verified TikTok creator known for her comedic skits, and has successfully pursued a career in fashion, owning her own business which sells exquisite dresses worldwide.

During the few hours she finds between her eleven-hour days and seven-day work weeks, she can be found reading a book, writing her own, or laughing with her friends.

Kaymie's dream is to live on a mountain with her friends and family, all while visiting far away worlds through the written word.

Printed in Great Britain
by Amazon

DIVERSE WORDS AND VOICES

EDITED BY
BENNIE KARA

OXFORD
UNIVERSITY PRESS

OXFORD
UNIVERSITY PRESS

Great Clarendon Street, Oxford, OX2 6DP, United Kingdom

Oxford University Press is a department of the University of Oxford.
It furthers the University's objective of excellence in research, scholarship,
and education by publishing worldwide. Oxford is a registered trade mark
of Oxford University Press in the UK and in certain other countries

© Oxford University Press 2024

The moral rights of the author have been asserted

First published in 2024

All rights reserved. No part of this publication may be reproduced, stored in a
retrieval system, or transmitted, used for text and data mining, or used for
training artificial intelligence, in any form or by any means, without the prior
permission in writing of Oxford University Press, or as expressly permitted
by law, by licence or under terms agreed with the appropriate reprographics
rights organization. Enquiries concerning reproduction outside the scope of
the above should be sent to the Rights Department, Oxford University Press,
at the address above.

You must not circulate this work in any other form and you must impose
this same condition on any acquirer

British Library Cataloguing in Publication Data

Data available

ISBN 978-1-38-203837-9

1 3 5 7 9 10 8 6 4 2

The manufacturing process conforms to the environmental regulations
of the country of origin.

Printed in China by Golden Cup

Texts and extracts

Crime and consequences	**1**
Mic Drop by Sharna Jackson	3
Forensics: The Anatomy of Crime by Val McDermid	6
Smart by Kim Slater	9
In Cold Blood by Truman Capote	13
Journeys and discoveries	**19**
Arctic explorer Matthew Alexander Henson's memoir	21
Around the World in 80 Trains: A 45,000-Mile	
Adventure by Monisha Rajesh	25
City of Stolen Magic by Nazneen Ahmed Pathak	30
What Are You Doing Here?	
by Baroness Floella Benjamin	34
Power and influence	**39**
Stella Young's letter to herself at 80 years old	41
To Sir, With Love by E. R. Braithwaite	46
Malala Yousafzai's Nobel Peace Prize speech, 2014	49
Megan Rapinoe's Women's World Cup speech, 2019	53
A Kind of Spark by Elle McNicoll	55

Terror and wonder	**61**
The Picture of Dorian Gray by Oscar Wilde	63
The Haunting of Tyrese Walker by J. P. Rose	68
'I think the human race has no future if it doesn't go to space' by Stephen Hawking	73
The Sky at Night: The Art of Stargazing by Dame Maggie Aderin-Pocock	77
Mrs Death Misses Death by Salena Godden	80
Wild places and urban landscapes	**85**
Poverty Safari by Darren McGarvey	87
The Right Sort of Girl by Anita Rani	93
The Waves by Virginia Woolf	98
Diary of a Young Naturalist by Dara McAnulty	103
'My Girl and the City' by Sam Selvon	107
Manhattan '45 by Jan Morris	112
Truth and reality	**117**
'A moment that changed me' by Samira Ahmed	119
Trumpet by Jackie Kay	122
The Left Hand of Darkness by Ursula K. Le Guin	126
Spectacles by Sue Perkins	130
We, the Survivors by Tash Aw	136
'It's time to regulate social media sites that publish news' by Sharon White	139

Dystopia and other worlds	**143**
The Knife of Never Letting Go by Patrick Ness	145
'Writing Fantasy Lets Me Show the Whole Truth	
of Disability' by Ross Showalter	149
The Island of Missing Trees by Elif Shafak	155
Klara and the Sun by Kazuo Ishiguro	159
'Uncertainty Principle' by K. Tempest Bradford	165

Youth and experience	**169**
Becoming Dinah by Kit de Waal	171
My Name is Why by Lemn Sissay	176
Red Leaves by Sita Brahmachari	182
My Left Foot by Christy Brown	188

Crime and consequences

People have always been fascinated by crime and its consequences. Crime dramas have become increasingly popular and gripping: people continue to watch and read them because they want to find out *what* happened, *where* it happened, *how* it happened and – perhaps most of all – how it was solved. Some of the most beloved characters from literature, film and television are detectives, from Sherlock Holmes to Scooby Doo. It is hard to know what brings people back to reading about crime and its consequences. These texts can be a window into a world that's difficult to understand and better kept at arm's length – even though it can affect anyone at any time.

This chapter explores crime and its consequences in many forms. In the extract from her novel *Mic Drop*, Sharna Jackson shows us aspiring detectives, who are seeking to uncover the truth. For those of you that like crime writing, there is a non-fiction extract that looks at forensics from the point of view of Val McDermid, one of the most famous crime writers in the UK. In a novel extract from Kim Slater's *Smart*, the narrator is reflecting

DIVERSE WORDS AND VOICES

on what he has seen. The non-fiction piece *In Cold Blood* explores what happens after an extreme crime has been committed.

Extract from *Mic Drop* by Sharna Jackson

FICTION

The following extract is taken from the opening of the novel *Mic Drop* by Sharna Jackson. The sequel to *High-Rise Mystery*, the story is about two sisters – Nik, aged 11, and Norva, aged 13 – who investigate a murder in The Tri, the high-rise building in London where they live. When *High-Rise Mystery* was published in 2020, the characters of Nik and Norva were hailed as the first Black detective duo in UK children's fiction. *Mic Drop* sees Nik, Norva and their friend George investigating a tragic incident that befalls pop star TrojKat while she is filming a music video in The Tri. Written in the first person, this opening section describes Nik's view of the incident. Readers should note that the extract describes someone dying and may be upsetting.

They didn't listen to me.

If they had, perhaps this wouldn't be happening.

*Perhaps she wouldn't be looking me in the eye, her face twisted with terror, as she **succumbed** to the inevitable.*

I will never forget that face. Never.

Katarzyna 'Kat' Clarke. 23. Better known as TrojKat.

Her talent was undoubtedly on the rise, but her body was mere milliseconds away from a fatal fall.

DIVERSE WORDS AND VOICES

This former resident of The Tri was definitely about to die. Katarzyna fell.

I stood still, frozen on the spot. My heart raced in my chest. 500 beats per minute. I didn't lean to look over the side. Why would I? Zero desire. There were exactly 0.0 recurring reasons to witness her body meet the concrete. For what reason?

No, her expression was enough trauma. Enough trauma for an entire lifetime. Somewhere, in another dimension, possibly, Future Me was thanking Current Me for this wise decision.

Why were we here at all? How did all the small decisions we made through our lives lead us here tonight? Standing on the edge of a tower block, with Katarzyna's film crew – her four friends and colleagues – witnessing a pop star lose her life? My sister and fellow investigator Norva had said. 'Nik, you defo have to be involved, it's going to be awesome.'

It was 'awesome' in all the negative ways 'awesome' could be. Wait, let me give you the facts.

The Tri – better known as The Triangle, consisting of three tall towers called Corners – is the estate where we live. We being Norva and I, and her best friend George.

Tonight, we found ourselves on the roof of Corner Three. Many metres in the sky, overlooking the entire city, participating in a video shoot for Katarzyna's new song, Cusp.

The song that was supposed to break her into the big leagues. Katarzyna's scream curdled my blood, twisted my stomach, implanted itself in my brain, never to leave. It was followed by a smacking, echoing thud I would never forget.

The worst sound I've ever heard.
It was the rope that broke this evening. Along with thousands
of hearts – and Katarzyna's body.
TrojKat was dead. 31/10. 19:56.
A terrible, terrible accident.
Or so it seemed.
That's what everyone else said.
But not us.

succumbed gave in to something overwhelming

Extract from *Forensics: The Anatomy of Crime* by Val McDermid

> In her non-fiction book *Forensics: the Anatomy of Crime*, published in 2014, the crime writer Val McDermid explores the history of the forensic techniques used by real-life detectives to solve gruesome crimes. The following extract looks at the clues that traces of blood have given to both fictional and real-life investigators.

Blood. It's the key to life. Without it, we die. It's the thread that runs through history, transferring property and power from one generation to the next. From the earliest times, man has understood blood both as a tribal marker and as an individual **blazon**. In some societies, inheritance flowed not from father to son, but from father to sister's son, because you could be sure that your sister's son was of the same blood as you. You knew for a fact his grandmother was your mother; you couldn't be certain your own sons shared your blood.

It's also been at the beating heart of crime fiction from the beginning. When Doctor Watson first lays eyes on Sherlock Holmes, he is bent over a table perfecting a test for **haemoglobin**. Watson's slowness in grasping

CRIME AND CONSEQUENCES

the test's brilliance makes the consulting detective **fume**. 'Why, man, it is the most practical medico-legal discovery for years. Don't you see that it gives us an **infallible** test for bloodstains. Come over here now!' Then he stabs a needle into his own finger and uses the resulting drop of blood to show the test in action.

'Criminal cases are continually hinging upon this one point,' he declares. 'A man is suspected of a crime months perhaps after it has been committed. His linen or clothes are examined, and brownish stains discovered upon them. Are they blood stains, or mud stains, or rust stains, or fruit stains? That is a question which has puzzled many an expert, and why? Because there was no reliable test. Now we have the Sherlock Holmes test, and there will no longer be any difficulty.'

The very title of Arthur Conan Doyle's first novel, *A Study in Scarlet*, comes from Holmes's lecture to Watson on the meaning of detective work. 'There's the scarlet thread of murder running through the colourless **skein** of life, and our duty is to unravel it, and isolate it, and expose every inch of it.' When, shortly afterwards, the pair discover a 'scarlet thread' beginning in a lonely house off the **Brixton Road**, Watson is nearly sick at the scene, which seems frankly improbable given he's a medical practitioner who has served in the Afghan Wars. But then, I am a writer whose work features blood and gore and yet I am squeamish about blood.

But back to the book. A man has been stabbed in the

DIVERSE WORDS AND VOICES

side as he lay in bed and the blade has pierced his heart. 'From under the door there curled a little red ribbon of blood, which had **meandered** across the passage and formed a little pool along the skirting at the other side.' This time, there is no need for his new test; instead Holmes **assimilates** all the physical evidence in the house, and listens to a policeman's take on the anonymous assassin. 'He must have stayed in the room for some little time after the murder, for we found bloodstained water in the basin, where he had washed his hands, and marks on the sheets where he had deliberately wiped his knife.'

Reconstructing past evens from blood found at a crime scene is known as Bloodstain Pattern Analysis. Conan Doyle's imagination barely touched the edges of what spilled blood can tell modern experts.

[...]

The police still use blood splatter analysis every day: to date, it has helped solve thousands of crimes. But the **seismic** change in the significance of bloodstains came in the 1980s with the discovery of genetic fingerprinting. The question of 'who' could now be added to the list of 'what', 'where' and 'how'.

---

assimilates sees and understands
blazon an old term for a coat of arms that represents a family
Brixton Road a street in London
fume be extremely angry
haemoglobin a substance in blood that carries oxygen
infallible cannot fail
meandered moved slowly in a random way
seismic something massive that has a big impact
skein a coil of thread

Extract from *Smart* by Kim Slater

FICTION

> In Kim Slater's novel *Smart*, published in 2019, the lead character is an art-loving 14-year-old called Kieran Woods, who can be read as being on the autism spectrum, although this is never explicitly stated in the novel. A keen reader of crime fiction and a fan of Sky TV's crime correspondent Martin Brunt, Kieran lives with his mum, his stepdad Tony and Tony's son, Ryan. At the start of the novel, Kieran and Jean, a homeless woman, find the body of a man in the river. Kieran suspects that the man has been murdered, but the police dismiss his suspicions. In this extract, Kieran is in his bedroom drawing a picture of the crime scene.

Ryan's video game was booming downstairs. I could tell if he had shot someone or detonated a bomb by the different noises. While I was drawing, I thought about Mrs Cartwright next door. She has **ulcerated** legs so can't get upstairs. She even sleeps in her living room, which is joined on to ours, so she can never escape Ryan's noise. […]

I drew from when I first got down to the river and saw Jean crying on the bench, to the divers getting the body out of the water. It took up two full pages of my sketchpad.

DIVERSE WORDS AND VOICES

When I was finished, I had very detailed notes and drawings.

I had remembered all the little bits of evidence. I packed matchstick people into the scenes, but I kept the background white like **Lowry** mostly did and just drew the river and close-ups of where the murder took place. This would make any clues much easier to spot.

Martin Brunt was going to be very pleased.

*

The gunfire sounds from downstairs cut off suddenly. That's how I knew Tony had a visitor.

I went to my bedroom door and opened it a tiny bit. I heard Tony coughing and spluttering. I heard the kitchen door shut behind him.

I used to be allowed downstairs. Now people have started visiting, Tony says I have to stay in my room.

My window overlooks the road, so I can still see everything. Sometimes, I sit with my notebook at the window and write stuff down. It feels like I'm in charge of the street.

There was a red Ford Focus outside the house. The passenger window was down and I could see a man's hand and arm flapping about to music that was booming out.

I got out my binoculars that Grandma gave me, from right at the back of my wardrobe. I hide anything I have that's good, so Ryan can't steal it.

CRIME AND CONSEQUENCES

You should never look at the sun with binoculars or you could go blind.

My binoculars are very good ones. I know this because the magnification is 10 x 50. The '10' bit means that whatever you are looking at will appear ten times larger than with your own eyes. The '50' bit means the wide distance across, on the lenses.

'The diameter', **Miss Crane** calls it.

When the diameter of the lenses is bigger, you get more light into your eyes and you can see stuff better. We learned this in science.

[...]

When I saw the man's hand ten times bigger through my binoculars, I spotted that his fingertips were all yellow and his nails were bitten. I wrote this down in my notebook and put an equals sign, like this:

smoker = nervous type

Sherlock Holmes always looked at the tiny clues that most people missed. These can tell you important things about someone. Holmes is old-fashioned now but people still love him.

When you notice little things about people, it is called 'the skill of observation'. Not everyone is good at it.

I heard the back door slam and a man walked down the path. He had a grey hoodie and sweatpants on. The

DIVERSE WORDS AND VOICES

hood was pulled up and he looked left and right as he walked, then back down at the pavement.

He jumped in the car and zoomed off. I had to keep saying the number plate in my head until I had it written down because I only got one look at it.

It had nothing to do with the murder at the embankment but it made me feel good to record the information. I pretended I was on a special mission and it was my job. Tony might make me stay in my room but I am in charge up here. I can sit at the window and do my observation work and he can't say anything.

I heard someone coming upstairs so I jumped on to my bed and hid my notebook, my sketchbook and my binoculars under the pillow. Then I lay down on top of my covers and looked at the ceiling.

Lowry L. S. Lowry was an English artist whose distinct style focused on industrial scenes of northern England and so-called 'matchstick' people
Miss Crane Kieran's teaching assistant at school
ulcerated covered with sores

Extract from *In Cold Blood* by Truman Capote

> The non-fiction book *In Cold Blood* by the American writer Truman Capote, published in 1966, tells the true story of the horrifying murder of the Clutter family in the small town of Holcomb, Kansas, in 1959. Two ex-convicts, Richard Hickock and Perry Smith, confessed to the killings and were later executed for the crime. This extract describes their arrival at the Finney County Courthouse, which was the county jail in Garden City, Kansas, after their arrest. The jail was unusual as it was located directly next to the Sheriff's Residence, an apartment where the under-sheriff Wendle Meier and his wife Josie lived.

The jail contains six cells; the sixth, the one reserved for female prisoners, is actually an isolated unit situated inside the Sheriff's Residence—indeed, it adjoins the Meiers' kitchen. 'But,' says Josie Meier, 'that don't worry me. I enjoy the company. Having somebody to talk to while I'm doing my kitchen work. Most of those women, you got to feel sorry for them. Just met up with Old Man Trouble is all. Course, Hickock and Smith was a different matter. Far as I know, Perry Smith was the first man ever stayed in the ladies' cell. The reason was the sheriff wanted to keep him and Hickock separated from each other until after their

DIVERSE WORDS AND VOICES

trial.' Perry Edward Smith and Richard Eugene Hickock were a young pair of ex-**convicts** who had confessed that in November of 1959 they murdered in his home a **prominent** Finney County farm rancher, Herbert W. Clutter, and three members of his family: his wife, Bonnie; their sixteen-year-old daughter, Nancy; and a son, Kenyon, fifteen. Smith and Hickock were arrested on December 30, 1959, in Las Vegas, Nevada; on January 6, 1960, they were returned to Garden City to await trial. Robbery and a desire to avoid the consequences of possible identification were the confessed **motives** for the crime.

'The afternoon they brought them in, I made six apple pies and baked some bread and all the while kept track of the goings on down there on Courthouse Square,' Josie recalls. 'My kitchen window overlooks the square; you couldn't want a better view. I'm no judge of crowds, but I'd guess there were several hundred people waiting to see the boys that killed the Clutter family. I never met any of the Clutters myself, but from everything I've ever heard about them they must have been very fine people. What happened to them is hard to forgive, and I know Wendle was worried how the crowd might act when they caught sight of Smith and Hickock. He was afraid somebody might try to get at them. So I kind of had my heart in my mouth when I saw the cars arrive, saw the reporters – all the newspaper fellows running and pushing. But by then it was dark, after six, and bitter cold, and more than half

14

CRIME AND CONSEQUENCES

the crowd had given up and gone home. The ones that stayed, they didn't say boo. Only stared.

'Later, when they brought the boys upstairs, the first one I saw was Hickock. He had on light summer pants and just an old cloth shirt. Surprised he didn't catch pneumonia, considering how cold it was. But he looked sick, all right White as a ghost. Well, it must be a terrible experience – to be stared at by a **horde** of strangers, to have to walk among them, and them knowing who you are and what you did. Then they brought up Smith. I had some supper ready to serve them in their cells – hot soup and coffee and some sandwiches and pie. Ordinarily, we feed just twice a day – breakfast at seven-thirty, and at four-thirty we serve the main meal – but I didn't want those fellows going to bed on an empty stomach; seemed to me they must be feeling bad enough without that. But when I took Smith his supper – carried it in on a tray – he said he wasn't hungry. He was looking out the window of the ladies' cell. Standing with his back to me. That window has the same view as my kitchen window – trees and the square and the tops of houses. I told him, "Just taste the soup – it's vegetable, and not out of a can. I made it myself. The pie, too."

'In about an hour, I went back for the tray, and he hadn't touched a crumb. He was still at the window. Like he hadn't moved. It was snowing, and I remember saying it was the first snow of the year, and how we'd

DIVERSE WORDS AND VOICES

had such a beautiful long autumn right till then. And now the snow had come. And then I asked him if he had any special dish he liked – if he did, I'd try and fix it for him the next day. He turned round and looked at me. Suspicious. Like I might be mocking him. Then he said something about a movie; he had such a quiet way of speaking – almost a whisper. Wanted to know if I had seen a movie – I forget the name. Anyway, I hadn't seen it; never have been much for picture shows. He said this show took place in Biblical times, and there was a scene where a man was flung off a balcony, thrown to a mob of men and women, who tore him to pieces. And he said that was what came to mind when he saw the crowd on the square. The man being torn apart. And the idea that maybe that was what they might do to him. Said it scared him so bad his stomach still hurt. Which was why he couldn't eat. Course, he was wrong, and I told him so – nobody was going to harm him, regardless of what he'd done; folks around here aren't like that. We talked some – he was very shy – but after a while he said, "One thing I really like is Spanish rice." So I promised to make him some, and he smiled, kind of, and I decided – well, he wasn't the worst young man I ever saw.

'That night, after I'd gone to bed, I said as much to my husband. But Wendle snorted. Wendle was one of the first on the scene after the crime was discovered. He said he wished I'd been out at the Clutter place when they

CRIME AND CONSEQUENCES

found the bodies. Then I could've judged for myself just how *gentle* Mr. Smith was. Him and his friend Hickock. He said they'd cut out your heart and never bat an eye. There was no denying it. Not with four people dead. And I lay awake wondering if either one was bothered by it – the thought of those four graves.'

convicts criminals
horde a large group of people
motives reasons for doing something
prominent well-known and important

Journeys and discoveries

The prospect of a journey can bring excitement, anticipation, dread or fear. For many people, journeys can lead to new adventures and discoveries. For others, they can be unwanted and or even dangerous. We may be taught that journeys awaken characters to new worlds, even though they can face peril in the unknown; or we may learn that a journey will take us away from everything we have ever known but help us to grow. For those with the privilege to do so, journeys are for leisure to seek out unfamiliar places, and for others, they are only taken out of necessity, and with a sense of dread. Some journeys are less literal and help us to grow and develop within ourselves. This kind of journey can happen without travelling anywhere.

This chapter includes many texts that explore journeys and making new discoveries. The first is an extract set in the treacherous Arctic, following the travels of African American explorer, Matthew A. Henson, in his memoir. Monisha Rajesh travelled around the world by train, and in the travel writing extract, we hear one specific anecdote from this journey, which covered 45,000 miles.

DIVERSE WORDS AND VOICES

In *City of Stolen Magic*, the reader is transported to Dacca in Bangladesh, and is exploring a bazaar. And Baroness Floella Benjamin takes us on her journey to London as a migrant in childhood, as part of her autobiography.

The journeys in this chapter are both real and imagined, both physical and emotional – no matter where they do or don't lead.

Extract from Arctic explorer Matthew Alexander Henson's memoir

Matthew A. Henson was an African American explorer who was one of the first people to reach the geographic North Pole in 1909. American explorer and naval officer Commander Robert Peary was the expedition lead publicly, but Henson was an integral member of the party, and they had worked together many times in the past. The expedition party included a number of Inuit explorers, including Ootah and Kudlooktoo, four of whom remained on the final stretch. Following the success of their expedition, racial division meant there was controversy over who reached the pole first, and Henson did not get the recognition he deserved until many years later. In this extract from Henson's memoir, published in 1912, he describes part of their treacherous journey.

Following the trail made by **Captain Bartlett**, we pushed off, every man at the **upstander** of his sledge to urge his team by whip and voice. It was only when we had perfect going over sheets of young ice that we were able to steal a ride on the sledges.

DIVERSE WORDS AND VOICES

The trail led us over the **glacial fringe** for a quarter of a mile, and the going was fairly easy, but, after leaving the land ice-foot, the trail plunged into ice so rough that we had to use pickaxes to make a pathway. It took only about one mile of such going, and my sledge split.

'Number one,' said I to myself, and I came to a halt. The gale was still blowing, but I started to work on the necessary repairs. I have practically built one sledge out of two broken ones, while out on the ice and in weather almost as bad as this; and I have almost daily during the journey had to repair broken sledges, sometimes under fiercer conditions; and so I will describe this one job and hereafter, when writing about repairing a sledge, let it go at that.

Cold and windy. Undo the **lashings**, unload the load, get out the **brace and bit** and bore new holes, taking plenty of time, for, in such cold, there is danger of the steel bit breaking. Then, with ungloved hands, thread the sealskin thongs through the hole. The fingers freeze. Stop work, pull the hand through the sleeve, and take your icy fingers to your heart; that is, put your hand under your armpit, and when you feel it burning you know it has thawed out. Then start to work again. By this time the party has advanced beyond you and, as orders are orders, and you have been ordered to take the lead, you have to start, catch up, and pass the column before you have reached your station.

JOURNEYS AND DISCOVERIES

Of course, in catching up and overtaking the party, you have the advantage of the well-marked trail they have made. Once again in the lead; and my boy, Ootah, had to up and break his sledge, and there was some more **tall talking** when the Commander caught up with us and left us there mending it. A little farther on, and the amiable Kudlooktoo, who was in my party at the time, busted his sledge. You would have thought that Kudlooktoo was the last person in Commander Peary's estimation, when he got through talking to him and telling him what he thought of him. The sledge was so badly broken it had to be abandoned. The load was left on the spot where the accident happened, and Kudlooktoo, much **chastened** and **crestfallen**, drove his team of dogs back to the land for a new sledge.

We did not wait for him, but kept on for about two hours longer, when we reached the Captain's first igloo, twelve miles out; a small day's travelling, but we were almost dead-beat, from having battled all day with the wind, which had blown a full-sized gale. No other but a Peary party would have attempted to travel in such weather. Our breath was frozen to our hoods of fur and our cheeks and noses frozen. Spreading our furs upon the snow, we dropped down and endeavoured to sleep, but sound sleep was impossible. It was a night of **Plutonian Purgatory**. All through the night I would wake from the cold and beat my arms or feet to keep the circulation

DIVERSE WORDS AND VOICES

going, and I would hear one or both of my boys doing the same. I did not make any entries in the diary that day, and there was many a day like it after that.

brace and bit a type of hand drill used to make holes
Captain Bartlett Robert Bartlett, who was Captain of the steamship, the SS Roosevelt, which took Henson and his colleagues on their 1908 voyage to the North Pole
chastened when a person is told they have done something wrong
crestfallen disappointed and sad
glacial fringe a continuous ice shelf
lashings ropes used to tie things down
Plutonian Purgatory in ancient Greek mythology, a place where a person's soul underwent purification
tall talking boasting or exaggerated storytelling
upstander in this context it means at the speaking position, or at the head of the sledge

Extract from *Around the World in 80 Trains: A 45,000-Mile Adventure* by Monisha Rajesh

NON-FICTION

> Monisha Rajesh is a British journalist who set out with her fiancé, Jeremy, to travel around the world by train. With a title inspired by Jules Verne's 1872 adventure novel, *Around the World in Eighty Days*, she chronicled her journey in the award-winning travel book, *Around the World in 80 Trains: A 45,000-Mile Adventure*, published in 2019. In the following extract, Rajesh describes her experience travelling on the Trans-Mongolian Railway, a route that stretches from Russia to China.

'You are the first English people I have ever met on board this train,' said Aleksandr. 'And you are the first English people that he has ever met on board this train,' he continued, pointing to his roommate, who was also called Aleksandr. That afternoon we had boarded the Trans-Siberian, the godfather of trains. Strictly speaking the Trans-Siberian is not a train, but a route, spanning more than 9170 kilometres from Moscow to Vladivostok. Featuring high on bucket lists, the train is the benchmark by which rail enthusiasts measure one another. If you say you haven't taken it – but that you will one day – their

DIVERSE WORDS AND VOICES

eyes glaze over as you cease to exist. In fact, we were travelling on the Trans-Mongolian, a more interesting route that drops down through Mongolia and ends in Beijing. Riding all the way to Vladivostok held no appeal other than that we could then tell people we'd ridden all the way to Vladivostok. There was nothing we wished to see at the end of the line, and the last thing we wanted to do once we'd arrived was turn around and come back. On the other hand, the Trans-Mongolian opened up far more opportunities for onward travel than simply wandering around the edge of the world map looking at Orthodox churches. We'd already stood in awe overlooking the Disneyland domes of **St Basil's Cathedral on Red Square**, and from then on, all other architecture was underwhelming. In spite of being one of the most familiar images in existence, the presence of the colourful domes – like big beautiful swirls of gelato – striped, **latticed** and topped with gold crosses, was glorious to behold. Via the Trans-Mongolian route, Jem and I could break up the journey in Irkutsk for two nights, then carry on to Ulaanbaatar in Mongolia, before eventually arriving in Beijing – 11 days after leaving Moscow. After our first Russian-train experience, we had boarded the Trans-Mongolian with **trepidation**, anticipating a mix of Russians, backpackers, students, weirdos, train geeks, and retired couples ticking off their bucket list. Met with familiar stares, we quickly realised we were the only foreigners on board. Having looked through travel-agency photos of the **Rossiya** service, we'd expected air-conditioned cars with soft berths, power sockets and flat-screen TVs, only to find ourselves staring down a grubby hard **sleeper** with a broken window [...]

Taking temperatures to both extremes, Siberia's heat was crippling. The air-conditioning didn't work, and the windows served only to channel hot air into the compartments. Tangled in damp sheets, I spent a lot of the journey lying limply, watching leafless trees roll past like rows of unsharpened pencils. Every few hours a farmhouse or two would appear with a **Lada** parked outside. Scarecrows tilted in potato patches, and dirt tracks wound into woods. Having picked up our location on Google maps in Moscow, I followed the blue sphere as it bobbed across blank territory. It was as though we were crossing a hinge in the Earth. By air, the notion of being in-between was constant, but by rail there were always villages, towns, and seas emerging like stepping stones between destinations. Neither West, nor East, we were hurtling through the borderlands. At dusk, halos of mist swirled above ground, orbiting forests like a magical force. Five days on board a continuous train had presented the rare opportunity to read great **tomes**, and, in keeping with our surroundings, I'd downloaded *War and Peace, Crime and Punishment* and *Young Stalin*, hoping to emerge in China a more refined and cultured person.

DIVERSE WORDS AND VOICES

But the heat and the swaying did nothing but lull me to sleep each time I began *War and Peace* […].

Between Moscow and Irkutsk, the train stopped at around 80 stations, for no more than two minutes at a time, with the odd one-hour break when the toilets were bolted and anyone inside was **collared** and hauled out to continue their **ablutions** on the platform. These hour-long stops presented an opportunity to break free from the **tedium**, to stretch our legs, and to remember that a world existed beyond the four corners of our compartment, which had begun to smell like an old laundry basket. Russian stations are handsome affairs painted peppermint with white piping, and adorned with old clock towers. Wandering from one […] **babushka** to the next, I'd buy a hunk of cheese or cake, or pass the time watching large women in small shorts selling rows of **omul** fish bunched like keys and hooked through the eyes. At one such stop I rifled through the trolley of a lady too busy chatting to a friend to bother with me, and offered her 90 roubles ($2) for a pack of playing cards. She laughed in my face, nudging her friend, who also laughed in my face. Even her son, who was sitting in the bottom of the trolley, covered his eyes with disbelief that anyone would offer more than a cursory glance for what turned out to be a pack of 36 cards.

By Wednesday evening I'd stopped bothering to change my clothes or brush my hair, and lounged in my

JOURNEYS AND DISCOVERIES

pyjamas in the drinking car where the air-conditioning worked, and it was marginally cooler than the sun. Oksana kept bringing me plates of fried mushrooms covered in dill, patting my head and flapping her cloth at anyone who came near me, watching closely as an elderly man offered me cottage-cheese blinis, repulsed by my instant mash. She chatted in Russian, wholly unbothered that I replied in English, neither of us understanding the other, but happy in each other's company.

ablutions washing yourself
babushka a Russian word for elderly woman or grandmother
collared grabbed by the collar
Lada a car brand from Russia
latticed an overlapping, criss-cross pattern
omul a type of fish common in parts of Russia
Rossiya the train service that operates on the route from Moscow to Vladivostok
sleeper a private train carriage with a bed for overnight journeys
St Basil's Cathedral on Red Square a well-known Russian Orthodox church in Moscow, Russia
tedium a boring time or experience
tomes large, heavy books
trepidation fear and nervousness

Extract from *City of Stolen Magic* by Nazneen Ahmed Pathak

The following extract is from a novel entitled *City of Stolen Magic* by British Bangladeshi author Nazneen Ahmed Pathak, published in 2023. In the story, Chompa's mother, Ammi, has been abducted by 'men, all pale in the moonlight'. In order to find her mother – as well as learning more about her life and the magic she practises – Chompa, the hero of the story, sets off travelling. In the journey described below, Chompa makes her way with her new friend Leeza, a maid who is also alone, to a bookshop in Dacca, Bangladesh, where Ammi seems to have purchased the spellbook she gave to her daughter.

She raised her hand and, for the first time in her life, hailed a **rickshaw**. A cyclist slowed and raised his head in enquiry.

'**Old Dacca Chowk Bazaar**,' she said **haughtily**, with a deeply satisfyingly rush of grown-upness.

The breeze blew playfully through Chompa's hair as the rickshaw wheeled along the wide streets, darting and weaving between the lumbering horse-drawn carriages like a little silver fish. Leeza grabbed Chompa's waist tightly as she waved her hand through the air.

'You should hold the edge of the hood. Any bump and you'll go flying into the street – and how will we explain your injuries, huh?'

JOURNEYS AND DISCOVERIES

'Chup- chup, Leeza, I'm fine. I won't fall!'

Chompa pulled herself up to standing, both hands reaching to the sky. The **rickshaw-wallah** muttered in rough, accented **Bangla** to Leeza.

'He's agreeing with me – sit down. He thinks you might be mad. I know you are.'

Soon the streets started to narrow, and the buildings became disordered, tumbling structures of tiles, brick, aluminium – anything that was spare, cheap and would hold off heavy monsoon rains. And people – suddenly there were people *everywhere*. It didn't seem possible, but the noise seemed to grow louder as they approached a slightly more uniform set of buildings packed into a tight grid. The rickshaw slowed to a stop.

Chompa jumped out and paid the driver. Her nerves thrilled with excitement.

[...]

The pair searched the market for the bookstall, munching on sweet, crisp spirals of amber-coloured **jalebi** from a banana-leaf packet. It was chaos here, but as with the rest of the city it was of an ordered kind. One row of stalls was for vegetable sellers, the air heavy with the heady green scent of coriander, then came a row of butchers' stalls, where flies buzzed about hung carcasses enthusiastically, and blood ran in **rivulets** across the earth. Each row was teeming with customers, but Chompa was looking for only one particular place.

At the very edge of the market, they found it.

DIVERSE WORDS AND VOICES

The last row had a single dusty dark stool with not a single customer. It was run by a **wizened** old woman, her entire face concealed by the end of her black **sari**. Chompa walked slowly in silence as she browsed the items on show: bottles of various shapes in vivid colours; cooking equipment and trinkets; bowls and grinding stones made from old discoloured brass; little carved boxes; ceramic dishes of silver necklaces and bracelets. The **wares** varied in age, beauty, and quality, but all of them were completely covered in **Farsi** writing.

On the final table lay neat stacks of crisp, unblemished books, all with familiar sari-silk covers and silver clasps. Chompa's heart leapt with excitement. She might meet the person who had sold Ammi her book.

'Excuse me, Auntie-ji, but can you tell me who makes these books, please?'

The woman raised her head sharply in Chompa's direction, her crooked, ancient back suddenly snapping straight. The end of the sari flapped away from her face for a moment, and Chompa had the briefest impression of an unlined face surrounded by **incongruously** short curls.

'Why do you ask?' she growled in a deep, low, strong voice as she tucked the sari end back behind her ear tightly.

'I – I've just seen one before.'

The woman turned away, muttering. 'It's of no business to a nosy little child like you – this is not a toyshop. Go find another place to spend your coins.'

32

JOURNEYS AND DISCOVERIES

Chompa snapped. 'I am not a nosy child, thank you. I'm here to find out about my mother. Her name was Amina Begum, and she bought books from this stall.'

The woman gasped and then stumbled, clutching the table. Chompa looked over her shoulder, confused, thinking that something must have frightened the old woman. But the alley was empty, Leeza clearly having **traipsed** off to friendlier stalls. Chompa turned back and jumped to find the stallholder right in front of her, pulling at the sari end, unveiling herself.

She was young, perhaps in her early thirties. She raised her gloved hands to Chompa's face and cupped it gently.

'**Mash'Allah**', the woman breathed. 'It's like a young mirror. As if Amina never left.'

Left?

'Did you know my mother?' Chompa spluttered.

Bangla the main language spoken in Bangladesh and West Bengal in India
Farsi the official language spoken in Iran and nearby countries
haughtily proudly and arrogantly
incongruously in a way that seems out of place
jalebi a sweet dish made of fried batter soaked in syrup
Mash'Allah an Arabic expression used to express a feeling of awe
Old Dacca Chowk Bazaar a busy market in the old town of Dhaka in Bangladesh
rickshaw a two-wheeled cart pulled by a person on foot or riding a bicycle
rickshaw-wallah a rickshaw driver
rivulets small streams
sari a type of dress worn by women in South Asia
traipsed walked somewhere slowly because you are unwilling to go
wares items for sale
wizened small with lots of wrinkles in the skin because of old age

Extract from *What Are You Doing Here?* by Baroness Floella Benjamin

NON-FICTION

> Baroness Floella Benjamin is a broadcaster, actress, television presenter and member of the House of Lords. Born in Trinidad in 1949, she moved to England and became famous as a children's television presenter in the 1970s and 1980s, inspiring many young people through her work on entertaining and educational programmes such as *Play School*. In the following extract from her autobiography *What Are You Doing Here?*, published in 2022, she describes the journey she made by ship in 1960 to join her mother, Marmie, her father, Dardie, and her two youngest siblings in London. She travelled with her sister, Sandra, and two brothers, Lester and Ellington.

I was actually on my way to the fabled **Motherland**. It felt as if we were stepping into one of Dardie's exciting adventure stories. Everything I cared about most was in England. That was where I was meant to be. That was where I had been told I belonged. Though we were to travel for two weeks or more over four thousand miles of ocean, in our heads we were simply moving from one part of Britain to another, where the streets were paved with gold.

The ships always left at night, and the **wharf** at **Port of Spain** was dark, noisy and crowded. I remember a

JOURNEYS AND DISCOVERIES

lot of shouting and shoving, as the night air crackled with emotion – worry and hope and sadness and fear all muddling together. People **fretted** loudly over their trunks and suitcases, or 'grips' as we called them. Others said prayers for a safe passage. Many were embracing and crying as they said goodbye to loved ones, maybe for the last time. We hugged Auntie Olive tightly, and I quickly found myself in tears too.

The harbour at Port of Spain was too shallow for the big ships to approach, so little motorboats ferried passengers out to the *Marqués de Comillas*. Lowering myself down into the **tender** as it bobbed on inky black water seemed an impossible step that filled me with terror. The liquid reflections of the quayside lights fractured over and over again. At last Sandra and my brothers **coaxed** me aboard, and we sped into the unknown, clinging tightly to one another and feeling terribly alone. Even more terrifying was bumping in darkness against the towering **bow** of the anchored ship, far away from the twinkling lights onshore, and realizing that to get on board I would now have to clamber up a shaky rope ladder.

'*Venga! Venga!*'

From above and below, kind Spanish sailors urged me on and offered helping hands, but again I felt wobbly with fear and found it hard to move. I was convinced that at any moment I would slip and plunge into the menacing depths of the swelling seas.

DIVERSE WORDS AND VOICES

Departure remains a blur. There was so much to take in. Stairs in all directions, numbers, signs, loudspeakers, the thundering bellow of the horn as we began to move. Once a luxury ocean liner travelling between Spain and New York, the *Marqués de Comillas* had been converted into a passenger cargo-ship after the Second World War; now over eight hundred passengers could be accommodated on board. This voyage had already picked up lots of other British citizens in Grenada and Barbados. The tiny cabin we all shared was between decks, right in the belly of the ship, and we took to our bunks gratefully.

My first shock on waking was the dizzying nausea that immediately overwhelmed me. Nobody had warned us about seasickness. Tomato soup and corn puffs were all we could stomach. Sandra took even longer to find her sea legs than I did, but by day five I was able to start exploring and bring her back reports, as Lester, Ellington and I rushed around the ship, investigating every corner of the vessel from the **cargo hold** to the ballroom. How fascinating it all was! What freedom we had! We were four youngsters aged seven to eleven travelling all on our own! Although Marmie had apparently paid someone to take care of us, nobody ever appeared, and we were left to run wild, until Ellington got into a fight with another boy. They punched and kicked each other, rolling around on deck together locked in combat without a thought of danger.

'Stop! Stop!' Sandra and I were horrified. Even when the captain shouted a furious warning from the bridge, they kept on fighting. Finally, he came down in person, and dragged them from the edge just before they fell overboard.

That voyage was a real adventure, and a time out of time. I remember peeling hundreds of potatoes in the galleys for the Spanish cooks. I didn't realize I was doing their job for them. I remember an eruption of glittering flying fish, leaping at the **prow** in a golden sunset. At night we would sneak out of bed to watch the grown-ups dancing. The ship lit up with laughter and music and lights as it throbbed across a changing sea. From the heat of the **tropics**, we passed into the cooler Atlantic Ocean and sailed past Spain into the English Channel. Then, as Marmie had warned us, the temperature began to drop so much that we had to run around the decks to keep warm. Lester thought we were about to crash into an iceberg, thanks to some story he'd heard in Trinidad about the cold in England, and his **agitation** only increased as we got closer to Southampton.

On our last night at sea, there was a huge party which went on late into the night. The final hours on board were agonizingly slow, and it was hard to be patient. We woke up in port on the morning of 2 September 1960. We all washed carefully, and put on the special arrival outfits Auntie Olive had given us. I plaited my hair and Sandra's in a stylish way, and decorated it with ribbons, as Marmie

DIVERSE WORDS AND VOICES

used to do. No prince or princess could have felt better. Everyone wanted to look their best when they first set foot in England, so we emerged onto a deck crowded with luggage and people **dressed to the nines**. The men wore **trilbies** and wide-shouldered suits with baggy trousers. The women were all in hats and gloves and colourful dresses puffed out with full, **starched petticoats**.

The docks were **bewilderingly** huge – a great mass of cranes and rail containers and iron-roofed sheds, and hundreds of people, some busy working, some recently **disembarked** themselves or about to set off on voyages of their own, others anxiously looking for loved ones. I gripped the rail and shivered, wondering how we'd ever find Marmie.

---

agitation a feeling of anxiety and upset
bewilderingly confusing or difficult to understand
bow the front part of a ship or boat
cargo hold a storage space inside a ship or airplane
coaxed persuaded someone gently
disembarked left a ship
dressed to the nines wearing glamorous and fashionable clothes (informal)
fretted worried and felt unable to relax
Marqués de Comillas the ship Baroness Benjamin is travelling on with her siblings
Motherland the country you were born in or feel a strong connection with
Port of Spain the capital city of Trinidad and Tobago
prow the pointed part at the front of a ship or boat
starched petticoats underwear dresses or skirts, washed with starch to make them stiff, worn beneath dresses or skirts
tender a small boat used to carry people or things between land and a large ship
trilbies hats made of soft felt with a narrow edge or 'brim'
tropics hot regions of the world near the equator
Venga a Spanish expression meaning 'Come on!'
wharf a quay where ships are loaded or unloaded

Power and influence

There are many ways that power and influence work together. The power of one person or group can be exerted over others, such as leaders in the Government or employers in the workplace. Sometimes people seize their own power and use it to live their lives with greater success. Influence can spark immediate action, or it may be felt years later. Think about how small acts of resistance against something can affect events later in time, such as people that have stood up for something in history. There are many ways to find our own power – big or small – even if our voices appear to be tiny. How can you use your voice to make change? Everyone's actions have influence and are connected.

In this chapter, we hear many voices that are using their power to influence others. Disability activist Stella Young strives for change in the future in her letter to her 80-year-old self. People who are knowledgeable and passionate about a topic can be powerful, such as Malala Yousafzai in her Nobel Prize acceptance speech. Megan Rapinoe's speech is also empowering, as she talks about success in the Women's World Cup. Power also exists in

DIVERSE WORDS AND VOICES

the everyday, as explored in E. R. Braithwaite's extract
from *To Sir, With Love* – a classic text about a Black teacher
in London's East End.

Stella Young's letter to herself at 80 years old

NON-FICTION

Stella Young was a comedian, journalist and disability rights activist who challenged the pitying and exceptional views of disabled people. She died unexpectedly at the age of 32. In this letter to her 80-year-old self, written two years before her death, Young talks about the expectations that are put on disabled people and shares her understanding of the social model of disability and the value she has in the world (although, as her TEDX talk eloquently explains, 'I'm not your inspiration, thank you very much!'). This letter takes on a different meaning from when it was first published (before Young's death) but the message it contains is still as powerful.

Eighty, hey? Eighty.

Eighty is a long way from where I write to you now. Fifty years, in fact.

To be honest, I've never thought a great deal about you, eighty-year-old Stell. I tend not to think about living to some grand old age. Then again, I don't think about dying either. I suppose you do; you're eighty. You've done a lot of things. Seen a lot of things. You almost certainly have a hover-chair by now. [...]

DIVERSE WORDS AND VOICES

I suppose I can't really write this letter to you without talking about the assumption, the expectation, that people like us die young.

One of my most beloved **crip** heroes, Harriet McBryde Johnson, wrote in her memoir about her realisation at four years old, while watching a Muscular Dystrophy Telethon, that she was a little girl who was going to die young. The telethon was famous for its host, Jerry Lewis, trotting out adorable disabled children and telling us all that they were going to die. Most disability charity hinges on that notion – that you need to send your money in quick before all these poor, pitiful people die. […]

When it comes time for Harriet to start **kindergarten** and she isn't dead yet, she says to herself, 'Well, I might as well die a kindergartener.' When she starts high school and she isn't dead yet, she thinks, 'Well, I might as well die educated.' When she graduates from law school and she still isn't dead yet, at twenty-seven, she decides, 'Well, I might as well die a lawyer.' Harriet is thirty before she realises that it is, in fact, too late to die young. And so she spends the rest of her life protesting against that awful Muscular Dystrophy Telethon. Not just because it handed her a false death sentence, but because pity gets in the way of our rights. There's been much talk of Lewis bringing his telethon to Australia, but don't worry, eighty-year-old Stell, you totally kicked that one in the privates.

I fall into this trap of talking about Harriet as though she was a friend. She was, in a way. Hers was one of

42

POWER AND INFLUENCE

your 'coming out' books. Remember those days back before you came out as a disabled woman? You used to spend a lot of energy on 'passing'. Pretending you were just like everyone else, that you didn't need any 'special treatment', that your life experience didn't mean anything in particular. It certainly didn't make you different from other people. Difference, as you knew it then, was a terrible thing. I used to think of myself in terms of who I'd be if I didn't have this pesky old disability.

Then, at seventeen, something shifted. To borrow from Janis Ian, I learned the truth at seventeen.

That I was not wrong for the world I live in. The world I live in was not yet right for me.

I started learning about the social model of disability. Reading all the disability studies resources I could lay my hands on. I devoured the memoirs of other disabled people. And I completely changed the way I thought about myself.

I stopped unconsciously apologising for taking up space. I'm sure you can scarcely imagine that now; a world where disabled people, women in particular, are made to feel like we're not really entitled to inhabit public spaces.

I started changing my language. […] Somehow, we're supposed to buy this notion that if we use the term disabled too much, it might strip us of our personhood. But that shame that has become attached to the notion of disability, it's not your shame. It took a while to learn that, so I hope that you've never forgotten.

DIVERSE WORDS AND VOICES

I started calling myself a disabled woman, and a crip. A good thirteen years after seventeen-year-old me started saying crip, it still horrifies people. I do it because it's a word that makes me feel strong and powerful. It's a word other activists have used before me, and I use it to honour them.

[…]

I will do everything I can to meet you, eighty-year-old Stell.

By the time I get to you, I will have loved with every tiny little bit of my heart and soul. […] Whether there's one great love or many, you will have loved and been loved, obscenely well.

[…]

By the time I get to you, I will have lost people I love. […] Losing someone is the thing that terrifies you more than anything. You will have been through that terror, and survived.

By the time I get to you, I'll probably have lost Mum and Dad. Dear Mum and Dad, who never wanted me to be anything other than what I am. Who never expressed a scrap of disappointment that I wasn't quite what they were told to expect. Who, despite being told not to have any more children because of the risk they'd have my condition, went on to have my two beautiful sisters. I think that's the thing I love them for the most; that they didn't see disaster, when those around them could speak of little else.

By the time I get to you, I'll have written things that change the way people think about disability. I'll have been part of a strong, beautiful, proud movement of disabled people in Australia. I'll have said and written things that annoyed people, disabled and non-disabled people. You will never, ever stop challenging the things you think are unfair.

[...] By the time I get to you, I'll be so proud. The late Laura Hershey once wrote about disability pride, and how hard it is to achieve in a world that teaches us shame. She said, 'You get proud by practising'. Thanks to my family, my friends, my crip comrades and my community, I'm already really proud. But I promise to keep practising, every day.

Listen, Stell. I can't tell you for certain that you and I will ever meet. [...]

But on my path to reach you, I promise to grab every opportunity with both hands, to say yes as often as I can, to take risks, to scare myself stupid, and to have loads of fun.

See you in our hover-chair, lady.

Love, Stell x

---

crip a slang term of endearment that some disabled people use to refer to other disabled people
kindergarten nursery

Extract from *To Sir, With Love* by E. R. Braithwaite

> Set in the aftermath of the Second World War, *To Sir, With Love* by E. R. Braithwaite, published in 1959, is an autobiographical novel based on Braithwaite's experiences as a Black teacher in a secondary school in the East End of London. In the following extract, Braithwaite has just arrived at Greenslade Secondary School, where he is starting as a new teacher.

From the Headmaster's office a short flight of stairs led down to a narrow corridor between the auditorium on one side and some classrooms on the other. I paused for a moment outside the first of these classrooms, not sure where to begin, when the door was pushed violently outwards and a tall, red-headed girl rushed out into the corridor closely pursued by two others. In such a narrow space I was quite unable to dodge her wild progress, so I quickly grabbed her by the arms to avoid being bowled over and to steady her. Quickly recovering herself she shook loose, smiled **impudently** in my face, and with a quick 'Sorry' raced down the corridor and out of sight. Her companions pulled up hastily, stopped a moment to look at me, then quickly re-entered the classroom, letting the door bang loudly shut behind them.

POWER AND INFLUENCE

I was staggered by this unexpected encounter and remained where I was for a moment, unsure of what to do next. Then, deciding to take a closer look at what went on in that room, I knocked on the door, opened it and walked in. There was a general **hubbub** and for a little while no one seemed aware of my entry, and then, very gradually, one by one the **occupants** turned to stare at me.

There was no sign of anyone who looked like a teacher. About forty boys and girls were in the room. Perhaps it would be more accurate to call them young men and women, for there was about most of them a degree of adulthood, not only in terms of obvious physical development, but also in the way their clothes were worn to emphasize that development whenever possible. They stood around the room in casual **postures**; some were clustered around a large open empty fireplace in one corner; a few were sitting on desks or chairs in careless **unscholarly** attitudes. They nearly all wore a kind of unofficial uniform. […] A wide variety of hairstyles **paid tribute** to their particular screen favorite. It was all a bit soiled and untidy, as if too little attention were paid to washing either themselves or their flashy **finery**. The boys wore blue jeans and T-shirts or open-necked plaid shirts.

A large, round-faced, freckled girl left the group by the fireplace and approached me.

'If you're looking for Mr. Hackman, he's not here, he's in the staffroom,' she announced. 'He said when we are ready to behave one of us can go and call him.'

47

DIVERSE WORDS AND VOICES

The various groups began to **disintegrate** and reform on either side of this self-elected spokesman, and I was subjected to their bold, **unabashed** scrutiny. God, I thought, what a crowd! Suddenly they were talking all at once, as if a penny had finally dropped somewhere; the questions came thick and fast.

'Are you the new teacher?'

'Are you taking Old Hack's place?'

'Is old Hackman really leaving?'

Taking my cue from the girl's first remark I said: 'I think I'll look in at the staffroom,' and slipped quickly through the door. I felt shocked by the encounter. My vision of teaching in a school was one of straight rows of desks, and neat, well-mannered, obedient children. The room I had just left seemed like a **menagerie**. What kind of fellow could this Hackman be who would stand for that sort of behaviour? Was it the accepted thing here? Would I have to accept it too?

---

disintegrate break up
finery fine clothes
hubbub a loud, confused noise of many voices
impudently cheekily or disrespectfully
menagerie a small zoo
occupants people who occupy a place
paid tribute done to show respect or admiration for someone or something
postures ways of standing and sitting
unabashed not ashamed, embarrassed or shy
unscholarly not suitable for a scholar or learned person

48

Malala Yousafzai's Nobel Peace Prize speech, 2014

NON-FICTION

In 2014, Malala Yousafzai became the youngest ever recipient of the Nobel Peace Prize. It was awarded to her for her inspirational work as a human rights activist and advocate for female education. Malala grew up in the Swat Valley in north-western Pakistan, which was taken over by the Taliban when she was ten. Girls were banned from going to school and Malala was shot by a Taliban gunman for campaigning for girls' rights to education. The following extract is taken from her speech accepting the Nobel Peace Prize.

Dear brothers and sisters, I was named after the inspirational **Malalai of Maiwand**, who is the **Pashtun Joan of Arc**. The word Malala means grief-stricken, sad, but in order to lend some happiness to it, my grandfather would always call me Malala, the happiest girl in the world and today, I'm very happy that we are together fighting for an important cause. This award is not just for me. It is for those forgotten children who want education. It is for those frightened children who want peace. It is for those voiceless children who want change. I'm here to stand up for their rights, to raise their voice. It is not time to pity them. It is not time to pity them. It is time to take action,

DIVERSE WORDS AND VOICES

so it becomes the last time, the last time, so it becomes the last time that we see a child deprived of education.

I have found that people describe me in many different ways. Some people call me the girl who was shot by the **Taliban**, and some the girl who fought for her rights. Some people call me a **Nobel Laureate** now. However, my brothers still call me that annoying bossy sister. As far as I know, I'm just a committed and even stubborn person who wants to see every child getting quality education, who wants to see women having equal rights, and who wants peace in every corner of the world.

Education is one of the blessings of life and one of its necessities. That has been my experience during the 17 years of my life. In my paradise home, Swat, I always loved learning and discovering new things. I remember when my friends and I would decorate our hands with henna on special occasions and instead of drawing flowers and patterns, we would paint our hands with mathematical formulas and equations. We had a thirst for education. We had a thirst for education because our future was right there in that classroom. We would sit, and learn, and read together. We loved to wear neat and tidy school uniforms and we would sit there with big dreams in our eyes. We wanted to make our parents proud and prove that we could also excel in our studies and achieve those goals, which some people think only boys can.

But things did not remain the same. When I was in Swat, which was a place of tourism and beauty [it] suddenly changed into a place of terrorism, I was just 10 [when] more than 400 schools were destroyed. Women were flogged. People were killed. And our beautiful dreams turned into nightmares. Education went from being a right to being a crime. Girls were stopped from going to school. When my world suddenly changed, my priorities changed too. I had two options. One was to remain silent and wait to be killed. And the second was to speak up and then be killed. I chose the second one. I decided to speak up.

We could not just stand by and see those injustices of the terrorists denying our rights, ruthlessly killing people, and misusing the name of Islam. We decided to raise our voice and tell them, 'Have you not learnt, have you not learnt that in the Holy **Quran Allah** says if you kill one person it is as if you kill the whole humanity? Do you not know that **Mohammad**, peace be upon him, the prophet of mercy, he says, do not harm yourself or others. And do you not know that the very first word of the Holy Quran is the word Iqra, which means read?' The terrorists tried to stop us and attacked me and my friends who are here today on our school bus in 2012, but neither their ideas, nor their bullets could win. We survived. And since that day, our voices have grown louder and louder.

I tell my story, not because it is unique, but because it is not. It is the story of many girls. Today, I tell their stories too. I have brought with me some of my sisters from Pakistan, from Nigeria, and from Syria who share this story. My brave sisters, Shazia and Kainat, who were

51

DIVERSE WORDS AND VOICES

also shot [that] day on our school bus, but they have not stopped learning. And my brave sister, Kainat Soomro, who went through severe abuse and extreme violence, even her brother was killed, but she did not **succumb**. Also my sisters here, whom I have met during my Malala Fund Campaign. My 16-year-old courageous sister, Mezon from Syria, who now lives in Jordan as a refugee and she goes from tent to tent encouraging girls and boys to learn. And my sister, Amina from the north of Nigeria, where **Boko Haram** threatens, and stops girls, and even kidnaps girls just for wanting to go to school.

Though I appear as one girl, though I appear as one girl, one person, who is five foot, two inches tall if you include my high heels. It means I'm five foot only. I am not a lone voice. I'm not a lone voice. I am many. I am Malala. But I'm also Shazia. I'm Kainat. I'm Kainat Soomro. I am Mezon. I am Amina. I am those 66 million girls who are deprived of education. And today, I'm not raising my voice. It is the voice of those 66 million girls.

Allah the name of God in Islam

Boko Haram an Islamist militant organization based in north-eastern Nigeria

Joan of Arc a saint and national hero of France who fought to establish the rightful king of France in 15th Century

Malalai of Maiwand a national folk hero of Afghanistan who rallied Pashtun fighters during the Battle of Maiwand in the 19th century

Mohammad prophet and founder of Islam

Nobel Laureate someone who has been awarded a Nobel Prize

Pashtun one of the ethnic group of Pashtuns, primarily living in northwestern Pakistan and southern Afghanistan

Quran the holy book of Islam

succumb give in to something overwhelming

Taliban a militant Pashtun organisation in Afghanistan

Megan Rapinoe's Women's World Cup speech, 2019

NON-FICTION

> Megan Rapinoe is a former co-captain of the US women's national soccer team and an LGBTQ+ campaigner. The extract is from a speech she gave after a parade that celebrated the US national team winning the 2019 FIFA Women's World Cup. A few months before this speech, the team players had taken US Soccer to court, saying that they should receive the same pay as their male counterparts, while Rapinoe had also been critical of national politicians in the United States.

I think I'll just end with this. This is my charge to everyone. We have to be better. We have to love more, hate less. We got to listen more, and talk less. We got to know this is everybody's responsibility, every single person here. Every single person who is not here. Every single person who doesn't want to be here. Every single person who agrees and doesn't agree. It is our responsibility to make this world a better place. I think this team does an incredible job of taking that on our shoulders and understanding the position that we have and the platform we have within this world.

DIVERSE WORDS AND VOICES

Yes, we play sports. Yes, we play soccer. Yes, we're female athletes but we're so much more than that. You're so much more than that. You're more than a fan. You're more than someone who just supports sport. You're more than someone who tunes in every four years. You're someone who walks these streets every single day. You interact with your community every single day. How do you make your community better? How do you make the people around you better? Your family? Your closest friends? The 10 closest people to you? The 20 closest people to you? The most 100 closest people to you? It's every single person's responsibility.

There's been so much **contention** in these last years. I've been a victim of that. I've been a **perpetrator** of that.

[…]

But it's time to come together. This conversation is at the next step. We have to collaborate. It takes everybody. This is my charge to everybody: Do what you can. Do what you have to do. Step outside of yourself. Be more. Be better. Be bigger than you've ever been before. If this team is any representation of what you can be when you do that, please take this as an example. This group is incredible. We took so much on our shoulders to be here today, to celebrate with you today. And we did it with a smile. So do the same for us. Please, I ask you.

---

contention strong disagreement or arguing
perpetrator someone who performs or is responsible for an act

Extract from *A Kind of Spark* by Elle McNicoll

FICTION

> The following extract is taken from the novel *A Kind of Spark* by Elle McNicoll, published in 2020, which tells the story of 11-year-old Addie who campaigns for a memorial to honour the women who were tried as witches in her Scottish hometown centuries earlier. Addie is autistic, as is her sister Keedie, and this extract describes her experience of school, drawing on Elle McNicoll's own experiences of being neurodivergent.

'This handwriting is utterly disgraceful.'

I hear the words but they seem far away. As if they are being shouted through a wall. I continue to stare at the piece of paper in front of me. I can read it. I can make out every word, even through the blurriness of tears. I can feel everyone in the classroom watching me. My best friend. Her new friend. The new girl. Some of the boys are laughing.

I just keep staring at my writing. Then, suddenly, it's gone.

Miss Murphy has snatched it from my desk and is now ripping it up. The sound of the paper being torn is overly loud. Right in my ears. The characters in the story I was

DIVERSE WORDS AND VOICES

writing beg her to stop, but she doesn't. She crumples it all together and throws it towards the classroom bin. She misses. My story lies in a heap on the scratchy carpet.

'Do not EVER write so lazily again,' she shouts. Maybe she isn't even shouting, but it feels that way. 'Do you hear me, Adeline?' I prefer being called Addie. 'Not ever. A girl your age knows better than to write like that; your handwriting is like a baby's.'

I wish my sister was here. Keedie always explains the things that I cannot control or explain for myself. She makes sense of them. She understands.

'Tell me that you understand?'

Her shouts are so loud and the moments after are so quiet. I nod, shakily. Even though I don't understand. I just know it's what I'm supposed to do.

She says nothing more. She moves to the front of the class and I am dismissed. I can feel the new girl glancing at me, and my friend Jenna is whispering to her new friend, Emily.

We were supposed to have Mrs Bright this year; we met her briefly before the summer holidays. She would draw a little sun with a smiling face beside her name and would hold your hand if you looked nervous. But she got sick and Miss Murphy came to teach our class instead.

I thought this new school year would be better. That I would be better.

POWER AND INFLUENCE

I take out my pocket thesaurus. It was a Christmas present from Keedie. She knows how much I love using different words and we laughed because the word 'thesaurus' sounds like a dinosaur. I read different word combinations to calm down, to process the shouting and the ripping.

I find one that I like. **Diminished**.

*

On days like this, I spend lunchtime in the library. I feel the other children in the class watching me as we tuck in our chairs and leave the room, the school bell screeching so loudly. Loud noises make my head spin, they feel like a drill against a sensitive nerve. I walk through the corridors, practising my breathing and keeping my eyes straight ahead. People talk so loudly to their friends, who are right next to them. They get too close, they push and **clamour**, and it makes my neck hot and my heart too quick.

But, when I finally get to the library, it's all quiet. There is so much space. There is one window open to let in a little fresh air. There is no loud talking allowed. The books are all categorised and labelled in their proper places.

And Mr Allison is at his desk.

'Addie!'

He has curly dark hair and big glasses, and he is tall and skinny for a man. He wears old jumpers. If I were to

DIVERSE WORDS AND VOICES

use my thesaurus to describe Mr Allison, I would say he was kindly.

But I like to just say that he is nice. Because he is. My brain is very visual. I see everything in specific pictures, and when people use the word 'nice', I think of Mr Allison, the librarian.

'I have just the thing for you!'

I like that he never asks boring questions. He doesn't ask how my holidays were or how my sisters are doing. He just gets straight to talking about books.

'Here we go.' He walks over to one of the reading tables and puts a large hardback book down in front of me. I feel all the horrid feelings from earlier disappear.

'Sharks!'

I flip it open immediately and stroke the first glossy page. I told Mr Allison last year that I love sharks. That they are the most interesting thing to me, even more than the ancient Egyptians and the dinosaurs.

He remembered.

'It's a sort of encyclopedia,' he tells me, as I sit down with the book. 'An encyclopedia is a book that tells you a lot about one subject, or one area of study. This one is all about sharks.'

I nod, somewhat dazed from excitement.

'I suspect you know everything that's in there already though,' he says, and he laughs after he says it so I know that he's joking.

58

POWER AND INFLUENCE

'Sharks don't have bones,' I tell him, caressing the photograph of what I know is a blue shark. 'And they have six senses. Not five. They can sort of sense electricity in the atmosphere. The electricity of life! They can also smell blood from miles away.'

Their senses are sometimes overpowering. Too loud, too strong, too much of everything.

I turn the page to a large photograph of a solitary Greenland shark, swimming alone in the ice-cold water.

'People don't understand them.' I touch the shark's fin. 'They hate them, actually. A lot of people. They're afraid of them and don't understand them. So, they try to hurt them.'

Mr Allison doesn't say anything for a while, as I read the first page.

'You take that home with you for as long as you would like, Addie.'

I look up at him. He is smiling, but his eyes don't match his mouth.

'Thank you!' I make sure to put all the glad that I am feeling into my voice so that he knows I really mean it. He moves back to his desk and I become **engrossed** in the book. Reading is the most calming thing after an overly loud and unkind classroom. I can take my time. There is no one rushing me or barking at me. The words all follow rules. The pictures are bright and alive. But they do not overpower me.

DIVERSE WORDS AND VOICES

When I am trying to sleep at night, I like to imagine diving beneath the cold waves of the ocean and swimming with a shark. We explore abandoned shipwrecks, underwater caves and coral reefs. All of the colour, but in a wide-open space. No crowds, no pushing and no taking. I would not grab their **dorsal fin**. We would swim alongside one another.

And we would not have to speak a word. We could just be.

---

clamour loudly protest or demand
diminished became smaller or less
dorsal fin a single fin on the back of a shark
engrossed absorbed in something

Terror and wonder

What is the line between terror and wonder? On its own, terror can rattle us to the bone. On its own, wonder can be linked to admiration, awe and inspiration. The Romantic poets wrote about terror and wonder combined; they called it the Sublime. The essence of terror and wonder combined are when something amazes but terrifies at the same time, or when something is horrifying, but we still can't seem to look away. There is a whole industry built on the concept: horror films actively work on the idea that people want to be scared and will probably continue watching regardless.

In this chapter, Oscar Wilde's classic text *The Picture of Dorian Gray* explores terror and wonder combined, as a picture triggers both fear and intrigue in the protagonist. In J.P. Rose's extract, the reader is left wondering whether hauntings are real, as unnerving as that might be. The wonder of science is expressed by both Stephen Hawking and Dame Maggie Aderin-Pocock, who discuss the vastness of space, a place

DIVERSE WORDS AND VOICES

associated with curiosity and fear of the unknown, which combine to make people want to explore it. In the last extract, we are challenged to consider the wonder and terror of death itself, through Salena Godden's book, *Mrs Death Misses Death*.

Extract from *The Picture of Dorian Gray* by Oscar Wilde

FICTION

This extract is taken from the novel *The Picture of Dorian Gray* by Oscar Wilde, first published in 1891. In the novel, a vain man named Dorian Gray has his portrait painted and, fearing his beauty will fade over time, sells his soul to ensure that he will stay forever youthful and his portrait will age and fade instead. Here, Dorian reveals the aged portrait to his friend, Basil Hallward, the artist who painted it originally.

He passed out of the room and began the ascent, Basil Hallward following close behind. They walked softly, as men do **instinctively** at night. The lamp cast fantastic shadows on the wall and staircase. A rising wind made some of the windows rattle.

When they reached the top landing, Dorian set the lamp down on the floor, and taking out the key, turned it in the lock. 'You insist on knowing, Basil?' he asked in a low voice.

'Yes.'

'I am delighted,' he answered, smiling. Then he added, somewhat harshly, 'You are the one man in the world who is entitled to know everything about me. You

DIVERSE WORDS AND VOICES

have had more to do with my life than you think'; and, taking up the lamp, he opened the door and went in. A cold current of air passed them, and the light shot up for a moment in a flame of murky orange. He shuddered. 'Shut the door behind you,' he whispered, as he placed the lamp on the table.

Hallward glanced round him with a puzzled expression. The room looked as if it had not been lived in for years. A faded **Flemish tapestry**, a curtained picture, an old Italian *cassone*, and an almost empty book-case – that was all that it seemed to contain, besides a chair and a table. As Dorian Gray was lighting a half-burned candle that was standing on the mantelshelf, he saw that the whole place was covered with dust and that the carpet was in holes. A mouse ran scuffling behind the **wainscoting**. There was a damp odour of mildew.

'So you think that it is only God who sees the soul, Basil? Draw that curtain back, and you will see mine.'

The voice that spoke was cold and cruel.

'You are mad, Dorian, or playing a part,' muttered Hallward, frowning.

'You won't? Then I must do it myself,' said the young man, and he tore the curtain from its rod and flung it on the ground.

An exclamation of horror broke from the painter's lips as he saw in the dim light the hideous face on the canvas grinning at him. There was something in its expression

TERROR AND WONDER

that filled him with disgust and loathing. Good heavens! it was Dorian Gray's own face that he was looking at! The horror, whatever it was, had not yet entirely spoiled that marvellous beauty. There was still some gold in the thinning hair and some scarlet on the sensual mouth. The sodden eyes had kept something of the loveliness of their blue, the noble curves had not yet completely passed away from chiselled nostrils and from plastic throat. Yes, it was Dorian himself. But who had done it? He seemed to recognize his own brushwork, and the frame was his own design. The idea was monstrous, yet he felt afraid. He seized the lighted candle, and held it to the picture. In the left-hand corner was his own name, traced in long letters of bright **vermilion**.

It was some foul **parody**, some **infamous**, **ignoble satire**. He had never done that. Still, it was his own picture. He knew it, and he felt as if his blood had changed in a moment from fire to sluggish ice. His own picture! What did it mean? Why had it altered? He turned and looked at Dorian Gray with the eyes of a sick man. His mouth twitched, and his **parched** tongue seemed unable to **articulate**. He passed his hand across his forehead. It was dank with clammy sweat.

The young man was leaning against the mantelshelf, watching him with that strange expression that one sees on the faces of those who are absorbed in a play when some great artist is acting. There was neither real sorrow

DIVERSE WORDS AND VOICES

in it nor real joy. There was simply the passion of the spectator, with perhaps a flicker of triumph in his eyes. He had taken the flower out of his coat, and was smelling it, or pretending to do so.

'What does this mean?' cried Hallward, at last. His own voice sounded shrill and curious in his ears.

'Years ago, when I was a boy,' said Dorian Gray, crushing the flower in his hand, 'you met me, flattered me, and taught me to be vain of my good looks. One day you introduced me to a friend of yours, who explained to me the wonder of youth, and you finished a portrait of me that revealed to me the wonder of beauty. In a mad moment that, even now, I don't know whether I regret or not, I made a wish, perhaps you would call it a prayer...'

'I remember it! Oh, how well I remember it! No! the thing is impossible. The room is damp. Mildew has got into the canvas. The paints I used had some wretched mineral poison in them. I tell you the thing is impossible.'

'Ah, what is impossible?' murmured the young man, going over to the window and leaning his forehead against the cold, mist-stained glass.

'You told me you had destroyed it.'

'I was wrong. It has destroyed me.'

'I don't believe it is my picture.'

'Can't you see your ideal in it?' said Dorian bitterly.

'My ideal, as you call it...'

'As you called it.'

TERROR AND WONDER

'There was nothing evil in it, nothing shameful. You were to me such an ideal as I shall never meet again. This is the face of a **satyr**.'

'It is the face of my soul.'

articulate express things clearly and fluently
cassone an Italian wooden marriage chest
Flemish tapestry a large piece of heavy cloth with a picture sewn on it using coloured threads from the Flanders region of Belgium
ignoble not honourable
infamous having a bad reputation
instinctively doing something naturally or automatically
parched very dry
parody an exaggerated imitation
satire exaggeration used to show what is bad or weak about a person or thing
satyr in Greek mythology, a woodland god with a man's body and a goat's ears, tail and legs; satrys were supposed to be wild and drunken and were known for attacking
vermilion bright red
wainscoting wooden panelling on the wall of a room

Extract from *The Haunting of Tyrese Walker* by J. P. Rose

FICTION

> The novel *The Haunting of Tyrese Walker* by J. P. Rose, published in 2022, is a supernatural horror story that draws on Jamaican folklore. In the story, Tyrese and his mother have left their home in Manchester to visit family in Jamaica. Tyrese's father has recently died and, on his first night in Jamica, exploring the wild landscape around his grandmother's house, Tyrese discovers a mysterious grave hidden deep in the forest.

Not wanting to make a noise, Tyrese kept still. Fleetingly, he wondered if he should just make a run for it, but curiosity overrode his initial fear. He stepped towards the edge, looking down the steep forested mountainside, the creeping mist weaving upwards.

For a moment, Tyrese felt like something was staring back at him. The sense he wasn't alone tapped into his imagination, slipping it into endless possibilities.

A shape darted through the trees. Startled, he jerked back, holding his breath as if somehow that would protect him from whatever it was.

His eyes stayed locked on the mountainside, and although there was nothing moving now, Tyrese caught sight of something else. Hidden behind a broken tree which leaned against a jutting out boulder – like a blister erupting from the face of the mountain – Tyrese could see something dark and solid.

Puzzled, he quickly scanned the descent. Then, careful not to get his feet tangled in the twisting plants which snatched at his ankles, Tyrese began to climb down the side of the slope, using the blue mahoe trees for balance.

Getting to the boulder, he stopped. Concealed within the tall ferns and between the fallen tree and the rock, he saw that the dark and solid shape was in fact a long stone slab sunken in the undergrowth.

Tentatively he moved closer to get a better look…

A neglected grave.

Frowning, he glanced up the mountainside. Strange to have one here. Why would anyone want to have a grave on such a steep slope, hidden from everyone?

Everything about it looked homemade; the tombstone, misshapen, and even though he couldn't make out the **inscription** which had mainly been worn away, he could still see the remains of some letters which had been crudely and unskilfully chiselled into the stone.

Tyrese pushed his glasses up. The grave was choked by creeping vines, and lichen and moss spread across it but there was something else carved into the stone. Kneeling, he began to rub away the heavily ingrained dirt, then leaned back on his heels examining what he'd revealed.

DIVERSE WORDS AND VOICES

Although faded, there was no mistaking what he was looking at. Carved into the stone was a large, simple etching of a snake in a circle devouring its own tail. There was something unsettling about it, and once again a sudden uneasy chill scurried down his spine, spider-like. His gaze darted around once more and he swallowed. It sounded too loud in the quietness. And maybe it was his imagination, but had the air just become stiller? Heavier? Like the aftermath of a fire.

Slowly, Tyrese stood and began to edge away, but a sound of rustling coming from the bushes had him spinning round and scrambling as fast as he could back up the slope and through the blue mahoe trees to the track at the top.

Panting, he let out a relieved sigh, brushed himself quickly off, wanting to get back to Grammy's as soon as he could.

'Ty?'

'Mum!' He jumped at the sound of her voice right behind him. 'Mum, did you have to sneak up on me like that?'

His mum rested her hands on her hips, catching her breath. 'Sorry, I didn't mean to... Are you all right, Ty? What were you doing down there?' She peeked over the edge. 'Oh my goodness, you could have fallen, look how steep it is.' Concern rippled over her face and a thin film of sweat sat above her top lip.

'It's not that steep.'

'It is, and I'd rather you didn't go off like that.'

'I thought you wanted me to get some fresh air,' Tyrese muttered **sullenly**.

'I do, but you don't know the place yet. It's so easy to get lost. Look how dense the trees are, you could've ended up walking round and round in circles for hours.' She pushed back her fringe. 'Are you sure you're OK, Ty?'

'I'm fine.' He wasn't in the mood to talk but it didn't stop his mum wanting to have a conversation. It never did.

Her face became **animated** as she launched into an unwanted speech. 'You know, I'd forgotten how amazing this place is. Can you imagine having all this nature right on your doorstep all the time? It makes a lovely change from the **Salford Quays dockyards**, doesn't it?'

He didn't think it did. He just wanted to go back home to Manchester. So he just shrugged, shoving his hands in his pocket. Then he felt something. The photo. He'd forgotten he still had it.

As soon as his mum glanced the other way, Tyrese pulled out the crumpled-up photo and quickly dropped it behind him, where it rolled down the slope.

'Come on, let's go, it gets dark much earlier here,' his mum said, turning back to him and resting an arm round his shoulders. 'And, Ty, when we get back, try not to get so upset when Marvin or Grammy talk about –'

DIVERSE WORDS AND VOICES

'… OK, I get it,' Tyrese said quickly, knowing *exactly* what she was going to say.

They began to walk back down the track but Tyrese glanced over his shoulder towards the trees on the mountainside. Even though it was hot and humid, he shivered, his skin tingling. Why couldn't he shake off the feeling that something or… *someone* was watching him?

---

animated lively and excited
inscription words written or carved on an object
Salford Quays dockyards the open area with docks and equipment for building or repairing ships in the city of Salford in Greater Manchester
sullenly sulking and gloomy
tentatively approaching something cautiously

'I think the human race has no future if it doesn't go to space' by Stephen Hawking

NON-FICTION

> Professor Stephen Hawking was a world-renowned physicist whose scientific work transformed humanity's understanding of the universe. His book, *A Brief History of Time*, first published in 1988, sold more than 25 million copies. At the age of 21, Hawking was diagnosed with amyotrophic lateral sclerosis (ALS), a progressive condition that affects the nerve cells in the brain and spinal cord that control muscle movements and breathing, which meant that by his late 20s he used a wheelchair to get around. He later used a speech-generating device to communicate, controlled by a muscle in his cheek. In the following text, Hawking explains why he wished to travel into space and the opportunities that space travel gives the human race.

I have no fear of adventure. I have taken daredevil opportunities when they presented themselves. Years ago I barrelled down the steepest hills of San Francisco in my motorised wheelchair. I travel widely and have been to Antarctica and Easter Island and down in a submarine.

On April 26, 2007, three months after my sixty-fifth birthday, I did something special: I experienced zero

DIVERSE WORDS AND VOICES

gravity. It temporarily stripped me of my disability and gave me a feeling of true freedom. After forty years in a wheelchair, I was floating. I had four wonderful minutes of weightlessness, thanks to Peter Diamandis and the team at the Zero Gravity Corporation. I rode in a modified Boeing 727 jet, which travelled over the ocean off Florida and did a series of manoeuvres that took me into this state of welcome weightlessness.

It has always been my dream to travel into space, and Peter Diamandis told me, 'For now, I can take you into weightlessness.' The experience was amazing. I could have gone on and on.

Now I have a chance to travel to the start of space aboard Richard Branson's Virgin Galactic SpaceShipTwo vehicle, VSS Unity. SpaceShipTwo would not exist without the X prize or without Burt Rutan, who shared a vision that space should be open to all, not just astronauts and the lucky few. Richard Branson is close to opening spaceflight for ordinary citizens, and if I am lucky, I will be among the early passengers.

I immediately said yes to Richard when he offered me a seat on SpaceShipTwo. I have lived with ALS, amyotrophic lateral sclerosis, for fifty years. When I was diagnosed at age twenty-one, I was given two years to live. I was starting my PhD at Cambridge and embarking on the scientific challenge of determining whether the universe had always existed and would

74

always exist or had begun with a big explosion. As my body grew weaker, my mind grew stronger. I lost the use of my hands and could no longer write equations, but I developed ways of travelling through the universe in my mind and visualising how it all worked.

Keeping an active mind has been vital to my survival. Living two thirds of my life with the threat of death hanging over me has taught me to make the most of every minute. As a child, I spent a lot of time looking at the sky and stars and wondering where eternity came to an end. As an adult, I have asked questions, including Why are we here? Where did we come from? Did God create the universe? What is the meaning of life? Why does the universe exist? Some questions I have answered; others I am still asking.

Like Peter Diamandis, I believe that we need a new generation of explorers to **venture** out into our solar system and beyond. These first private astronauts will be **pioneers**, and I hope to be among them. We are entering a new space age, one in which we will help to change the world for good.

I believe in the possibility of commercial space travel – for exploration and for the **preservation** of humanity. I believe that life on Earth is at an ever-increasing risk of being wiped out by a disaster, such as a sudden nuclear war, a **genetically engineered** virus, or other dangers. I think the human race has no future if it doesn't go to

DIVERSE WORDS AND VOICES

space. We need to inspire the next generation to become engaged in space and in science in general, to ask questions: What will we find when we go to space? Is there alien life, or are we alone? What will a sunset on Mars look like?

My wheels are here on Earth, but I will keep dreaming. It is my belief [...] that there is no boundary of human **endeavour**. Raise your sights. Be courageous and kind. Remember to look up at the stars and not at your feet. Space, here I come!

---

endeavour an attempt to do something
genetically engineered containing genes that have been artificially altered
pioneers the first people to go to a place or do something
preservation keeping something safe
venture to go somewhere when this may be risky

Extract from *The Sky at Night: The Art of Stargazing* by Dame Maggie Aderin-Pocock

NON-FICTION

> Dame Maggie Aderin-Pocock is a British space scientist and chancellor of the University of Leicester. She credits her deep passion for science for allowing her to overcome the disadvantages of being a Black woman working in a field dominated by white men. The following extract is from the introduction to her book on stargazing.

Next time you notice it is a clear bright night, wherever you are – in a city or in the countryside – step outside if you can or just get to a window and look up for a few minutes. The view will help put you at peace, and you'll be following in a long tradition that probably spans back to a time before we could communicate with words, but when we could still share the wonder and majesty of the **cosmos.**

Looking up at the stars has been a constant quest in my life. Someone once commented that even when trying on a **VR** headset to enter a virtual world, the first thing I do is look up to see the stars.

I spent my teenage years growing up in a council flat in London, but that did not deter me from looking up

DIVERSE WORDS AND VOICES

whenever I got the opportunity. In one of the places we lived, I would run up to the upper floors of the building, where I could look out across the iconic London skyline, serene against a **canopy** of stars that was only slightly diminished by the city lights.

I remember one particularly clear night, feeling limited by the barrier of the window, I ventured outside for a better view. I stood between the blocks of flats to look up and take in the awe-inspiring vista. When I had had my fill and was starting to feel cold, I turned to go back inside ... only to realise that the door had shut behind me, locking me out. It was 3am, I was standing outside in my nightdress and now I was anticipating the wrath of my father when I tried to explain why I had woken him up at such an ungodly hour to let me back in, and why I was half-dressed and standing out in the cold. Luckily, I avoided that conversation as a door to another level of the flats had been left open, so I sneaked back into bed with Dad none the wiser and, once the **adrenaline** jolt had subsided, I drifted off to sleep with a **contented** smile on my face.

Since then, I have experienced the joy of working at and visiting some of the largest telescopes in the world. They are generally built on locations atop mountains that give the clearest possible views of the universe.

One of the great joys I currently experience is speaking to school children of all ages. When I first started doing

TERROR AND WONDER

this, I pondered on the hook that would get a 4-year-old excited about space. The answer came to me like a gift:

Twinkle, twinkle, little star,
How I wonder what you are…

We learn this rhyme as children without really thinking about it, but 'wonder' truly is the right word to describe the sky on a clear night, with its thousands of stars glimmering bright in the vast blackness of space. Through the ages, this awesome spectacle has inspired great art as well as scientific inquiry. It has shaped civilisations.

---

adrenaline a hormone produced when you are afraid or excited
canopy a hanging cover forming a shelter
contented happy with what you have
cosmos the universe
VR virtual reality

Extract from *Mrs Death Misses Death* by Salena Godden

> This extract is taken from the opening of the novel *Mrs Death Misses Death* by Salena Godden, published in 2021. In the novel, Mrs Death is a personification of death and presented as a Black woman, who takes on a number of different guises as she moves through the world. Befriending a writer, Mrs Death begins work on her memoir and, in this opening section of the novel, the author outlines what readers will find in the pages that follow.

Disclaimer:

This book contains dead people.

This book cannot see the future. This book is dabbling in the past. This book is not about funerals although funerals are mentioned. You do not have to wear black to read this work. You do not have to bring flowers.

Caution: This work contains traces of **eulogy**.

Warning: This work contains violent deaths.

Spoiler alert: We will all die in the end.

This book cannot change the ending or your ending or its own ending. This book does not know how to switch on the light at the end of the tunnel. This book cannot contact the other side. This book cannot speak to the dead or for the dead. This book will not confirm if there is an afterlife or an alternative universe. This book will not improve your karma. This book will not nag you to live a healthier life. This book will not help you quit smoking. This book is not going to urge you to age gracefully. This book does not **advocate** the use of that **funereal** phrase 'he had a good innings'. This book does not contain any person or persons clapping their hands and singing *kum-by-yah-mi-lord*. This book may be used for mild to moderate relief from grief, fear and pain, however if symptoms persist please buy a ticket to see a live reading of this work where you will *find the others*.

Caution: Do not exceed death.

This work has a very high dead and death count. Take with caution. Take your time. Do your lifetime in your own life time. If you are sensitive or allergic to talk of the dead or non-living things use this work in small doses. This is not a self-help brochure. This is not a guide to avoiding dying. If you think you are about to drop dead, please seek medical advice immediately.

This work has very little to do with God, the Gods, Goddesses, Satan or the Devil. This work is not focused on a battle of good and evil or right and wrong. This is not about morality or heaven and hell or sinners and saints. This book does not judge you or your choices. This book is not connected to or promoting any religion

DIVERSE WORDS AND VOICES

or cult. This is not a map to the way out of here. This is not a compass. This book does not contain directions to heaven or hell – see also **Elysium, Valhalla, Gan Eden, The Fields of Aaru, Vaikuntha, Tír na nÓg, Cockaigne, Big Rock Candy Mountain** or any other world versions of otherworld.

This work calls the **righteous** spirits of all of our mighty ancestors now and in the hour of our need. We take a breath and look back in amazement and wonder at how our ancestors survived so we may also survive. We take another deep breath, we feel our hearts beating inside our bodies, and we celebrate that the same empowerment and spirit runs in our blood now and can be found in our DNA today. We give thanks to our ancestors, thanks for giving us life, for being alive to feel alive and to share this one magnificent connection to life and all living things.

This book does not mention every person that has ever died – if you wished this book to have mentioned another death, we can only apologise now in advance, for not knowing which death or dead celebrity you wanted mentioned and celebrated in this book at time of writing and printing. At the time of writing this book mourns for **Prince, David Bowie, Leonard Cohen, Toni Morrison and Aretha Franklin**. And this book sincerely hopes there aren't any more inspirational human beings, bold souls, brave hearts and superheroes to add to that dead list before we go to print. Amen.

This book contains traces of ghosts. This book may contain bones and other human remains. This book has been haunting me. This book may haunt you. This book is about you and me and all of us. We will use the term 'human' or 'human being' to mean people who identify as human, that is being 'alive' and 'living', and furthermore discuss how they are now 'dead' and use the word 'dead' to mean that the heart stopped beating and the brain ceased functioning and they are not breathing any more. This work does not contain zombies but has no prejudices against those that choose to be living dead.

This book knows loss and feels your pain. This book shares your fears and anxieties. This book will explore the worst-case scenarios. This book is afraid of death, but not afraid to speak about it. This book is in mourning and trying to understand this process of grieving. This book sends you all its love. This book says it's alright to cry on its shoulder.

This book is short because life is short. The time it took for us to evolve from *Homo sapiens* to modern civilisation, from the first cave paintings and words and stories and songs to the first book and the first bookshop, is a wonder and also relatively short. Any book with the word Death in the title must be light enough to carry in your hand luggage. It must be short enough to be read cover to cover on a train up from London to Liverpool. It must be loud enough to read during the length of a

83

DIVERSE WORDS AND VOICES

good **belter** of a thunderstorm, then when the storm passes and the clouds clear and the skies open up, the train doors open, and so will your heart.

advocate to speak in favour of something
belter thrilling
Elysium, Valhalla, Gan Eden, The Fields of Aaru, Vaikuntha, Tír na nÓg, Cockaigne, Big Rock Candy Mountain places people are believed to go after death in the stories or beliefs of various cultures
eulogy a speech or piece of writing in praise of a person or thing
funereal suitable for a funeral; gloomy or depressing
Homo sapiens human beings regarded as a species
kum-by-yah-mi-lord lyrics from the song 'Kumbaya My Lord'
Prince, David Bowie, Leonard Cohen, Toni Morrison and Aretha Franklin famous artists from the worlds of music and writing who are no longer alive
righteous virtuous

Wild places and urban landscapes

Whether in the middle of a busy city or standing in an open field surrounded by nature, there is always something to notice. Stopping to appreciate our surroundings is fundamental to living: it helps us connect to the world around us and improves our wellbeing. Some of the greatest thinkers in science and nature have spent years observing their surroundings and produced amazing texts as a result. We don't need to be in the countryside to develop our understanding of the environment either. All spaces have beauty if we are willing to look for it, from the great outdoors to the local shopping precinct to the urban spaces of a big city – if we stop and notice, we might find the extraordinary right in front of our eyes. Have you ever looked above the shop names in a town or city? You will often find reminders of its history: older parts of buildings and clocks of all shapes and sizes, stopped or working, reminding us of a distant past.

In this chapter, each text includes an insight into a wild place or an urban landscape, and what it means to the narrator or character. In the first extract, Darren

DIVERSE WORDS AND VOICES

McGarvey shows the contrast of the urban spaces of his youth. Anita Rani goes on an adventure after passing her driving test. Dara McAnulty keeps us by the sea, describing the natural landscape in Northern Ireland, with the birds as a constant connection to nature. In Sam Selvon's extract, the reader sees the urban landscape of London through his eyes.

Extract from *Poverty Safari* by Darren McGarvey

NON-FICTION

> Darren McGarvey is a writer, performer, columnist and former rapper-in-residence at Police Scotland's Violence Reduction Unit. He grew up in Pollok, a large housing estate on the south-western side of the city of Glasgow. His mother was an alcoholic who left the family home when Darren was ten years old. In this extract from his non fiction book and memoir *Poverty Safari*, published in 2017, McGarvey describes how he first experienced a different side of Glasgow when attending anger management classes in Hillhead, an affluent suburb of the city.

Near the end of my school career, I was venturing beyond the borders of Pollok and across the **Clyde** to the fabled, almost mythical, West End, where I attended weekly sessions with a child psychologist. The appointment was something to look forward to and, apart from breaking up the **monotony** of a regular school day, it also gave me a couple of hours off the leash to explore the city unsupervised. At lunchtime on Thursday I would leave school and take a short bus trip to **Govan** before jumping the **Underground** to Hillhead.

DIVERSE WORDS AND VOICES

The first thing I remember upon stepping off the escalator and onto the busy street was an odd feeling of relaxation. People here looked and sounded different in a way that was immediately **apparent**. Where I grew up it was unusual to see people of colour, unless they were behind a shop counter, but here it was very multi-cultural, like the world described in my modern studies class. Where I grew up it was unusual to see clean pavements, but here the streets were in **pristine** condition and nothing like the turd **gauntlet** I was accustomed to running every day. Here dogs were attached to leads and walked by their owners, as opposed to the collarless, **feral** hounds running around outside the shopfront along the road from my house.

Having taken a few moments to catch my breath, adjusting my eyes to the world in wonderful technicolour, I remember my first thought being, 'So, this is how people dress when they aren't afraid of being stabbed?'

The Notre Dame Centre, where I attended my counselling, was five minutes from the **affluent** strip of town, known as Byres Road. You know when you and your friends attempt to **impersonate** a **stereotypically** 'posh' person? Well, the people on Byers Road are what that impersonation is based on. On Byres Road it is not unusual to find a small, fashionable dog waiting in the retro wicker basket of an up-cycled **penny-farthing** while its owner proceeds into a café to politely complain

WILD PLACES AND URBAN LANDSCAPES

to a **barista** named Felix about being undercharged for **artisan** sausage. Byres Road is where I learned that there was more than one type of coffee and that you could drink it in a glass. It's where I discovered fruit was a pleasure in its own right and not merely a cheap alternative to Haribo. But more importantly, this part of the city was where I was first confronted by the strange idea that living in fear of violence was not, as I had been led to believe, an **immaculate** fact. Bizarre as this place seemed to me, I was also **captivated** by it because I would never have thought such an easygoing place could exist – especially in Glasgow. Ironic that I only found myself in this **serene** part of town because I had to attend anger management.

Using the only thing culturally familiar to me as a means of navigation (the famous Greggs bakery chain), I waded deeper into this unknown territory. Though not before purchasing an **obligatory** sausage roll, bottle of Coke and a fudge doughnut. Then, up the leafy road I went, feeling very pleased with myself as I charged past local kids nibbling on rabbit food.

Despite this being a densely populated **residential** area, mature trees **flanked** slanted **tenement** flats, leering clumsily over the pavements like lanky security guards. This wasn't the first time I had seen tenement housing of this type, but never had I witnessed it in such a grand scale. It was the attention to detail that distinguished the

89

DIVERSE WORDS AND VOICES

buildings here. It seemed like things gained more value the older they got, as opposed to falling into **dereliction**. Here things were built to last and the architecture seemed to project that quality outwards. The planners had not foreseen a time when every family here would own at least two cars, but this cramped feeling, rather than a source of stress, merely **accentuated** the exclusivity and **prestige** of the area and, by extension, the social status of all therein.

The oddest thing, however, was that you never saw anybody coming or going from those tenements and you never saw neighbours talking to each other. It was almost as if people never grew up here, but instead bought their way in and that their houses were all lying empty because everyone was out at work.

Mind-boggling.

As I continued upwards to the Notre Dame Centre, children from a local school were walking down towards me, on the other side of the road. I immediately sensed they were non-threatening and as they drew closer I overheard them talking. I couldn't quite follow the thread but I could hear enough to know they were using the kind of words that I always had in my head but felt too **inhibited** to speak. They were expressive and uninhibited with each other. A part of me wanted so much to walk over and join the conversation, as it seemed like we would probably have had a lot of things in common, but as I passed them they suddenly went quiet. Instantly

WILD PLACES AND URBAN LANDSCAPES

I knew why: that's what you did when you were walking past something that made you anxious.

Falling silent, and perhaps a head bow, was a way of showing **deference** to a potential threat; a signal you weren't looking for trouble and wished to pass without incident. So often I had executed this exact **manoeuvre** on my own turf to avoid **confrontation**. The signal was always a gamble because, once a potential attacker knew for certain that you didn't want to fight, they often took it as a green light to get more aggressive. In this **inversion** of my usual experience, these kids seemed to perceive me as the threat. It was a **jarring** role reversal and I experienced a mixture of pride at being feared and **resentment** at feeling misunderstood as I continued up the hill, short of breath, to my destination.

accentuated emphasised something or made it more obvious
affluent wealthy, rich
apparent clear, obvious
artisan goods produced on a small scale using traditional methods
barista a person who makes and serves coffee in a coffee shop
captivated charmed or delighted by
Clyde river that runs through the city of Glasgow
confrontation a challenge to fight or argue face to face
deference out of respect for
dereliction abandoned and left to fall into ruin
feral wild and untamed
flanked positioned at the side of something
gauntlet a testing ordeal; trial
Govan a district of Glasgow
immaculate without any faults or mistakes
impersonate to pretend to be another person dishonestly or for entertainment

DIVERSE WORDS AND VOICES

inhibited feeling embarrassed and worried about doing something or expressing your emotions
inversion turned upside down
jarring striking or shocking
manoeuvre careful or skilful move
monotony when something is dull and tedious because it does not change
obligatory compulsory, not optional
penny-farthing an early type of bicycle
prestige great reputation gained from achievements
pristine in its original condition; unspoilt
resentment feeling insulted by something said or done
residential an area that contains or is suitable for private houses
serene calm and peaceful
stereotypically a fixed image or idea of a type of person or thing that is widely held
tenement a large house or building divided into separate flats or rooms
Underground train system that runs under Glasgow

Extract from *The Right Sort of Girl* by Anita Rani

> Anita Rani is a British television and radio presenter, who was born and grew up in Bradford, West Yorkshire. Her parents were Punjabi immigrants who built up and ran a clothing business in the city, including a three-storey factory. But with a mass shift to offshore manufacturing in the 1990s, their business vanished and they had to close the factory. In this extract from her autobiography, *The Right Sort of Girl*, published in 2021, Rani describes the liberating journey she took from the heart of the city into the countryside on the day she passed her driving test.

The day I passed my driving test, aged 17, may well have been the most **liberating** day of my life and I knew exactly where I was heading. Now I didn't need to ask for a lift, I didn't need to wait for the bus, I didn't need to ask anyone to pick me up. No friends, no family, just me, my beat-up Vauxhall Astra and a selection of **cassettes**. The day I'd been dreaming of had finally arrived. With no one else in the car with me, I pushed it more than was safe. Which really wasn't that fast as the car started rattling over 40 miles an hour. I was a bit of a teenage speed demon. Driving for me was independence. Driving is freedom still.

DIVERSE WORDS AND VOICES

The journey to freedom takes me from home through Bradford city centre, past the **imposing edifice** of Bradford Town Hall, the **iconic** Alhambra Theatre, past my mum and dad's old shop and factory. Traffic lights are red on the steep hill, so I attempt **clutch control** and hope and pray that no cars pull up behind as I might roll backwards. I just about find the **biting point**, I push the accelerator too hard, but I'm off again with a jerky vrooom. There's the eighties concrete block of the Arndale Centre and up beyond the seventies single-storey John Street market. I know these streets, I've pounded them my entire life. I don't need a map, I've memorised the route. It is in me through **osmosis**. Today, I'm seeing them all from a new perspective, in my **peripheral** vision. Today, my eyes and mind are focused on driving, buzzing with excitement, adrenalin coursing through my veins, riding the edge between the pure terror of being in complete control and on my own for the first time in my life and the pure exhilaration and excitement of being in complete control and on my own for the first time in my life. I've waited for this moment. Dreamt of doing this. Onwards to my destination!

I've been a passenger for this journey since I was in the womb, so instinct kicks in with each gear change. Once out of the city centre, I go past the Victorian terraced houses of inner-city Bradford, curry houses, newsagents that sell fruit and veg, Asian women's clothing shops,

WILD PLACES AND URBAN LANDSCAPES

and I drive further past the larger magnificent Victorian homes around Manningham Park, made of sturdy yellow Yorkshire stone, once homes for wealthy **merchants**, now large enough to house extended Asian families. Keep going, not there yet! Things are beginning to open up though as we round the corner and descend another hill. Got to keep an eye on my speed, driving through new build housing estates for the **upwardly mobile middle classes**, full of Asians who'd done well and their flash cars parked on concrete driveways, then slip into a lower gear to get up the steep hill to the more affluent villages in Baildon, Eldwick, big solid homes behind Yorkshire walls, with driveways and large gardens with stunning views. These areas are **predominantly** white in the nineties. Then, all of a sudden, the road opens up to reveal what I've been driving towards: the West Yorkshire countryside.

You only need to do this drive for 20 minutes in any direction, from pretty much anywhere in Bradford city centre, and your eyes open a little wider and your lungs breathe a little deeper as you leave the **urban** sprawl behind and the magnificent splendour greets you with a nod of the flat-capped head and an 'Ey up?'

If you head up to Shipley Glen or Baildon Moor for a run around, as we often did as kids, you can see Bradford sitting in its bowl beneath you. Rows and rows of terraced houses, peppered with '**those dark**

95

DIVERSE WORDS AND VOICES

satanic mills'. The mills that built this city, that fuelled the city, that choked the city, that created communities, that are the reason I am a Yorkshire **lass**. The mills that kept us locked to the concrete and stone and are also the reason for our need to escape. That used to cough up a right mess but now just sit there quietly and proud, polished up and turned into art galleries and flats.

It's on these same Moors that Bradfordians have been escaping to get away from the oppression of the city since the **Industrial Revolution**. But I'm not stopping just yet though. Not this time. My destination is a little further still. The road opens up before me with **Dales** and sheep and the odd farmhouse on either side. My music gets turned up too.

[...]

There's the converted barn to my right, but today, I haven't got time to imagine me and my family living in it. I'm now officially on the move, squeezing through Burley in Wharfedale and slowing down to give the Hermit pub a little wave, then, just up a little further, on top of the **moorland** over a couple of cattle grids, I see her grey craggy face, giving me a knowing smile in the distance. Awaiting my arrival. As she does everyone. Well aware we all need to break free from our concrete prisons and come seek her embrace. Ilkley Moor. The Cow and Calf rocks.

WILD PLACES AND URBAN LANDSCAPES

The car judders to a stop. I slam the door shut with a tinny clunk. Do I go left for a slow walk up the path or do I go right to scramble up and over the rocks as I always did as a kid? No-brainer. I bust a right and walk towards the pile of fallen rocks that make for a perfect scramble up to the top of the **crag**.

'I knew this day would come. I've been waiting for you,' she says. (It's my story and in my story, the moors talk.)

At the top, out of breath, I turn to take in the view, out to the horizon, over the posh little town of Ilkley, and just stare and breathe deep. Let it all go.

---

biting point / clutch control terms used to describe the process of starting to drive a manual car
cassettes plastic cases that were used to play music
crag a steep piece of rough rock
Dales the Yorkshire Dales, a series of valleys
iconic famous and highly admired
imposing edifice grand and impressive large building
Industrial Revolution the expansion of British industry by the use of machines in the late 18th and early 19th centuries
lass a girl or young woman (informal)
liberating freeing
merchants people involved in trade
moorland an area of rough land covered with bushes
osmosis gained gradually and without any obvious effort
peripheral happening at the edge of your vision
predominantly more noticeable or important, or larger in number, than others
those dark satanic mills a phrase from the poem 'Jerusalem' by William Blake that people often use refer to the Industrial Revolution and its destruction of nature and people's livelihoods
upwardly mobile middle classes people moving to a higher social class
urban relating to a town or city, as opposed to rural

Extract from *The Waves* by Virginia Woolf

FICTION

> This extract is taken from a novel titled *The Waves* by the acclaimed English writer Virginia Woolf, one of the most important authors of the 20th century. Published in 1931, the novel follows six friends' lives from childhood to old age by making parallels to the changing position of the sun and the tides. The extract below follows a conversation between the six friends – Bernard, Susan, Rhoda, Neville, Jinny and Louis – when they are children. They each describe what they saw and heard as the sun rose.

The sun had not yet risen. The sea was **indistinguishable** from the sky, except that the sea was slightly creased as if a cloth had wrinkles in it. Gradually as the sky whitened a dark line lay on the horizon dividing the sea from the sky and the grey cloth became **barred** with thick strokes moving, one after another, beneath the surface, following each other, pursuing each other, **perpetually.**

As they neared the shore each bar rose, heaped itself, broke and swept a thin veil of white water across the sand. The wave paused, and then drew out again, sighing like a sleeper whose breath comes and goes unconsciously.

WILD PLACES AND URBAN LANDSCAPES

Gradually the dark bar on the horizon became clear as if the **sediment** in an old wine-bottle had sunk and left the glass green. Behind it, too, the sky cleared as if the white sediment there had sunk, or as if the arm of a woman couched beneath the horizon had raised a lamp and flat bars of white, green and yellow spread across the sky like the blades of a fan. Then she raised her lamp higher and the air seemed to become **fibrous** and to tear away from the green surface flickering and flaming in red and yellow fibres like the smoky fire that roars from a bonfire. Gradually the fibres of the burning bonfire were fused into one haze, one **incandescence** which lifted the weight of the woollen grey sky on top of it and turned it to a million atoms of soft blue. The surface of the sea slowly became transparent and lay rippling and sparkling until the dark stripes were almost rubbed out. Slowly the arm that held the lamp raised it higher and then higher until a broad flame became visible; an arc of fire burnt on the rim of the horizon, and all round it the sea **blazed** gold.

The light struck upon the trees in the garden, making one leaf transparent and then another. One bird chirped high up; there was a pause; another chirped lower down. The sun sharpened the walls of the house, and rested like the tip of a fan upon a white blind and made a blue finger-print of shadow under the leaf by the bedroom window. The blind stirred slightly, but all within was dim and **unsubstantial**. The birds sang their blank melody outside.

DIVERSE WORDS AND VOICES

'I see a ring,' said Bernard, 'hanging above me. It **quivers** and hangs in a loop of light.'

'I see a slab of pale yellow,' said Susan, 'spreading away until it meets a purple stripe.'

'I hear a sound,' said Rhoda, 'cheep, chirp; cheep chirp; going up and down.'

'I see a globe,' said Neville, 'hanging down in a drop against the enormous flanks of some hill.'

'I see a **crimson tassel**,' said Jinny, 'twisted with gold threads.'

'I hear something stamping,' said Louis. 'A great beast's foot is chained. It stamps, and stamps, and stamps.'

'Look at the spider's web on the corner of the balcony,' said Bernard. 'It has beads of water on it, drops of white light.'

'The leaves are gathered round the window like pointed ears,' said Susan.

'A shadow falls on the path,' said Louis, 'like an elbow bent.'

'Islands of light are swimming on the grass,' said Rhoda. 'They have fallen through the trees.'

'The birds' eyes are bright in the tunnels between the leaves,' said Neville.

'The stalks are covered with harsh, short hairs,' said Jinny, 'and drops of water have stuck to them.'

'A caterpillar is curled in a green ring,' said Susan, '**notched** with blunt feet.'

WILD PLACES AND URBAN LANDSCAPES

'The grey-shelled snail draws across the path and flattens the blades behind him,' said Rhoda.

'And burning lights from the window-panes flash in and out on the grasses,' said Louis.

'Stones are cold to my feet,' said Neville. 'I feel each one, round or pointed, separately.'

'The back of my hand burns,' said Jinny, 'but the palm is clammy and damp with dew.'

'Now the cock crows like a spurt of hard, red water in the white tide,' said Bernard.

'Birds are singing up and down and in and out all round us,' said Susan.

'The beast stamps; the elephant with its foot chained; the great brute on the beach stamps,' said Louis.

'Look at the house,' said Jinny, 'with all its windows white with blinds.'

'Cold water begins to run from the **scullery** tap,' said Rhoda, 'over the mackerel in the bowl.'

'The walls are cracked with gold cracks,' said Bernard, 'and there are blue, finger-shaped shadows of leaves beneath the windows.'

'Now Mrs. Constable pulls up her thick black stockings,' said Susan.

'When the smoke rises, sleep curls off the roof like a mist,' said Louis.

DIVERSE WORDS AND VOICES

'The birds sang in chorus first,' said Rhoda. 'Now the scullery door is **unbarred**. Off they fly. Off they fly like a fling of seed. But one sings by the bedroom window alone.'

barred having bars or stripes
blazed brightly lit
crimson tassel a bundle of threads tied together at the top and used to decorate something, deep red in colour
fibrous containing a lot of fibres or fibre, or looking as if it does
incandescence shining light
indistinguishable not able to be told apart; not distinguishable
notched a small V-shape cut into a surface
perpetually repeatedly
quivers shakes slightly
scullery a small kitchen or room for washing dishes and doing other household work
sediment fine particles of solid matter that float in liquid or sink to the bottom of it
unbarred not provided or fastened with a bar or bars
unsubstantial lacking weight, strength or firmness

Extract from *Diary of a Young Naturalist* by Dara McAnulty

NON-FICTION

> In 2020, Dara McAnulty became the youngest-ever winner of the Wainwright Prize for nature writing for his debut book, *Diary of a Young Naturalist*. This memoir details McAnulty's deep connection with the natural world and his campaigning work as an environmentalist from his perspective as an autistic teenager. The following extract describes a birthday trip that McAnulty took with his family to Rathlin Island, a small island off the coast of County Antrim in Northern Ireland.

In late-afternoon light, with wind rising from the sea, we sail on the ferry the few miles from **Ballycastle** on the north-east coast to Rathlin Island. **Guillemots** and **gulls** scrabble the air with screeching and cackling. My excitement is intense.

Today is my birthday, and this morning I lay awake in bed for hours before the actual birth time (11.20am) listening to a screeching fox in the distance. All week I've been like this, intensely excited, nervous, for reasons I may never truly understand. Perhaps it's because I love new places and hate new places all at once. The smells, the sounds. Things that nobody else notices. The people,

DIVERSE WORDS AND VOICES

too. And the right and wrong of things. Small things, like how we'd line up for the ferry, or what was expected of me on Rathlin when we arrived. Though I always do the usual mop-up operation in my mind after any journey, look back and usually think how **ludicrous** it all was, still the anxiety floods in. Mum assures me that our time on Rathlin will be spent either outside or alone with the family. 'It'll all be okay,' she says.

Eider ducks congregate at the harbour on our arrival, and as we head out to the cottage that we'll be staying in for a few days, my usual dislike of new surroundings softens. This place has something special. It feels so calm here. The air is fresh, the landscape extra-worldly in its **abundance**. **Lapwing** circle to our right, a **buzzard** to our left. The windows are rolled down and the sound circulates through our limbs, stiff from the three-hour drive and ferry ride. We relax and radiate as hares abound and geese honk above. The car climbs above sea level towards the west of the island.

When we reach our **roosting place**, it looks perfect in the distance: traditional stone with no other **dwellings** around for miles, and on arrival I jump out to walk and explore. I soon discover a lake with **tufted duck** and **greylag geese**. As I walk, hares seem to keep popping up everywhere and my eyes struggle to keep up with all the movement, my brain whirring with all the senses.

I can hear the cries of seabirds in the distance. **Gannets** fly on the horizon, the squeak of **kittiwakes** becomes louder. I stand and look out to sea and watch the waves gently swirling, and in the dusk sky a **skein** of white-fronted geese fly in dagger formation. Although we've just arrived and have a few days here, I start wondering how empty I'll feel when it's time to leave. I feel panic.

My childhood, although wonderful, is still confined. I'm not free. Daily life is all busy roads and lots of people. Schedules, expectations, stress. Yes, there is **unfettered** joy, too, but right now, standing in an extraordinary and beautiful place, so full of life, there is this terrible angst rising in my chest. I walk back to the cottage in a trance, watching shadows moving in golden fields.

After dinner, song bursts from every corner of the sky and we stop to listen in the twilight. Isolating each and every melody, I feel suddenly rooted. **Skylark** spirals. **Blackbird** harmonies. Bubbling **meadow pipits**. The **winnowing** wings of **snipe**. And always the sound of seabirds. We are in the other world. No cars. No people. Just wildlife and the magnificence of nature.

It's the best birthday.

A full moon beams from behind clouds as we watch Venus above the distant houses, and I stand there with numb hands and a numb nose but a bursting heart. This is the kind of place I can be happy in. I wrap my coat tightly around my chest, inhaling it all in, not wanting

DIVERSE WORDS AND VOICES

to go to bed, storing the moment up with all the other memories I keep **cached**. When I'm **ambushed** by the anxiety army, when it comes stomping back, I'll be ready to fight, armed with the wild cries of Rathlin Island.

---

abundance a large amount of something, often more than you need
ambushed attacked by surprise
Ballycastle a town in Northern Ireland
cached hidden in a store of valuable things
congregate to assemble or come together
dwellings houses or other buildings to live in
guillemots, gulls, eider ducks, lapwing, buzzard, tufted duck, greylag geese, gannets, kittiwakes, skylark, blackbird, meadow pipits, snipe types of birds
ludicrous ridiculous or laughable
roosting place a place where birds rest and sleep
skein a coil of yarn or thread
unfettered not controlled or limited by anyone or anything
winnowing beating (wings)

Extract from 'My Girl and the City' by Sam Selvon

FICTION

> Sam Selvon was a Trinidad-born author who moved to London in 1950, and his novels and short stories often explored the experiences of Caribbean immigrants in the city. The following extract is taken from his short story 'My Girl and the City', published in 1957. In this story, he describes a man's relationship with his girlfriend and his feelings towards the city of London.

Sometimes you are in the **underground** and you have no idea what the weather is like, and the train shoots out of a tunnel and sunlight floods you, falls across your newspaper, makes the passengers squint and look up.

There is a face you have for sitting at home and talking, there is a face you have for working in the office, there is a face, a **bearing**, a **demeanour** for each time and place. There is above all a face for travelling, and when you have seen one you have seen all. In a rush hour, when we are breathing down each other's neck, we look at each other and glance quickly away. There is not a great deal to look at in the narrow **confines** of a carriage except people, and the faces of people, but no one deserves a glass of Hall's

DIVERSE WORDS AND VOICES

wine more than you do. We **jostle** in the subway from train to lift, we wait, shifting our feet.

When we are all herded inside we hear the footsteps of a straggler for whom the operator waits, and we try to figure out what sort of a footstep it is, if he feels the lift will wait for him; we are glad if he is left waiting while we shoot upwards. Out of the lift, down the street, up the road: in ten seconds flat it is over, and we have to begin again.

One morning I am coming into the city by the night bus 287 from **Streatham**. It is after one o'clock; I have been stranded again after seeing my girl home. When we get to **Westminster Bridge** the sky is marvellously clear with a few stray patches of beautiful cloud among which stars sparkle. The moon stands over **Waterloo Bridge**, above the Houses of Parliament sharply outlined, and it throws gold on the waters of the **Thames**. The **Embankment** is quiet, only a few people loiter around the public convenience near to the **Charing Cross** underground which is open all night. A man sleeps on a bench. His head is resting under headlines: Suez Deadlock.

Going back to that same spot about five o'clock in the evening, there was absolutely nothing to recall the atmosphere of the early morning hours. Life had taken over completely, and there was nothing but people. People waiting for buses, people hustling for trains.

I go to Waterloo Bridge and they come pouring out of the offices and they bob up and down as they walk across the bridge. From the station green trains come and go relentlessly. Motion **mesmerises** me into **immobility**. There are lines of motion across the river, on the river.

Sometimes we sat on a bench near the river, and if the tide was out you could see the muddy bed of the river and the swans **grubbing**. Such spots, when found, are pleasant to **loiter** in. Sitting in one of those places – choose one, and choose a time – […] I have known a great frustration and weariness. All these things, said, have been said before, the river seen, […] the lunch hour eating apples in the **sphinx's lap** under **Cleopatra's Needle** observed and duly registered: even to talk of the frustration is a repetition. What am I to do, am I to take each circumstance, each thing seen, noted, and **mill** them in my mind and spit out something entirely different from the reality?

My girl is very real. She hated the city, I don't know why. It's like that sometimes, a person doesn't have to have a reason. A lot of people don't like London that way, you ask them why and they shrug, and a shrug is sometimes a powerful reply to a question.

She shrugged when I asked her why, and when she asked me why I loved London I too shrugged. But after a minute I thought I would try to explain, because too often a shrug is an easy way out of a lot of things.

Falteringly, I told her how one night it was late and I found a fish and chips shop open in the **East End** and I bought and ate in the dark street walking; and of the cup of tea in an all-night café in **Kensington** one grim winter morning; and of the first time I ever queued in this country in 1950 to see the Swan Lake ballet, and the friend who was with me gave a **busker two and six** because he was playing 'Sentimental Journey' on a mouth-organ.

But why do you love London, she said.

You can't talk about a thing like that, not really. Maybe I could have told her because one evening in the summer I was waiting for her, only it wasn't like summer at all. Rain had been falling all day, and a haze hung about the bridges across the river, and the water was muddy and brown, and there was a kind of **wistfulness** and sadness about the evening. The way **St Paul's** was, half-hidden in the rain, the motionless trees along the Embankment. But you say a thing like that and people don't understand at all. How sometimes a surge of greatness could sweep over you when you see something.

But even if I had said all that and much more, it would not have been what I meant. You could be lonely as hell in the city, then one day you look around you and you realise everybody else is lonely too, withdrawn, locked,

WILD PLACES AND URBAN LANDSCAPES

rushing home out of the chaos: blank faces, unseeing eyes, millions and millions of them, up **the Strand**, down the Strand, jostling in Charing Cross for **the 5.20** […].

bearing the way that you stand, walk or behave
busker a person who plays music in the street for money
confines the limits or boundaries of an area
demeanour the way a person behaves
falteringly hesitantly
grubbing searching
immobility inability to move
jostle to push someone roughly or carelessly, especially in a crowd
loiter to linger or stand about idly
mesmerises fascinates or holds a person's attention completely
mill turn over
sphinx's lap, Cleopatra's Needle a landmark in London
St Paul's a large cathedral in London
Streatham, Embankment, Charing Cross, East End, Kensington, the Strand places in London
Thames the main river in London
the 5.20 a train
two and six two shillings and sixpence (currency used in the UK before 1971)
underground the train system that runs under London
Westminster Bridge, Waterloo Bridge bridges over the Thames
wistfulness a sad longing for something

Extract from *Manhattan '45* by Jan Morris

> Jan Morris was a Welsh author, travel writer and historian, and the following extract is taken from her book *Manhattan '45*, published in 1987. This work of non-fiction describes the city of New York in 1945, a time considered to be the city's Golden Age, even though the author didn't visit the city herself until 1953. Instead, she wrote the piece based on facts from archives. In this extract, Morris describes her impressions of the place and the contrasts the city contains.

Suddenly in the distance there stand the skyscrapers, shimmering in the sun, like **monuments** in a more antique land. A little drunk from the sight, you drive breathlessly into the great tunnel beneath the **Hudson River**. You must not drive faster than thirty-five miles an hour in the tunnel, nor slower than thirty, so that you progress like something in an assembly line, soullessly; but when you emerge into the daylight, then a miracle occurs, a sort of daily **renaissance**, a flowering of the spirit. The cars and trucks and buses, no longer confined in channels, suddenly spring away in all directions with a burst of engines and black clouds of exhaust. At once,

WILD PLACES AND URBAN LANDSCAPES

instead of discipline, there is a **profusion** of **enterprise**. There are policemen shouting and **gesticulating** irritably, men pushing racks of summer **frocks**, trains rumbling along railway lines, great **liners** blowing their sirens, **dowdy** dark-haired women with shopping bags and men hurling **imprecations** out of taxi windows, shops with improbable Polish names and huge racks of strange newspapers; bold colours and noises and indefinable smells, skinny cats and very old dustcarts and bus drivers with patient weary faces. Almost before you know it, the **mystique** of Manhattan is all around you.

Everyone has read of the magical glitter of this place, but until you have been here it is difficult to conceive of a city so sparkling that at any time Mr **Fred Astaire** might quite reasonably come dancing his **urbane** way down **Fifth Avenue**. It is a marvellously **exuberant** city, even when the bitter winds of the **fall** howl through its **canyons**. The taxi-drivers talk long and fluently, about **pogroms** in old Russia, about Ireland in its bad days, about the Naples their fathers came from. The waiters urge you to eat more, you look so thin. The girl in the **drug store** asks **pertly** but very politely if she may borrow the comic section of your newspaper. On the skating rink at **Rockefeller Center** there is always something pleasant to see: pretty girls showing off their **pirouettes**, children staggering about in helpless **paroxysms**, an **eccentric** sailing by with a look of **profoundest contempt** upon his

DIVERSE WORDS AND VOICES

face, an elderly lady in tweeds excitedly arm-in-arm with an instructor.

[…]

The traffic swirls through New York like a rather slobby mixture running through a cake-mould. Some seventy-five years ago an observer described New York traffic as being 'everywhere close-spread, thick-tangled (yet no collisions, no trouble) with masses of bright colour [and] action […]'. The description is not so far from the mark today, and the colours especially are still bright and agreeable. The women are not afraid of colour in their clothes, the shop windows are gorgeous, the cars are painted with a peacock dazzle. From upstairs the streets of Manhattan are alive with shifting colours.

[…]

[…] the city itself, with its sharp edges and fiery colours, is a thing of beauty; especially seen from above, with Central Park startlingly green among the skyscrapers, with the tall towers of **Wall Street** hazy in the distance, with the two waterways blue and sunny and the long line of an Atlantic liner slipping away to sea. It is a majestic sight, with no Wordsworth at hand to honour it, only a man with a loudspeaker or a fifty-cent guide book.

So leaving Manhattan is like retreating from a snow summit. The very air seems to relax about you. The electric atmosphere softens, the noise stills, the colours blur and fade, the pressure eases, the traffic thins. Soon

WILD PLACES AND URBAN LANDSCAPES

you are out of the city's spell, pausing only to look behind, over the tenements and marshes, to see the lights of the skyscrapers riding the night.

canyons deep valleys, in this case between the tall buildings
dowdy shabby and unfashionable; not stylish
drug store a shop that sells medicines as well as other general items; in the USA they often had a cafe area called a soda fountain
eccentric someone who behaves strangely
enterprise activity
exuberant very lively and cheerful
fall autumn
Fifth Avenue, Rockefeller Center, Wall Street places in New York City
Fred Astaire a famous American dancer, actor and singer
frocks dresses
gesticulating making dramatic movements with your hands and arms as a way of emphasising what you are saying
Hudson River a river that flows through the state of New York
imprecations rude, angry or hostile things said to someone
liners large ships in which people travel long distances, often on holiday
monuments statues, buildings or columns put up as a memorial of a person or event
mystique an aura of mystery, power and awe that surrounds a person or thing
paroxysms sudden outbursts of laughter, crying or strong feeling
pertly cheekily in a lively and attractive way
pirouettes spinning around
pogroms organised massacres of an ethnic group, in particular Jewish people
profoundest contempt the deepest feeling that a person or thing is worthless and does not deserve any respect
profusion a plentiful amount
renaissance rebirth
urbane having smoothly polite manners

Truth and reality

Truth and reality are connected in many ways but can also be different and unique to each person. The word 'truth' seems to have only positive connotations, but truth can often mean facing up to harsh realities. The truth can become difficult or dangerous to navigate, and reality is sometimes hidden through fear or shame. Our modern society is interested in truth and reality: while we live with fake news and reality television in the media, we also explore artificial intelligence and feel empowered to question the reality. How do we work out ultimately what is real and what is not? We are compelled, perhaps, to consider that there might be many perspectives on truth. In some cases, reality may not always be what it seems.

In this chapter, the ideas of truth and reality are uncovered and challenged. When Jackie Kay tells the story of Millie and her grief in losing her spouse, we see how truth and reality can become a nightmare. Ursula K. Le Guin explores science fiction, truth and lies. Justice and truth are connected in Tash Aw's tale of a murder trial in Malaysia. In Sharon White's article about social media, there is a clear call for more regulation of what is

DIVERSE WORDS AND VOICES

posted online, where the lines between truth and reality can often become very blurred.

'A moment that changed me' by Samira Ahmed

NON-FICTION

> The British broadcaster and writer Samira Ahmed started her career in journalism aged 19, with a two-week work experience placement at her local newspaper in south-west London. In this article from 2019, she reflects on the time when she and an experienced reporter visited a family after the death of their son in order to find out more about him.

It was my first day on a local paper when I went to visit a **bereaved** family with a **seasoned** reporter. It shaped all the values I took into my journalistic career.

I was 19 when, in September 1987, I got a fortnight's work experience on my local free newspaper, the Kingston Guardian, in south-west London. It was a small but dedicated team of reporters operating out of an office in Twickenham and they were incredibly generous, taking me under their collective wing and sending me out on all kinds of assignments. By the end of the two weeks, I had a handful of **bylined** pieces and had written my first investigative feature – a tug-of-love dog ownership **dispute** over a **whippet**. But the moment that changed me came on the very first day, on a story that I didn't even write.

DIVERSE WORDS AND VOICES

The team had suggested I go out in the evening with an older reporter on a 'death knock' – going to visit a family after a death. They didn't call it a death knock and it wasn't one of those **notorious tabloid** visits, when a reporter turns up out of the blue and confronts a bereaved family. It had been agreed in advance with the parents of the **deceased**, a 17-year-old schoolboy who had died in a car accident, not long after passing his driving test. It was the kind of awful, accidental death that happens regularly, all over the country.

The reporter drove us to the house and we rang the bell. I was very nervous at the idea of meeting people suffering such grief. But when the father came to the door, he shook our hands, smiled and welcomed us in. He had been waiting for us and was happy to tell us all about the kind, wonderful young man his son had been. We sat on the sofa and I listened while he talked about his son: what a good person he had been, all his achievements at school, his hopes and plans. I still remember that he had got a place at the University of York, because that was where my brother had studied.

The reporter was kind and professional and took it all down in **shorthand**. He asked more questions to make sure he had enough details. It probably took about half an hour. When we had finished, the reporter asked if the family had had a chance to think about a photo for the paper to use. Again, they had asked in advance of the visit. The father had remembered the request and had a lovely portrait ready on

120

TRUTH AND REALITY

the mantelpiece, which he handed over. The reporter said he would make sure it was returned to them.

It was very matter-of-fact and very English. The father seemed calm and polite. The reporter was kind and sensitive. I had never confronted death with a stranger before. There were no tears. I felt there might be some small comfort in knowing your child's life and death were going to be marked and **commemorated** in the paper. It made me realise how journalists could provide an important service to their community, that they could be welcomed into the home of a bereaved family to help remember a life and record how a loved one mattered.

I have taken that memory into every crime story I have covered. […]

I still have all my early clippings in a cuttings book. The story of that first death knock isn't in it, of course, as I didn't write up the report. But it is the experience that made me the journalist I am. Or at least try to be.

---

bereaved someone who is bereaved has recently suffered the death of a loved one
bylined to be credited as the writer of an article
commemorated celebrated or reminded of a person
deceased the person who has died
dispute argument
notorious well known for something bad
seasoned experienced
shorthand a set of special signs for writing words down as quickly as people say them
tabloid a newspaper with pages that are half the size of broadsheet newspapers, usually popular in style with many photographs and large headlines; considered less serious than other newspapers
whippet a breed of dog

Extract from *Trumpet* by Jackie Kay

FICTION

> The following extract is taken from the novel *Trumpet* by Jackie Kay, which was first published in 1998. In this novel, the death of legendary jazz trumpeter Joss Moody leads to personal information about his gender becoming public and being portrayed as a scandal. Prior to this, Joss's wife, Millie, was the only person who knew that he was a transgender man. The revelation of this private information, and their adopted son Colman's reaction to it, brings the press to Millie's doorstep, leading her to retreat to a house in a remote Scottish village. In the following extract, Millie reflects on the way the press has treated her since Joss's death.

I pull back the curtain an inch and see their heads bent together. I have no idea how long they have been there. It is getting dark. I keep expecting them to vanish; then I would know that they were all in my mind. I would know that I imagined them just as surely as I imagined my life. But they are still there, wearing real clothes, looking as **conspicuous** as they please. Each time I look at the photographs in the papers, I look unreal. I look unlike the memory of myself. I feel strange now. It used to be such a certain thing, just being myself. It was so easy, so painless.

TRUTH AND REALITY

I have to get back to our **den**, and hide myself away from it all. Animals are luckier; they can bury their heads in sand, hide their heads under their coats, pretend they have no head at all. I feel pain in the exact place Joss complained of for months. A stabbing pain on my left side. We couldn't die of the same thing?

There's a film I watched once, *Double Indemnity*, where the guy is telling his story into a tape, dying and breathless. I feel like him. I haven't killed anyone. I haven't done anything wrong. If I was going to make a tape, I'd make it for Colman.

*

I crept out of my house in the middle of the night with a thief's racing heart. Nobody watching. I drove into dawn. Relief as I crossed the border into Scotland. I let down the windows to sniff the different air. I am exhausted. Every morning for the past ten days, someone has been waiting outside my house with cameras and questions. I have seen the most awful looking pictures of myself in the newspapers looking **deranged** and shocked. Of course you are going to look **demented** if some hack hides behind your hedge, snaps and flashes the moment you appear. How else are you going to look?

Even here now the sound of cameras, like the assault of a machine-gun, is still playing inside my head. I can't get the noise to go no matter what I do. I hear it over music,

over the sound of a tap running, over the kettle's whistle –
the cameras' rapid bullets. Their fingers on the triggers,
they don't take them off till they finish the film, till I've
been shot over and over again. They stop for the briefest
of **frantic** seconds, reload the **cartridge** and then start up
again. What can they want with all those pictures? With
every snap and flash and whirr, I felt myself, the core
of myself, being eaten away. My soul. I met a man once
who wouldn't let me take his picture with Joss. He said
it would be stealing his soul. I remember thinking, how
ridiculous, a soul cannot be stolen. Strange how things
like that stay with you as if life is waiting for a chance to
prove you wrong. Joss's soul has gone and mine has been
stolen. It is as simple and as true as that.

Once, I came out of my house and at least ten of them
were waiting, two days after Joss's funeral. I was still
in a daze. I didn't react quickly enough. I couldn't find
cover. I couldn't hide. They took me walking towards my
car, entering my car, wild behind the steering wheel. I
looked like an actress in an old black and white movie
who has just bumped off her husband and is escaping.
The wipers on, the rain on the windowscreen, my face,
crazy, at the wheel. The blinding white light, flashing and
illuminating me. I could barely see to drive off. Of course,
the minute I am placed in front of that raging white light,
I am not myself any longer. I am no more myself than a
rabbit is itself trapped in front of **glaring** headlights. The

TRUTH AND REALITY

rabbit freezes and what you see most on the road is fear itself, not a furry rabbit, fear flashed up before you for a second until your brakes screech to a halt. I have stared at the woman who was captured by the light for ages and ages to try to find myself in her. I have never seen my own fear. Most people don't get a chance to see what they look like terrified. If I had died they would have continued shooting, one shot after another. They would have taken me dead. The next day I was splattered all over the papers again, more lies, more **lurid** headlines.

cartridge a case containing the explosive for a bullet or shell; in this case, it may also refer to camera film
conspicuous easily seen; noticeable
demented mad; crazy
den a wild animal's lair
deranged insane; wild and out of control
frantic wildly agitated or excited
glaring very bright and dazzling
illuminating lighting something up or making it bright
lurid sensational and shocking

Extract from *The Left Hand of Darkness* by Ursula K. Le Guin

> Ursula K. Le Guin was an award-winning American author whose novels and short stories spanned many genres, including science fiction and fantasy. Her novel *The Left Hand of Darkness* is a science fiction story set on a planet where the inhabitants are mostly non-binary but can become either male or female to reproduce. The following extract is taken from Le Guin's introduction to the novel, in which she considers the role of science fiction and its relationship with truth and lies.

Science fiction is not **predictive**; it is descriptive.

Predictions are **uttered** by **prophets** (free of charge), by **clairvoyants** (who usually charge a fee, and are therefore more honoured in their day than prophets), and by **futurologists** (**salaried**). Prediction is the business of prophets, clairvoyants, and futurologists. It is not the business of novelists. A novelist's business is lying.

The weather bureau will tell you what next Tuesday will be like, and the **Rand Corporation** will tell you what the twenty-first century will be like. I don't recommend that you turn to the writers of fiction for such information. It's none of their business. All they're trying to do is tell you what they're like, and what you're like – what's going on – what the weather is now, today, this moment, the rain, the sunlight, look! Open your eyes; listen, listen. That is what the novelists say. But they don't tell you what you will see and hear. All they can tell you is what they have seen and heard, in their time in this world, a third of it spent in sleep and dreaming, another third of it spent in telling lies.

'The truth against the world!' – Yes. Certainly. Fiction writers, at least in their braver moments, do desire the truth: to know it, speak it, serve it. But they go about it in a **peculiar** and **devious** way, which consists in inventing persons, places, and events which never did and never will exist or occur, and telling about these fictions in detail and at length and with a great deal of emotion, and then when they are done writing down this pack of lies, they say, There! That's the truth!

They may use all kinds of facts to support their tissue of lies. They may describe the Marshalsea Prison, which was a real place, or the battle of Borodino, which really was fought, or the process of cloning, which really takes place in laboratories, or the **deterioration** of a personality, which is described in real textbooks of psychology, and so on. This weight of **verifiable** place-event-phenomenon-behavior makes the reader forget that he is reading a pure invention, a history that never took place anywhere but in [...] the author's mind. In fact, while we read a

DIVERSE WORDS AND VOICES

novel, we [...] believe in the existence of people who aren't there, we hear their voices, we watch the battle of Borodino with them, we may even become **Napoleon**. [...]

Is it any wonder that no truly respectable society has ever trusted its artists?

But our society, being troubled and **bewildered**, seeking guidance, sometimes puts an entirely mistaken trust in its artists, using them as prophets and futurologists.

[...]

This book is not about the future. Yes, it begins by announcing that it's set in the 'Ekumenical Year 1490–97,' but surely you don't *believe* that?

Yes, indeed the people in it are **androgynous**, but that doesn't mean that I'm predicting that in a **millennium** or so we will all be androgynous, or announcing that I think we damned well ought to be androgynous. I'm merely observing, in the peculiar, devious, and thought-experimental manner proper to science fiction, that if you look at us at certain odd times of day in certain weathers, we already are. I am not predicting, or prescribing. I am describing. I am describing certain aspects of psychological reality in the novelist's way, which is by inventing elaborately **circumstantial** lies.

In reading a novel, any novel, we have to know perfectly well that the whole thing is nonsense, and then,

TRUTH AND REALITY

while reading, believe every word of it. Finally, when we're done with it, we may find – if it's a good novel – that we're a bit different from what we were before we read it, that we have been changed a little, as if by having met a new face, crossed a street we never crossed before. But it's very hard to *say* just what we learned, how we were changed.

The artist deals with what cannot be said in words.

androgynous not distinctly male or female in appearance or in behaviour
bewildered puzzled or confused
circumstantial evidence consisting of facts that suggest something without actually proving it
clairvoyants people who are said to be able to predict future events or know about things that are happening out of sight
deterioration becoming worse
devious underhand and cunning
futurologists people whose job is to attempt to predict future events
millennium a period of 1,000 years
Napoleon a military commander, leader of the French Republic and then emperor of the French empire in the late 18th and early 19th centuries
peculiar strange or unusual
predictive saying what will happen in the future
prophets people who make prophecies (predictions about the future)
Rand Corporation an American non-profit organisation that carries out research and analysis to inform US policies and government decision-making
salaried a person who earns a regular wage, usually for a year's work, paid in monthly instalments
uttered spoken
verifiable able to be checked that it is true by careful investigation

Extract from *Spectacles* by Sue Perkins

> Sue Perkins is a comedian, television presenter, broadcaster and writer, who famously co-presented *The Great British Bake Off*. This extract is taken from the opening of her memoir *Spectacles*, published in 2015. In the extract she humorously describes the origins of the book and the approach she's taken to writing it.

Most of this book is true.

I have, however, changed a few names to protect the innocent, and the odd location too. I've **skewed** some details for comic effect, swapped timelines and generally **embellished** and embroidered some of the duller moments in my past. I have sometimes created **punchlines** where real life failed to provide them, and occasionally invented characters **wholesale**. I have **amplified** my more positive characteristics in an effort to make you like me. I have hidden the worst of my flaws in an effort to make you like me. I may at one point have pretended to have been an Olympic fencing champion.

Other than that, as I say – I've told it like it is.

[...]

TRUTH AND REALITY

I've always wanted to be a writer; since I first felt the **precarious** wobble of a book in my hand, since I first heard the phrase 'Once upon a time', since I first realized that fairies, wizards and seafarers could transport you from the endless grey of 1970s south London. I was a **prolific** child. By the age of seven, I had produced several **anthologies** of poems about God, death and aquatic birds. I was prolific right up to the point I received a B- for a haiku I'd written about a heron. The **uninitiated** can be so unkind.

As an adult I started writing articles, reviews and **glib** little pieces for glossy magazines. I'd hide away in my room on the days I wasn't on set and continue work on *Ra'anui and the Enchanted Otter*, the intense, magic-realist novel set in Tahiti I'd been working on for the best part of a decade. By the time it neared completion, it was clear that there was never going to be an appetite for it and that the book world had changed beyond recognition. Almost to prove that point, I had a meeting in the autumn of 2010 with a well-known publishing house to discuss the possibility of writing something. I'd been invited to a **swanky** restaurant in **St Martin's Lane**. I arrived late, as always, in full wet-weather gear to find a semicircle of unspeakably beautiful people sat at the table waiting for me.

'Hi, I'm Tamara,' said the **immaculate** blonde to my left, **proffering** a manicured hand. I'm head of **talent acquisitions**.'

DIVERSE WORDS AND VOICES

I leant forward to greet her. Dried mud **cascaded** from my sleeve into the *amuse-bouche*. 'Sorry, I've been walking the dog on the **heath**.'

'I'm Sarah-Jane,' said the immaculate blonde to my right. 'I'm the publishing director.'

'Nice to meet you. Ooh, I wouldn't hug me – I'm a little damp around the edges.'

'Hi, I'm Dorcas,' said the immaculate blonde dead ahead of me. 'I'm the managing director.'

'Hello – oops!' I said, as a roll of poo bags **unfurled** from my coat pocket.

It wasn't the best first impression I'd ever made. I sat down and panic-nibbled on some **artisanal** micro-loaves.

'So, Sue...' said one of the immaculate blondes, staring at me as if I were a monkey smearing itself with excrement at the zoo. 'What would you like to write?'

It was the question I had been waiting all my life to answer. Twenty-five minutes later I finished speaking, having **evoked**, in minute detail, my **proposed epic**:

'...so Ra'anui finally tames the beast with his uncle's amulet and marries Puatea. It's essentially a **meditation** on climate change.'

There followed a long pause during which I awkwardly pushed some 'textures of artichoke' around my plate.

'Well...' said one immaculate blonde, breaking the silence, '...that's great!'

'Really, really great,' chimed the second.

'Great!' said the third.

132

TRUTH AND REALITY

This was going so well. All three had said 'great'. In a row! Then came the stinger.

Blonde 1: Now, you see, what *we'd* like you to write…
Me: Oh…
Blonde 2: No, hear us out…
Blonde 1: We've looked at what generates mass sales – you know, what really works piled up at Tesco and Asda. And we've developed a formula…
Blonde 2: [*blurting*] Death is really hot right now…
Blonde 3: And pets…
Blonde 1: So either of those would make a great starting point.

By now I thought we were all having a laugh, that I was among friends. We'd ordered *sharing plates* for goodness' sake. I'd dug my fork into Blonde 1's sweet anchovies. Blonde 2 had tried my avocado tian. I mean, we were *mates*. In that spirit of fun I joined in.

Me: [*grinning*] Well, what about combining the two?
Blonde 1: [*intrigued*] What? Death *and* pets?
Me: Yes, why not? [*Carrying on*] A kind of *Lovely Bones* meets *Lassie*.
Blonde 3: [*squealing*] Amazing! Amazing!
Me: We could call it…*Angel Dog*.

DIVERSE WORDS AND VOICES

Blonde 3: Oh my God – *Angel Dog*!
Me: The dog dies, doesn't go straight to heaven –
           ends up in some kind of canine **purgatory** […]
           – and ends up guarding his owners from the
           plane of the undead. *Angel Dog*.
Blonde 1: *Angel Dog*…
Blonde 2: Wow. *Angel Dog*.
Blonde 3: I love it. I love it!

I roared with laughter. Roared. It took me nearly a minute to realize no one else was roaring with me. The penny finally dropped – they were being serious.

*

Well, I'm sorry, but this book isn't *Angel Dog*. There is a dog in it, later on, although she was far from an angel, as you shall see. I doubt this book will ever disappear in huge numbers from supermarket shelves, or that shoppers will **scuffle** over the last discounted copy in a frenzied **Black Friday** riot. But neither is it the **Polynesian pan-generational** epic I **pitched** all those years ago. It's something in the middle. Mid-range. Comfy. The sort of book that turns up to a meeting covered in mud […] having not changed into something more appropriate.

Something a little more me.

TRUTH AND REALITY

amplified increased in strength or volume

amuse-bouche the small amount of food that is the first course of a meal

anthologies collections of writings

artisanal goods produced on a small scale using traditional methods

Black Friday the day after the US holiday of Thanksgiving, regarded as the first day of the Christmas shopping season, on which retailers make many special offers

cascaded poured down in large amounts

embellished added details to something

epic a story written on a grand or heroic scale, usually very long

evoked produced or inspired a memory or feelings

glib fluently said or written, but not sincere or well thought out; flippant

heath an area of flat open land with low shrubs

immaculate perfectly clean or tidy

meditation thinking deeply and quietly

pan-generational relating to different generations

pitched proposed or attempted to sell

Polynesian of or relating to an area in the South Pacific Ocean called Polynesia, its people, or any of their languages

precarious not very safe or secure

proffering offering something

prolific producing a lot of work

proposed suggested (an idea or plan)

punchlines words that give the climax of a joke or story

purgatory in Roman Catholic belief, a place in which souls are purified by punishment before they can enter heaven

scuffle a confused fight or struggle

skewed not balanced or accurate; biased

St Martin's Lane a street in London

swanky very luxurious or expensive (informal)

talent acquisitions getting skilled people for jobs

unfurled unrolled or spread out

uninitiated people who have no knowledge or experience of a particular subject or activity

wholesale on a large scale; including everybody or everything

Extract from *We, the Survivors* by Tash Aw

> *We, the Survivors* by Tash Aw, published in 2020, is set in Malaysia. The novel is about a man called Ah Hock, who tries to improve his life after an impoverished childhood, but becomes trapped in a series of unfulfilling jobs, concluding with him murdering a fellow worker. This extract describes the end of his murder trial, where Ah Hock's lawyer tries to defend him to the jury by sharing the truth about his childhood.

Towards the end of the trial my lawyer tried to explain to the jury the kind of childhood I had experienced. She was young and clever, she worked for free, she wanted to help me. I understood that my life was being used as an excuse for many things. I listened to her speak about me, and though the facts were true, I felt as if she was describing someone else, someone who had grown up close to me, maybe in a village a couple of miles up the coast. Another guy who shared my name, which she kept repeating. Lee Hock Lye. Lee Hock Lye. Always my full name. Sometimes she said, Lee Hock Lye, *also known as* Jayden Lee, which made the name sound fake, as if I'd made it up – which I had. But still, it was my name –

had become my name. I had chosen it when I'd found proper work and things were going well, just before I got married. It sounded good, people liked it – they hadn't heard anything like it before. It was a cool name that looked professional on the **calling cards** that I had printed when business started going well. Jayden – that was me, but each time she pronounced the name in front of the entire courtroom it felt as though she was referring to someone else, because she said it as two separate words. *Jay, Den*. As if she found it unnatural. Every time I heard it, I felt as though the name was being **prised** away from me, and that I never truly owned it. *Also known as*. I should never have taken that name, I was foolish to have chosen it.

The person she talked about was miserable, badly educated, hopeless. Someone who had no choices in life. Anyone listening would have pitied him. A woman in the jury was nodding her head slowly, her face twisted in a frown. Even I nearly felt sorry for the person being described. But then I thought: Wait, this is wrong. I also thought: I was happy. I was normal. I knew my lawyer was trying to help me, but I wanted her to stop talking. I started humming a tune to block out the noise of her words. I closed my eyes and tried to imagine being back in the village as a child. I tried to remember what it was like to be myself again, but it was ridiculous. That life was gone. What a stupid thing to do, trying to recapture

DIVERSE WORDS AND VOICES

your childhood while you're being tried for killing someone. **Recalling** my life wouldn't make it any more real – the truth of it existed in the version being described by my lawyer. I laughed at my own stupidity. I laughed quite loudly, and couldn't stop, so I had to put my face in my hands. The lawyer turned around to look at me. She stopped speaking in the middle of a sentence and stared at me – the kind of look you give someone when you think he might be having a heart attack but you're not yet sure what's happening. The judge said, 'I don't think the **defendant**'s life story is relevant. Please continue with your legal arguments.' My lawyer tried to dispute this, but my laughing and the judge's **scolding** made her lose her concentration; all the intelligence and **conviction** and **vigour** I had admired up to that point dissolved in that stuffy courtroom. It was very hot that day, the **air-con** wasn't working, I had trouble breathing. She stumbled over her words a couple of times, and couldn't hold her thoughts together. I was glad it was all going to end soon.

---

air-con a system for controlling the temperature and humidity of the air in a room or building
calling cards small cards with personal information about you on them, such as your name and address, which you can give to people when you go to visit them
conviction the feeling of being firmly convinced of something
defendant a person accused of something in a law court
prised forced something out
recalling bringing something back into your mind; remembering something
scolding speaking angrily to someone because they have done wrong
vigour strength and energy

'It's time to regulate social media sites that publish news' by Sharon White

NON-FICTION

> Dame Sharon White is a Black British businesswoman and the former CEO of Ofcom, the organisation in charge of regulating the broadcasting and telecommunications industries in the UK. In this article, which she wrote in 2018 for *The Times* newspaper, she sets out her view about the need to regulate social media sites that publish news in order to crack down on 'fake news' and disinformation.

Picking up a newspaper with a morning coffee. Settling down to watch TV news after a day's work. Reading the sections of the Sunday papers in your favourite order.

For decades, habit and routine have helped to define our relationship with the news. In the past, people **consumed** news at set times of day, but heard little in between. But for many people, those habits, and the news landscape that shapes them, have now changed fundamentally.

Vast numbers of news stories are now available 24/7, through a wide range of online platforms and devices, with social media now the most popular way of accessing news on the Internet. Today's readers and viewers face the challenge to keep up. So too, importantly, does **regulation**.

The fluid environment of social media certainly brings benefits to news, offering more choice, real-time updates, and a platform for different voices and perspectives. But it also presents new challenges for readers and regulators alike – something that Ofcom, as a regulator of editorial standards in TV and radio, is now giving thought to in the online world.

In new Ofcom research, we asked people about their relationship with news in our 'always-on' society, and the findings are fascinating. People feel there is more news than ever before, which presents a challenge for their time and attention. This, combined with 'fear of missing out', means many feel **compelled** to engage with several sources of news, but only have the capacity to do so **superficially**.

Similarly, as many of us now read news through social media on our smartphones, we're constantly scrolling, swiping and clearing at speed. We're exposed to 'breaking news' notifications, newsfeeds, shared news and stories mixed with other types of content. This limits our ability to process, or even recognise, the news we see. It means we often engage with it **incidentally**, rather than actively.

In fact, our study showed that, after being exposed to news stories online, many participants had no **conscious recollection** of them at all. For example, one recalled seeing

TRUTH AND REALITY

nine news stories online over a week – she had actually viewed 13 in one day alone. Others remembered reading particular articles, but couldn't recall any of the detail.

Social media's attraction as a source of news also raises questions of trust, with people much more likely to doubt what they see on these platforms. Our research shows only 39 per cent consider social media to be a trustworthy news source, compared to 63 per cent for newspapers, and 70 per cent for TV. 'Fake news' and '**clickbait**' articles persist as common concerns among the people taking part in our research, but many struggle to check the **validity** of online news content.

Some rely on gut instinct to tell fact from fiction, while others seek second opinions from friends and family, or look for established news logos, such as *The Times*. Many people admit they simply don't have the time or **inclination** to think **critically** when engaging with news, which has important **implications** for our **democracy**.

Education on how to navigate online news effectively is, of course, important. But the **onus** shouldn't be on the public to detect and deal with fake and harmful content. Online companies need to be much more **accountable** when it comes to **curating** and **policing** the content on their platforms, where this risks harm to the public.

[...]

When it comes to trust and **accountability**, public service broadcasters like the BBC also have a **vital** role

DIVERSE WORDS AND VOICES

to play. Their news operations provide the **bedrock** for much of the news content we see online, and as the broadcasting regulator, Ofcom will continue to hold them to the highest standards.

Ofcom's research can help inform the debate about how to regulate effectively in an online world. We will continue to shine a light on the behavioural trends that emerge, as people's complex and evolving relationship with the media continues to evolve.

---

accountable, accountability being able to or having to explain why you have carried out an action
bedrock something solid on which an idea or belief is based
clickbait something on a website that encourages people to click on a link
compelled forced to do something
conscious recollection ability to remember
consumed took in something
critically being able to point out faults or weaknesses in a person or thing
curating carefully choosing, arranging and presenting different items in order to get a particular effect
democracy government of a country by representatives elected by all the people
implications things that are implied or can be concluded from something said
incidentally happening as a less important additional part of something else
inclination a tendency
onus the duty or responsibility of doing something
policing the job of controlling the way in which something is done
regulation a rule or law
superficially not deeply or thoroughly
validity the quality of being based on truth or reason, or of being able to be accepted
vital essential

Dystopia and other worlds

What does the future hold for us? The question has intrigued fiction and non-fiction writers for centuries. Dystopian writing reveals people's deepest, darkest fears. It is an exploration of troubled worlds in which oppression and tyranny rule with an iron fist. The genre also encompasses science and fears about how the world is changing. Novels such as Margaret Atwood's *The Handmaid's Tale* or *The Hunger Games* show how the extremes of a dystopian world could become a nightmare. The opposite of dystopia is utopia, which is a place of perfection and amazement. Literally, it means 'no place', suggesting perhaps a perfect place may never exist. Humans could always try to find another world to inhabit, but space is vast and who knows what it holds.

In this chapter, the texts explore a variety of utopian and dystopian worlds. In *The Knife of Never Letting Go*, readers are flown to another planet, where the characters have amazing abilities that earthlings do not possess. In Shafak's *The Island of Missing Trees*, the utopian and

DIVERSE WORDS AND VOICES

dystopian space is combined. And in a world where AI is growing, it is fascinating to read Kazuo Ishiguro's extract on 'Artificial Friends'.

Extract from *The Knife of Never Letting Go* by Patrick Ness

FICTION

> *The Knife of Never Letting Go* by Patrick Ness, published in 2008, is set on an alien planet that was colonised by humans ten years previously. Through war with the indigenous occupants, men and boys are affected with a germ that means that their thoughts are broadcast out loud; this is referred to as Noise. The thoughts of animals are also audible. Women are thought to be extinct. The narrator, Todd Hewitt, is about to turn thirteen. He lives in what is thought to be the only remaining settlement, Prentisstown, ruled by Mayor Prentiss. In this extract Todd is making his way towards the town with his dog, Manchee.

We get ourselves outta the swamp and head back towards town and the world feels all black and grey no matter what the sun is saying. Even Manchee barely says nothing as we make our way back up thru the fields. My Noise churns and bubbles like a stew on the boil till finally I have to stop for a minute to calm myself down a little.

There's just no such thing as silence. Not here, not nowhere. Not when yer asleep, not when yer by yerself, never.

DIVERSE WORDS AND VOICES

I am Todd Hewitt, I think to myself with my eyes closed. *I am twelve years and twelve months old. I live in Prentisstown on New World. I will be a man in one month's time exactly.*

It's a trick Ben taught me to help settle my Noise. You close yer eyes and as clearly and calmly as you can you tell yerself who you are, cuz that's what gets lost in all that Noise.

I am Todd Hewitt.

'Todd Hewitt,' Manchee murmurs to himself beside me.

I take a deep breath and open my eyes.

That's who I am. I'm Todd Hewitt.

We walk on up away from the swamp and the river, up the slope of the wild fields to the small ridge at the south of town where the school used to be for the brief and useless time it existed. Before I was born, boys were taught by their ma at home and then when there were only boys and men left, we just got sat down in front of vids and learning modules till Mayor Prentiss **outlawed** such things as '**detrimental** to the discipline of our minds'.

Mayor Prentiss, see, has a Point of View.

And so for almost half a stupid year, all the boys were gathered up by sad-faced Mr Royal and **plonked** out here in an out-building away from the main Noise of the town. Not that it helped. It's nearly impossible to teach anything in a classroom full of boys' Noise and *completely*

DYSTOPIA AND OTHER WORLDS

impossible to give out any sort of test. You cheat even if you don't mean to and *everybody* means to. [...]

Ben taught me the rest at home. Mechanics and food prep and clothes repair and farming basics and things like that. Also a lot of survival stuff like hunting and which fruits you can eat and how to follow the moons for **direkshuns** and how to use a knife and a gun and snakebite **remedies** and how to calm yer Noise as best you can.

He tried to teach me reading and writing, too, but Mayor Prentiss caught wind of it in my Noise one morning and locked Ben up for a week and that was the end of my book-learning and what with all that other stuff to learn and all the working on the farm that still has to be done every day and all the just plain surviving, I never ended up reading too good.

Don't matter. Ain't nobody in Prentisstown ever gonna write a book.

Manchee and me get past the school building and up on the little ridge and look north and there's the town in question. Not that there's all that much left of it no more. One shop, used to be two. One pub, used to be two. One clinic, one jail, one non-working petrol **stayshun**, one big house for the Mayor, one police stayshun. The Church. One short bit of road running thru the centre, paved back in the day, never upkept since, goes to gravel right quick. All the houses and such are out and about, outskirts

DIVERSE WORDS AND VOICES

like, farms, *meant* to be farms, some still are, some stand empty, some stand worse than empty.

And that's all there is of Prentisstown. **Populayshun** 147 and falling, falling, falling. 146 men and one almost-man.

---

detrimental harmful or disadvantageous
direkshuns this is how the narrator says 'directions'
outlawed forbidden
plonked put something down clumsily or heavily
populayshun this is how the narrator says 'population'
remedies things that cure or relieve diseases and illnesses
stayshun this is how the narrator says 'station'

Extract from 'Writing Fantasy Lets Me Show the Whole Truth of Disability' by Ross Showalter

NON-FICTION

> The following extract is from an essay published by a nonprofit online magazine in 2020. The writer, Ross Showalter, is deaf, and reflects on his search for representation in speculative fiction – a genre whose stories do not take place in real world, for example dystopian futures or worlds inhabited by werewolves.

The first time I saw deaf people in mainstream storytelling was in the Freeform family drama *Switched at Birth*. *Switched at Birth* is a TV show where two young women learn that, as babies, they went home and grew up with the other's family. Almost two decades after the switch, they meet their biological families and get to know them.

One of the women, Daphne, is deaf. When we meet her in the **pilot** episode, she both signs and speaks, "it's nice to meet you." She wears hearing aids.

The show aired in 2011, when I was on the cusp of entering my **senior year of high school**. I devoured the first season – it was a lifeline for me. I was the only deaf person both in my family and my school district. My deafness felt like a veil between me and everyone else, one I couldn't tear down. I found solace in the existence of a TV show that featured deaf people, people like me.

When the second season came around, I wasn't the only deaf person in school anymore. There were other deaf students at my university, and we'd found each other. My signing had improved. I had learned the difference between Deaf (a cultural label) and deaf (a medical label), and I was starting to claim my Deaf identity and affirm myself under that label, within that community.

I stopped watching *Switched at Birth* because I was preoccupied with the Deaf people I met in real life. But there was talk about the ninth episode in the second season, "Uprising," which would be presented in only sign language. We all decided to watch.

When I watched that all-signed episode, I felt my heart plunge into disappointment. It was no longer the lifeline it was in high school. The signing is stiff, the characters are **stereotypical**. Apart from the presentation, the episode is standard teenage drama […]. It felt like a faint shadow of a culture and a community that I now knew was richer than what was on the screen. I was disappointed.

I tried to find a replacement for a show I'd outgrown. I wanted to find representation, something that could comfort and validate me as I move through a world that doesn't accommodate me. I couldn't find anything that reflected my real experience.

DYSTOPIA AND OTHER WORLDS

What I found instead was horror and fantasy.

Instead of real-world dramas like *Switched at Birth*, I started watching darker fare like *Hannibal* and *Teen Wolf*. […] I related with the emotional arcs these shows presented; both shows follow their **protagonist** trying to find their place in a world that either **persecuted** them or paid them little attention. I found myself **rapt** at the way they presented identity and community. […]

Horror and fantasy let me see my struggle when I couldn't find any other representation. *Teen Wolf*, in particular, has moments where the protagonist, Scott McCall, struggles with the demands that being a werewolf places on him; he is asked to be responsible, to **assimilate**, to go through the world without causing trouble. He clings to human friendships and resents the werewolf bonds he builds. He claims his identity as a creature of the night while struggling with a werewolf's bloodlust. I understood his frustration, because I wanted to be part of a community without losing parts of myself that aren't directly tied to Deafness. When I watched *Teen Wolf*, I almost felt like Scott too, part of a community that was both visible and yet hidden to the world at large.

[…] Often, authors sideline disabled people in literary fiction. Narrators or authority figures see them as unfulfilled, powerless, or saints. They are in need of saving either by God or by another person who might move through society with fewer barriers. This viewpoint upon disabled characters persists in work from decades past to contemporary work today, from novels like Carson McCullers's *The Heart Is a Lonely Hunter* to Lara Vapnyar's story "Deaf and Blind." Seeing people like me with little agency or **autonomy** tells me that fiction does not recognize that disabled people can gain, wield, and enact power in a narrative. As a result, I don't feel represented in those stories, even if the characters are superficially like me.

[…]

I found a new direction in **speculative fiction**. I read Karen Russell's story "St. Lucy's Home for Girls Raised by Wolves" in a fiction workshop, and the story stayed in my consciousness long after I'd moved to other readings. In that story, a group of werewolves are brought to a school to learn how to be human women. The werewolves felt pressure from the human nuns to erase their werewolf selves; the pressure to assimilate from the overseeing class, even as it was wrapped up in metaphor, resonated with me. I had read speculative fiction before, but never stories that negotiated ideas of identity so urgently and efficiently.

There has been plenty of speculative fiction that shows **systematic** oppression in all its different forms, or, alternatively, that makes the invisible visible. Modern writers like Rivers Solomon and Helen Oyeyemi have highlighted systemic racism through science-fiction and fairy tales, respectively; Carmen Maria Machado and Leni Zumas have explored gender equality and gender expectations using surrealist and dystopian frameworks. In years past, writers like Octavia Butler and Angela Carter snuck revolutionary ideas and sensibilities about race and gender into science fiction, fantasy, and fairy tales.

When I read those writers, I saw ways to center disability in speculative fiction. I saw frameworks and **tropes** that could springboard conversations I wanted to have about disability. […] I could connect to these stories because speculative fiction allowed main characters to not only be human beings, but also otherworldly creatures. In speculative fiction, humans and creatures alike are given the same space to feel a wide range of emotions and to struggle against limiting decrees and ideas – instead of being weak or helpless. […]

When I write about disability, I want to show the real experiences of people like me without having to lay out all the societal pressures and oppressions. I want that situation to be accessible to anyone. I don't want to explain disabled experiences. I want to show them.

[…]

I love being represented and seeing Deaf people in literature and media today. I love seeing disabled people take on challenges and overcoming them. But, as a reader, what I love more is people like me being seen as

DIVERSE WORDS AND VOICES

someone full of possibility and full of power. When I am given space to speculate about people like me, it makes me feel included. That kind of inclusion makes me feel proud to be myself.

assimilate become absorbed and integrated into a society or culture
autonomy the freedom to act as you want to; independence
persecuted to treat someone cruelly because of their, background, identity or beliefs
pilot the first episode of a TV series
protagonist main character
rapt completely fascinated or absorbed by what one is seeing or hearing
senior year of high school the final year of secondary school; year 11
speculative fiction a genre of fiction that is set in somewhere other than the real world, e.g. a dystopian future
stereotypical relating to an oversimplified image or idea that has become fixed through being widely held
systematic methodical; carefully planned
tropes figures of speech or plot devices that are predictable or familiar because of overuse

Extract from *The Island of Missing Trees* by Elif Shafak

> The novel *The Island of Missing Trees* by Elif Shafak, published in 2021, is a love story set on the divided island of Cyprus. In this opening section of the novel, Shafak sets the scene, describing both the beauty of the place and the way it has been damaged by conflict, presenting the island in both utopian and dystopian terms.

Once upon a memory, at the far end of the Mediterranean Sea, there lay an island so beautiful and blue that the many travellers, **pilgrims**, **crusaders** and **merchants** who fell in love with it either wanted never to leave or tried to tow it with **hemp** ropes all the way back to their own countries.

Legends, perhaps.

But legends are there to tell us what history has forgotten.

It has been many years since I fled that place on board a plane, inside a suitcase made of soft black leather, never to return. I have since adopted another land, England, where I have grown and **thrived**, but not a single day passes that I do not yearn to be back. Home. Motherland.

It must still be there where I left it, rising and sinking with the waves that break and foam upon its **rugged**

DIVERSE WORDS AND VOICES

coastline. At the crossroads of three continents – Europe, Africa, Asia – and the **Levant**, that **vast** and **impenetrable** region, vanished entirely from the maps of today.

A map is a two-dimensional representation with **arbitrary** symbols and **incised** lines that decide who is to be our enemy and who is to be our friend, who deserves our love and who deserves our hatred and who, our sheer **indifference**.

Cartography is another name for stories told by winners.

For stories told by those who have lost, there isn't one.

*

Here is how I remember it: golden beaches, turquoise waters, **lucid** skies. Every year sea turtles would come ashore to lay their eggs in the powdery sand. The late-afternoon wind brought along the scent of **gardenia**, **cyclamen**, **lavender**, **honeysuckle**. Branching ropes of **wisteria** climbed up whitewashed walls, **aspiring** to reach the clouds, hopeful in the way only dreamers are. When the night kissed your skin, as it always did, you could smell the jasmine on its breath. The moon, here closer to earth, hung bright and gentle over the rooftops, casting a **vivid** glow on the narrow alleys and **cobblestoned** streets. And yet shadows found a way to creep through the light. Whispers of distrust and **conspiracy** rippled in the dark. For the island was **riven** into two pieces – the north and the south. A different language, a different

DYSTOPIA AND OTHER WORLDS

script, a different memory **prevailed** in each, and when they prayed, the islanders, it was **seldom** to the same god.

The capital was split by a **partition** which sliced right through it like a slash to the heart. Along the **demarcation line** – the **frontier** – were **dilapidated** houses riddled with bullet holes, empty courtyards scarred with grenade bursts, boarded stores gone to ruin, ornamented gates hanging at angles from broken hinges, luxury cars from another era rusting away under layers of dust… Roads were blocked by coils of barbed wire, piles of sandbags, barrels full of concrete, anti-tank ditches and watchtowers. Streets ended abruptly, like unfinished thoughts, unresolved feelings.

Soldiers stood guard with machine guns, when they were not making the rounds; young, bored, lonesome men from various corners of the world who had known little about the island and its complex history until they found themselves posted to this unfamiliar environment. Walls were plastered with official signs in bold colours and capital letters:

NO ENTRY BEYOND THIS POINT
KEEP AWAY, RESTRICTED AREA!
NO PHOTOGRAPHS, NO FILMING ALLOWED

Then, further along the **barricade**, an **illicit** addition in chalk scribbled on a barrel by a passer-by:

WELCOME TO NO MAN'S LAND

DIVERSE WORDS AND VOICES

arbitrary chosen or done on an impulse, not according to a rule or law
aspiring having an ambition to achieve something
barricade a barrier, especially one put up hastily across a street or door
cartography the art or activity of making maps and geographical charts
cobblestoned street surface made with stones that have a rounded upper surface
conspiracy a secret plan made by a group of people to do something illegal
crusaders soldiers who fought in the Crusades, a series of military expeditions made by Christians in the Middle Ages to recover the Holy Land from the Muslims who had conquered it
demarcation line a marked boundary or limits of something
dilapidated falling to pieces
frontier the boundary between two countries or regions
gardenia, cyclamen, lavender, honeysuckle, wisteria types of flowers
hemp a plant that produces coarse fibres from which cloth and ropes are made
illicit forbidden by law or rules
impenetrable impossible to get through
incised cut or engraved into a surface
indifference lack of care or interest
Levant a former name of an area in the eastern Mediterranean
lucid clear
merchants people involved in trade
partition division
pilgrims people who travel to a holy place for religious reasons
prevailed succeeded
riven divided
rugged having an uneven surface or outline
seldom not often
thrived grown strongly; prospered or been successful
vast very great
vivid bright and clear

Extract from *Klara and the Sun* by Kazuo Ishiguro

FICTION

> *Klara and the Sun* by Kazuo Ishiguro, published in 2021, takes place in a future time when solar-powered androids known as AFs, or Artificial Friends, have been created to provide companionship for human children. In the following extract, Klara, who is one of the AFs, is moved into the window of the shop from which she is to be sold, alongside another AF called Rosa.

That was one reason why we always thought so much about being in the window. Each of us had been promised our turn, and each of us longed for it to come. That was partly to do with what Manager called the 'special honour' of representing the store to the outside. Also, of course, whatever Manager said, we all knew we were more likely to be chosen while in the window. But the big thing, silently understood by us all, was the Sun and his **nourishment**. Rosa did once bring it up with me, in a whisper, a little while before our turn came around.

'Klara, do you think once we're in the window, we'll receive so much goodness we'll never get short again?'

I was still quite new then, so didn't know how to answer, even though the same question had been in my mind.

DIVERSE WORDS AND VOICES

Then our turn finally came, and Rosa and I stepped into the window one morning, making sure not to knock over any of the display the way the pair before us had done the previous week. The store, of course, had yet to open, and I thought the grid would be fully down. But once we'd seated ourselves on the Striped Sofa, I saw there was a narrow gap running along the bottom of the grid – Manager must have raised it a little when checking everything was ready for us – and the Sun's light was making a bright rectangle that came up onto the platform and finished in a straight line just in front of us. We only needed to stretch our feet a little to place them within its warmth. I knew then that whatever the answer to Rosa's question, we were about to get all the nourishment we would need for some time to come. And once Manager touched the switch and the grid climbed up all the way, we became covered in dazzling light.

I should confess here that for me, there'd always been another reason for wanting to be in the window which had nothing to do with the Sun's nourishment or being chosen. Unlike most AFs, unlike Rosa, I'd always longed to see more of the outside – and to see it in all its detail. So once the grid went up, the realisation that there was now only the glass between me and the **sidewalk**, that I was free to see, close up and whole, so many things I'd seen before only as corners and edges, made me so excited that for a moment I nearly forgot about the Sun and his kindness to us.

I could see for the first time that the RPO Building was in fact made of separate bricks, and that it wasn't white, as I'd always thought, but a pale yellow. I could now see too that it was even taller than I'd imagined – twenty-two storeys – and that each repeating window was underlined by its own special ledge. I saw how the Sun had drawn a diagonal line right across the face of the RPO Building, so that on one side of it there was a triangle that looked almost white, while on the other was one that looked very dark, even though I now knew it was all the pale yellow colour. And not only could I see every window right up to the rooftop, I could sometimes see the people inside, standing, sitting, moving around. Then down on the street, I could see the passers-by, their different kinds of shoes, paper cups, shoulder bags, little dogs, and if I wanted, I could follow with my eyes any one of them all the way past the pedestrian crossing and beyond the second Tow-Away Zone sign, to where two **overhaul men** were standing beside a drain and pointing. I could see right inside the taxis as they slowed to let the crowd go over the crossing – a driver's hand tapping on his steering wheel, a cap worn by a passenger.

The day went on, the Sun kept us warm, and I could see Rosa was very happy. But I noticed too that she hardly looked at anything, fixing her eyes constantly on the first Tow-Away Zone sign just in front of us. Only when I pointed out something to her would she turn her head, but then she'd lose interest and go back to looking at the sidewalk outside and the sign.

Rosa only looked elsewhere for any length of time when a passer-by paused in front of the window. In those circumstances, we both did as Manager had taught us: we put on 'neutral' smiles and fixed our gazes across the street, on a spot midway up the RPO Building. It was very tempting to look more closely at a passer-by who came up, but Manager had explained that it was highly **vulgar** to make eye contact at such a moment. Only when a passer-by specifically signalled to us, or spoke to us through the glass, were we to respond, but never before.

Some of the people who paused turned out not to be interested in us at all. They'd just wanted to take off their sports shoe and do something to it, or to press their **oblongs**. Some though came right up to the glass and gazed in. Many of these would be children, of around the age for which we were most suitable, and they seemed happy to see us. A child would come up excitedly, alone or with their adult, then point, laugh, pull a strange face, tap the glass, wave.

Once in a while – and I soon got better at watching those at the window while appearing to gaze at the

DYSTOPIA AND OTHER WORLDS

RPO Building – a child would come to stare at us, and there would be a sadness there, or sometimes an anger, as though we'd done something wrong. A child like this could easily change the next moment and begin laughing or waving like the rest of them, but after our second day in the window, I learned quickly to tell the difference.

I tried to talk to Rosa about this, the third or fourth time a child like that had come, but she smiled and said: 'Klara, you worry too much. I'm sure that child was perfectly happy. How could she not be on a day like this? The whole city's so happy today.'

But I brought it up with Manager, at the end of our third day. She had been praising us, saying we'd been 'beautiful and **dignified**' in the window. The lights in the store had been dimmed by then, and we were rear-store, leaning against the wall, some of us browsing through the interesting magazines before our sleep. Rosa was next to me, and I could see from her shoulders that she was already half asleep. So when Manager asked if I'd enjoyed the day, I took the chance to tell her about the sad children who'd come to the window.

'Klara, you're quite remarkable,' Manager said, keeping her voice soft so as not to disturb Rosa and the others. 'You notice and absorb so much.' She shook her head as though in wonder. Then she said: 'What you must understand is that we're a very special store. There

DIVERSE WORDS AND VOICES

are many children out there who would love to be able to choose you, choose Rosa, any one of you here. But it's not possible for them. You're beyond their reach. That's why they come to the window, to dream about having you. But then they get sad.'

dignified having or showing dignity
nourishment food; something that sustains you
oblongs how the character refers to mobile phones
overhaul men men doing repairs
sidewalk footpath
vulgar rude

Extract from 'Uncertainty Principle' by K. Tempest Bradford

FICTION

> The short story 'Uncertainty Principle' by K. Tempest Bradford, published in 2012, is about a young person called Iliana who notices reality shifting around her, even though these changes are noticed by nobody else. This extract describes Iliana's experiences of different dystopian futures as the world keeps changing around her.

The changing didn't stop, though it did pause for a long time. Two years went by before it happened again – just long enough for Iliana to start mistrusting her own memories. Certainty came rushing back along with that sound, now familiar and dreaded, in the middle of math class.

Less severe than the last, the pain **dissipated** almost as soon as she felt it. Her eyes stayed open, so she saw the classroom walls turn from white to dingy gray. The desks changed, too, now looking older and more abused than they had before. Panic bloomed in her stomach. What, or who, had she lost this time?

No one, it turned out. None of the kids she knew had disappeared. Her house was still there when she got home. Her parents came home in time for dinner, like always. But even that little change at school had to mean something, she decided. So she started keeping track.

DIVERSE WORDS AND VOICES

She bought an old-fashioned pocket notebook from the **paperie** in the mall and wrote down all the dates and times she could remember in one column and any changes she could think of in the other. Next to her birthday she wrote just one word in bold, green letters: *Grayson*.

After the day in math class, the changes came faster. The next one happened months later, not years. Same as the one after that. Sometimes the only indication came from the sound and the pain; the differences weren't always immediately **apparent**. They still affected her, just the same.

The day she had to bring home a report card with a big red C next to Social Studies she wanted to tell her parents how hard it was keeping up with current events and history when the details kept changing on her. And the textbooks. But how could they possibly believe her? It's not like they or anyone else noticed how much the world changed around them.

Like the way their neighborhood went from a community where everyone knew each other to one where people barely talked and then to one where chain-link fences separated increasingly **unkempt** yards and the only interactions happened when someone's dog or cat **violated** the boundaries. Peeling paint now scarred every house on her street and the neighbouring blocks. Iliana missed flowers the most and the delight of walking home from school in the spring, the air full of bees and fragrance. All over the space of four changes in middle school.

Her parents went from encouraging her to go outside and play with her friends from the block to grounding her if she didn't make it home before the 4:00 p.m. Under-13 curfew that hadn't existed just a week before.

At home, the problems always centred around money. It felt as if funding at the university where her parents worked always shrank after a change. They worried about their department **downsizing** or having to give up their research. Apparently things were the same at other schools, so no point in moving, according to her father.

Iliana obsessed over news feeds on the family computer or the ones at school, trying to track changes in the wider world. It sometimes took days or weeks of reading and rereading news reports, Wikipedia entries, and magazine archives to find the differences between events and people that she remembered. Though there were plenty of obvious ones.

The US went to war, then a change hit and that war didn't exist. There had been one five years before that caused a major oil shortage. Now they only had one car – an old **prehybrid** style – that they rarely drove because they couldn't afford the **gas**.

Cities on the coasts had to turn off all electricity during planned hours to save energy. Then a change swept

DIVERSE WORDS AND VOICES

through and the same had been true for **Ohio** and the rest of the **Midwest** for over a year.

By the time Iliana started high school, changes might come just weeks apart, keeping her off balance and in a constant state of anxiety. Still, she kept her log faithfully, copying it to multiple pocket notebooks after the morning she woke up to discover the furniture in her room completely rearranged. Nothing was permanent.

apparent obvious
dissipated went away
downsizing reducing in size
gas petrol
Midwest an area in the centre of the USA that includes Ohio, Indiana, Michigan, Illinois, Wisconsin, Iowa, Minnesota, Nebraska, Missouri and Kansas
Ohio a state in the USA
paperie a shop that sells pens, paper and notebooks
prehybrid from a time before vehicles that run on both petrol and electricity; a car that runs just on petrol
unkempt untidy
violated crossed without permission

168

Youth and experience

What would you do if you could stay young forever? Would you even want to? Being young has advantages and disadvantages; it is a time when we may feel wildly free and at the same time, not free at all. Youth can be simultaneously brilliant and terrifying – and literature often focuses on the transition into adulthood. With experience often comes wisdom and freedom, but new challenges too. For example., many people are portrayed as fearing aging because of changes in how they look. But is the fear really more than skin deep? We might also fear being forgotten; we fear our bodies letting us down; we fear being neglected by society. Whatever stage of life, our experiences are intrinsically linked to our relationships.

In this chapter, the ideas of youth and experience are explored in each text. In the extract from *Becoming Dinah* by Kit de Waal, teenager Dinah struggles with her sense of identity and sets out on an epic journey. Lemn Sissay recounts his challenging childhood, including his relationship with his foster parents and navigating

DIVERSE WORDS AND VOICES

the social care system as a young Black man. In Christy Brown's *My Left Foot*, he reveals one of the most profound and unforgettable moments of his youth.

Extract from *Becoming Dinah* by Kit de Waal

FICTION

> In the novel *Becoming Dinah* by Kit de Waal, published in 2019, 17-year-old Dinah struggles with her sense of identity. She is mixed race, but feels neither Black nor white, and she's attracted to both boys and girls. In this extract from the opening of the novel, Dinah uses blunt scissors and a razor to shave off her hair, even though these are dangerous tools to use for the task, before leaving the commune where she's grown up to set out on an epic journey.

Cut your hair off? Not as easy as you think. You need the right stuff for a start.

Electric shaver? No. Proper scissors? No. If you haven't got them, you'd better think hard. Think fast.

First thing, get rid of the weight, get it from long to short. And if your hair lies the whole length of your back, as thick and heavy as a blanket, this could take forever. So make a start.

Grab a great big hank of hair, wind it around your hand and pull it upwards, away from your scalp. Go carefully with the redhandled scissors, the ones that you took out of the kitchen drawer that your mum uses for cutting coupons out of newspapers or cutting the string off a parcel. They're not sharp and the blades are bent but it's all you've got.

DIVERSE WORDS AND VOICES

So get in close as you can. If you'd thought about it you might have bought a hair cutting kit from somewhere but you didn't think and anyway the nearest shop is seven miles away and this is happening right here, right now, and it's too late for wishing what you might have done…

You cut. And you cut. You have to do this over and over again, cut and cut and cut, hair on the left, hair on the right. Chop into the top sections, pulling and cutting and trying not to leave any long bits as you go. Ignore the tremble of your fingers and the bump of your heart asking over and over if this is the right thing to do. Because you know it is. You know it is.

The back of the head is the hardest because you can't see. Balance a mirror behind you, hang it off the hook on the bathroom door. Try not to block out your own reflection or get in your own way as you snip and cut and scratch. It's hard to make your hands do the right thing when you can only see them in reverse and it takes forever and the muscles in your arms ache and the muscles in your shoulders ache and it's the biggest thing you've done so far in your whole life. Well, it was until yesterday. But you don't want to think about yesterday so you carry on.

Then when it's as short as you can get it, you stare at the new you in the mirror and you see yourself for the first time. You look like someone you don't recognise. And it's not good. But you look different and that was the

172

point, wasn't it? All that's left where your beautiful hair used to be is clumps and wisps and wavy tufts sticking up at strange angles, and painful scratches where the dull blade of the scissors caught your skin. And even though you're tired there's still more to do.

So you fill the sink, bend over and dip your head in the water. Add a squeeze of shampoo. Make a lather on the tufts, all white and soft as a cloud, and you look like an advert on the telly for someone having a really good time in the shower, except you're not having a really good time. Tough. It's too late to turn back now. You make the suds thick and creamy and you're just flying blind now because you don't know if it will work but you've got no choice.

You get your mum's razor, the one she's been using under her arms and on her legs for months, the one with little rusty bits on the corners, the one that's been sitting on the side of the bath forever, the one you have to hope is still sharp.

You start by making long tracks along the great curve of your head and the razor keeps snagging and getting clogged up with your tufty hair. The soap stings and the blood turns the suds to pink like no advert you've ever seen.

And you really know now, you're more certain than ever that you should have had a better plan.

You rinse the razor under the tap to make it clean again and you keep going even though it hurts with

DIVERSE WORDS AND VOICES

all the tangles and pulls and you feel like you're on the verge of tears but you choke them down. It wouldn't take much more to make you cry. Not today.

It seems to take forever. Your arms hurt even more than before. As the suds and the lather disappear you see that your scalp isn't as brown as your face. It's not even brown at all, it's the same colour as your mum's face in winter, white and pale. Your stomach lurches. You're going to look ridiculous with non-matching skin with cuts and scratches all over the place and your eyes red from not sleeping all night, or like someone who's had cancer, like someone who's dying not someone on the brink of a new life. But you stick with it, keep making tracks with the razor until the tracks take over and suddenly there are no more tracks to be made.

You rinse your head under the tap and feel the tickle of the water like cold fingers dancing on your new skin. Then you stand up and dry your face. Then you look. Look again. Look again and keep looking because it's worked. There you are. You're not boring old Dinah any more. You're someone completely new. Or you will be.

But there's no time to stand admiring your new self in the mirror. You have to clean the silky, black, wet tufts out of the plughole, pick the long **tresses** up off the bathroom floor, and make sure you don't look too hard because you'll wonder at the colour of your hair, like the bark of a tree, and the shine of your hair, like the sleek coat of a

YOUTH AND EXPERIENCE

cat, and you'll remember the weight of your hair and the feel of it, soft and heavy against your skin, warm on your back. And you might remember all the times people said they loved it and how they wanted to touch it and how it made you beautiful and how it made you feel.

And you think about putting your hair in the bin, but you realise you can't and you don't know why so you bundle the tresses into a small, soft pillow and you take it downstairs with you and put it in a carrier bag. And you put the carrier bag in your rucksack and you put your coat on and say goodbye to the only life you've ever known.

Now it really is time to go.

---

tresses locks of hair

Extract from *My Name is Why* by Lemn Sissay

NON-FICTION

> Lemn Sissay is an award-winning author, poet and playwright of Ethiopian heritage. He grew up in Greater Manchester after being fostered as a baby. His white foster parents gave him the name Norman and went on to have three children of their own, the eldest of whom was called Christopher. The following extract is taken from Lemn Sissay's autobiography, *My Name is Why*, published in 2019, and describes the harsh treatment that he received from his foster parents. Interspersed with poetry, the extract includes dated extracts from social worker files written when he was a child, the first of which reveals that his birth mother had asked for Lemn to be returned to her.

19 April 1978

There is a letter on file from Norman's mother, written in 1968, requesting he be returned to her in Ethiopia – perhaps Norman should be made aware of this?

    – NOT YET I THINK.

The Greenwoods are seen by Norman as his parents, and they and their natural children meet his needs in every way [...].

Jean Jones, Social Worker

YOUTH AND EXPERIENCE

Why would the social worker, Jean Jones, say that my mum and dad 'are seen by Norman as his parents'? They told me they were my parents for ever. Why would I think anything else? But why would she make the comment now? In two months' time they would send me away for ever as if I were a stranger.

As with most brothers close in age, Christopher and I fought like snakes on each other's territory. […] He was an **introvert.** I had no idea that Mum thought it was my fault. We raced each other home from school every day, and every day I beat him.

I waited in the kitchen by my mum. He dived into Mum's arms and said, 'Mum, I beat Norman, didn't I?' She stroked his head and said, 'Yes, you did.' And then she looked at me. 'Yes, you did.'

Over the past few years I had begun to sense that I had done something wrong and yet didn't know what it was. There were times when Dad was charged with punishing me in the front room with the cane. He asked me to yelp so it sounded like I was being punished. Other weird things started to happen.

I was ten, and we were off to a wedding in our new clothes. Chris, Sarah and I were on top of the world. Sarah looked pretty as a picture in her blue floral dress and flower basket. Just before leaving the house, Mum looked at me for a second; something pinched her features. She said, 'Take them off and give them to him.' I didn't understand. I took off my trousers and gave them to my

DIVERSE WORDS AND VOICES

brother. These moments stuck in my memory. It was the sense of an underlying unkindness that stayed with me. [...]

He lost touch at night
Their fingertips withdrew
Nobody touched him, light,
Except you

It was the end of December 1979 and I was excited when I entered the front room for the family meeting. I was excited because the family meeting was just me and Mum and Dad. Just me. No brothers and sisters. I felt important. I sat at the table and my mum looked at me intensely.

'You don't love us, do you?'

I said, 'Yeees, I do love you.'

'We want you to spend the next day thinking about love and what it is. Read the scriptures and give us your most honest and truthful answer tomorrow.'

That was it! It was a clear instruction from Mum and Dad. I studied the question for a day and a night, I prayed to God, and I read the Bible to see if a passage would answer the question. It was a question to which I already had the answer. Of course I loved them. Mum had always said that love was never in question. I started thinking all over again.

If they were asking me whether I loved them or not, and if they were the ones who taught me about love, then maybe I didn't love them, otherwise they wouldn't ask.

This led me to the answer I thought they wanted me to get to. They wanted me to ask God for forgiveness and through Him I would learn to love them. His love would shine through me to them. And in the Baptist faith a sinner must ask forgiveness for his sins. The **theology** was perfect, the timing unquestionable, and the answer as honest as a sinner could get.

The next day came and I said it with pride because I thought I had found the answer they wanted me to find. 'I mustn't love you,' I said. I looked at their faces to see if I had said the right thing. 'But I will ask God for forgiveness... and *learn* to love you.' This was the perfect answer. 'Seek and ye shall find.' This is what they wanted me to seek. And this is what I had found. I had found the answer.

She looked at me as if I had wounded her. 'You don't love us? You don't want to be with us?'

All of this happened the day after they had made this call to the social worker.

31 December 1979
'Message left after Christmas saying that the Greenwoods wanted Norman removed without further discussion.

Spoke to foster parents on telephone. Both almost insisted that Norman had to leave today.' […]

2 January 1980
'A long discussion ensues but attitudes seemed hardened and therefore I arranged to take Norman to **Woodfields**. […]'

DIVERSE WORDS AND VOICES

My mum wouldn't hug me as I left, so I hugged her. Norman Mills, my new social worker, waited at the gate. He ushered me gently in the car. I looked back but they were already turning to go indoors, mindful of the neighbours. The car filled with a quiet loss. Mum told me they would never visit me because it is my choice to leave them because I didn't love them.

We passed the butcher's and the chemist's and Wigan Road and passed the Flower Park and the main park, past the junior school, past Byrchall High School, and then unfamiliar territory unfolded before me. The East Lancashire Road: one dual carriageway, with a single destination: Woodfields

This was the beginning of the end of open arms and warm hugs. This was the beginning of empty Christmas time and hollow birthdays. This was the beginning of not being touched. I'm 12. And it is my fault. This is what I have chosen. The journey took about 45 minutes, or 45 seconds. Or 45 years.

I said to Norman Mills in the car, 'I know this is my fault and I will ask God for forgiveness.' He kept his eyes on the road, but his hands gripped tighter on the wheel. He tapped the indicator and pulled quietly into a **lay-by** and turned the engine off. 'None, none of this is your fault. None of it.' I had no idea what he meant.

[…]

There'd be many times in future that I would play table tennis with myself by pushing the table against the

YOUTH AND EXPERIENCE

wall. Backhand and forehand smash, defend and attack, spin, cut, lob and slice. My body will skip around the table like a sprite on the solid stone floor. I would **narrate** the game against Christopher, my invisible brother, and I'd let him win.

Mum and Dad must have told everyone in my family to stay away from me. I hadn't realised then that none of them would contact me ever again for the rest of my life.

My grandparents, aunts and uncles and cousins. Mum and Dad must have gone back to the family and said, 'We cannot contact him. He has left us. He chose to leave us. After everything we gave him.'

Whenever I got a call to leave the table-tennis table in the middle of a game against my invisible brother I'd say, 'I'll play you later, Chris. Okay?'

All my personal belongings were to go in the locker by the bed. I asked when my clothes and toys would be arriving. They were in the trunk back at home, the one with my name on it, the one Granddad Munro made. But nothing was coming here from there. Not even a Bible. I had nothing to put in the locker by my bed in the dormitory.

Over the next few weeks the children's home filled up with teenagers. Most children in care have someone they can call family. I had no one.

introvert a quiet or shy person who often prefers to spend time alone rather than with a lot of other people
lay-by a place where vehicles can stop beside a main road
narrate tell
theology the study of religion
Woodfields a children's home in Lancashire, England

Extract from *Red Leaves* by Sita Brahmachari

Red Leaves by Sita Brahmachari, published in 2014, is about a 13-year-old girl called Aisha who lives in London with her foster mother, Liliana. Aisha is a refugee from Somalia, but has found a loving home with Liliana. In this extract, the two of them are looking through the pages of Aisha's life story book – a scrapbook that charts key moments in her life.

Liliana shrugged, and smiled to herself as she turned the pages of Aisha's life story book – Liliana had taken to calling it a 'story book' and sometimes 'a scrapbook', because somehow these names seemed less **daunting**. Every child she had cared for had one. It was a personal history in words and pictures, made so that they, and future carers, could chart their life's journey, record progress and give the children a joined-up sense of their own history.

Some foster-carers she knew didn't bother too much with them, but Liliana always felt that making sure these little details were filled in was the very least that she could do for the children she welcomed into her home.

Aisha's earliest drawings in the book were from the time when she had refused to speak. There was one of

YOUTH AND EXPERIENCE

Aisha as a baby curled up in a **foetal position** inside a giant image of her mother. That always choked Liliana up the most. When she had first seen it she'd cried. Who could blame the child for wanting to crawl back inside her mother and be born all over again? Aisha's 'life story' already looked too long and complicated. It was hard to believe that she was not yet even thirteen.

Aisha's description of leaving Somalia and travelling to Britain had broken Liliana's heart. At just ten years old she had managed to convince the authorities that she was twelve. Liliana would never forget the day that the little girl had finally **confided** in her.

'"It will go better for you if you pretend you are a few years older." That's what the guide said to me.'

'And how did you pretend to be older?' Liliana asked.

'Like this!' Aisha stood taller and made her face into a kind of expressionless mask that no clouds of emotion could **penetrate**.

It had taken a long time before she let down her guard and removed that mask.

Now Liliana studied Aisha's smiling face. She was in awe of how far her foster-daughter had come from those painful early days. 'Sure you don't want to start writing in this yourself now?'

Aisha shook her head.

If I were to write a life story book for myself, I would make so many things different, she thought. No matter how pretty

183

DIVERSE WORDS AND VOICES

Liliana tried to make the book, with all her decorations it was a constant reminder to Aisha of all the times that she had been uprooted and torn away from the people she loved.

Liliana glanced at her foster-daughter as she stuck down the last photos of Aisha's 'band' then wrote their names underneath – Aisha, Muna, Somaya, Mariam – and closed the book. This felt like the right moment to raise the subject.

'Can I see?' Aisha asked, leaning over Liliana.

'Of course! It's your story!'

Liliana gently handed the book to Aisha. Maybe she could talk to her as they read over the pages together.

It had been a while since Aisha had really looked at the book, but now she noticed how Liliana had **adorned** their story so carefully, sticking in little **mementos** and memories of times they had shared. In fact, Aisha now realized Liliana was working her way backwards through the book, adding her own paintings, sketches and swatches of material from the clothes that Aisha had been wearing in a particular photo on a particular day. Liliana rarely threw anything away. These little scraps of material were the sorts of details that **transported** you back.

Aisha reached out to touch the piece of red velvet skirt that she remembered wearing, soft and comforting against her skin, and Liliana patted the cushion on the

YOUTH AND EXPERIENCE

chair next to her. Aisha sat down and Liliana budged up closer so that they now sat shoulder to shoulder.

'I can't believe that I've been here for two and a half years already.' Aisha flicked back to the formal, typed entries from before she had come to live here and felt relieved that Liliana had not been tempted to decorate these stark pages. *Nothing could be added to that time to make it feel better*, she thought as she read over the facts of her own life.

'Aisha arrived at Heathrow Airport alone.'

'Aisha's first day at Monmouth House care home…'

'Aisha's first day at Bishop's Primary School…'

'Aisha granted **Refugee Status**.'

In this section the photos were mostly official passport shots of a shy-looking little girl with long thin plaits who did not want her image captured. Without her **hijab**, she looked odd even to herself. Looking at her unveiled ten-year-old face, so exposed to the world, so alone, the weight and chill of the cold stone she'd felt lying in her stomach at that time returned to her. Occasionally one of the staff in the home had tried to capture her in a photo with the other children, but Aisha had always stood slightly aside, as if she was living in another dimension. Which was exactly how it had felt as she'd hugged her stomach tight and ached for the heat of home.

'A sad chapter.' Liliana placed a soothing hand on Aisha's back as she leafed forward again to the beginning of

DIVERSE WORDS AND VOICES

their time together and Liliana's own careful handcrafted pages. 'But look at all of these happy memories!'

Aisha hugged Liliana close. 'You made them for me.'

'*We* made them!' Liliana corrected.

In the time that they had been together, everything had changed for Aisha. She had gone from being a **traumatised** child to a confident young woman, and it was Liliana who had held her hand every step of the way.

Liliana leaned forward and ran her finger over a sentence on the page.

'Remember? Your first words!'

'"I feel safe here",' Aisha read out loud. 'I would never have said that to anyone except you.'

Liliana wiped a tear from her eye. She feared that just bringing up the subject of meeting this family who might adopt Aisha would rock her sense of safety. But maybe she was only thinking of herself. She had promised her own children, now grown-up, that Aisha would be her last foster-child, but in her mind she had always imagined that she would keep Aisha with her until she was old enough to go off to college or university. Liliana had even pictured the graduation photos – '*Such a clever girl*' – and she had no doubt that Aisha would one day fulfil her dream of becoming a lawyer. In her own mind Liliana had decided that the two of them would graduate together: Aisha from university and Liliana from foster-caring into a well-earned **retirement**.

YOUTH AND EXPERIENCE

Liliana sighed deeply. *I should have learned by now that life isn't as neat and tidy as that! But who'd have thought that anyone would come forward to offer a home to a Somali teenager with a traumatic past?* She shook herself. *This is just an introductory meeting. If Aisha doesn't want to go, no one will force her. Anyway, it might not come to anything.* As these arguments sifted through her mind, Liliana felt ashamed of her own selfishness. She attempted to **savour** the sight of Aisha's **serene**, trusting face but the **spectre** of the mask the child had once worn haunted Liliana and the memory seemed now to cast them both in a long **brooding** shadow.

It'll have to wait till tomorrow. I'll tell her tomorrow.

---

adorned decorated
brooding looking or seeming dangerous or threatening
confided told something to someone confidentially
daunting making a person feel discouraged or not confident about doing something
foetal position curled up
hijab a scarf worn by some Muslim women, usually covering the head and neck
mementos souvenirs
penetrate make or find a way through or into something
Refugee Status an official recognition that someone can stay in a country for a period of time because they have had to leave their home country due to conflict
retirement the time after a worker has stopped working
savour enjoy
serene calm and peaceful
spectre ghost
transported felt carried away by a strong emotion
traumatised feels ongoing shock following a disturbing experience

Extract from *My Left Foot* by Christy Brown

NON-FICTION

> Christy Brown was an Irish writer and painter who was born in Dublin in 1932. Complications during his birth led to him developing cerebral palsy, which in his case meant that he needed support to hold his head up and had minimal control over his body movements. He was also unable to speak. Christy lived with his father, mother and siblings, and was supported and encouraged by his mother. In the following extract from his autobiography, *My Left Foot*, Christy Brown describes the moment that he was able to demonstrate that he was capable of communicating.

I was now five, and still I showed no real sign of intelligence. I showed no **apparent** interest in things except with my toes – more especially those of my left foot. Although my natural habits were clean I could not aid myself, but in this respect my father took care of me. I used to lie on my back all the time in the kitchen or, on bright warm days, out in the garden, a little bundle of crooked muscles and twisted nerves, surrounded by a family that loved me and hoped for me and that made me part of their own warmth and humanity. I was lonely, imprisoned in a world of my own, unable to

YOUTH AND EXPERIENCE

communicate with others, cut off, separated from them as though a glass wall stood between my existence and theirs, thrusting me beyond the sphere of their lives and activities. I longed to run about and play with the rest, but I was unable to break loose from my **bondage**.

Then, suddenly, it happened! In a moment everything was changed, my future life molded into a definite shape, my mother's faith in me rewarded and her secret fear changed into open triumph.

It happened so quickly, so simply after all the years of waiting and uncertainty that I can see and feel the whole scene as if it had happened last week. It was the afternoon of a cold, grey December day. The streets outside glistened with snow; the white sparkling flakes stuck and melted on the window-panes and hung on the boughs of the trees like molten silver. The wind howled **dismally**, whipping up little whirling columns of snow that rose and fell at every fresh gust. And over all, the dull, murky sky stretched like a dark **canopy**, a **vast infinity** of greyness.

Inside, all the family were gathered round the big kitchen fire that lit up the little room with a warm glow and made giant shadows dance on the walls and ceiling.

In a corner Mona and Paddy were sitting huddled together, a few torn school **primers** before them. They were writing down little sums on to an old chipped slate, using a bright piece of yellow chalk. I was close to them, propped up by a few pillows against the wall, watching.

189

DIVERSE WORDS AND VOICES

It was the chalk that attracted me so much. It was a long, slender stick of vivid yellow. I had never seen anything like it before, and it showed up so well against the black surface of the slate that I was fascinated by it as much as if it had been a stick of gold.

Suddenly I wanted desperately to do what my sister was doing. Then – without thinking or knowing exactly what I was doing, I reached out and took the stick of chalk out of my sister's hand – *with my left foot*.

I do not know why I used my left foot to do this. It is a puzzle to many people as well as to myself, for, although I had displayed a curious interest in my toes at an early age, I had never attempted before this to use either of my feet in any way. They could have been as useless to me as were my hands. That day, however, my left foot, apparently on its own **volition**, reached out and very impolitely took the chalk out of my sister's hand.

I held it tightly between my toes, and, acting on an **impulse**, made a wild sort of scribble with it on the slate. Next moment I stopped, a bit dazed, surprised, looking down at the stick of yellow chalk stuck between my toes, not knowing what to do with it next, hardly knowing how it got there. Then I looked up and became aware that everyone had stopped talking and were staring at me silently. Nobody stirred. Mona, her black curls framing her chubby little face, stared at me with great big eyes and open mouth. Across the open **hearth**, his face lit by

YOUTH AND EXPERIENCE

flames, sat my father, leaning forward, hands outspread on his knees, his shoulders tense. I felt the sweat break out on my forehead.

My mother came in from the **pantry** with a steaming pot in her hand. She stopped midway between the table and the fire, feeling the tension flowing through the room. She followed their stare and saw me, in the corner. Her eyes looked from my face down to my foot, with the chalk gripped between my toes. She put down the pot.

Then she crossed over to me and knelt down beside me, as she had done so many times before.

'I'll show you what to do with it, Chris,' she said, very slowly and in a **queer**, jerky way, her face flushed as if with some inner excitement.

Taking another piece of chalk from Mona, she hesitated, then very deliberately drew, on the floor in front of me, *the single letter 'A'*.

'Copy that,' she said, looking steadily at me. 'Copy it, Christy.'

I couldn't.

I looked about me, looked around at the faces that were turned towards me, tense, excited faces that were at that moment frozen, immobile, eager, waiting for a miracle in their midst.

The stillness was **profound**. The room was full of flame and shadow that danced before my eyes and **lulled** my **taut** nerves into a sort of waking sleep. I could hear

DIVERSE WORDS AND VOICES

the sound of the water-tap dripping in the pantry, the loud ticking of the clock on the mantelshelf, and the soft hiss and crackle of the logs on the open hearth.

I tried again. I put out my foot and made a wild jerking stab with the chalk which produced a very crooked line and nothing more. Mother held the slate steady for me.

'Try again, Chris,' she whispered in my ear. 'Again.'

I did. I stiffened my body and put my left foot out again, for the third time. I drew one side of the letter. I drew half the other side. Then the stick of chalk broke and I was left with a stump. I wanted to fling it away and give up. Then I felt my mother's hand on my shoulder. I tried once more. Out went my foot. I shook, I sweated and strained every muscle. My hands were so tightly clenched that my fingernails bit into the flesh. I set my teeth so hard that I nearly pierced my lower lip. Everything in the room swam till the faces around me were mere patches of white. But – I drew it – *the letter 'A'*. There it was on the floor before me. Shaky, with awkward, wobbly sides and a very uneven centre line. But it *was* the letter 'A'. I looked up. I saw my mother's face for a moment, tears on her cheeks. Then my father stooped down and **hoisted** me on to his shoulder.

I had done it! It had started – the thing that was to give my mind its chance of expressing itself. True, I couldn't speak with my lips, but now I would speak

YOUTH AND EXPERIENCE

through something more lasting than spoken words – written words.

That one letter, scrawled on the floor with a broken bit of yellow chalk gripped between my toes, was my road to a new world, my key to mental freedom. It was to provide a source of relaxation to the tense, taut thing that was me which panted for expression behind a twisted mouth.

apparent obvious
bondage captivity
canopy a hanging cover
dismally gloomily
hearth floor of a fireplace, or the area in front of it
hoisted lifted
impulse a sudden desire or urge to do something
lulled calmed
pantry a small room for storing food and crockery
primers small books for teaching young learners reading, writing and maths
profound very deep or intense
queer an old-fashioned word for strange
taut stretched tightly
vast infinity endless
volition to choose to do something

ACKNOWLEDGEMENTS

The publisher and author would like to thank the following for permission to use the following material:

Extract from *Mic Drop: A High Rise Mystery* by Sharna Jackson published by Knights Of in 2020. Reproduced by permission of Knights Of.

Extract from *Forensics: The Anatomy of Crime* by Val McDermid published by Profile Books in 2015. Reproduced by permission of Wellcome Collection and Val McDermid.

Extract from *Smart: A mysterious crime, a different detective* by Kim Slater published by Macmillan Children's Books in 2014. Reproduced by permission of Macmillan Children's Books.

Extract from *In Cold Blood by Truman Capote* published by Penguin Classics on 3 February 2000. Reproduced by permission of Penguin Books Limited.

Extract from *Around the World in Eighty Trains* by Monisha Rajesh published by Bloomsbury Publishing in 2019. Reproduced by permission of Bloomsbury Publishing.

Extract from *City of Stolen Magic* by Nazneen Ahmed Pathak published by Puffin in 2023. Reproduced by permission of Penguin Books Limited.

Extract from *What Are You Doing Here?* by Baroness Floella Benjamin published by Macmillan Books in 2022. Reproduced by permission of Pan Macmillan.

Extract from 'Stella Young's letter to herself at 80 years old' by Stella Young published by The Sydney Morning Herald in November 2014. Reproduced by permission of Sydney Morning Herald.

Extract from *To Sir, With Love* by E. R. Braithwaite published by Vintage in 2005. Reproduced by permission of David Higham Associates.

Extract from a Nobel Peace Prize speech by Malala Yousafzai published by The Nobel Foundation in 2014. Reproduced by permission of Nobel Prize Outreach 2024.

Extract from Megan Rapinoe's speech in women's world cup 2019. Reproduced by permission of Wasserman Media Group.

Extract from *A Kind of Spark* by Ellie McNicoll published by Knights Of in 2020. Reproduced by permission of Knights Of.

Extract from *The Haunting of Tyrese Walker* by J. P. Rose published by Andersen Press in 2022. Reproduced by permission of Andersen Press Ltd.

Extract from 'I think the human race has no future if it doesn't go to space' by Stephen Hawking published by The Guardian in 2016. Reproduced by permission of Stephen Hawking.

Extract from *The Sky at Night: The Art of Stargazing* by Maggie Aderin-Pocock published by Ebury in 2023. Reproduced by permission of Penguin Books Limited.

Extract from *Mrs Death Misses Death* by Salena Godden published by Canongate Books on 28 January 2021. Reproduced by permission of Canongate Books.

Extract from *Poverty Safari: Understanding the Anger of Britain's Underclass* by Darren McGarvey published by Picador in 2018. Reproduced by permission of Pan Macmillan.

Extract from *The Right Sort of Girl* by Anita Rani published by Blink Publishing in 2001. Reproduced by permission of Bonnier Books.

Extract from *Diary of a Young Naturalist* by Dara McAnulty published by Little Toller Books in 2020. Reproduced by permission of Curtis Brown.

Extract from *My Girl and the City* by Sam Selvon published in 1957. Reproduced by permission of the estate of Sam Selvon.

Extract from *Manhattan '45* by Jan Morris published by Faber & Faber in 2011. Reproduced by permission of Faber & Faber.

Extract from 'A moment that changed me' by Samira Ahmed published by The Guardian in 2011. Reproduced by permission of The Guardian.

Extract from *Trumpet* by Jackie Kay published by Picador in 2011. Reproduced by permission of Pan Macmillan.

Extract from *The Left Hand of Darkness* by Ursula Le Guin published by Orion Publishers in 1981. Reproduced by permission of Orion Publishers.

Extract from *Spectacles* by Sue Perkins published by Penguin Random House in 2016. Reproduced by permission of Penguin Books Limited.

Extract from *We, the Survivors* by Tash Aw published by Fourth Estate in 2020. Reproduced by permission of Harper Collins.

Extract from 'It's time to regulate social media sites that publish news' by Sharon White published by The Times in 2018. Reproduced by permission of The Times.

Extract from *The Knife of Never Letting Go* by Patrick Ness published by Walker in 2008. Reproduced by permission of Walker Books.

Extract from 'Writing Fantasy Lets Me Show the Whole Truth of Disability' by Ross Showalter published by Electric Literature in 2020. Reproduced by permission of Ross Showalter.

Extract from *The Island of Missing Trees* by Elif Shafak published by Penguin Random House in 2022. Reproduced by permission of Penguin Books Limited.

Extract from *Klara and the Sun* by Kazuo Ishiguro published by Faber & Faber in 2021. Reproduced by permission of RCW Literary Agency.

Extract from 'Uncertainty Principle' by K. Tempest Bradford published by Tu Books in 2012. Reproduced by permission of K. Tempest Bradford.

Extract from *Becoming Dinah* by Kit de Waal published by Orion Publisher in 2019. Reproduced by permission of Orion Publisher.

Extract from *My Name is Why: A Memoir* by Lemn Sissay published by Canongate Books in 2019. Reproduced by permission of Canongate Books.

Extract from *Red Leaves* by Sita Brahmachari published by Macmillan Childrens Books in 2014. Reproduced by permission of MBA Literary Agents.

Extract from *My Left Foot* by Christy Brown published by Vintage in 1990. Reproduced by permission of Penguin Books Limited.

Although we have made every effort to trace and contact all copyright holders before publication this has not been possible in all cases. If notified, the publisher will rectify any errors or omissions at the earliest opportunity.

Links to third party websites are provided by Oxford in good faith and for information only. Oxford disclaims any responsibility for the materials contained in any third party website referenced in this work.

Cover: Oxford University Press